MW01122545

Letting Go

To Silvia -
the best friend
A person could hope
For - with love -
Linda aka
Madelyn

Letting Go

A NOVEL

Madelyn Heller

Library of Congress Control Number: 2012904988
ISBN: Hardcover 978-1-4691-8567-5
Softcover 978-1-4691-8566-8
Ebook 978-1-4691-8568-2

This book was printed in the United States of America.

To order additional copies of this book, contact:
Xlibris Corporation
1-888-795-4274
www.Xlibris.com
Orders@Xlibris.com
110059

Dedication

To the Simon Family, whose residence in both my imagination and my heart has been a refuge and safe haven for most of my life.

Acknowledgments

First, I am beholden to Barbara Smith Leigh, whose editorial skills, patience, encouragement, and generosity of time turned my story from what it aspired to be into what it is. Second, I am grateful to Suzanne Loveland, my dear friend and sole support on the homefront. Third, to the creators of the Internet and the multitude of websites upon which I relied for my copious research: Thanks for providing research sources that I trust were accurate.

Part 1

<u>*Chicago, September 1972*</u>

As soon as my sister Katherine turned eighteen, she announced to our parents that she was moving to Chicago to work. They were horrified, not only at the idea of her moving away from home at her age, but at her boldness in making an independent decision about her own life. Never imagining that their approval made no difference to Kathy, they allowed the move only because I was already living in the city. I was appointed guardian of this pretty and outgoing nineteen-year-old woman whom I knew mainly as the subteen she had been when I had last lived with her.

My little sister didn't worry about the oppressive dreariness of the room she insisted on finding for herself. She didn't worry about the dingy building or her neighborhood. She didn't worry about anything. Apparently it was enough to be free of our parents and Clearyville. Besides, she liked her filing job at a local television station; and she liked being with her niece, Jennifer, and with me. It wasn't long before I was convinced that she was able to take care of herself.

It was amazing to me how well we got along despite the big difference in our ages. Kathy loved people and made a lot of new friends, whom she often brought over to my place for dinner. I suppose I really didn't mind. Though I would rather have spent my evenings alone and her constant chatter could be nerve-wracking, I had to admit her enthusiasm for life was cheering, and she was fun most of the time. I've never been able to figure out how she and I came from the same humorless family, though it was less a mystery to me that I came from it. I really didn't want the responsibility of keeping an eye on her, but she was such a great help with Jennifer, I don't know how I ever did without her. If there was anything that concerned me about her, it was her easy acceptance of strangers.

With good reason.

"I wasn't even in the door," I gasped, knowing it was Kathy on the other end of the phone. I had subliminally registered fifteen rings during the time it took me to fumble my key into the lock, open the door, deposit my groceries, kick off my shoes, and dash across the room. Only Kathy would hang on that long.

"You're late," she said.

"I know. I had to go to the post office and stop at the store. I haven't even picked up Jennifer yet."

"Well, you'd better move it," she informed me, "because I'm bringing someone home for dinner."

I sank down on the floor, feeling familiar prickly fingers of resentment. "What do you mean, bringing home? You don't live here, you know."

"I know," she said defensively, "but you can't expect me to bring anyone to my place. Besides, he happens to live in your building, so it's more convenient."

He. My mind raced over those tenants I had seen, but I couldn't bring up a single face under seventy years of age. Not that I paid much attention. "Here? Who is it?"

"Only the most incredibly handsome man I've ever met."

"Not in this building." I'd noticed that much.

"Oh yes. In your building. But listen, we don't have time. I'll pick up dessert and make a salad. You just make an extra special meal, okay? We'll be there in an hour."

"Kathy—"

"The line was dead. "What's his name?" I said to myself into the receiver, then returned the phone and got to my feet. A magic meal for a magnificent man, a child to be picked up, bathed, and fed, all in an hour. There wouldn't even be time to change from my uniform. A little ache started up in the back of my head, which meant that I was irritated with Kathy and would have to mask it. She should understand by now how much I hated anything that intruded on my routine. It was this ticktock wake-work, day-to-day-to-day routine that had enabled me to survive Steve's absence, and she knew it. How could she not have sensed that anybody she brought over spontaneously represented an intrusion? I'd never said so, but it should have been obvious. But I didn't panic, because I'd been trained to believe that nurses are resourceful and competent. This had been proved over and over by my mother, the ultimate nurse and last word in competence, in whose image I had apparently been created. So within a half hour, while these thoughts were blazing a painful pathway through my brain, I had retrieved my daughter, bathed her, set her to getting the table ready, and gotten the meal under way. It was not elegant, but it would have to do, since I had no idea what a "most incredibly handsome" man would want to eat. I also had no idea how this man had come into Kathy's life. Just another of her strays. As I finished changing out of my uniform, the doorbell rang. Kathy was alone. Reprieve.

"Where's the guest of honor?"

"He went down to his place. I told him I'd pick him up when dinner was ready."

My head was still aching, but at least it hadn't gotten worse. Nevertheless, I was angrier now about her cutting into my life so casually, and there was a moment awkward and frosty enough for even her to notice it. "Maggie," she said slowly, "I know you're furious with me for imposing on you."

"I love your sensitivity."

"But the coincidence was practically an omen. Admit it."

"What?"

"Well, that he lives in this building and doesn't know a soul and that you live in this building and don't know a soul."

"I don't want to know anyone. What's his excuse?"

"He doesn't want to know anyone." She emitted that little giggle she sometimes inserts like a punctuation mark when she thinks she's being witty.

"Kathy," I said evenly, "I don't know what all this is about, but I wish you'd stop doing things like this."

"I know, and it's not about anything. I just want to get to know him."

"Well, don't use me!" I took a deep breath. "Okay. Tell me about him."

"I can't. I don't know anything about him."

"God, Kathy. You've got to quit picking up strays. Someday you're going to get into trouble. You're going to get all of us into trouble."

"And you've got to start trusting people, Mag." I didn't say anything. "Look, don't worry. I met him at the station, in the cafeteria. He just started at the news station and he was eating by himself and you know how I can't stand to see people eating alone."

"Maybe he didn't want company. Did you ever think of that?"

"He probably didn't," she admitted. "I mean, he was studying or something. But he only started there on Monday, and I thought somebody should be friendly." I turned with my hand on a stove control and just looked at her, and she added with a little smile, "Actually I would have been happy just to sit and look at him."

Visions of male models, the kind in magazines, popped into my head. Not my taste in men.

"There were three tables of girls. You know, all gaping and giggling, but not one had the decency to go over to him to say hello."

"Except you."

As usual, all she needed was a grain of encouragement from me before she launched into an animated recital of what she had learned about him, the fact that most impressed her being that he had ridden all the way to Chicago from his home in New York on a motorcycle. *A motorcycle*, I thought. I was not feeling comfortable about this. "He goes to school, I guess at night, and he said he studies a lot, but I didn't ask what. He lives in the west wing." At this point I checked my watch and found it was close to six thirty. Jennifer was ready to eat, and I was anxious to get this thing started and over with.

"Everything's ready, Kath. Why don't you go get this guy?" After she'd left, I realized I had still not heard his name. Not that it mattered.

The building I live in is unusual. It is a turn-of-the-century mansion with two two-floor wings, each of which has maybe fifteen rooms on each floor. Some of the rooms had been joined to make larger units. Ours was pretty small, but I considered it adequate for a woman with a six-year-old child. The rent is moderate by city standards, and the building is in reasonably good repair. Some of the tenants look as if they've lived here since the building was converted sometime around 1928.

Jennifer is the only child in the building. The first year of her life had been spent with my parents in their rural-industrial community, about forty miles from the city, while I tried to create a life here alone. I was newly capped then, newly independent, new to motherhood. Steve should already have been home with us, and we should have been a family, together and happy. Instead he was still over there, maybe alive, maybe not. Nobody knew for sure, not even the army; and so here I was in the city, full-time nurse, weekend mother, and trying desperately to pull it all together into some kind of workable arrangement.

Jennifer was a year old before I was able to bring her back with me, and I had to go to great lengths to persuade the management that she would rarely be seen and never be heard. The younger tenants are couples, nearly all in retirement range. People come and go noiselessly on the ancient carpeting, and the atmosphere is that of an old dignified hotel, more than slightly faded, but with a kind of charm. Kathy insists that she hates my building, that it gives her the creeps. I don't think there is another place like it anywhere. It suits my needs, and I feel lucky to have found it. The west wing is a healthy distance from my apartment at the far end of the east wing. You have to pass the central staircases, which, at the second level, form a gallery over the lobby. Sometimes I will see the super down in the lobby gossiping quietly with a tenant. I've never been interested in joining them.

Kathy came back with her friend while I was still in the kitchen, thinking that nobody in real life can be incredibly handsome, at least no one I ever knew. But Kathy sees what Kathy wants to see, and I was prepared for anything. I took Jennifer by the hand, and we went into the living room. Kathy and the man stood with their backs to us, looking at a wall hanging she had given us the Christmas before. From this angle, there was nothing extraordinary about a fairly tall man in old jeans and a denim work shirt. Dark hair, long enough to wisp over his collar. It occurred to me that if Steve's hair was long, it might fall just like that. He looked like any ordinary young man from the back.

Kathy turned then, all rosy and smiling. "Maggie."

Oh boy. I could recognize the earmarks of a latent crush. She was hooked. "Maggie, um, this is Rick Simon? He works in my office building. Rick, this is my sister, Mary Grace McLean, and my niece, Jenny."

Rick turned, came forward with a polite smile, and put out his hand.

"Hello, Rick, nice to meet you. I smiled back and shook it, suddenly at a loss for something else to say. My daughter, an extremely shy six-year-old, moved close to me and nuzzled my hip. He must have sensed her reticence immediately, because he quickly turned his attention to her, telling her right off that he had a little brother about her age.

"Why don't you get comfortable while I get supper on," I suggested awkwardly and hurried into the kitchen.

My headache left with the familiarity of serving the meal. Kathy and Rick took their places while I was putting the food on the table. At first conversation did not come easily; Rick appeared to be more interested in Jennifer than in us and seemed to enjoy drawing her out. Someone who didn't know Jennifer would say he was not successful, but I could see her responding to him. Eventually we managed to discuss a variety of superficial things: our jobs, the city, the apartment house. Neither Kathy nor I had ever been east of Illinois, and we pumped Rick about New York and about his family there. He had a good sense of humor and automatic and unself-conscious charm. And Lord, he was good-looking, with his dental-ad teeth and guileless dark eyes. I'll admit it: if this man was ordinary, he was the best-looking ordinary I'd ever seen. With his smoky, soft, slightly hoarse voice, I found him as appealing as Kathy did. Should warning bells have gone off in my head? Of course. Did they? No. Kathy tried every way to get him to talk about himself, but the more inquisitive she got, the more he withdrew, until she clearly got so personal that I was ready to pull her into the kitchen and tell her to back off. Certainly Rick was entitled to his privacy, but it seemed throughout the meal, he would come forward, then retreat, so that by the time we were done, it was obvious, to me at least, that even if he ate every meal with us every day, he would still be a stranger. But it wouldn't matter. I'd never met anyone remotely like him, and I was fascinated.

I kept thinking about Rick after he had taken Kathy home and I was cleaning up. I kept trying to decide just what made him so intriguing. Handsome, yes. But in the end, I decided it wasn't his appearance that earned him high marks but some intangible thing that was just part of his natural makeup: a gentleness, a kind of sweet reserve, at least until you violated his boundaries, as Kathy had, more than once during dinner. I like gentleness. Steve is a gentle man, a little reserved too, and he has a sweet calm nature. And yet it wasn't the same. Rick definitely had an indefinable something more.

In spite of myself, I felt a genuine spark of interest stir in me, the first I had felt in anything or anybody in years, and I knew instinctively that it would be better for me if I didn't see Rick Simon again.

We didn't see Rick again for a month. Despite my better judgment, for a short while I found myself looking for him in the lobby or on the stairs, but I guess our hours were different. I thought about him sometimes and wondered again who he was, with his curious gentleness and beautiful eyes. I can't say I'd ever had an analytical nature, but this was an interesting person. Kathy was developing a serious crush, so I couldn't help but be reminded of him; she found a hundred ways of injecting him into conversation, which more and more revolved around her lunchtimes with him. Everything was "Rick said" and "Rick did." You didn't have to be analytical to recognize the signals I'd gotten from him at dinner that night, like electrified barbed wire ready to spark as soon as someone came too close. Kathy obviously wasn't getting the message, and I wondered how he felt about her.

"Signals about what?" she asked, surprised and delighted that I was finally interested in talking about him.

"It seemed to me like he was saying, 'Stay away.' The only one I thought he was interested in was Jennifer."

"That's silly, Maggie."

"Maybe. But I got the impression he was sort of afraid of women. I don't know, maybe he's gay." I had never met a gay man, but I imagined they might not be too comfortable at a table of women.

Kathy gasped. “You’re crazy! He’s so masculine. How could you even think anything like that?” She had never met a gay man either. “He’s just shy, maybe, but gay! God, Maggie.” It bothered me that she was getting so intense about this guy. I didn’t want her to be hurt. And I didn’t want to hear about him anymore. From then on I refused to talk about him or listen to her stories; and gradually, what with work and my absorption in my own world, he slipped from my mind. The month passed, beautifully quiet and uneventful.

My schedule at that time called for me to work alternate weekends. When I was on, I took Jennifer to my parents’ in the country. When I was off, we went to the library or did little projects together. We spent a lot of time in the park on the other side of the boulevard.

It was on the Saturday morning of an off weekend that my doorbell rang. Rick stood there in his denims and long thick hair, looking as though he’d been put on earth solely to stop women’s hearts, and being totally unaware of it. I hadn’t seen him in a month, and the sight of him stunned me speechless. Without Kathy there, I was struck by something else, that he really was young, probably ten years younger than I was. After a moment of awkward silence, he said, “I’m on my way to the laundromat”—I saw then that he was carrying a stuffed pillowcase—“and I wondered if Jennifer isn’t doing anything else, maybe she’d like to go to the zoo with me.” My mouth fell open, but he pretended not to notice. “I’m taking a break today, and I thought, well, my little brother really likes the zoo, maybe she does too.”

I drew back a little, and he stepped into the apartment and put his sack down. Jennifer wandered in then and smiled shyly at him. He said, “Hi, Jenny,” softly, and she averted her eyes in her way, but I knew she would accept Rick’s invitation with joy.

“Remember Rick? He came to ask if you’d like to go with him to the zoo today.” She nodded vigorously and took my hand. “I guess she’d like to go,” I said. He smiled, and there were those wonderful creases under his eyes that I’d noticed that night at dinner.

“Great. I’ll take my laundry over and—in fact Jenny can come with me. It’s right next to the bus stop.”

But I had realized how impulsive I was being and had begun to reconsider. What was I doing, turning my child over to someone I barely knew? I looked at him uncertainly. He misunderstood my hesitation.

“Don’t worry. No motorcycle. We’ll get the bus and stop for lunch. We’ll be back later.”

“When?”

"I don't know. We'll see how it goes."

This was a little too vague for me, which made me even sorrier I'd gotten involved in it. "Listen, Rick," I said tentatively, "are you sure you want to do this?"

"Sure. I'm due for an afternoon off. The zoo's a good place to spend it." He looked at Jennifer. "Don't you think she wants to go?" The little squeeze of her hand in mine very plainly said, "Please, Mommy." I thought it might be a good idea to find out a little more about Rick at this point; for instance, what was he taking an afternoon off from? It was Saturday morning. But I was so confused that I couldn't get a word out, and we stood in silence once more.

"Yeah, well," he said finally and looked directly at me for the first time, as though he actually saw me, "we'll get going, if Jenny's ready."

Jenny was ready, and I got her jacket and went to the door with them. Rick and I inadvertently came close, and I noticed that he was wearing something that smelled soapy and delicious. My heart began to pound, and invisible lights flashed "danger" in my brain. I wanted to believe they were warning me about sending my child out alone with a stranger, but I knew there was more to it than that. I went to the window and watched them vanish around the corner. Then I sat thinking for a long time. I knew I should have been worrying about Jennifer, but I wasn't. I was thinking about Mary Grace McLean and her years of self-imposed insusceptibility, of her carefully devised fortresslike existence, and how it was in danger of falling apart. And all because a young stranger who smelled like soap had almost touched her when he came to take her daughter away for the afternoon. I was thirty-two years old, a mother, a nurse, a . . . what? A widow-wife. And above all, highly sensible and proper, but I was acting like a teenager over a kid I knew nothing about. It was absurd.

But I did know something about him. I knew what he had told us at dinner, about the large family, the big house on the north shore of Long Island in New York, the father who was a lawyer. I knew he was a doctoral candidate at the University of Chicago and that he worked at the television station. I knew he wasn't a drifter, only looked like one. I knew he loved his little brother. So, assuming all this was true—and I couldn't even begin to think that maybe it wasn't—Jennifer would be safe with him. The real problem was that for the first time in six years, I did not feel safe. Because in all that time, I had never looked twice at a patient, hospital staff member, or stranger on the street. And now I was so confused and excited by a mysterious kid in jeans that I couldn't think straight or make sensible decisions about my child's safety. This was too stupid to allow. Therefore it would not be allowed.

Rick brought Jennifer back at four, and she was more animated and happy than I had ever seen her. He thanked me politely for letting her go with him, shouldered his sack of laundry, and disappeared down the hall.

I felt I should do something to reciprocate for Rick's generosity toward Jennifer, so I invited him to dinner. He said Saturday would be good but it would have to be lunch and that he would be happy with a sandwich. During the meal, we talked a little about his job, my love for nursing, and which television programs Jennifer liked the best. Lunch lasted less than an hour because he needed to get to the library.

A couple of Saturdays later, he came by and took Jennifer out again. Those days were highlights in her life; she really adored this man, and nobody could have done a better thing for me than to make her happy. At last she had a friend. An unlikely one, but a friend nevertheless.

I suppose with some people, you feel as if you've known them all your life after only a few minutes' conversation. With others, it takes longer. Rick was always easy to be with, and fun, yet I continued to sense the distance. I had the feeling that with him, it would be never. Kathy finally admitted she felt the same way and eventually stopped referring to him in our conversations. She wasn't defensive about him anymore either, and I was relieved that the crush had ended with no serious injury to her heart. On the nights I worked late and she babysat Jennifer, she still rode over with him on his motorcycle after work.

As for Rick, for all we knew, he came home from work and studied late into the night. His subject had something to do with news broadcasting, what he called mass media. He wasn't very specific, but it sounded interesting. I was curious, but I didn't ask any questions or try to discuss it with him, because I never considered myself a well-read person and thought that whatever I said would sound stupid.

Rick was so good with Jennifer that I began to accept him at face value and soon no longer found him threatening. In fact, the uneasiness I had felt that first Saturday morning now seemed ridiculous. Instead I saw him as a homesick kid and me as the mother of a little girl who reminded him of the brother he missed.

In the almost six years I'd been in Chicago, my life had consisted of home, study, and work. When I first arrived, I tried attending a support group for wives of servicemen missing in action, but after only five meetings, I still felt uncomfortable among these warm and welcoming women. Even though every one of them shared my pain and loneliness, they were strangers, and I had been taught early in life that we were never to reveal our feelings to strangers. God knew our pain and loneliness, and that must be enough for us. Everything was once again under control, and I could settle back into my routine.

During those years, I rarely ventured downtown. Occasionally I wanted to see a movie but couldn't bring myself to go alone. Once I began working at the hospital, I enjoyed the camaraderie of the other nurses, but I was never tempted to get together with them after work or on weekends. The only people I really knew well enough to call on the telephone were Carol and Jerry Hauser. They were a couple who had hired me to work nights at their small medical clinic when I first moved here and was going to school during the day. After I brought Jennifer home to stay, I was perfectly content to spend my evenings keeping Steve alive and with us through photo albums and his letters from Vietnam. It was important to me that Jennifer knew about her father, and I worked hard at it. Almost every weekend, when we went to Clearyville to visit my parents, we talked about him so often that it was almost as if he were there somewhere just out of sight.

Mother never approved of my bringing my year-old daughter to live in the city. She didn't like the idea of the baby spending her days in day care with a stranger and her evenings with me at the clinic. Even after I explained that the caregiver was a very kind and nurturing woman who took in two or three other children as well, she made it clear that I was a negligent mother. Fortunately I found a much-needed sense of security in my regimented routine. It was difficult at first, and I soon learned that juggling school, work, and a small baby wasn't an ideal situation, but the strict schedule of our lives got us through the next few years. And then along came my extroverted sister, a free spirit who met people wherever she went and did not have any problem going out anywhere by herself.

One night, just after Thanksgiving, Kathy talked me into joining her for a movie, and Rick offered to stay with Jennifer. In return, Kathy insisted on cleaning his apartment for him. Afterward, she and I shared a cup of tea while she cheerfully described the disaster she had walked into. Making order out of the mess had been a lot of hard work, but as she excitedly told me about his clothing, furniture, and dirty dishes, I could tell she was not sorry she'd offered to do it. Rick told us later that everything in the apartment, except for his books, clothes, and toothbrush, had been chosen by a decorator from the store that had rented the furnishings to him. We had never known anybody who could afford that kind of luxury, and it occurred to me his background was so alien to ours that no matter how much he told us about himself, we would never really understand who he was. When I teased Kathy about her excitement over his apartment, she assured me it had more to do with curiosity than puppy love. There were plenty of other fish in her ocean.

It was Christmas Eve, and 1972 was only one week away from being history. As I had done every year, I asked for, and got, my vacation between Christmas and New Year's. My parents came in from Clearyville to help Jennifer trim the tree. They had picked her up at day care, and when I got home at three thirty, she and Grandaddy were hard at work, sharing some eggnog and hanging ornaments on our little tabletop tree. Mother sat nearby drinking her superstrong coffee, supervising, and making sure the trimmers followed her specifications. Steve's mother hadn't felt up to making the trip, but her younger son, Bobby, came in her place. Knowing how depressing holidays would be for me if I couldn't share them with family or friends, I felt sad for Rick and wondered to Kathy if she thought he might care to join us. I was surprised by her enthusiasm when she indicated that she would consider our little party a "bomb" without him. *So much for those other fish in the ocean.* As it turned out, Rick accepted the invitation, explaining that his family didn't celebrate Christmas and he had never trimmed a tree. I was pleased that he would be with us because, though he liked to come across as totally independent, I sensed there were times when he missed his family a lot. I was a little worried about Bobby though. He had been sweet on Kathy for years. Now it appeared she hadn't given up on Rick after all. I hoped she wouldn't make it apparent when Rick got here.

Rick rang the bell at about six but wouldn't come in. He was in a mood I'd never seen before. Jack Ryan, who I knew was his boss, had ordered him to do the ten o'clock news broadcast because the regular man had suddenly come down with the flu. To say Rick was annoyed would be an understatement. He was so furious that I could almost imagine sparks shooting from his eyes. "I don't want to do this. I'm not a professional, and I have no interest in working that side of the lights," he fumed. "The only camera I've ever been in front of is my parents' 8mm in their backyard."

Did this mean he wouldn't be able to be with us? "Can't Ryan ask someone else?" I asked, then held my breath.

"If there were someone else to ask, would he have asked me?"

"Then why—"

"He said he was really strapped, and that lesson one in broadcasting is the show goes on no matter what. I wanted to tell him to do it himself, but he's such a personality-challenged schmuck, it wouldn't help the station. When I tried to get out of it, he asked me if I was interested in keeping my job. I hate this job, but I don't want to lose it. I'm learning everything there is to know about what *not* to do in management. Where could I find another one like this?"

I could only guess by his tone what a schmuck was. "And?"

"I said I'd do it."

No matter what he said, I thought it was ridiculous for him to stay at that crummy station. It wasn't like he needed the money. But I didn't say anything.

He was on his way to his apartment for his suit, which he claimed not to have seen in months. How lucky for him, I thought, that Kathy had straightened up his place. When he said he'd be going directly back to the station, my heart fell in a thud of disappointment, followed by a small queasiness of fear at feeling it. Lucky for me, he was too preoccupied with himself to notice my reaction. On top of this, he didn't look exactly right to me, and when I mentioned it, he admitted that he didn't feel too well. It was bitter cold and windy out, and I was relieved that he had garaged the motorcycle for the winter and was taking the bus. I figured Christmas Eve with us was the last thing on his mind at that moment, but as he went down the hall, he called back over his shoulder that he was going to stop off for a drink after work. My mood brightened, but just for a moment, as I realized we'd most likely be in Clearyville by the time he got back.

Kathy came rushing over at seven. She'd heard the news about Rick. It was all over the Holt Building, where the station was located, and "every" female employee—Kathy was given to exaggeration—was planning to tune in. Kathy said, "So he doesn't have experience. What difference does that make? He can talk pig Latin for all anyone cares, just as long as he's facing the camera." Actually nothing mattered, since he was working at the lowest-rated station in Chicago. I was glad Rick didn't hear her say what she did; I doubted he would appreciate being exploited like that.

Kathy, Jennifer, and I were going to Clearyville for Christmas Day, and Mother and Dad wanted us all to leave by seven. Kathy threatened not to leave until tomorrow if she couldn't watch the broadcast tonight, and not wanting her to be alone in the city overnight, they stayed, sitting side by side on the couch with ramrod postures and grudging looks on their faces. The news broadcast, while not totally professional—even for this channel—wasn't a disaster either. Rick's peculiar hoarse voice came over well, and he looked especially handsome in a suit that looked black on my old black-and-white set, but which was actually navy. He must have forgotten his glasses and seemed to have trouble seeing the prompter. Kathy and I laughed too loudly when he squinted into the camera, then began an item, stopped with a puzzled look, and muttered, "Huh? Let me take that again." He didn't seem nervous, exactly, just different, and I commented on it when the first commercial came on.

"He seems drunk to me," my father said peevishly. He had been watching the intense interest Kathy and I were taking in this outsider.

"I've never seen him drink," my sister declared defensively at the same moment my mother said, "He is good looking, isn't he?" My father ignored Kathy and scowled at my mother, who added quickly, "Anyone could tell he has a cold though."

"He looks fine to me," Kathy barked. I'd already noticed Bobby sunk sullenly in his seat, desolately watching her instead of the set.

I agreed with Mother; Rick was sick. It didn't take two nurses to figure that out. His eyes were too bright, and I suspected he had a fever. I would feel a lot better when I saw him back here, where it was warm. As soon as the program ended, my parents got their coats. Bobby got ready to carry Jennifer, who was asleep on the rug, to the car. The nurse in me didn't want to leave until I had seen Rick and was sure he was okay, so I suggested they go on without me. They said nothing but looked at me suspiciously. When Kathy said she'd wait with me, they took off their coats and sat back down. They had learned the year before that arguing with Kathy was useless. Their expressions had turned to out-and-out disapproval; we all sat silently watching the now dark screen, waiting for someone who might not even show up at all. I felt a little off balance myself.

It was close to eleven when the doorbell rang. As I almost leaped at the door, I caught my parents exchanging a look of dismay. "Why are you so late?" I whispered as Rick entered the apartment.

"I walked."

"Walked! It's more than three miles."

"What's three miles?"

He looked worse than he had earlier, and his voice was now a croak. He had no hat, no scarf, no gloves, and he was perspiring. Automatically I cupped my hand over his forehead. "You've got a temperature."

He pulled my hand away impatiently and said with quiet, but definite, anger, "Don't you ever take off that damn uniform?"

By this time, a good deal of the evening's cozy charm had evaporated under my parents' displeasure, and now Rick's unexpected rudeness took care of the rest. I'd never thought of myself as a supersensitive person, but his sharpness stung me. I hung back as he moved into the living room, where Kathy introduced him to our parents and Bobby. Instantly Rick reverted to his normally polite manner and even smiled at me as though not a word had passed between us. For me, however, the evening was spoiled, and I felt depressed and confused. Worse, I felt angry with myself for feeling that way. Who was Rick Simon, and what did he have to do with me? I had invited him to join my family on Christmas Eve, and he had responded with insult. He had disappointed my daughter by not being here while she was awake and had thrown a well-meant gesture back in my face. Now that I thought about it, his breath had smelled strongly of mint. Had he been drinking? I refused to believe it. Once again, though Rick had been our friend for three months and had eaten at my dinner table, I felt as if I didn't really know him.

In the end, the only thing that kept my evening from being completely spoiled was that Kathy decided to ride back to Clearyville with Bobby. At least someone was happy.

The ride out to the country was heavy with silent reproof. The heater was not doing much for the backseat and I was cold. Jennifer was asleep against me and the arm she was leaning on was beginning to get numb. I knew that my parents were irritated about Kathy forcing them to stay longer than had planned; once their plans were made, my mother couldn't abide changes and my father just went long with her. I'd never learned how to get around their anger, which is probably the reason I was outwardly so obedient and compliant with them. Somehow I had managed to avoid taking part in the battle that surrounded Kathy's leaving home the year before, and recognizing that same sort of contention in the air, I was not anxious to be involved now either. Besides, they should have known that their approval was not necessary where Kathy was concerned, so why did they bother to express it, even in silence? I, on the other hand, was feeling less and less comfortable with the passage of each minute and each mile.

We were almost off the tollway when my father's voice cut through the darkness, startling me. "Who is that man?"

It would have been silly to pretend I didn't know who he was referring to. "A kid Kathy met at the station," I answered in as neutral a voice as I could muster. "It happens that he lives in my building and we've had him to dinner a couple of times." My voice sounded loud in the stillness and unnaturally offhand.

I saw the silhouettes of my parents turn briefly toward each other. "What's he to you?" My father was a man who had always preferred directness to subtlety. I thought I detected a note of accusation. "He's taken a liking to Jennifer, that's all," I managed.

"I see," he said with an implication in his tone that made me realize it was me and not Kathy he was angry with after all. I couldn't imagine what I had done to provoke him, and I was glad I couldn't see his face, which when disapproving had always intimidated me.

After a few minutes of silence, my mother spoke. "Kathy tells us this man's family doesn't celebrate Christmas. What does that mean?" Well, wait, maybe it was Rick that they were annoyed with. Then I lost patience with the whole stupid situation as I realized what was really on their minds.

"I don't know, Mother. I think it means he doesn't celebrate Christmas." I knew insolence would not ease the awkwardness between us, but we were now on familiar ground, the one area in which Kathy and I were united in our criticism of not only our parents but most of the people we had grown up with. Nonpracticing Christians didn't exist in my parents' world; nor did Jews, Catholics, black people, or anyone not cut from the hometown mold. I, in some unexplained way, had recognized early on that my background was small-minded and racist and at some point in my teens realized that I didn't agree with the views of those Anglo-Saxon Protestant types with whom we were expected to associate. (Steve was fighting the same ongoing battle with his parents when we started dating.) I couldn't have cared less about Rick's ethnic or religious background. My parents were aware of my peculiar tolerance, and my mother used it more than once as an example of how living in the city had corrupted me. I'd never had the courage to disagree while I lived with them, but nothing in this world could make me change my mind now.

In the intermittent flashes of light from the highway lamps, I could see my middle-American, arch-conservative parents stacking the deck against Rick. I think they would rather have seen Kathy or me hopping into bed with him four nights a week than find out he was not one of us. They were genuinely impressed by his education—unlike many people who didn't have much education, they had respect for people who were educated—and it must have been hard for them to come to a decision about him. I said nothing more, but my father had a final word. "Man drinks too much," he grumbled. My instinct was to protest, as Kathy had earlier, that this was the first time I'd ever seen Rick take a drink, but that would've sounded defensive, and I didn't want to be defending him for fear of sounding as if I cared. Right then, in the uncomfortable isolation in my parents' car, the idea that I might care for Rick filled me with apprehension.

Being at home that Christmas Day was like finding my way out of a maze. For the first time since we'd moved to the city, more than a month had gone by since we'd been in Clearyville, and now that I was back here, it was easy to straighten out my bent perspective. Here I was surrounded by memories of Steve, and it was suddenly clear as glass that my attraction to Rick was a temporary weakness, not worth the effort of forcing myself to ignore it, certainly not worth the sense of lost stability because of my denial. Here I was on solid ground once again, safe in the certainty that Steve was still the major force in my life; it was on him that my future and Jennifer's depended. It was so obvious to me that Rick was just a diversion, someone who would be in our lives one day and out the next, just as we would be for him. I could truly believe that once he overcame his shyness or homesickness or found the time or whatever it was that was holding him back, he would no longer need us and would seek more appropriate company. Here in Clearyville, I could admit to myself that it was inevitable that I should be drawn to someone sometime, that that attraction did not have to take over my life; it could easily happen and as easily be gone. Here at home, with Steve all around me, my feelings for Rick no longer seemed scary but foolish. I did want to be friends with him, not only for Jennifer's sake, but because he represented a glamour mystery that my life had always lacked. And right at that moment, I knew I could handle it.

I returned to Chicago and woke the next day feeling lighter and happier. I cleaned the apartment for most of the day. It was good to be doing the things I wanted to be doing, remembering Steve a lot, unburdened with thoughts about Rick that frightened me. Then in the middle of the afternoon, Kathy called, sounding troubled. Rick had not come to work, and no one was answering the phone at his apartment. Ryan knew she knew him and asked her to try to find out what was going on. She wanted me to go down and check.

"Did you try calling him?" I asked, instantly feeling put-upon.

"I just told you we did," she said impatiently, "but there's no answer."

"Then he obviously isn't there." *I really don't want to be involved.*

"But where is he?" she asked irritably. "He'd never just not show up."

I was sure that was true, felt a tiny prickle of alarm, but I was determined to keep my distance from her *friend* from now on. "Calm down, for heaven's sake. Maybe his cold got worse he just wanted to stay home. Maybe he doesn't feel like answering the phone. I don't know."

"Not call in? Come on, Maggie, it'll only take you a minute. Please?"

In the end I gave in, went down the hall, past the main stairs along the length of the west wing. Rick's apartment was a tiny efficiency at the end. The corridor was very quiet, not a soul in sight. I can't say why I was relieved, outside of recognizing what a Puritan prude I was and always had been. So I was going to the man's apartment. He'd come to mine. Still I felt vaguely uncomfortable.

Rick's door was ajar. *Okay, that was strange.* I knocked timidly. When there was no answer, I knocked again, more boldly. When there was still no answer, I became even more uneasy than I already was. I entered gingerly, my heart beginning to beat fast. "Rick?"

The room was a mess. The beautiful furniture Kathy had described lay buried under clothing, books, papers; I immediately found Rick nearly hidden beneath a tangle of blankets on the sofa. It was scary. I thought at once that someone had broken in, attacked him, ransacked his place. "Rick?" I went toward him fearfully, with great relief found that he was not half dead but asleep. His chest moved up and down with labored breathing. I touched his neck and instantly knew he was very sick. I relaxed. I could handle sickness.

Some minutes passed before I could wake him, more minutes still before he focused his eyes and recognized me. He looked awful, pale, and flushed at the same time, eyes overly bright in a way that only a high fever can produce. When he appeared to be registering, I said, "What's going on here?"

He shook his head as if to clear it. "I don't know," he croaked. "I'm sick."

"I see that. How long have you been like this?"

"I think . . ." His eyes went out of focus for a second, and he seemed uncertain. "Maybe last night?" I looked at him steadily, my heart beginning to thump again in a way it had never done over a patient. "After I left your place," he continued slowly, "I went out again."

"Out. What for?"

"A drink. I needed a drink."

"Rick—"

"I really got wasted." He shook his head again. "I guess I can't do it anymore. I was sick. I think,"—he lowered his eyes—"I think I passed out."

"Rick. What are you talking about?"

"The thing at your place. Last night."

"But that wasn't last night. It was Saturday."

"What's today?"

"Monday."

He sank back on the pillow and closed his eyes. After a moment, he sighed. "I'm supposed to be at work."

"Forget that now. Let's get you cleaned up. Do you have a thermometer?"

"No."

"Okay, I'll get one." I looked around me. "Oh dear! This place should be condemned." He shrugged. "Can you sit up?" With some pulling and pushing, we finally succeeded in getting him into a sitting position. He closed his eyes, and I knew the room was spinning around him. "Can you get to the chair?"

"I don't know. I think I'm going to throw up."

He was weak and dizzy and probably couldn't stand, but moving a patient from a bed is about as basic as nursing gets. I grabbed a half-empty wastepaper basket and set it on his lap. "I'll tell you what." I pulled a chair close to the bed. "Just lean on me when we get you up on your feet."

"If I *can* get up on my feet . . . my legs seem to have a mind of their own."

"Have you ever slept for thirty hours before?"

He sank crookedly onto the chair and, in answer to my next question, pointed to where I could find a clean sheet. Then he sat quietly with the basket on his lap and watched me open the sofa and make the bed up.

When I was done, I threw the blankets in a heap at the foot of the sofa. "Now you," I said in my brisk nurse voice.

"Let me just sit here, okay? I'm okay."

"You get a bath, clean pajamas, and back into bed." I could have been talking to my daughter. Was I this parental with my patients?

"A bath?"

"Don't worry. I'm a nurse and I've bathed men before."

He smiled then, slowly, and in such a way that I felt a tremor. It was not a girl-shy smile. "I'm not worried." My professionalism seemed to evaporate in the face of that smile, and he saw it go. "Well, you don't have to worry either. I'm too sick to make the most of the situation," he said and leaned into the basket, gagging.

I helped him back onto the bed and went to the tiny kitchenette, filled a large bowl with soap and water, and grabbed a towel. After locating his pajamas, still in pins and store plastic, I bathed and dressed him, things I'd done thousands of times, but for the first time since nursing school, I did them with trembling hands. The wariness I'd felt during the preceding months crept back, and I tried to chase it away by conjuring Steve's image in my head. I couldn't. Steve had deserted me, and only Rick was here. As soon as the job was done and he was installed beneath the blankets, I grabbed the bath equipment and quickly turned away. I didn't have to worry; he was asleep again. I let myself out silently.

On the way down the hall to my apartment, I thought about what I should do with him. I hadn't taken his temp yet, but he clearly needed to be seen by a doctor, and my guess was that he didn't know one in town. I did, and it would be plain stupid to disregard his condition. Yet I sensed he would resent my taking the liberty of calling one for him. I couldn't blame him. We didn't know each other that well.

When I called Kathy back, she seemed both relieved and alarmed. "Maybe I should come over and stay with him," she offered. "He needs attention and there doesn't seem to be anybody else . . . After all, this is your vacation."

There was an awkward silence when I assured her I could handle the thing myself, and that's when I recognized a hint of competition for Rick. My entire body flushed with the realization, and I quickly pushed the thought away. We puzzled for a few minutes over the idea that Rick didn't seem to know anyone in Chicago besides us. Was he a loner who had gone through his entire life without friends or dates? Kathy had to get back to work, so we ended our conversation, and I sat there, trying to decide how best to handle Rick. To leave him to himself in that condition might end up in complications, so I made up my mind to let the thermometer make the decision. If the fever ran high for the next few hours, I'd get up my nerve and call a doctor; if it went down and nothing else happened, I'd take care of him myself. Neither of these possibilities made me very comfortable.

When a half hour had gone by since I'd left him, I found my thermometer and slipped quickly back to his apartment. The telephone was ringing as I opened the door, but he was so deeply asleep that the noise had not even penetrated. I lifted the receiver tentatively and spoke. There was a pause on the other end, the kind that often happens when people think they've dialed a wrong number. Finally a woman's voice asked, "Is Ricky there?" *See? Of course there are women.* But . . . Ricky?

"Yes," I answered, using my most no-nonsense professional voice. "May I ask who's calling?"

The voice said, "This is his mother."

"Oh," I gasped, startled. It occurred to me that I should use the thermometer on myself; my own temperature seemed to be rising and falling with regularity. Struggling to get myself back on track, I explained that I was Mrs. McLean, Rick's neighbor, emphasizing the "Mrs." in a dumb effort not to sound guilty about answering the telephone in her son's apartment. "Rick hasn't been feeling well and I've been helping out a little. I'm a registered nurse." *Did I sound defensive? Why should I?*

"Is he okay? What's wrong?" his mother asked anxiously.

"I've only just gotten here so I'm not exactly sure yet. But it's probably just a flu or something. He's running a little fever and says he's been sleeping most of the weekend. I'm sure it's nothing. He's sleeping now."

"Should he call a doctor?"

"Well, I think so, but he doesn't want to. I could call one for him, but I have a feeling he wouldn't like me interfering."

She sort of laughed. "I'm sure he wouldn't."

There was a small silence, during which I experienced a strange mixture of uneasiness and excitement. Yes, excitement. Finally, she said, "Don't mind me, Mrs. McLean. I'm sure it's nothing to worry about. He's twenty-two years old, but he's far away and alone and I can't seem to stop acting like a mother."

"You don't have to apologize. I'm a mother too," I said, feeling instant empathy with this woman I didn't know. "But he's not alone. Rick has been very kind to my daughter and me. I'll keep an eye on him, so don't worry."

"Thank you, I feel better then. It's silly how they never stop being your children no matter how old they are." This was not a comforting thought for the future. After a moment she added, "Maybe it would be better if you didn't tell him you talked with me. He'd probably be annoyed and we're at a point with him where it'd be easier if he weren't annoyed with me."

I couldn't guess what that was all about, and I was confused enough already. It's very difficult to equate a sexy man who makes your heart pound with somebody's touchy little boy. Somebody's rebellious little boy. Somebody's little boy. *Stop it, Maggie. You're losing your mind.*

After I hung up, I stood beside the couch, watching Rick sleep and thinking over the phone call. It had, in some way, involved me more deeply with him, the real him, the Ricky his mother had wanted to speak to, not just the mysterious guy who had taken an interest in my daughter and had dinner at my table. I felt like I had been given some insight into a part of him that, for his own reasons, he had withheld from us. Something didn't feel right. I stood looking at him, trying to see beyond his face, his skin, the sweet huskiness of his quiet voice, trying to figure out what it was in him that made me feel like I had never felt before.

I sat with him for the rest of the day, reading and thinking about whether I really wanted to get involved in this situation. Steve's wife said no. Maggie the Nurse said I couldn't not. At suppertime I tried to get a little soup into him. He hadn't eaten in two days and still couldn't keep the food down. In the evening, he had chills again; he'd had chills, he said, when he'd first come home from his drinking binge, before he'd passed out. Rick's fever hovered somewhere between what it should've been and what I'd expected. I told him he should see a doctor, and he, predictably, refused. I didn't tell him his mother had called.

I was sort of troubled by the drinking. No, that's not exactly true. I was really very disturbed by it. I wanted him to tell me about it, but I knew he couldn't; talking nauseated him. Besides, even if he could have, he wouldn't. I wanted to know about what he'd done that night, where he'd been, why he'd gone. I felt repelled in a way and frightened, as I felt about alcohol itself. I had strong feelings about alcoholics after years of dealing with them. I had to keep reminding myself that one night of drinking too much did not make this man an alcoholic. I felt again his unexpected, unexplained anger at the door after he returned from the news station, the way he basically disregarded without a word the invitation that he had accepted from us. He was certainly nothing like the person we thought he was that night he came to dinner. Except for Jennifer. Rick's fondness for her seemed truly genuine, and for a young man to be that good with a child says a lot. Maybe this had just been a whim or something.

I went home, made myself a sandwich and a cup of coffee, stripped the beds, and made them up fresh. Mine looked so inviting that, feeling worn out and put-upon as I did, I thought for a minute about chucking everything and just getting in it. But dutiful Nurse Maggie would never do that, not without one last check on her patient, and so back I went. Bad move for me, though probably a good one for the patient. As Steve liked to say, the gods were scowling. It took about one second for me to determine that Rick's condition had deteriorated. His color was worse, his lips dry and beginning to crack, his face fever flushed and slick with perspiration. The sheets were soaked. I could see that he was laboring to get air into his lungs. He was fidgeting uncomfortably and coughing in intermittent, short bursts that were as painful to hear as they probably were to experience. I was looking at another hour, maybe two, before I saw my bed again.

I located a clean towel in a cabinet in the bathroom and sponged his forehead, face, and neck. He didn't wake up. Then I sat down on the chair I'd pulled over earlier and watched him, automatically recording my observations and assessing the severity of his condition. The next time I looked, my watch told me that almost an hour had passed, and I had that logy, sawdust-brain sensation you get sometimes when you wake up from an unintentional doze.

Rick was quieter now. I leaned forward and gently laid my fingers on his cheek, held them there, suddenly aware of the roughness of the glistening stubble outlining the shape of his jaw, the heat emanating from his body, and the erotic sensations invading my own.

I sat up stiffly and forced myself to take stock of the situation, which, in my opinion, was not good. What had appeared to be a bad cold, helped along by walking three miles in subfreezing weather without proper protection, had now escalated to something that needed medical attention. But how to make that happen?

Actually the answer had been skirting the edges of my mind all day. It was something I probably should have done hours ago, but now it was no longer a question of alienating him. I started searching for the phone book, finally locating it under another pile of dirty laundry. The phone itself was hiding in plain sight, on the floor of the alcove leading to the bathroom. I found Jerry's clinic number and dialed.

Jerry was a doctor I had known for several years, a good friend whose small clinic I had worked in evenings while I was in nursing school. After graduation, I had continued there until I was hired by the hospital. Though I saw and talked with them only occasionally now, Jerry and his wife Carol were still the only real friends I had in the city.

At this time of night, Jerry was probably closing up, and it was almost five minutes before he came on the line. I laid out the situation before he had a chance to say anything more than hello.

"He'll need an x-ray," he said when I finally gave him the opportunity. "Can you get him to emergency?"

"He's not comatose. I'm afraid if I call an ambulance, the attendants will wake him in the process and he'll refuse to go. They can't take him against his will."

"Anybody who could persuade him? Family, friends?"

"Nobody I know of. His family is in New York and I've never heard him mention anyone here."

After a moment, he sighed. "I don't know what to tell you, Maggie. If he refuses, I don't see that there's anything to talk about."

"Well," I offered somewhat hesitantly, "I've been thinking there might be a way. I'm off this week and Jennifer's at my folks'. If I could get him to stay at my place, he could use her room. Then at least I could keep my eye on him without having to run back and forth."

Jerry considered this for a moment and then asked, "How old is this guy, Maggie?"

"Oh, not young, not old. I don't know. What difference does it make?"

"Well, you wouldn't want to cause a scandal in that biddy retreat you live in."

I felt the blood rush to my head. "For heaven's sake, Jerry, all I'm trying to do is get him well."

"Umm . . . might there be a man-woman thing happening here, I hope?"

Now I wanted to kill him. "What on earth are you talking about?" I snapped. "I have a very sick patient here. Why are you wasting time?"

"Okay, okay. Cool down. D'you think you can manage it? Getting him over to your place?"

I swallowed. "I don't know. He was too weak to get to the bathroom this afternoon."

I waited for some kind of smart remark, but mercifully, he was all business now.

"Listen, how about this? If you can get him to your apartment, Carol and I will come for dinner tomorrow night."

I hated to look a gift horse in the mouth, but tomorrow night was a long way off. "You couldn't possibly make it tonight?"

"I'm here until eleven tonight. But don't sweat it. If anyone can get him through this, you can. You just detach yourself emotionally and do that thing you do so well. And don't hesitate to call me here or at home if you need to. Got it?"

His calm confidence had neutralized my annoyance, and it was beginning to subside. "Got it, Jerry. Thanks."

For years, Jerry and Carol had been encouraging me to start dating. They had never believed that Steve would come home. I'd always resented their lack of faith when I was so sure he would, and had seen them less often in recent years. They were both kind and caring people, traits that put Jerry a definite cut above most of the physicians I'd worked with. True, his inappropriate remarks tied me in knots, and it was sometimes hard to overlook the nonsense and concentrate on his good qualities, but if something is worthwhile to you, you just take the bad with the good.

Rick was still quiet when I hung up, not coughing as violently and sleeping more peacefully. There was nothing else for me to do here, and I had dinner preparations to make, so I went home.

I did some serious thinking while I readied Jennifer's room for Rick. The situation was turning out to be a lot more complicated than it seemed, and I was beginning to wish I hadn't gotten involved. All Rick had to do was get an x-ray taken. Why did he have to make things so difficult by refusing to see a doctor? I had definite reservations about Jerry and my plan, had had them even as I had proposed it to Jerry, but as things stood, there seemed no other way; I just wasn't made to sit around and watch someone suffer when he might not have to. A more immediate concern, however, was how I was going to get Rick back here. No way was I going to ask anyone in the building to help me. I could have called Kathy, I supposed, but Monday was the night she went to her Bible study group. Well, I was not a small woman, and I was fairly strong. I would manage somehow. And there was kind of a funny side to the situation. The corridor between my apartment down the east wing and Rick's at the end of west was quite long, and the chances of meeting another resident along the way were pretty good. Passing the staircase was definitely risky, though, since there was usually somebody in the lobby minding everyone else's business: Mr. Wagner, the super, or his son, Tim, or—worst case—his wife, who loved to gossip with the tenants when they came down for their mail in the mornings. I could picture it: Woman Helps Staggering, Half-Dressed Young Male to Her Apartment. What would they think? Nothing probably, nothing at all. At any rate, it wasn't even worth wondering about. It was unlikely that anyone would be around anyway, since it was nearly eleven.

When I got back to Rick's, he was mumbling in his sleep, and his eyes were moving rapidly beneath the lids. I touched his shoulder and said his name, and his eyes, bright but unfocused, popped open and fastened on me.

"Rick, I'm going to take you to my apartment," I said softly.

"No. I'm okay," he responded in a hoarse whisper, triggering a brief but obviously rib-jolting coughing fit.

"You shouldn't be here alone and you won't let me get you to a doctor. Somebody's got to take care of you and this is the only way I can think of."

"I don't need any help." He closed his eyes and tried to take a deep breath, which caused groans and some more coughing. "I'll be okay tomorrow. Don't worry about me."

"Go on and argue if it makes you happy. I'm just going to swing your legs around and get you upright."

"And carry me down the hall—" His voice sounded small, weak.

"No. You're going to walk down the hall and I'm going to help you."

He lay still for a minute, looking at me. Then, to my surprise, he said docilely, "Yeah, all right. I don't feel very good."

He was steadier on his feet than I had expected, but he was bigger too, and heavier. He must have been determined not to make a fool of himself because he made it all the way across the building, faltering once or twice, but not falling. Pretty amazing considering he hadn't eaten or been on his feet for three days. I led him directly to Jennifer's room, where he collapsed on the bed and, panting shallowly, gasped what sounded like "pail." I handed him the waste bucket, but without medication to loosen the stuff in his lungs, nothing came up. Then he sank down into the pillows; I relieved him of his soggy pajamas and covered him up. He didn't say a word.

"Just go back to sleep and I'll see you in the morning. Okay?"

"Thanks, McLean," he whispered and squeezed my hand. My heart began to pound.

Later, before turning out my light, I went in to take just one more look at him. Having him asleep in Jennifer's room gave me a sense of profound relief. He was in my territory now, and it felt good.

Rick seemed better the next day. He sat up and drank a little broth without it coming back up. The fever was still high, and his wrenching cough and aching ribs continued, but I left him for a while in the morning to shop for dinner. He didn't say anything when I told him I was having company for dinner. I was too timid to ask him if he felt up to coming to the table, nor did I mention that one of my guests was a doctor. This cloak-and-dagger act I'd cooked up wasn't fair, but it was the only sensible thing I could see to do, under the circumstances. I just hoped the evening wouldn't be wrecked when he found out.

At the store, I had an urge to buy something for him, a book or a magazine. He would be in bed for a few more days, and he'd probably get bored. I didn't know which to choose; I had no idea what he might like. I stood at the rack for a couple of minutes, then walked away with nothing but a foolish feeling; and a few minutes later, I left the store with a bag of groceries and a head full of confusion. Everything that used to seem right seemed wrong since I'd met Rick. I had always been the decisive Mary Grace, the woman who knew what she wanted, the bedside nurse with administrative ability. I hated this craziness I was feeling. And yet how would I want things to be with him? These last couple of days, finding him sick, volunteering to take care of him, bringing him to my apartment, had been exciting, in a way. Here I was, alone in my apartment with a very attractive and enigmatic young man who was completely dependent on me. Wasn't this the stuff that romance novels were made of?

The roast was in the oven, the table was set, and the living room was straight. All I had left to do was get through the remainder of the afternoon. When I went in to sponge Rick off and change his pillowcases, he was lying quietly, staring at the ceiling. He assured me he was feeling a little better today, wasn't as sore, and then asked me if I would sit with him for a while. I brought Jennifer's rocking chair over, figuring that if he wanted to talk, okay, and if he didn't, that was fine too. He didn't. I leaned back in the chair and thought of the thousands of hours I had spent sitting with other patients, sitting like this, just passing time, of how often they had told me I was easy to talk to and how they seemed able to confide in me as though they knew me and knew they could trust me. I liked people and got pleasure out of helping them, letting them get things off their chest if that's what they needed, being a friend to them for however brief the time. But here was Rick, sick and away from home, and he didn't seem to need a friend. Not that I thought he considered me a friend, of course, but I was disappointed.

After a while, however, we did kind of slip into conversation, a few words about this or that, Jennifer, my job, his job, almost a rerun of that first dinner talk. We chatted in clumps, quietly, at sick-person speed. He told me that being around Jennifer kept him rooted; it was like having his little brother around. I already knew about the little boy called Jody, who was close in age to Jennifer. Rick was warm and loving when he talked about his brother. So gentle. I had once loved a gentle man, still did. I took a deep breath, hoping to slow the throbbing pulse in my neck. *Steve, where are you?*

I asked him to tell me about his other siblings. He told me that he'd always felt closest to his sister Susan, who was about a year younger than him and who had been his best friend until he'd left for college. As he spoke, so softly, a feeling of peace settled over me, intensified by the soft light in the room, the strangeness of his being here in Jennifer's bed, how easy he was to talk to, as if we were two people who'd known and trusted each other for a long time and were secure in that trust. This—could I call it a bond?—enabled me to loosen up too.

"I always wished I had a sister like that," I confessed. "Kathy was so much younger that it was more like having a niece or a cousin. I've always felt like an only child, in fact."

Rick nodded sympathetically, then surprised me by saying, "Most of my life, I wished I was an only child."

"But from what you've told us, your family sounds like a really good one to be in."

"It is if you like living in a circus."

I didn't believe that for a minute and prodded him to tell me more. He obliged by describing their big white house, being careful to play it down by saying it was just ordinary. Ordinary, I thought, is relative. The house Kathy and I had grown up in could be described as ordinary too, but it had to be a far different ordinary than Rick's. He told me he had shared a bedroom with one of his brothers until he was sixteen, when he moved into a small storage room off the landing below the attic; it had been called a box room in the old days. This change must have meant freedom and privacy for him. I guess I had never thought about the value of privacy, since privacy was about the only thing I hadn't lacked growing up. I began to understand why Rick guarded his private thoughts and the details of his life so carefully. When I said this to him, he simply shrugged. "The move was more for convenience than privacy. I wanted to be out at night and it was easier to sneak around from the attic."

It crossed my mind to ask what it was he did when he sneaked out, but I didn't. Maybe I really didn't want to know.

At this point, he drifted off for a while. I took advantage of the time to gather the dirty laundry and take it to the machine in the basement. When I returned, he was awake and began to talk about his parents. His father was a lawyer, as were his grandfather and a number of their relatives. All of them worked for the family firm, which was very large and had several offices in the United States, as well as overseas connections. This was exciting to me; in Clearyville, lawyers still had old-fashioned, one-man offices over shops and drugstores downtown. The talk about Rick's family started me wondering about the call from his mother and how I wished I had an image to put with the voice on the telephone. Somehow I got up the nerve to ask him what she was like. He wanted to know why I was asking, and still not comfortable about mentioning the phone call, I replied lamely, "Oh, I don't know. I'm always interested in people's mothers. Maybe it's because I'm one myself."

"Ah," he said with a teasing smile. "Then you'll also want to know about the nurse who took care of me when I was born." I thought for a moment he was making fun of me, or maybe rich easterners had a certain kind of humor I wasn't familiar with. He looked at me curiously. "I don't know what you want to know."

The pulse in my neck started up again. I didn't know either

"She's smart," he answered, "and funny. She's not your typical country-club matron. She reads a lot, volunteers at the library. She used to be a teacher, so she likes to work with children. Oh, and she still treats me like I'm six years old. Will that do it?" I nodded.

"I can't imagine having seven children, and still having time to read."

He snorted. "Some mothers have other people to change diapers and wipe noses for them, so they have time to do other things. From the time I was seven or eight, we've had a housekeeper who did it for us. Though," he added quickly, "there was never any doubt who our real mother was. We've always known she was there if we needed her." He reached for the water glass on the bedside table, and as he sipped, I caught myself watching his throat, then his chin, and then his mouth—*don't do this, Maggie*—and again experiencing the embarrassing reaction I'd had last night.

I quickly excused myself and escaped to the kitchen, where I checked the roast and found it doing better than I was. To my relief and frustration, his eyes were closed when I returned to Jennifer's room, but he came awake instantly and insisted he wasn't tired. We sat in silence for a while, but I had this insatiable need to know everything, and time was growing short. I asked him about his father.

"I guess you could say that my father is a successful man, though he's had his disappointments. Even successful people do, you know. He thought he was spawning another generation of lawyers in the firm, but I wasn't interested and Andrew and Matthew haven't been either. I don't know what will happen with the kids, but so far, our branch of the family isn't even in the race."

"The race?"

He sighed. "It's a Simon thing. There's always been competition, first between my grandfather and his brothers, and now my father with his brothers and the cousins. We are talking about very competitive people. It looks like my brothers and I have screwed up his chance to win the 'Who Will Father the Most Junior Partners in the Family Firm?' race and he isn't too happy about it." He laughed, and it seemed a little nasty to me for him to be treating his father's dreams so lightly. After all, my mother was a nurse, and I knew she'd always wanted me to be one. I would never have disappointed her in something that was so important to her. But Rick seemed to think it was funny to hurt his father. Welcome to the '70s, Mary Grace. I had heard a lot of stories from my coworkers who had kids Rick's age, stories of behavior that was so incredible to me that I'd been sure the mothers were exaggerating. After all, my sister is a young adult in the '70s, and she's never shown that kind of disrespect for authority or for our parents or even for me. Unless you count her moving away from home, but that was different.

"The thing is," Rick continues, "the man has five sons and there's only one other male in our generation. Those are pretty stiff odds. It's not sitting well with him."

"Does it have to be a male?" I asked seriously.

"Who? Susan?" He laughed even harder, which started a prolonged coughing spasm. "Susan, the social worker?" he went on, after resting for a few minutes. "She's a smart kid, but her idea of serving humanity is spending the summer ruining her manicure grinding meal in some Mexican village. It doesn't have much to do with helping humanity, but it says a lot about Susan."

Rick was resting for longer and longer periods, so it was clear he was running down. I don't know if it was because I was put off by Rick's sarcasm or I was getting tired too, but I didn't want to talk anymore either. I sat in the chair, dreamily rocking back and forth, thinking about what would happen with Jerry tonight, half wishing I was nowhere near Rick, half wishing I was lying beside him . . . *This is wrong* . . . One thing was encouraging though: some of Rick's behaviors—his attitude toward his father, for instance—seemed so childish that there actually were moments when he wasn't quite so attractive to me.

I was hardly aware that he was talking again when the word "war" jumped out at me, and I literally snapped to attention. Suddenly Steve was in the room with us, insisting that I remember something he had said to me before he left for boot camp. He had been a reluctant soldier, bitter because he was already twenty-five and in the middle of the courses that he hoped would eventually get us out of the factory and Clearyville for sure. I told Rick how Steve had felt about the rich boys, the college students who were biding their time until their parents managed to buy their way out of the draft, while guys like Steve, who were willing to work for what they got—I stopped in midsentence because it had been a long time ago and I had hated hearing Steve say such angry things. If I had to be reminded of him now, I didn't want it to be about bitterness and resentment.

Rick had been watching me solemnly. Now he nodded. "Yes. That's right," he agreed. "A lot of the guys I knew bought their way out or used whatever influence their families had." He snorted again. "But not the Simons. The Simons are full of Ideals and 'What's the Right Thing to Do.' It never matters to them what anybody else does. It's their ethic. I mean, my grandfather is so totally ethical, so completely above reproach, it's unreal. Though it's really my grandmother who runs the show, when it comes to things like God, Mother, and apple pie, my grandfather makes the rules." He stopped suddenly, looked into my face. "Look, you don't really want to hear all this, right?"

"I do. Really," I said, managing somehow to get a tone of clinical detachment into my voice but thinking, *It's about you, I want to hear it.* As if I hadn't written him off as an obnoxious brat just minutes ago. I was a fish with a hook in its mouth.

His eyes locked on mine for another second, then went toward the ceiling as he settled back into the pillows. "They're all like that, you know? I mean, about that ideals crap. My uncle was in the army in World War II. Another uncle died in Korea and sometimes I think my grandfather was never prouder of his sons. My father was on a ship somewhere when Susan and I were born. I mean, who really wants to get shot up for nothing in some dumb-ass war? That's crazy."

He had been going on about himself for almost the whole afternoon. His voice was ragged, and he looked very tired. I knew I should leave so he could sleep. But I couldn't. I couldn't let him or his life or the afternoon go.

Not yet. The hook was more deeply imbedded in the fish's mouth than it had been two hours earlier.

Instead of doing what I should have done, which was to straighten the pillows, pull up the covers, and leave the room, I said, "Why do you hate your family so much?" I don't know where it came from; I was not even conscious of thinking such a thing.

His eyes widened for a second. "I don't hate my family," he answered softly. "It's just that there are two things that have been a pain in the ass to me all my life and the second one is my family."

The fish took what it thought was bait, and I started to ask what the first thing was, but he didn't even hear me.

"I don't hate my family," he repeated. "I just can't agree with what they believe in." He smiled at the ceiling. "My father, Susan, Andy, and I have had some pretty wild arguments. He's really something. He takes us all on at once. He's such a damn good trial lawyer, he just talks circles around us and we get so frustrated, we eventually just give up. But he can't really convince us that he's right, so nobody wins. This crap about patriotic duty and responsibility and all that garbage. Morals, ethics—" He yawned.

Not yet, not when we're finally getting to Rick.

"So he blames our lack of principles," he continued. "That's what he calls it, our lack of principles. He blames it on our youth. That's the usual excuse. 'It's the generation,'" he mimicked mockingly. It was just like listening to my colleagues complaining about their kids.

"And you, Rick? What do you believe?" His answer was important to me, yet I didn't know what I wanted to hear. *Something so profound and mature that it would justify my fascination with him?* If that was it, I was in for a disappointment.

"That life is for living," he said quietly.

"And war?" I prompted, still hoping. "What's that for?" Maybe it was for Steve that I was pushing it, a sort of giving the rich kid a chance to validate his position.

"For other people." He was silent for a minute, then asked, "How did you feel about losing your husband in the war? Did it make you feel idealistic?"

"I haven't lost my husband," I protested. "At least I don't know it."

"Don't you?"

Dear Lord, how could he ask me such a hurtful question? It wasn't talking about war that hurt; it was the wishing and waiting for Steve to come home. I had found a way years ago of disconnecting Steve from the war.

He was away; that was all. As far as I was concerned, he could have been on a long business trip; it didn't make any difference where. All that mattered, the thing that hurt, was that he wasn't home yet.

Rick must have realized. "I'm sorry, Maggie," he said. "I don't know how we got into this."

"Your family," I reminded him, trying to be casual, but all the while clenching my trembling hands in the pockets of my apron.

There was a space, a brief suspension of time, when, though he kept his eyes on me, everything between us seemed to have stopped. Then he shrugged, and a little smile curled the corners of his mouth. He was satisfied that a difficult moment had passed like a drifting cloud. He looked at me curiously. "Yes," he said slowly, "you might."

"Might what?"

Instead of answering, he said, "Maggie, do you expect to spend the rest of your life alone?"

My heart skipped a beat and I stood up abruptly and turned away. "I'm having company for dinner, Rick. You're welcome to join us if you feel up to it." There was no response, and I turned back to him. His eyes were closed. "Do you?"

"No," he whispered. "I feel sick again. Too much talking."

He was right; there had been too much talking. At least one question too many. "Sleep now," I said and hurried from the room.

Rick didn't come to the table; in fact, he didn't even eat. The awareness of him lying silently in the next room, staring at the ceiling, distracted me and made me restless. I was also worried about how Jerry would do what he was here to do without making Rick so angry that he would haul himself out of bed and back down to his own apartment. Though the food was good and the company was trying their best to liven me up, I wasn't really hungry, and most of the time I felt out of synch with the conversation. Carol, who had obviously noticed my preoccupation the minute she had arrived, was watching me warily all evening.

We'd been sitting with coffee and dessert for a while when Jerry put his napkin aside and announced he was going to the bathroom. After he had been gone for what seemed a long time by anyone's standard, I said nervously, "Do you think he found the patient, or does he have stomach trouble?"

"Both," Carol answered, rolling her eyes. I don't do humor very well, and she can be very tough when she's not in a patient mood. She caught her upper lip in her lower teeth and continued to watch me so intensely that I felt as if she was x-raying my face. "You are really off the wall tonight," she said quietly.

Now I knew this whole evening had been a mistake and that I just should have left Rick to his own devices. I'd known this woman for eight years; did I think she wouldn't probe? Did I think at all? I sighed, fixed my eyes on the cold coffee and the dirty plates.

"No games please, Maggie. It's him, isn't it, this guy you have in the other room." I said nothing. "In reality, he might be in Jennifer's bed, but for you he's been at the table all evening. What's going on?"

I wished that I could clench my hands in the pockets of my apron, but since I had left it in the kitchen, I had to make do with clasping them firmly on the table while I raised my face and looked her steadily in the eye. "There is absolutely nothing going on," I hedged.

She shook her head wearily. "Oh, I must have it mixed up then. Maybe you've mentally been in the bedroom with him. Is that it?"

I gave up. Carol is both a nurse and a clinical therapist and one of the most patiently persistent people in, possibly, the entire universe. She could sit out stubbornness, reluctance, even sheer refusal to cooperate longer and more calmly than seemed humanly possible. It was no use trying to put her off, and I desperately needed to bounce these last few weeks off somebody, so I gave in. But as soon as I opened my mouth to tell her how confused I'd been feeling, I couldn't make the words come. "If I'm edgy tonight, I'm sorry, Carol," I stalled. "I guess I wish I hadn't gotten myself into this. It's my vacation and who knows what this is going to turn into? I don't think I want the responsibility for the kid after all." That sounded good for starters, so I went on. "I don't know anything about him. It's just that he's been nice to us, especially to Jennifer. And he's sick and alone." I shrugged.

"No," she said. "There's more to it and I have the feeling you need to unload whatever it is." She smiled. "You're not like yourself tonight, Maggie. You act like you're harboring a fugitive."

What was the use? I let out a deep, defeated sigh, knowing that in less than five minutes, she was going to know what a pathetic fool I was. "He's twenty-two years old," I said miserably.

"Ah, starting with the biggies," she murmured. "So he's twenty-two years old. That's not a crime."

"Maybe not to you." I breathed hard and plunged. "He's . . . Kathy brought him home for dinner one night. He works at the television station in her building. She'd met him in the cafeteria. He's a doctoral candidate at the university. He's from New York. She thought he needed a friend—you know Kathy—and he lives in the other wing. He was nice, interesting in a different sort of way, attractive . . . Well, that's it."

"Go on."

"I don't know. He began taking Jennifer out on Saturdays. She likes him, trusts him. I didn't like it at first. You know how you'd feel with Sarah, letting a stranger take her off for an afternoon, but he's the oldest in a large family and he's so good with her. It was dangerous and irresponsible of me, but I let her go."

"I don't want to hear about him and Jennifer. I want to hear about him and you. That's what's really bothering you, isn't it?"

"There is no him and me. It's just that he's so . . . It's strange. He talks to us, tells us about himself, but he's not really saying anything, you know? And when he looks at me, I feel as if he's looking right into me, that he knows me, but I can't get to him. It's, well, it's disturbing."

"And?"

"And nothing. I just know—no, I don't know what I know." I turned away from her, too embarrassed to say more.

"Maggie." She put her hand over mine and looked at me earnestly. "Let me tell you something. You're the fugitive. You've been hiding inside your shell for—what—six, seven years? You're only human. You can't keep doing this to yourself. You have to let yourself out. Do you expect to spend the rest of your life alone?"

Startled, I told her, "He said that to me."

"Well?"

"Am I so transparent, Carol? Is it so obvious to everybody, even to strangers, that I—"

"Need people? Need men?"

"He's a kid!"

"I doubt his youth has any effect on his equipment. Don't blush. It's normal, Maggie."

"I love Steve," I whispered, tears starting.

You haven't seen Steve for years. Too many years. You're not the same person you were when you last saw him. What you love is his memory. Look, is there any way I can convince you? One thing has nothing to do with the other. If you are attracted to this man—what's his name?"

"Rick."

"To Rick, it's okay. You don't have to feel guilty. You owe it to yourself. You only have one life."

"But when Steve comes back—"

"Maggie—"

"He will, Carol. I felt it when I was home over the weekend. He was all around me. He will come back."

"Believe it then, if you have to. But you still have to live here now, and if you want Rick to be a part of your life, it's okay."

I heard her saying the words, but I knew it didn't make any difference. There was Steve, and there was Rick. One belonged, the other didn't. "But I don't!" I argued. "Sometimes he acts like a kid. I'm not interested in that. And," I added, "whether you believe me or not, I'm not really interested in testing his equipment either."

"Then what's the problem?"

Yes, what? Suddenly the whole thing seemed absurd, as though I were a thirty-two-year-old teenager in love with a movie star, as though it were that kind of ridiculous, obsessive one-way fantasy thing. I was so ashamed of myself. That was the problem. "I guess it's what you said. Me. Feeling guilty over finding him attractive."

"Is he?"

I shrugged, childish about admitting what was so obviously true. "So-so."

Carol opened her mouth to speak again but was interrupted by Jerry calling for her from Jennifer's room. "Okay," she challenged as she left the room. "I'll see for myself."

I got up to clear the table, feeling exhausted and disgusted with myself. Already I regretted having opened up to Carol. I never should have exposed myself like that, even to her.

She soon reappeared with a paper in her hand. "The doctor says the patient will live. I'm going to get this prescription filled."

"What is it?"

"Just an antibiotic. There's a lot of stuff in the lungs and Jerry thinks it's pneumonia, but without an x-ray he can't be sure." She put on her coat, stamped into her boots.

"Carol, I'll go."

"No, I think Jerry has other plans for you." Just before she went through the door, she said, "God sure knows how to make twenty-two-year-old doctoral candidates. I think I'm in love."

After she had returned from the drugstore and Jerry had given me instructions, Carol followed me into the kitchen. "Don't be so uptight, Maggie. Honest, it doesn't matter. You're not being foolish, only human."

She put her hand on my shoulder. “Look, he’s cute, he’s sweet, he’s smart, he’s clean, and for as long as he needs you and you need him, just let it happen. Enjoy it.” I said nothing. “I mean it,” she insisted. “That’s what I’d do . . . Oh, just one thing more,” she added as she left the room. “You were lucky this time, kiddo. Don’t ever trust Jennifer to anyone else you don’t know. Promise?”

I nodded. *Take three parts pathetic foolishness and add two parts guilt.*

I guess they let themselves out.

The kitchen was finished, and I forced myself to go into Jennifer’s room. Rick was lying quietly, watching the door, as if waiting for me.

“Feel any better?” I asked with false nursely cheerfulness.

“You had no right to do that, Maggie,” he croaked.

“I would have had no right to stand by and see you get sicker. It’s my job.”

“Then you’re a credit to your profession.”

I’d expected him to be annoyed, but I hadn’t counted on more sarcasm. My heart rose into my throat, and I couldn’t speak right away. With great effort, I moved to the bedside table and picked up the glass, intending to refill it. Rick grasped my wrist angrily, but he was weak. Jerry had probably shot him with something. “Maggie,” he said drowsily, “what are you going to do with the rest of your life?”

It didn’t take much to free my arm. “That has nothing to do with you, Rick. You sleep now.”

Once again I ran from my daughter’s room.

I barely slept, my mind racing for hours, Rick’s face haunting me through the night. Over and over their words repeating themselves in my head: “the rest of your life,” “spend it alone,” “expect to,” fragments floating around me, tossing me and turning me hour after hour. I was angry at Carol’s encouragement, Rick’s drugged presumptuousness. I felt trapped by the situation I had let myself into, disabled by my guilt. I wanted my old life back. I wanted Jennifer. She wasn’t here to make me know I was still me, and without her presence, I felt less in control than ever.

When I dragged myself into her room the next morning, it was close to noon. I dreaded seeing Rick’s face in the daylight, dreaded some unprovoked cruelty, feared still more his usual gentleness. I had done a number of unnecessary things that morning, even calling Jerry at the clinic to discuss Rick's condition. Pneumonia was not a new nursing experience for me, and I couldn't have felt stupider than I sounded asking questions about fever and long heavy sleeps. If I had been looking around for a way to punish myself for my foolishness, I couldn't have come to a better place. Jerry was one of the few people who could really exasperate me, and he was in fine facetious form, starting with his explanation for Rick's prolonged fever, "He has the hots for you," and ending with an exchange that almost guaranteed I wouldn't talk to him for the rest of my life—"Did Carol tell you she's in love?"

"Yes. She was joking."

"Did she also tell you that you are still a woman and entitled to a life—?"

"Jerry, stop it please."

"And that you are free to do, think, and feel as you wish?"

"Jerry, I'm going to hang up."

"I have a prescription for you, Maggie. It's a little unorthodox, perhaps, but I promise it's what you need, even though it can be habit-forming—"

I slammed the receiver down. Even seeing Rick couldn't be that humiliating.

So here I was, bustling around efficiently, opening the blinds, and messing around with the blankets. An automatic phony "good morning" came from my mouth before I could stop it.

Rick smiled sleepily.

"You look better," I chirped. He just grinned, didn't respond. "You hardly coughed all night," I reported. Still nothing from him but the grin. "That's a good sign." My last word. Three strikes and you're out.

But he caught the ball. "How do you know?" Still grinning, but we were making progress.

"That it's a good sign?"

"No, that I didn't cough all night. Didn't you sleep?"

"I've had better nights," I admitted.

This time I was ready for a sarcastic comment, but he only said, and in a shy and endearing way, "I'm sorry. If it was because you were worrying about me, look, I appreciate your going to all that trouble to get that doctor here. He must have put something good into me. The pain I had whenever I breathed is gone."

"Good."

"But you'd better get some rest. He says I'll have to stay here until the throat culture comes back."

Jerry! "It will take a few days. And you're the one who'd better rest. I'm going to need that bed back at the end of the week."

He nodded slowly, and our eyes connected and held. "I'll get your medication now," I said quickly, "and then you can give yourself a bath and have some breakfast."

"I have to wash myself?" he protested.

"I think you're strong enough today. And anyway, I thought you didn't want me to play nurse."

That smile again. There was no winning against this man. I stuck the thermometer in his mouth and took his arm to check his pulse. When I brought over the basin, cloth, and towels, he asked, "Am I being punished for being bad last night?"

I gave a front lock of his hair a maternal tug. "Don't forget to wash behind your ears, lady-killer."

The next few days moved along quickly. Rick's recuperation progressed at a steady rate so that by Friday he was out of bed for short periods of time. He ate and took his pills and was pleasant and undemanding. He kept his suggestive smiles to himself and avoided any references to the personal conversation we'd had that first afternoon. I called my mother to ask how Jennifer was doing. It was a short call. An awkward word or two with Mother, a few words with Jennifer, good-bye. Kathy announced a few times that she was coming over, and I hastily made up some excuses. I told her I was feeling the need for complete solitude so she wouldn't be suspicious. Of course she was anyway. In the end, I think she decided I was going through some kind of mood or that I was annoyed with her for some reason, and this kept her from just popping in after work. She asked about Rick each time I talked with her, and when I assured her that I was looking in on him and he was doing fine, there was an uncertain silence, but she didn't challenge what I told her.

Rick had been wearing the same pajamas for three days, and I wanted to put them in with my laundry that afternoon. I went down to his apartment for something else he could wear, and after a cursory search, I settled for some clean underwear that was jammed carelessly into the top drawer of his dresser. As I pulled a tee shirt free, a snapshot of a young woman fell on the floor. Kathy told me once she had once coerced Rick into telling her about a girl he had broken off with in New York, an English girl with an unusual name. I remember being irritated at Kathy's smugness about having pried this information out of him. Now I studied the picture, wondering if this could be that girl. The girl in the picture was plain and undistinguished, with blue eyes, long brown hair parted in the middle. She wore no makeup. She looked no different from many girls I saw walking around Clearyville or visiting at the hospital. I could even see her as one of his sisters. I turned the picture over, but there was nothing written on the back. It seemed to me that someone with Rick's looks and brains and money could have any girl he wanted and that the one he chose to go out with would be special. This one certainly didn't look special. I tried to put the picture back precisely where I had found it, but the image came home with me and refused to leave.

Rick's throat culture was negative, and he went back to his own place on Friday. I argued that he should stay in bed for a few more days, but he insisted that he felt completely well and reminded me that Jennifer would be coming home the next day. He still looked tired and weak, and I made him promise to stay in his own bed at least over the weekend. He promised. Then he picked up his clean laundry and took off down the hall. This time I didn't give a thought to anybody noticing him leaving my apartment with his pajamas in his hand; I was too busy wondering when I would see him again.

Without him in it, the apartment felt as empty as I did.

And so Jennifer returned, school began, my vacation was over. We settled into our normal routine, and my inner turmoil subsided. Kathy reported that Rick was working hard trying to make up the time lost on his thesis. It was two weeks before we saw him again. We asked him to dinner twice in that time, but he declined each invitation. I noted happily that I was not terribly disappointed.

As before, Kathy came over frequently, riding the bus with Rick in the most extreme Chicago winter weather. On the normally cold and windy days, Rick walked the three miles, as he had done on Christmas Eve, but he walked alone; Kathy's devotion didn't extend that far. She fished around a few times for an explanation for my distance over the vacation week, but I pretended I didn't know what she was talking about. Rick had obviously said nothing.

It was on a Tuesday toward the end of January when one of the nurses who was to take over the night duty on my service called in sick. The entire flying squad was either already assigned or out with the flu. I was late getting my coat to go off shift and so was the only one still around when the call came in. I always needed the extra money, so I agreed to take her place. I called Kathy, who was still at work, and asked her to pick up Jennifer and stay till I could get home.

She complained as she always did in this situation. "You've just done an eight-hour shift. You'll be exhausted."

"I know, but I'll be home by one. You can sleep in my bed and I'll collapse on the couch when I get in."

"I don't mind that, Maggie. I just don't see why you're always the one who has to do it."

"Because I'm always the one in the wrong place at the right time, that's why. With this flu epidemic, everyone's either filling in or home themselves. Anyway, I'm off tomorrow, so I'll catch up. I can't pass up time and a half."

"Well, I guess that's something. Okay. I'll take care of it. Just don't work too hard."

"I'll be on maternity ward. There won't be much to do, I hope."

"Unless there's a full moon."

"See you later."

As luck would have it, it was a wicked night. Nobody was normal, which is what always happens when the floor is short staffed. We did nine babies in three and a half hours, three of them premies and struggling. There were two emergency C-sections, in addition to the two electives we had done during the day, and by ten the recovery room was full. It was hectic. We were still short two nurses, and chaos is the only word to describe the mood on the floor. I must have begun half a dozen cups of coffee, only to leave them cooling after two harried gulps. Everyone had problems that night, but with it all, I would rather have been on the staff than in a bed. I don't think any of us had even one of our best feet forward. I finally left at one fifteen, close to exhaustion and praying that I would never have another shift like that.

When I got home, I found Rick asleep on my couch. Kathy was nowhere in the apartment, and there was no message to say why she wasn't. Jennifer was sleeping soundly in her bed. I kissed her lightly and returned to the living room. Rick's papers and things were spread around him, an indication that he had been there for a while. This was the first time I'd seen him in a couple of weeks, and a small sharp volt of excitement darted through me at the sight of his face. I stood watching him for a minute or two. He was slumped over on himself, as though he'd conked out suddenly without making an effort to get comfortable. He was wearing the old jeans and faded work shirt he'd worn the night I'd met him, and I noticed that one button had come undone on the front of his shirt and his sleeves were rolled below his elbows. There was a Band-Aid on his finger, and for some reason I fixed on it, maybe because looking at his face made my body feel funny in an old, half-remembered way I didn't want to associate with him. *Especially not with him.*

While I was standing there staring at him, his eyes popped open. He took a few seconds to focus. "Just get home?" he yawned.

"What are you doing here? I thought Kathy was babysitting."

"Agh, some guy propositioned her in the elevator after work and she couldn't refuse, so I said I'd do it for her."

"Oh, Kathy," I wailed. "Sometimes she's so . . . I think I can depend on her and then she does something like this. If I can't rely on her to help me out once in a while . . ."

Rick smiled. "It's only a date, Maggie. And it's not like she left Jenny by herself. I'm here."

I shook my head, the inside of which felt like a high-tension wire packed in cotton. If there's anything worse than being overstimulated and overtired at the same time, I don't know what it is. "I'm sorry, Rick, "I apologized weakly. "It's just that she makes me so . . . It's just that . . . God, I'm exhausted . . . What did you do about supper?" Scarcely five minutes in his presence and I couldn't get a coherent sentence out, except what did he do for supper.

"Jennifer made supper for both of us," he answered.

"Jennifer? What could she make?"

"She makes a mean peanut butter and jelly sandwich. And she found some chocolate milk."

I was too dumbfounded by the image of the Jennifer I knew preparing a sandwich or finding a carton of milk to think of anything more to say, and the conversation came to a standstill. It was awkward, but at last I managed to blurt, "I hope she behaved herself at least." Rick gave me a funny look because he knew well that Jennifer's hyperdocility was already a problem and that I sometimes wished she would break out of herself and act up a little.

"Yeah," he said, smiling again, "she was good."

All I wanted to do was fall into bed, but I was grateful to him for having been there when my sister had felt like being irresponsible. For lack of a better way to show my appreciation, I asked him if he would have a cup of tea with me. Hot tea probably didn't excite him too much, but at that point it sounded to me like the next best thing to deep sleep. He considered for a minute and accepted. "Rough night?" he asked.

"The worst." Fuzzily I went into the kitchen to put the water on, babbling all the while about the night's events. I spoke loudly from the kitchen, aware of the strangeness of a situation I had not been in for so many years. It was like being in a time warp because it had been this very way the times I had had night classes during the early days of my marriage. It was Steve on the couch in our old living room then, and I would be putting the water on, talking the whole time. I would go and sit with him until the kettle whistled, and he'd get up and fetch the tea. I had never worked this late in those days, but there were times when I'd been this worn out. And now, as if drawn by a magnet of memories, I came back to sit beside Rick on the couch to talk until the water boiled. But before I even knew I'd fallen asleep, I felt myself startled awake, not by the teakettle, but by something else, the awareness of Rick near me, very near me. His hand was on my face lightly, so lightly, and I jumped and gave a quiet little shriek. In that moment, I could feel his breath on my hair and could see the shadow of stubble on his jaw and smell a faint trace of soap smell. I knew that he had either just kissed me or was about to. "What are you doing?" I cried.

He drew back instantly and placed the steaming cup of tea on the table. "Your tea's ready," he said and moved a loose strand of hair from my eyes.

"Don't do that, Rick." I felt as if I were in a waking dream, acutely conscious of my surroundings, yet with a strong quality of unreality. I half expected him to protest that he hadn't done anything, but he didn't. He just looked at me. I realized that I was trembling.

He said quietly, "You know you don't mean that, Maggie."

"You'd better go."

"You don't mean that either."

"Yes I do," I insisted, but even I was not convinced.

"You can't go on wasting your life like this," he said, more softly still.

Why would an outsider say this? "It's my life and you don't know anything about it." *Why am I arguing with him?*

"I know you think you're waiting for Steve."

"That's right. He's my husband and he's coming back," I retorted with conviction.

"And you know he isn't. You haven't even heard from him or about him for six years."

"It doesn't matter. He's coming back. I believe that."

"You're making yourself believe that."

Tears came into my eyes and rolled down my face. I knew it was fatigue that had lowered my normally strong defenses, and his gentle hoarse voice that made me so depressed and deflated that I could not even control this embarrassing display of weakness. "Please don't do this," I pleaded. "It's all I have, Rick. If I can't believe that, I can't go on. You don't understand. It's taken me years to learn to survive. It's not fair for you to try to take it away."

"I understand that you're cheating yourself. What I can't figure out is why you want to throw your life away."

"It's my life."

"Yeah, it is, but sometimes other people can care about it too." *Did he mean him?* I couldn't ask him, and when I tried to find some answer in his face, I found nothing. "You're too good for that, Maggie. Don't you think you owe yourself something? All your best years are going by and you're sitting in your little cocoon, looking at old pictures."

The tears had passed now, and my head was clearer. It occurred to me somewhere outside myself that tact wasn't Rick's long suit, but like his father, I attributed this to his youth. After all, he had such a gentle way. I made a great effort to pull myself together, but it was too late. For months I had been losing large chunks of my precious self-control, and now, tonight, the last of it was slipping away, and I could do nothing about it. I felt weak with exhaustion and the fear of really getting close to Rick, which was the same to me as betraying Steve. To lose even the smallest particle of Steve terrified me. I hadn't really cried in years, but to my helpless horror, I had cried tonight. "You're taking advantage of me because I'm too tired to defend myself," I yammered accusingly.

"Defend yourself. Against what? I'd never do anything you didn't want me to."

Maybe I was too naïve to recognize a line and too trusting to believe that Rick would do this to me. Did it matter? All I knew at this moment was that I was tired and I was frightened and that I wanted him to touch me in any way he knew how and that I desperately wanted to touch him but didn't dare. I pulled myself up from the couch and picked up the cups of lukewarm tea, which had gone untouched.

"All you have to do is tell me to go home," he said.

"I did."

"But you have to mean it."

I refused to accept the faint tinge of arrogance in his voice. *Except there was no arrogance in his voice. My confusion was distorting everything.*

"I mean it," I insisted. "Go home." I took the cups into the kitchen, put them in the sink, stood waiting for the door to open and close. It didn't, and I walked dumbly back into the living room. He stood where I'd left him, rumpled, with sleepy creases beneath his eyes. He held out his hand to me.

Every instinct told me to make him leave my apartment right now, but I just couldn't do it. I couldn't muster the resistance tonight, wasn't sure I'd ever be able to. "I can't let myself do this, Rick," I whispered. He stood where he was and just looked at me with gentleness.

This is very wrong, Mary Grace. Don't do it. Oh, dear God, help me. I can't stop myself.

"It won't be anything you haven't done before, Maggie. I promise."

When I took his hand, I felt a terrible fear, as if God had turned away from me. But I couldn't help myself.

I have no idea how much time has passed, but it seems like forever. The clock on the night table is just beyond my shoulder, but I'm afraid if I turn over I'll wake him, this boy I hardly know who is lying beside me with his arm across my chest. He fell asleep almost instantly. I haven't been able to close my eyes—or have I? Maybe I've been asleep, and the whole thing is a dream. No, it couldn't be. He's too solid, too real. If I lie in this position much longer, my muscles are going to start cramping. On the other hand, maybe it's not him I'm afraid of disturbing but myself. Maybe I'm afraid that if I do move, I'll wake myself and find that he was never really here at all. And Steve. I keep seeing his face, heartsick, as if he knows that I've betrayed him. It was wrong. I know that. It will be light soon, and I will have to get up and face the day and do the things I have to do, and the world will go along as it always does. It's the way things are.

But, oh God, how will I ever live with what I've done?

I woke in full light, startled to discover that I'd finally fallen asleep and that Rick had left without my hearing him go. My brain automatically took up the inner monologue I'd been having when I dropped off, as if there had been no interruption at all. But I couldn't face it—my sinful betrayal of my husband, the guilt. I couldn't face myself in the daylight. I went into the kitchen, took a cup from the cabinet, and put water on for tea. Then I went to the bathroom to throw cold water on my face and back to the bedroom to make my bed. Passing the linen closet on my way back to the kitchen, something made me stop and open the door. For a moment, I went blank, had no idea what I was going to look for in there. After a minute or so, it came to me. Carefully, I lifted two blankets from the shelf above my head and set them on the floor, then rummaged around the back of the shelf until I found a small black cloth bag. My hands started to tremble as I brought it into view. I hadn't sought or seen the bag since the previous summer, but I needed to see it today.

The kettle started to whistle, and I took the bag into the kitchen, put a tea bag in the cup, and added the hot water. Slumping into my chair, I mindlessly watched the tea brew for a few minutes.The black bag was on the table to my left.—*Hold on, Mary Grace*—I looked at it for another minute, then opened it and took out the envelope.

The weather was perfect that Friday in September. Mother was over at church supervising the setup of the weekly potluck supper, Dad was at the mill, and Kathy was at school, where she had just begun her senior year. I was in the backyard with my beautiful daughter, Jennifer Elizabeth, who had been born five weeks earlier. I was nestled in the hammock that hung between two tall elm trees, and she was asleep in her carriage. She was a good baby, not at all fussy or demanding the way some new babies are, and I was idly musing over whether I should be worried about her being so quiet. Inwardly, though I that it wasn't the baby I was really concerned about, but Steve. Jennifer had been born amid devastating circumstances: Steve had disappeared while on a mission in Vietnam and had been declared missing in action. Though the birth had been easy and she was perfect in every way, I couldn't help thinking that her birthdays would always hold a taint of sadness connected with Steve's disappearance. By that time, I was worrying about anything I could think of in order not to obsess over him and where he might be, even if he was still alive. The army had informed us on June 13 and that he had been officially declared missing in action. They'd been kind and sympathetic, but they just didn't have much information. I had been horribly depressed for six weeks, had lost all interest in food, and could barely get up off the couch. Everybody in town was solicitous and helpful to us and to Steve's family. Even my mother, who was never the most sympathetic person in the world, seemed to understand that it was not a good time to badger me into pulling myself together, even for the baby's sake. Now, after three months, I was able to take care of Jennifer, and though the pain of Steve's situation was no less intense, I was handling it a little better. I was to return to nurse's training on Monday—two weeks late for the start of the semester—and I was once again thinking about possibly transferring to Chicago in January. Last month had been our third anniversary, which only intensified my grief, and though I was doing better overall, I still hadn't adjusted to Steve's not being here with me, to his not even knowing he had a daughter. I prayed to God every day to bring him back, and I refused to consider the possibility that He wouldn't or couldn't.

On this day, however, there was nothing but quiet and birdsong. The air was warm and sweet, and the sun felt good. I closed my eyes and tried to conjure up Steve lying in the hammock with me, as he so often had.

"Excuse me?" said a calm, quiet male voice. I blinked, slightly confused, as if I'd wakened from a dream, and turned slowly to find a tall black man standing about ten feet from me with his hat in his hand. To say I was startled would be a gross understatement. Our church, which comprised about 98.5 percent of Clearyville, did not accept minorities as being on an equal basis with us, and the factory hired only white men. It's the way it had always been, and we saw nothing wrong with it. So I was flabbergasted and alarmed to find a Negro in my backyard.

"Sorry," he said with a sheepish, toothy smile, "I rang the front doorbell several times, then came around here in case you were taking advantage of the beautiful weather. I didn't mean to scare you."

I hurriedly pulled my legs over the side of the hammock and stood up. "I . . . I was just daydreaming. Can I help you?" Mother had told us that we are always polite. We are not trash. *He stepped forward, and I instinctively took a step back, which was not polite, but I'd never been in this situation before. I had no idea how I should respond to a stranger—especially this particular stranger—appearing out of nowhere in my backyard.*

He was undaunted. "Are you Mrs. Mary Grace McLean?"

My stomach lurched. "Yes," I answered tentatively, at that moment realizing that he was wearing a military uniform. "Is this about my husband?"

"I'm Lt. Sam Munson, ma'am. Steve and I were good friends over in 'Nam. And well, no news, unfortunately, but I stopped by to bring you something I believe he meant for you to have."

When he said Steve's name, something I'd never experienced before came over me: a weak sensation that started in my legs and spread up through my body, turning my insides to jelly. My head felt as if it was shaking up and down like one of those bobble-head things on springs that you see in the back window of people's cars. I made it to a nearby lawn chair, dropped into it, and bent way forward so my head was hanging down past my knees. The world seemed to be suspended for a time, until I finally began to get my wits back. When I raised my head, the man was watching me with an expression I can only truthfully describe as compassion. I wouldn't have expected that.

"Are you okay, Mrs. McLean?" he asked anxiously.

I took a deep breath. "Yes, I'm all right now, thanks," I answered feebly, grasping the arms of the chair and pulling myself up. My legs were unsteady, but at least I was upright. "Nothing like that has ever happened to me before."

"You don't look so good," he said. "Is there anything I can do?"

My heart was beating thunderously. "No, it's okay. If you'll just give me a minute—" And then it came to me who this man was. I never would have imagined . . . "You're Lt. Munson? My husband wrote me about you." My voice sounded strange, distant, and my heart would not slow down. "What is it he gave you for me?"

Just then Jennifer started to cry, and I excused myself and shakily made my way over to the carriage. I tried to ignore a moment of dizziness when I bent to pick her up. As I brought her tiny body into my arms, a wave of such intense emotion swept over me that I couldn't move. Steve's child . . . Lord, please bring him home. *I wobbled back to the lawn chair and dropped into it, cradling her in my arms and unable to take my eyes off her.*

"She's a beautiful baby," the lieutenant said softly. "I think she resembles her daddy."

Thank you," I whispered. Am I crazy? The man isn't anything like he's supposed to be. If he hadn't cared about Steve, he wouldn't be here now. *In spite of what I'd been taught all my life, I wanted to trust him.*

Jennifer was picking up steam now, and even though her little face was all screwed up and red, the man was right. I, too, thought that she looked a lot like Steve. I squinted up at the sun to judge the time of day: just past midday. She was hungry. What had I done with her bottle? I started to rise but still felt weak. Nerves. The lieutenant came forward, I guess to help me, and again I recoiled. And felt ashamed. "Her bottle, it's in the carriage."

"May I get it for you?" Just trust him. He was Steve's friend, the last person to see Steve before he . . . what? *Jennifer was working herself into a frenzy. "If you would just pull the carriage over here. Thank you."*

"You're living with your parents?" I quickly retrieved the bottle before he could put his hands on it. He sat down in the chair across from mine. My parents would have a fit if they saw this. Please, God, don't let Mother come home before he leaves.

"Yes, but it's temporary. I have one more year to go for my nursing degree."

"Hey, that's great. My wife's a second-grade teacher. She moved back with her parents too. She didn't want to live alone."

I nodded my head in empathy. "Do you have children?"

"Not yet. First I get my master's degree. Then we'll think about a family."

"What are you studying?"

"Architecture."

"That's what Steve—"

"Yeah. We have a lot in common." He checked his watch. "Well, I have to get a bus back to Chicago in time to make my flight connection. I'd better give this to you and take off." He took an envelope from his breast pocket. My eyes flooded when I took it from him. "When I packed Steve's stuff so they could send it back to you, this must have fallen out of his bag. I never saw it until I was doing my own packing to come home."

My hand began to tremble, and my head started buzzing. I stared at the envelope, willing myself not to make another scene. But it was as if I was touching Steve himself.

I sensed the lieutenant rise to his feet. "I'll leave you alone now so you can read it."

"I'll never be able to thank you for bringing the letter to me in person," I said tearfully, and meant it. I knew it was wrong, but in that moment, I didn't want him to go. He was my last link with Steve, the last human link.

"No trouble at all." He smiled. "I'm on my way home to Cleveland."

"Your tour is up?"

"Sure is." He looked away for a second, then at Jennifer, then at me. "It was an honor for me to serve with Steve. All the men in our company had a lot of respect for him. We knew we could always rely on him to be there for us. He's a good soldier and a good man, and I'll be praying for him to get back and for you and your family to be together again before very long."

I watched him walk across the grass toward the path to the front of the house, stop suddenly, and come back. "There were five of us that day," he said as if it was an afterthought. "Myself and another guy were leading the way and Steve and the other two were a couple of yards behind us. The two of us were beating back the bush, trying to clear the way for the others. It was raining hard. It's noisy in the jungle, anyway, and with the rain and the way we were moving, we couldn't hear anything. We'd only gone thirty, maybe forty yards, when we checked behind us and didn't see them. We doubled back, even hacked into the bushes a ways in every direction, but there was no sign of them. They were gone and we'd never heard a sound." He turned his palms up in wonder and shrugged. "It happened on my watch . . . I'm so sorry."

"It wasn't your fault. They're calling him MIA and I know he'll come home. I feel it." He lowered his head and nodded. "God bless you and keep

you, Lieutenant," I continued, my voice shaking, "for knowing how much this letter means to me, for knowing how much I needed to have this small human connection with my husband." Impulsively—totally forgetting who he was—I put my hand out to him. He took it, and we shook, as though the three of us had formed a bridge, a bond—him to me to Steve. It felt right.

"Mary Grace! What in holy heaven are you doing?" My body jerked as if I'd had a spasm. It was my mother's sharp voice coming from the back door. Steve vanished, and the lieutenant looked up, startled, and pulled away. How long had she been there? My cheeks turned to flame.

"Mother, this is Lt. Munson of the United States Army. He was in Steve's company and he's been kind enough to come here and give me a letter from him."

My mother nodded stiffly in the lieutenant's direction. "Well, isn't that *nice. Everybody in the neighborhood's been wondering about that taxi that's been sitting out front for so long. I assume it's waiting for you, Lieutenant?"*

At that moment, I hated my mother, but the lieutenant simply smiled and bowed. "Delighted to meet you, Mrs.—"

She said nothing, so I offered weakly, "Hill."

"Miz Hill, ah yes." He looked at his watch again, then at me. "It's been a pleasure talking with you, Mrs. McLean."

Still holding Jennifer and the bottle, I walked to the taxi with him, wanting desperately to apologize for my mother, but unable to find the energy.

"Well, you keep well and take care of that little girl," he said. "Her daddy's going to be crazy about her when he gets back."

My mouth formed another "thank you," but nothing came out. He climbed into the cab and turned down the window. The motor started, and he smiled and waved. I lifted Jennifer upright and held her against me. This good man had been with Steve that last day . . . Thank you, Lord.

The taxi disappeared from sight. I went slowly into the house on still-shaky legs and, ignoring my mother's icy, disapproving glare, climbed the stairs to Jennifer's sunlit room. I settled her in her crib, then sank down on the bed, opened the letter carefully. I read it through over and over, I don't know how many times, all the while crying so hard I felt as if my eyes would never be dry again. When I finally woke up, the sunlit windows were now deep blue. Kathy was sitting in the rocking chair, feeding Jennifer her bottle. I heard Dad's radio downstairs and the clatter of dinner dishes, life going on as usual. I would go on with it too, the best I could, for Jennifer and for Steve, until he came home.

And I had no doubt he'd come home. We'd made a bond.

Two days passed, and we didn't see Rick at all; two days during which I went about my business at work and at home, trying, for Jennifer's sake, to remain steady despite the emotional upheaval inside me; two days in which I tried not to think about what would happen next or about how I could face Rick when I couldn't face myself. But I had to make peace with myself, and so on the second night, after supper was over and Jennifer was asleep, I went into the living room, turned off the lamps, lay down on the couch, and forced myself to confront what I'd been spending so much energy avoiding.

How did it happen in the first place? Had he seduced me? Had he taken advantage of my exhaustion, that weak moment? Or had it been coming for months and I just didn't have the strength to hold it off? All I'd wanted to do when I finally got home that night was get out of my uniform and fall into bed.

I remember him bringing me tea that I was too tired to drink. I remember him saying things that were hurtful, things that made me cry. And I remember letting him lead me into the bedroom, even though I knew I would probably lose the little self-control I had left. I dimly recall that he seemed to hesitate, as if he had had a change of heart, but instead of just leaving, he took me by the shoulders and sat me down on the bed.

"Maggie, I . . . I . . . ," he began, then sat down next to me, put his arm around my shoulders. His arm felt both heavy and soothing. He appeared to be pondering whether to stay or go. Minutes passed . . . I was so tired . . . I remember thinking how peaceful it would be if we could just lie together, maybe fall asleep holding each other.

Then he asked, "Have you ever been to Italy?"

Italy . . . what does that have to do with anything? I looked at him blankly.

"I was there a few years ago," he went on in a conversational tone, evidently not expecting an answer and as if I had asked him to tell me about a European vacation he had taken. "You can't believe how beautiful it is in some places. But, of course, you have to know where those places are"—*my stomach lurched as I saw, out of the corner of my eye, that he was unbuttoning his shirt*—"and how to get to them," *pulling it out of his pants, tossing it on the floor, kicking off his shoes, bending over to take off his socks.* "The thing you have to do if you want to learn your way around a foreign country is to hire a tour guide," he went on without missing a beat, his voice softer now, the smoky quality of it almost hypnotic. I longed to touch his smooth back, the ridges along his spine, his shoulder blades, which looked somehow vulnerable.

He straightened up and turned to me. "You like the light on or off?"

"Off," I said, shaking my head foggily. This whole thing was too surreal for me, the way he made it all seem so ordinary. Italy, tour guides, this man, any man, in my bed. This wasn't happening . . .

He swung his legs up onto the bed and lowered himself onto his back, maneuvered me down beside him. "Maggie," he asked earnestly, "do you think you could pretend that I'm a country you've never been to?"

What? What was he talking about? I was unable to imagine where he was going with this, but as though I had the wits of a puppet, I nodded anyway. He reached across me to the lamp. The switch clicked, and the room went black. I couldn't breathe. I felt him take my hand and place it on his chest. Once again my common sense told me not to let this continue. This time, however, my traitorous body told my common sense to get lost.

"We picked up the guide in Naples," he continued lazily, placing his hand over mine and moving it lightly in slow circles around his thorax, his abdomen, his ribs. "We were all into ruins, hiking, great scenery, all that stuff. One of the guys was a volcanologist and he said he would take us to Taormina, which is on the Mediterranean, close to Mount Etna." My heart was thumping like a kettledrum. I knew he could feel it, and I was embarrassed. He kept moving my hands up, down, back, forth, round and around, and I had this flash delusion that it was the first time I'd touched his body, that I'd never before felt the fine texture of his skin or the length of his bones or the contour of his muscles. It was so different from bathing him on a sickbed or watching him asleep in daylight, sensual in a way those chores could never be. I realized that he had stopped guiding me but that my hand, actually my fingertips now, were continuing to graze on their own. After a while, he brought my palm to his cheek, and my fingers, tentatively at first, then raptly, explored the fullness of his mouth, the firmness of his nose, the shape of his jaw, the little shallow indent in his chin. Then, suddenly, I became aware that he had somehow managed to get himself out of the rest of his clothes and me out of everything but my underwear—*where had my brain gone?*—and I panicked for a moment, but it was a reflex reaction, and I didn't resist when he relieved me of those too. Whatever inhibitions I still had vanished, and I could no longer deny what I'd wanted since that first night in my dining room when he turned to me and I saw his eyes. I think he knew even then what it was, but he took these last three months getting to it, just as he took his time tonight. And now, there was no turning back. I was getting what I wanted: the anticipation and expectation, the intensity of the feverish flush and acute sensitivity of every nerve in my body as it responded to his nearness, to his touch, his heartbeat, the act. It was all I had remembered and more than I could ever have imagined. And true to my perception of the difference between us, he had made it happen, and I had let it happen. When he finally withdrew, I collapsed like a deflated balloon against him, and we lay quietly for a time, letting our systems return to normal. Then he leaned over, kissed me, and rolled over on his stomach. Within minutes, he was asleep, leaving me slightly dazed and with a still slightly elevated heartbeat.

All I knew was that I was somewhere I'd never been before . . . and it wasn't Italy.

I must have fallen asleep at some point because the next thing I knew, it was six twenty, the light in the room was silvery, and Rick was gone. It wasn't time for Jennifer to get up yet, so I lay a while longer, staring at the ceiling and listening to Rick in my mind, his smoky voice repeating words about how life was for the living and war was for other people; about how I was existing in a self-imposed limbo, waiting for a man who had vanished from my life six and a half years ago; about how he would never do anything I didn't want him to; about how he would never hurt me. Maybe every word was true, but this was all too much for me to deal with right now. I sensed that change was being demanded of me and that I was the one making the demands. That was scary.

Everything was crowding in on me, and hovering over all of it was the humiliating possibility that all I had been was a one-night stand for a lonely kid with beautiful dark eyes and a good line.

I couldn't imagine that he would come to me again. There had to be girls, girls his age, girls whose numbers he kept in a book somewhere. Did they ever feel guilty? Probably not, the way things are nowadays. But I did. And I didn't want to. Every second we had spent together had been like nothing I had ever experienced, and I wanted more. I knew from all I had read and heard that these things rarely ended well, but I refused to think about that. I just wanted him to come back.

I had to admit to myself that the turmoil inside me was not only about betraying Steve, but also about me. Who I was, and what had made me me. I had figured out a long time ago that Kathy and I were the unlikeliest daughters our puritanical parents could have had. For Kathy, who reached puberty at a time when everyone you read about was rebelling against something, it was easier to free herself from the restrictiveness of our upbringing. Though total liberation from their ways was an idea I had often suppressed, the rules of our parents' straitlaced orthodoxy were deeply ingrained in me. I simply followed blindly in their footsteps and probably would have continued to do so if I had not been thrust into the position of single working mother. My mother had made it clear early on that I was expected to go into nursing, but the idea of having to touch people's bodies repelled me. I wasn't even in my teens yet when she started reminding me that a woman was to regard the human body as a tool to get a job done; nothing more, nothing less. When I asked what the job was that the body was supposed to do, she said simply, "Create children." When, at the age of eleven, I asked her exactly how that worked, she said I would find out when the time was right. I never brought the subject up again. It was at a sleepover at the house of a Sunday school friend when we were in the eighth grade that I got an inkling of what was involved. I didn't trust the explanation much, though, because the process was made to sound like fun, and I knew that couldn't be right. Not when my mother had made it sound like serious stuff. Even though I like my job and I've tried to be the best at it that I can be, I can't help wondering sometimes if there might have been something besides nursing that I would have liked to do.

Fortunately I married a patient man, so when the right time actually came, he understood my lack of abandon. Both of our families belonged to the same church, and he knew my mother's reputation for severity in all things. Steve, of course, helped me to loosen up, even let go. Still, I'd never experienced anything like the mixture of anxiety, joy, and exhilaration I felt with Rick. It was as if I was on sensory overload and as totally out of control as I had felt the night Marjorie Barr talked me into going on a roller coaster ride.

But old conditioning dies hard, and now I was feeling guilty and so ashamed, it had taken me days to even be able to think about myself with Rick. The realization that not once during those hours did I think of Steve or even of Jennifer in the next room didn't help much either. I didn't like me very much, nor did I feel comfortable wondering, for the first time ever, who I really was. At the same time, I sensed it was all part of the changes my instinct told me it was time to make, and I was kind of glad, in a way, that I'd been too weak to stop myself from giving in.

Rick came over around ten thirty the following night as if nothing at all had happened between us. His quiet rap on the door startled me, and the fantasy I usually had when someone came unexpectedly—that it would be Steve in his uniform, looking happy and healthy and home for good—never even occurred to me. When Rick hadn't stopped by during the past two days, I just assumed that he felt as uncomfortable with me as I did with him. That turned out not to be the case.

I was in my bathrobe and had no makeup on. When I looked through the peephole and saw him, my stomach instantly tied into knots. I opened the door a crack, and he smiled. I couldn't resist that smile and opened the door a bit wider.

"Is it all right if I come in?" he asked, the smile fading into a quizzical expression. I stepped aside. "You okay? You look funny."

"It's not my best time of day. I'm dressed for bed and I don't have makeup on."

"I see that. I didn't realize it was so late. I was hoping you'd offer me a cup of coffee."

"Oh. Well, come into the kitchen." He followed me across the living room. "Instant okay?"

"Anything. Just make a pot of it." He settled himself at the table.

I started the coffeemaker and stood at the counter with my back to him while it brewed. I knew I was making a mountain out of a molehill, but I couldn't face him. He waited in silence. When the pot clicked off, I filled two cups, took spoons from the drain board, and sat down opposite him. He blew across the rim of his cup and took a sip. "You're upset," he said.

"Yes."

"The other night."

"Yes." *Dear Lord, I don't want to talk about it.*

He sighed. "I hoped you wouldn't feel like this, Maggie. All I wanted to do—do you think you could look at me while I'm trying to make up with you?"

For some reason, the words "make up" struck me funny. Marjorie and I used to make up regularly. Steve and I had to "make up" a couple of times after disagreements. The words just, I don't know, sounded odd coming from Rick. I lifted my head and smiled weakly.

"Thanks. I would like to talk with you about this."

"I really don't want to talk about it, Rick."

"Why not?"

"I don't feel comfortable talking about it."

"Why not?"

"Because I don't and please don't ask me 'why not' again."

"Fine, then you listen and I'll talk."

"No. I've heard enough about how I'm wasting my life. It's caused me nothing but trouble."

"You think the other night was trouble? I'm sorry to hear you feel that way . . . Why was it trouble?" He looked at me with a wounded expression that seemed genuine. I wished I hadn't said it. For one thing, it wasn't true.

"Why do you think? I'm a married woman with a young child on the other side of the wall. Besides, doesn't it bother you that I'm ten years older than you are?"

He nodded his head slowly. "I see." He thought for a moment. "Are you aware that in some states a couple is automatically considered divorced after being apart for seven years? It's called the Enoch Arden law." That sounded like something he was making up, and I opened my mouth to tell him so, but he continued, "Regarding Jennifer, I thought I was being exceptionally quiet under the circumstances. Even at certain crucial moments, I was careful not to make noise. Did she say she heard anything?"

"No, but—"

"And as for the age thing, it's not like I'm fourteen." He sucked in a lungful of air and slowly let it out. "I'm sorry it bothers you so much, but there's nothing I can do about it."

He slugged the rest of his coffee, picked up his cup, took it to the sink, then walked past me and out of the room.

I caught up with him at the front door. "Rick, be reasonable. Think about it from my point of view."

He turned back to me. "I want to sleep with you again, Maggie."

I felt like crying, but never would I let him see me do that again. I didn't know what to say, so I settled for the first thing that came into my head. "Will you wear protection?"

"I'll pay for a diaphragm."

"And you promise Jennifer will never know?"

"I'll oil your bedsprings."

After all the guilt and confusion, how could I not simply say no? "I don't . . . I mean, I'm not sure—"

"Is that a yes?"

I looked at him, at the expectation on his guileless face. "Yes," I agreed, knowing it would probably end in disaster but unable to say anything else.

Within a month, he had stayed with me several times. He would go to the university or study in his apartment until eleven, then he would come down for a cup of coffee and the news and casually slip into my bed. He was always gone before I woke up. Even so, I continued to be concerned about Jennifer. Though I couldn't imagine what it could mean to her if she found Rick in my bed, I worried that she would innocently mention it to Kathy or the sitter or my mother. *Or Steve's mother.* Any responsible person would agree that it was inappropriate for a child's mother to be sleeping in the next room with a man who wasn't her father. There was never a night that I didn't think about that, but she was a sound sleeper and hadn't discovered it so far. Rick, of course, laughed and suggested I lock the door so he would have time to hide under the bed if she wanted to come into the room. I was not quite as casual as I tried to pretend I was, and didn't think he was very funny.

Once the rosy afterglow had worn off, I realized that guilt was going to be a very powerful opponent. Guilt was not something that Rick spent much time on, and sometimes it was as if he was doing his best to make mine worse. One evening when I expressed some discomfort about our situation, he was so impatient with me that I almost wound up in tears. The episode ended abruptly with him saying, "I'm not going to listen to this shit anymore, Maggie. Make up your mind. Do you want me to go or do you want me to stay? There's no room for Steve and me, so if you'd rather be with him, I'll leave." And I had to face the fact that where this had once been an impossible question, it was now an easy choice. After all, he was here, and Steve wasn't.

Early in March, I agreed to take the three-to-eleven shift, mainly for the extra pay. Rick agreed to split the babysitting with Kathy, who obviously had no idea about us.

He had let his guard down a lot by now. Once he even mentioned the girl he had been engaged to (*engaged?*), and again I wondered if she was the one whose picture I had found in his dresser. I didn't ask questions, just let him tell me what he chose to. Sometimes we spoke about our families and sometimes about the ordinary little things in our lives: his hours at the station, meeting with his dissertation advisor, his analysis of the world news, my days on the wards. I didn't understand his work or care much about what was going on elsewhere in the world, but lying in the dark with him, listening to his past, his family, his knowledge and intelligence, was like sitting in the audience of a wonderful and exciting play. He could be a good storyteller when he wanted to be, and I would lie there with a silly smile he couldn't see, visualizing the scenes he drew with his soft, hoarse voice. A lot of it was commonplace, even in towns like Clearyville. Parties, movies, bowling, miniature golf. He had been good at tennis, fair at golf, terrible at football. He had taken trumpet lessons for six years until his teacher had begged him to quit. It was the stuff camera commercials were made of. And there were other things: friends who had pool parties at their houses, friends who had their own boats, the country club—Clearyville did have a country club, but I had only glimpsed it when Marjorie and I sneaked peeks through the tall dense hedges surrounding it. Rick's father had taken him to New York City many times during the years he was in grade school and junior high. He had even seen shows on Broadway. As he talked, I recalled Steve's two dreams: to buy me a home and to take me on a vacation to New York City. It probably would have taken years for us to be able to do either, but for Rick, they were an ordinary part of life. And he'd actually gone on that trip to Italy. I asked him if he knew how lucky he was to have had all those opportunities.

"Lucky?" he asked after a long silence. "I don't know. It's the only way it ever was."

"But to have so much," I marveled.

He agreed that having all that was nice, but added, "It depends on what it is you have so much of. Maggie, don't wish yourself into another person's life. Nothing is perfect and you might find something in all that 'much' that you wouldn't really want." Though intense about his work and what he read in the papers, Rick rarely sounded so serious about himself, and I wondered if he was referring to his own life. I didn't pursue it, though, because to me, his life was like a fairy tale without wolves or wicked witches, and I wanted to continue to believe it was that way. Still, he had been a teenager in the '60s, so maybe he saw things differently than I did. The ten years between our ages could have been a century. And yet in spite of all the things that were alien to me, like wealth and sophistication, I could talk to him like he was an ordinary person, just someone I knew. There were times when we talked late into the night, but still I never saw him go. I would open my eyes and like magic he'd be gone.

By now I knew he seemed well-adjusted, what Kathy might call a "really together person," who knew where he had been and where he was going. I had once believed myself to be like that, but in a different way. I had always known where I was going because it was all set out for me, and I just followed the track. Rick, however, made choices and followed through.

I guess I let things work and he made things work. The pieces of the puzzle he had been were finally falling into place.

I didn't share any of what I learned him with anyone. I didn't know why he had opened up, but I was fascinated, and every new piece of information he whispered during those nights only increased my appetite for more.

There was a strange sense of unreality about this time, a floating sensation, a feeling of suspension. I was helplessly drawn to Rick, and it frightened me. I couldn't deny that the self-dependence I had spent years building was slowly slipping away from me, yet in spite of the uncertainties in our relationship, his presence gave me a wholeness I had lost when Steve didn't come back. Rick was not a supportive person, and he really had no desire to understand the challenges in my life. But he was here and I needed him. Yet sometimes, when I lay in bed alone disarmed by sleep, the cozy glow gone, I would have a feeling of falling, sort of losing my grip for a while. *Hold on*, I would say to myself over and over. *Mary Grace, hold on.*

I remember one time when the carnival came to my hometown, Clearyville, a factory town surrounded by farmland about forty miles northwest of Chicago. Those forty miles between us and the city might have been four hundred; we were as far removed from city influence as could be. Many people lived their entire lives within the town limits. There was not a lot to do, so every August, when Mitchell's Traveling Carnival set up in a big field about two miles east of town, it was the big event of the year.

I was thirteen or fourteen that summer, and my best friend was Marjorie Barr. She and I had been inseparable since fourth grade. The week before the carnival arrived, Marjorie had confessed to me that she'd been approached by Carolyn Cleary. Carolyn's family had owned the mill for generations and were the richest and most prominent members of the town, which, of course, had been named for them. Carolyn herself, being the most popular girl in our class, was an ever-present reminder of the hierarchy system that dominated every facet of town life, even school. Once in a while, I guess to show how magnanimous the Clearys were, she would suddenly invite some classmate from what my father called "the pavement" to join her clique. This time it was my friend Marjorie, pretty, fun-loving Marjorie Barr, who was everything I wasn't. Though I couldn't imagine she would ever let me down, I was secretly afraid that one day Carolyn would take her away from me. Marjorie said, however, she'd kind of shrugged her off. My father and Mr. Barr were accountants, not mill workers, at the factory, but he and my mother didn't associate with the Barrs; Mother and Dad bore the marks of their own childhoods and felt comfortable only with the people in our church. Neither Marjorie nor I cared whether the rich kids even knew who we were—at least I didn't—and knowing Marjorie so well, I felt sure that she didn't either. We were like sisters; I loved her.

It was the first time Marjorie and I had gone to the carnival together. My parents had never permitted me to go, so I lied and said I was going to Marjorie's house. We were too timid to go on the big rides, just enjoyed walking around, eating the usual carnival hot dogs, cotton candy, and ice cream. It was a beautiful night, and we hadn't yet outgrown the excitement of neon lights and carnival noise. The one thing that marred the freedom of the evening for both of us was that Marjorie's mother had made her bring along her eight-year-old brother. Still, he was behaving well, so we tried to make the best of it.

We ran into the Cleary crowd as they were about to board the new Thrillcoaster. Carolyn and the girls invited Marjorie to join up with them, and when I saw her actually considering it, my heart stopped while she made her decision. What she did was tell Carolyn flat out that she would go with them if Russell and I were invited too. I was relieved when I saw that Carolyn didn't seem to care much for those conditions and looked as if she was about to withdraw the offer. But Russell said he was afraid to go on the ride. I felt the same way and said that I would stay on the ground with him, but then Carolyn decreed that he and I sitting together would be "the perfect solution," and Marjorie begged him to ride. He gave in, and we all boarded. Marjorie's friendship was the most important thing on my mind as we struggled up to the top, but the moment the roller coaster went into its first dive, terror took first place, and I found myself holding on to Russell for dear life, while he sat with his face buried in my lap and cried. When it was over, Russell wouldn't stop crying until we said we'd take him home. Carolyn said Marjorie just couldn't leave, and Marjorie looked so torn, that I said she should go with them, that the ride had made me feel sick, and I would walk Russell home. And so the much-anticipated evening ended, and so, I thought, did my friendship with Marjorie.

Later I would have to admit that there had been a certain exhilaration to the roller coaster's grueling climbs and breath-stopping drops. Though engulfed by an overpowering numbing terror, I was still vaguely aware somewhere outside myself of the shouts and shrieks of the other riders. Still, the voice I most vividly recalled when I thought of that awful ride was my own, and it was screaming, Hold on, Mary Grace. Maggie, hold on. *Marjorie didn't last long in the clique, and when Carolyn dropped her, she turned back to me.*

I sometimes heard echoes of those shouts and calls in the darkness of the early mornings after Rick had gone and I lay awake and alone. *Hold on, Mary Grace. Hold on*. And I still remembered the enormous relief I felt when Marjorie came back to me after Carolyn lost interest in her.

But who will I turn to when Rick has gone for good?

Eventually the world righted itself, and everything got back to normal. My guilt had nearly faded, and at times the three of us seemed almost like a family. Weekends were especially nice because Rick made a point of taking Jennifer out somewhere a couple of Saturday mornings a month. I particularly liked their park days because the park was one of Jennifer's favorite places, and not being a fan of frigid temperatures or lake-effect winds, I couldn't handle it during the winter. Jennifer, however, seemed oblivious to blustery weather, and never once had I caught her huddled miserably in a corner of the sandbox or the kiddie rink with her hands in their red mittens, stuck up in her armpits. In Rick she had a real buddy; winter didn't bother him either.

So I always looked forward to April, the month when we would begin to see signs that the long Chicago winter was ending, the month when the skies would more often be blue than gray and Saturdays in the park would mean reading on a bench in chilly spring sunshine instead of bundling into myself wishing I was home with a cup of hot tea.

This year, April also meant a visit from Rick's parents.

Except for a momentary quake of apprehension, I felt nothing when he casually informed me that they would be coming out from New York. We discussed the logistics of our situation, and he readily agreed it would be best if he slept at his own place for the nights they would be in town. Despite my curiosity about them, I was actually hoping he wouldn't introduce us. I was too afraid our arrangement would be discovered or the telephone conversation I had had with his mother be revealed. After a couple of weeks went by and he hadn't mentioned their visit again, I began to relax, thinking they probably weren't going to come after all.

He must have said something to Kathy, though, because all of a sudden she couldn't talk about anything else. She was finding that life in the big city wasn't quite as glamorous as she had envisioned it before she'd left home, and now she appeared to be immersed in a daydream in which she saw herself actually rubbing elbows with the kind of worldly elegant people she imagined Rick's parents to be. Sometimes I just wanted to shake her.

A month or so earlier, she had begun dating a boy named Todd, whom she had met at a party she'd gone to, so we weren't seeing her as often as we had been. This worked out well for me since I always felt I had to be on my guard when she was around. I don't know why I was so anxious about her finding us out. After all, it was probably so inconceivable to her that Rick could be attracted to me that I assumed she had finally decided that he and I had nothing more than a friendship that revolved around Jennifer. Besides, Rick was good about not leaving telltale personal articles around my apartment, not because he thought it was a sensible idea, but because I had insisted. In any event, it wasn't likely he'd slip up since he usually showered, shaved, and dressed at his own place before he went to work.

One evening when they were both over for dinner, Rick asked us if we knew a good cleaning person he could hire before his parents arrived. Kathy, never one to pass up an opportunity, pounced. Forget the professionals; she would do the job, free of charge. Rick, in his wisdom, tried really hard to put her off, but she didn't hear a word he said, declaring emphatically that he could expect her at ten the following Saturday. He shrugged in defeat.

Later, after she had gone, he asked, "Does she even know the difference between a broom and a dishrag?"

About as much as you do, I said to myself, but answered, "I never thought so, but does it matter?" A mischievous smile sneaked onto my face. "How much worse can she make it?"

He blushed. It was one of my rare attempts at humor, and I was more embarrassed than he was.

Saturday morning came, and Rick took Jennifer with him to the public library. Kathy arrived on time for once, stopping at my place to pick up cleaning materials and stopping again a couple of hours later to bring them back and announce that she had done a great job and that his stuff really "blew her mind." I was in the middle of my own housecleaning, but I offered her a Coke, poured myself a cup of coffee, and sat down with her at the dining room table. Immediately she began to entertain me with a lengthy inventory of Rick's belongings. For weeks I'd listened to her carrying on about his parents' visit until I couldn't stand another minute of it, and now it didn't take long to know I would go crazy if she didn't shut up.

"For crying out loud, Kathy, will you please stop this foolishness? His this, his that. How, in the name of heaven can anyone go into raptures over somebody's dirty underwear?" She looked at me, dumbstruck—fits of temper had never been permitted in our family—then fled defensively into the bathroom and slammed the door behind her. The guilt was instant and enormous. Why did I do that? Because I felt threatened. Why would I feel threatened when there was no way on earth she could discover what was going on? And how could I lose control of myself that way? I put my head down on the table, covered it with my arms.

"Maggie?"

I looked up to find Kathy standing behind me, no longer dumbstruck, more like in shock. She was clutching a small leather case in both hands, and I didn't have to read the initials on the case to know who it belonged to. My worst nightmare. That's what I get for saving the bathroom for last on cleaning day.

"He's been staying here, hasn't he?" she said accusingly.

I could not take my eyes off that stupid little bag. *Keep cool*, I told myself. *Don't be defensive*. I raised my head and nodded.

"I knew it," she wailed, shaking her head dramatically from side to side. "I guessed it."

"Why didn't you say something before?"

"I couldn't believe it!"

A minor blow to my vanity, but I'd get over it. "Why couldn't you?"

"Well, because—" She shut her mouth.

I sighed. "Because he's young and I'm old?" I asked coolly. "Because he's smart and I'm a dumb nurse from the sticks? Why?"

A little of the color went out of her face, and she drew back. "Because you're married. To Steve, remember?"

"Yes, I remember," I assured her, not believing how calm I was. "I don't think you can understand this yet, but one thing has nothing to do with the other. Whatever Rick and I have now is just, I don't know, just for now, I guess. It has nothing to do with Steve or how I feel about him. Kathy, I have a life to live—" I almost choked. That couldn't be me, repeating words I had heard for months from Jerry and Carol and Rick. But it had been me, and I had repeated them, spontaneously and naturally.

"I know, but—"

"And sometimes age doesn't make any difference."

"It isn't that, Maggie," she protested, looking down at the black bag. "It's just, I don't know, sleeping together! You and Rick." She looked around the room as if it could give her some sort of support. "It's just so kind of . . . tacky."

"Thanks."

"I don't mean trashy, just kind of, like, inappropriate. I mean, he wears jeans and rides a motorcycle. It's . . . it's weird."

I couldn't help smiling a little. "And you call yourself a member of the younger generation? It's 1973, Kath. I thought everything goes now."

"It does," she retorted indignantly, "but not with my own sister."

Oh, I see. Living is for other people, just like war.

"And since you brought it up," she added, "don't you think he is a little young for you?"

"You act like I'm corrupting him," I said. "You don't know how funny that is."

She ignored me. "And what about Jennifer? How do you explain it to her?"

"I don't have to explain anything to her, because she knows nothing about it. And I hope it will stay that way."

"A kid can get hurt like that."

"Nobody is going to hurt Jennifer. You know how much Rick cares about her."

"Oh, sure, but she's a child," Kathy countered. "What about you? Maggie, I know Rick better than you think I do. You've freaked out if you really think he cares about you."

I was stunned that she would be so outspoken with me. For one thing, I'd been almost a mother to her. For another, she'd always treated me with a deference I took as respect. "I think he does," I said, trying to keep my voice steady.

"Well, you're wrong," she cried. "Rick Simon doesn't care about anyone but himself, and if you had your head on straight, you'd realize it."

"I know one thing," I retorted. "I know that you don't have enough experience to know what you're talking about."

Her mouth opened, but instead of more argument, she uttered a low moan, and her eyes shifted to a point beyond my left shoulder. I instinctively turned and found Rick standing in the doorway, holding Jennifer's hand. I didn't know how long he'd been there, but I'm sure that Kathy would not have spoken her last sentence if she had noticed him sooner.

"Rick—"

He let go of Jennifer and, ignoring me, strode toward Kathy and snatched the kit from her. "Listen, Kathy," he said with a quiet, almost menacing, anger, "I don't give a damn what you think about me. I don't give a damn what you think about me and your sister. But I have a real bad feeling that by 9:05 Monday morning, every switchboard operator, file clerk, and waitress in that office building is going to know something about my personal life that I wouldn't have told them myself, and since you're so hungry to know everything about me, I do give a damn about that." His blazing eyes strafed me as he stalked out the door, pulling it closed behind him.

Jennifer was still standing where Rick had left her, with a stricken stare willing me to notice her. I went to her, put my arm around her, and led her into the kitchen. She sat, mute, while I prepared a cup of hot chocolate for her to drink in the living room while she watched her Saturday cartoons. I didn't know how to explain what she had just seen and heard, so I said nothing.

When I came back to the table, Kathy's eyes fastened on mine, as if waiting for some signal that would tell her where we stood. For some bizarre reason, I felt like laughing, which, while it was considered to be a good tension releaser, didn't seem quite appropriate to the situation. Besides, I didn't want her to think I'd really freaked, to use her phrase. Instead I concentrated on breathing normally, as opposed to what she appeared to be doing, which was not breathing at all. Eventually I put my hand on hers and smiled.

"It's all right," I said softly, all of me fervently hoping it was, except for maybe that one tiny part that hated living in dread of being found out. It was ridiculous for either of us to be upset over such a trivial incident, but Rick had become so much a part of all of our lives, at least Jennifer's and mine, that I couldn't picture our lives without him. Kathy had left, and after lunch, I took Jennifer to the market in an effort to get myself back into one piece. I had replayed the morning again and again in the past couple of hours, each time regretting a little more that it had taken place. But it had. My major reaction, that I was glad it was over, beat out by only a hair my fear of Kathy letting anything slip to my mother.

I guess it was bound to happen. We ran into Rick and his parents in the lobby. They had a small boy with them, obviously his little brother. We squeezed past each other at the main door and nodded hellos. I couldn't guess from Rick's polite smile whether I would have a chance to formally meet his parents, and began to play that scene in my head. In fact, I spent most of the rest of the afternoon sitting in a living room chair imagining how it would go. I knew I was behaving like a fool, but at least it pushed the morning out of my mind. Mainly I focused on Rick's parents, especially the strong resemblance between him and his father. Mr. Simon had to be around fifty but looked younger, and he had the same confident, almost arrogant, glow of self-assurance as Rick. As we had maneuvered past each other, he looked right at me, into me, in the same unsettling way Rick did. His smile, however, seemed mechanical. Though Mrs. Simon was just as Rick had described her, she was a surprise: as unlike my concept of his mother or his father's wife as I could imagine. Her hair, while more natural than it was high style, had certainly been done professionally, and her clothes were unmistakably expensive. Her smile was warm and friendly. But as curious as I had been about her after speaking with her on the phone, it was her husband who drew my interest.

It was close to three thirty when Rick let himself into my apartment. I was washing my hair when he loomed up behind me in the medicine chest mirror. "Hi," I said tentatively, fearful that he would be different because of what had happened in the morning.

He asked, "What are you doing tonight?"

"Nothing."

"We're going out to dinner. My parents would like you to come."

I lowered my eyes to the sink so he wouldn't see my relief. "Me? Why?" My heart was leaping, but I was disgusted with myself. Wasn't I the one who didn't even want to meet them?

"They want to repay you for taking care of me when I was sick."

I straightened up and reached for the towel he held out to me. Little drops of water sprayed his light blue dress shirt, making tiny clusters of dark spots, and he backed up and perched on the rim of the bathtub.

"That was months ago."

"They're coming over from the hotel to pick us up at six."

"What about Jennifer and your brother? That is your brother, isn't it?"

"Can't you get Kathy to sit?"

"She has a date."

"We'll take them with us then. Or my mother can call an agency. Or we can leave them in the hotel and get someone to watch them there."

I toweled my hair hard, covering my face, wishing I didn't want to go with them, wishing Rick had reasons of his own for asking me. Whatever nursing I had done didn't merit any reward. "No," I said. "Tell them thanks, but my hair is wet and Jennifer won't stay with a stranger."

"Are you sure? It won't take an hour to dry your hair. You can use my blow-dryer. And Jenny will be okay. My brother'll be there and they can keep each other busy."

"I have my own dryer, thanks, and Jennifer, as you know, doesn't respond well to other children."

"No? They look like they're having a pretty good time in your living room right now."

I must admit I reconsidered for a moment, but then common sense took over. I simply couldn't see myself in my best seven-year-old polyester dress sitting down to dinner in a fancy Chicago restaurant with people like them. I just wouldn't fit. "You can leave your brother here with us."

He didn't say anything for a minute, just sort of peered up at me quizzically. Then he dragged himself up and ambled out of the bathroom. "Okay. Thanks for taking Jody."

"Wait a minute," I called, following him into the living room. "Will your mother want to leave him here? We haven't even met." This coming from a woman who had entrusted her own child to the first decent-seeming guy who had showed any kind of interest in them.

"I told her what a good caretaker you are." He looked back at me with one of those smirks I hated. "And I can vouch for how good you are at everything you do."

Jennifer and the little boy were playing with wooden building things and dozens of small figures that were unfamiliar to me. Jody was making little boy noises. Jennifer glanced shyly up at us. Jody was intent on his activity and took his time finishing what he was doing even after Rick told him he needed to go. Rick waited patiently, then said it again. Jody got to his feet lazily, his silky hair settling just short of his shoulders. Except for the blackness of his hair, he did not resemble Rick. I said so, and Rick shrugged. "None of us looks alike."

"You look like Daddy," the little boy contradicted.

"Go get your toys."

"I'm leaving them here for her to play with," Jody said with a slight emphasis on the "her." "I can come back, can't I?"

"I think so."

"Neat," he breathed, looking excitedly at Jennifer to see if she shared his enthusiasm. She remained impassive, eyes rooted to the carpet.

"Jody can have supper with us too," I said.

"Oh, cool. I get to eat here instead of a dumb restaurant. I'm gonna go tell Mom." He slammed out.

Rick said, "You asked for this yourself. You could have had a nice peaceful dinner at some expensive restaurant."

I didn't know why I was doing this to myself; I wanted so much to go with them. "We'll be fine here. You go and have a good time."

Rick leaned down and kissed my forehead lightly. "See you later, McLean."

I was so dizzy with relief I fell into the chair the minute the door closed behind him.

I spent most of the evening watching the children play. In spite of Jennifer's remoteness and her lukewarm response to Jody's efforts to involve her in his games, they managed to get through the hours pretty well. I recalled that the one time Jennifer had had another child over, when she was in kindergarten, the kid was begging to be taken home before an hour had passed. I couldn't blame her; she might as well have been alone in a strange place. Teachers invariably commented on Jennifer's lack of social initiative, her complete separateness from the rest of the class. They said when she works with other children, she works alone. It wasn't that others didn't make moves toward her, make spaces for her; it was this kind of inborn detachment, this solitariness, that kept her apart from them. It was the same with adults, except for me, Kathy, and her grandparents. And Rick Simon. I often worried about how she would get along in the world when she was older. I wondered how I could ever send her out into it.

But here she was, interacting with Jody better than I'd ever seen her do with other kids. Maybe it was because he was Rick's brother that she acknowledged he was there at all. Jody was a little older than she was; he was in second grade. He had that same shyness I'd seen in Rick at the beginning, that sweet reserve I'd mistaken for gentleness. About that, I knew better now. And I could see other signs of Rick in him too—the direct looks, the little smiles, they were obviously Simon traits. Jody was more inquisitive and talkative than Rick, but he was a child, and I'd always believed children—except my own, unfortunately—were more open than adults. I wondered if Rick had been like Jody when he was young and if Jody would become more like Rick as he grew older. I could've gotten so much insight into these people if I had just gone to dinner with them. Well, it's too late now; no use thinking about it.

Jody wasn't at all put off by Jennifer, and he kept trying. When he learned that she had no father, had never even seen him, his curiosity was piqued; and he asked her a lot of questions, which she answered in as few words as possible. She only knew what I'd told her anyway, and that wasn't very much. He wanted to see a picture of Steve, but by then Jennifer had already shared about as much as she was about to and acted as if he hadn't asked. I didn't interfere. Jody told her that most of his sisters and brothers were so old it was like having a lot of parents, and most of the time he wouldn't mind not having any of them. Everyone was always telling him what to do, and he hated it. I could tell that Jennifer thought this was pretty interesting and that she might like to hear more about it, but she didn't ask him to elaborate. After that, they played for a while in silence. Then I heard my daughter say softly, as if to no one in particular, "Sometimes I pretend Rick is my father." I tensed, afraid she might somehow reveal what I was sure she didn't know.

Jody looked at her like she had just sprouted wings and said, "You can have him." Nothing more was said between them. One private thought was about as much as Jennifer could part with in one day.

Around eight, both children were clearly running down, and I took them into my bedroom, where they curled up on the covers and let me read them a book from Jody's toy bag. At supper, he had told us about the long limousine ride from his home to Kennedy Airport, the plane trip, and the big airport in Chicago. He'd had lunch at their downtown hotel before coming to Rick's apartment. And I'd even seen him give one of his "fathers" away. It had been an exhausting day for a seven-year-old.

I made him comfortable on my bed and carried Jennifer to her own room and tucked her in. Then I moved into the living room to wait for Rick and his parents, whom I was now hoping to meet. But when Rick startled me out of a doze shortly after ten, he was alone.

"Did your parents go back to the hotel?" I asked, dopily forgetting about Jody.

"They're down at my place."

"Why didn't you bring them? I thought they'd want to meet the caretaker."

"They trust my judgment. Anyway, my mother's cleaning my apartment."

"Now? It's after ten."

He glanced at his watch automatically. "Yeah, well, she's frustrated." I didn't understand what that meant but was too sleepy to care.

"Kathy'll be crushed." I yawned. "She thought she did such a terrific job."

"She doesn't know my mother." He looked around at the littered floor. "They're tired and want to get back to the hotel. Where's Jody?"

"Sleeping on my bed."

"Oh." He started for the bedroom. "I'll get him."

"If it's all right with your mother, why don't you just let him stay, Rick? I think they'd both like that. They got along fine."

"Where will he sleep?"

"He can stay where he is. I'll sleep on the couch. Or you can move him to the couch. It doesn't matter."

"No." His tone of voice told me in no uncertain terms that there was nothing more to be said.

"But why?" I persisted. "Your parents aren't leaving that early, are they? There'll be plenty of time to get him ready to go."

Rick softened a bit. "That's not it."

"Then what is?"

"If he stays, I can't."

"I know. But it's just for one night. I thought we'd already decided about that." He glared at me. "Come on, Rick, it would make the children so happy."

"I don't want to make *the children* happy," he snapped. "I want to make *me* happy."

Any reasonable person would have been joking, but the intensity in his eyes and voice told me that he wasn't. Besides, a little muscle in his jaw was twitching, and that was a sure sign that he had made up his mind about something and was not about to be challenged. I'd been down that road with him several times, and right now I was not in the mood for another trip. "Rick, I've really had a difficult day. I don't want to argue about this anymore, and I don't want to play any games."

I guess I thought at this point that he would make the decision; he would go, or Jody would go. He didn't. He didn't do anything, just stood there, staring into me, waiting for me to make the next move. I stood my ground, said nothing. It was clear he only wanted his way, didn't much care where anyone slept, except himself. It came to me that this was happening a lot lately, and I was going to have to deal with it soon because it made me angry. But not now. Now I had to get some sleep, and as far as I was concerned, the sleeping arrangements had already been decided. "As far as I'm concerned, Jody can stay," I said resolutely. Rick's eyes widened, blazed just for a moment, then his face went passive.

"I see." He was furious with me, and his pride was probably hurt that I had chosen against him, but right now I didn't care. I just wanted the day to be over. This morning, this afternoon, and now. Just let it be over.

He waited.

I waited.

And at that moment, there were three quiet raps on the door.

Rick turned, opened it, and there stood his mother, ready to be introduced at last.

Almost before I could process it, he had exited and she had entered, so that she now stood precisely where he had a moment before. Sort of like an intricate ballet step. And when the door shut, she and I faced each other awkwardly, she not knowing what to make of his rapid and rude departure, and I, too tired to care. "Did I interrupt something?"

"Oh no, not really," I stammered. "I . . . he . . . I'm Mary Grace McLean."

"Lenore Simon." She held out her hand.

I took it. "Please call me Maggie."

"Hi, Maggie."

I smiled weakly. It was my turn, but nothing came out and there was an uncomfortable pause.

Finally, she said, "I hope my son behaved himself."

I wanted say, "One of them did," but restrained myself. "Jody was wonderful. We loved having him. Jennifer doesn't get to have children over very often, so it was a special treat for her." I felt as stiff as a wet woolen sock that had been hung outdoors to dry in the middle of winter.

Mrs. Simon smiled and looked around the room. For the first time, I became aware of the mess. Piles of books and toys, puzzles, games. Instead of straightening up so I could make the good impression I had dreamed about all day, I had spent hours on the couch watching the children and writing silly stories in my head. And now here she was, and here I was, like a zombie, in a room that looked as though it had been struck by a tornado. If I could have changed places with one of Jody's little plastic men, I'd have done it in a second. Because bone weary or not, I really did care. And there were just too many things to care about right then.

"It looks as if they had a wonderful time," she said tactfully. "Why don't I go and collect my son and let you get to bed. You look exhausted."

"It's been a long day."

"For us too."

"Jody fell asleep while I was reading to him and Jennifer."

"I'm not surprised. I hate to have to wake him up."

This could give me a chance to redeem myself. "Would you consider leaving him here overnight?" I suggested. "I noticed he had his things with him."

She smiled apologetically. "He insists on carrying that duffel bag everywhere he goes. It's his new 'thing.' Please believe that we didn't plan on imposing on you for more than the evening."

"I know that," I assured her. "But it is a shame to wake him, and Jennifer would be so happy to find him here tomorrow." I wasn't so sure about that, but it sounded like a good argument.

"If you're positive it wouldn't be any trouble." She hesitated. "I don't want to take advantage of your generosity."

"You're not and I'm sure."

She bobbed her head. "Okay then. I'll just go in and kiss him good night." I indicated the room.

The chill of fatigue took over then, and I went to the kitchen to put on the kettle. When I heard her call softly from the living room, I went back in and offered her a cup of tea. She declined. I told her I was having one and two cups were no more trouble than one. Again she refused, but said she would like to speak to me for a minute. She followed me into the kitchen and sat down at the table. I couldn't help thinking that for all her elegant grooming, she looked very much at home in a kitchen.

"I won't take much of your time," she said. "I can see you're tired and I am too, but we might not have another chance to talk before I leave."

I felt a pang of uneasiness. *She knows.* My stomach began to flip. She must have sensed my apprehension because she put a calming hand on my arm. A gesture I know well.

"First, Maggie, I know I have no right to speak to you about this. Ricky is a grown man and it's not up to me to judge what he does with his life. It's certainly none of my business what you do with yours." *Dear God, she knows. First Kathy, now them. But how—?* The kettle whistled. I rose and, forgetting that she'd refused tea, set a cup in front of her. She must have forgotten, too; she nodded at me gratefully. I didn't know what to say to her. I felt I had come out ahead with Kathy, but I didn't know this woman or how to avoid getting into a scene with her. On the other hand, I couldn't handle her; I could only handle me, and frank and direct was what I'd been brought up to be, I took the initiative.

"Mrs. Simon," I said steadily, "I know what you're going to say. But believe me, you don't have to say it. I know how it must look to you and your husband, but I want you to understand that I never planned for it to happen. At first it was only because Rick was so kind to my daughter and she responded to him more than I've ever seen her do with anyone else. I was grateful to him for that. The rest is something I never expected and certainly never asked for. I want you to believe that I understand how, how . . . indecent . . . it must seem to you—"

Her head snapped up from her cup, and she looked as if I had suddenly begun speaking in tongues. "Wait, Maggie," she interrupted. "This isn't—"

"No, I want you to understand," I continued. "I know what you're thinking, and I feel awful about it. I just want you to believe that I never set out to corrupt Rick."

She put her cup down and started to laugh. *Laugh.* "This is a joke," she said.

"It's not funny to me," I retorted with as much dignity as I could muster under the circumstances. That she could treat my confession so lightly stung. When she realized this, her laughter faded.

"Wait. Please let me go on," she said. I conceded. She took a sip of her tea. "Courage," she murmured, holding up the cup as if it was whiskey and not Lipton. "I know I shouldn't get involved in this, but since I have, I guess I'd better get it over with." She gulped down what was left. "The truth is I have to tell you something about Ricky. Today he talked to us a little about you, your husband, and what you've been through, and when he finished I just knew I couldn't stand by this time. I know it sounds melodramatic, but I have to tell you to be careful."

I heard myself gasp.

"I know," she hurried on. "I'm his mother. But there are things I don't understand about him, things that worry me, not only about him, but about the people he gets involved with. You see, as far as I know, Ricky has never had a relationship with a woman that didn't end in someone getting hurt. Also as far as I know, he's never been that someone. You know, Maggie, he was our first, and I was so careful with him. I tried so hard to do everything right and I thought I had. I have no idea why he's the way he is, but I can tell you that it's hard to be a parent and see things like this happen in spite of your best efforts. It's hard to know he'll probably do it again and you won't be able to do anything to stop it."

This was a situation I had never dealt with before. In Clearyville, things like murder, prison records, and cruel lovers were swept under the rug until they could be gossiped about as old scandal. "You came to warn me about him?" I asked incredulously.

"I guess I did," she admitted, not meeting my eyes. "I don't know what the answer is for him. I only know if we interfere with him, we might lose him and I couldn't live with that. We love him very much, in spite of some of the things he does. And yet I can't bear to see this happen again. So my only choice is to warn you. You don't need to be hurt any more than you already have been." She looked at me with great distress in her eyes. "Please forgive me if I've overstepped."

"You haven't. Only I don't know what I'm supposed to do. Drop him? How? It's not only me, it's what he does for Jennifer. He brings her out of her shell, and I think he'll eventually get her to where she can come out with other people too. I don't want her to go back to the way she was before we met him. Besides, she's too attached to him to have him just disappear from her life." I hesitated. "She's already lost one person in her life."

"I know that."

"Then what am I supposed to do?"

With a frown of deep concentration, she went to the sink and rinsed her cup, then to the front door. I followed her, hoping that she would say something, give me some clue. She was his mother for heaven's sake, and she had started this. She must have some advice for me. But all she said was, "Just don't ask for more than he can give," and walked out the door. Numbly I watched her small round figure as it moved down the long corridor toward the west wing.

It was close to noon when the Simons came for Jody. I looked awful. I had spent a tense, sleepless night agonizing over what Mrs. Simon had said and what I was going to do about it. Should I ignore her advice and take my chances? Should I end this right now and risk hurting Jennifer? Rick was only going to be here another year at most anyway, and a lot of things can change in a year. Changes don't necessarily have to be bad either.

By the time dawn had broken, I felt as if my head was stuffed with cotton, and I wasn't even sure anymore what was bad and what was good. At eight, I dragged myself out of bed and into the bathroom. I looked into the mirror and saw my face all blotchy and puffy, as if I'd been crying for hours. Cold water didn't help; neither did hot. I tried a compress; nothing. While the kids were having breakfast, I made a desperate effort at damage control, resorting to some foundation makeup that had been lying in a dresser drawer for years. It was cakey and streaky in the jar, and the shade was more orange than I remembered, but I rubbed it on, powdered over it, and told myself it was better than what was underneath. I didn't think I could feel any worse until I opened the door and found not only Mrs. Simon, but Rick and his father.

Their plane was due to leave O'Hare in two hours, and Mrs. Simon bustled about getting Jody's things together, chasing after him to get him dressed and get his hair brushed, all the while fussing and fretting about getting to the airport on time. The men ignored her.

I sat uncomfortably on the couch, trying to concentrate on the sporadic small talk between Rick and his father, which was awkward and strained, due mainly to Rick's somewhat hostile attitude. It seemed to me that he purposely took offense at whatever was said to him, though I didn't hear a single thing that was even remotely provocative. In fact, I would have said Mr. Simon was being especially careful not to cause friction. Rick reminded me of a belligerent teenage cousin of mine, and I felt embarrassed, not only for him and his father, but for myself. I didn't want to know this Ricky who seemed to be locked in some kind of power struggle with his parents. I certainly didn't want to sleep with him. Mr. Simon finally gave up and turned to me, asking about my nursing, my family, my life in Chicago. He was exactly the same with me as he had been with Rick, and I didn't feel I was being cross-examined. I was painfully aware of the way I looked and tried to keep my face averted, but he was a magnetic man, and it was hard not to respond to him. Flattering touches of silver in his hair framed the sides of his face, and he was wearing a sweater made from the kind of wool that is so fine you can't believe it's wool. He looked distinguished and dignified, like one of those political candidates who, as I once heard a doctor say, "has the Image." He looked like Rick all grown up. And he was being so kind and interested in me, with my limp hair and flaking orange face, that it just made me feel worse. When we were interrupted for a moment by his anxious, harassed wife, I tried to guess what she had looked like when they were first married. Younger of course, thinner, less dowdy, and I wondered, not for the first time, why Rick, so like his father physically, was bothering with me. *Don't, Maggie. Better not to think about it.*

At last Jody was ready to go. There were thank-yous and good-byes, a little gift for Jennifer, which I imagined had been hurriedly purchased at the hotel gift shop. The gesture touched me. Jody shook one of my hands like a little man, while his father squeezed the other, and Mrs. Simon kissed my cheek as if we were old friends. There was not the slightest hint of what had passed between us the night before. Rick followed them out, after pausing at the door to lean down, kiss my forehead, and whisper, "What's that gunk all over your face?"

"An experiment that failed," I said ruefully.

He pondered the ruins for a moment, screwing his own flawless face into an exaggerated expression of repulsion. I waited for him to say something like "gross," which I gathered from Kathy was worse than "yuck" or "ick." Instead he rearranged his mouth and his eyes, with their creases underneath, into a smile, shook his head, and said, "See you later, McLean."

I was more confused than ever.

Where I grew up, mothers don't warn strangers about their sons. No mother would imagine there was anything to warn about, or if she did, she'd never admit it to herself. At home, if you get caught talking to a fire hydrant on North Main Street or wearing snowshoes in July, people might say you're strange, but they'd right away justify you by saying that the Hills have always been strange, and that would be that. They might crucify you for it two generations later, but never while you're still breathing. Nor do parents sit around blaming themselves because their kids are behaving badly. The people I grew up with just accept whatever happens, and the concept of a mother blaming herself for her child's behavior would be foreign to any Clearyville mother I'd ever known, especially my own.

So it was peculiar to me that Mrs. Simon had said what she'd said about Rick, and days later, I still hadn't figured out what I was supposed to do with that information. True, Rick had said and done things that troubled or confused me, but after all, we'd been raised in different worlds and in different generations. Would it really be reckless to keep things as they were, which is what her warning seemed to imply? Sure, I might be hurt, but how much worse could it be than losing a husband? Besides, even considering ending our relationship was out of the question because of Jennifer. She missed Rick on days when we didn't see him and wanted to know why he hadn't come over. Just the fact that she felt enough attachment to him to be thinking about him when she hadn't seen him for a day or two must mean that he was important to her. I thought a lot about that and, as winter moved further and further behind us and spring began to take hold, I began to realize that it was probably just curiosity. It wasn't Jennifer who was hooked; it was me. I was the one who couldn't let go.

And so our routine resumed. I was working days again, home with Jennifer by five thirty every evening. As before, Rick came home with or without Kathy, ate dinner with us or didn't, worked on his dissertation at his place or mine. But he was always beside me during the night and gone before I woke up.

Once spring was really with us, Rick took the motorcycle out of mothballs for transportation to and from work or the university. It was garaged a few blocks from the building, so I neither saw nor heard it, but I often pictured the two of them, Rick and Kathy, coming home from work on it, their helmets gleaming in the late afternoon sun. Several times Rick invited me to ride with him, but somehow I couldn't see myself clinging desperately to his waist and praying for the ride to be over. He always smiled his little teasing smile when I declined.

The park we went to was across the boulevard and a few blocks from our building, and the three of us spent many weekend hours there when the weather was good, and sometimes even when it wasn't. Like Jennifer, Rick didn't mind getting wet. When it rained, he would raise his face to the gushing clouds, while I stood, sticky and uncomfortable, clutching my umbrella and wishing I was someplace dry. Rick seemed drawn to the air and the elements, and these outings were apparently the only recreation he needed. At least, he never took us anyplace else with him, and if he went anywhere without us, I didn't know about it.

It was a lovely spring, mild and sunny. We would sit on the grass and watch Jennifer on the playground. No matter how often we went, she could be counted on for a couple of uninterrupted hours of play. She would come to us occasionally for her juice or raisins, but mostly she was content to glide lazily on the swings or putter in the sandbox, always by herself.

I was thinking how easy and comfortable life had become again, when in the middle of May, I noticed that Rick was different, restless. He frequently talked about quitting his job at the television station, giving a different reason for every day of the workweek. The primary complaint was that he should be devoting all his time and energy to finishing his dissertation. It was a mystery to me that he was even working to begin with, but every time I asked him why he felt he had to put up with something that was so unsatisfying, he answered with a shrug. It was not as if he depended on the paycheck. He had told me that the education of each of the children in his family was paid for by trust funds set up by his grandfather. I couldn't figure him out, and being Rick, he wasn't about to explain himself.

It was on a beautiful summerlike Saturday in the park when Rick, for the first time, took me into a deep, dark place inside of himself, and I ended up understanding him even less than I had before. My patients had taught me what true complainers are, and Rick Simon was not one. He was probably too secretive. So when the restlessness became really apparent, I knew there had to be something serious troubling him. I didn't mind him unloading on me; I was still feeling flattered when he revealed anything about himself. But this time, as he spoke, a different Rick, another Rick that I didn't want to know, began to emerge.

It started with the station again, but that was okay; I was used to people voicing the same grievances over and over. It was at the point when he began using ugly words that I became concerned, because he was not applying them to the job, but to himself, and that was something I had never heard him do before.

I gaped at him. "What in heaven's name are you talking about?"

"Just because you're always so sure of yourself doesn't mean everyone else is, Maggie," he replied quietly.

This was so totally unlike him, it was as if the world had tilted. I didn't know what to say and responded to him as I would have responded to a depressed patient. With my usual gesture of comfort, I took his hand, and asked encouragingly, "Why don't you tell me about it? Maybe I can help."

"How?" he retorted sarcastically. "By taking my pulse?"

I drew back, my face flushing, and there was the usual silence as he waited for me to rescue the conversation. "I'm sorry, Rick, I've never heard you put yourself down before. I don't understand."

"You wouldn't," he said sullenly. "You're always so in control."

"I don't know what to say to you," I said in as steady a voice as I could manage. "Why on earth would you think these things about yourself? You have everything anybody could ever want in life."

"Such as?"

"Well, for starters, you've got a terrific family behind you, supporting you in whatever you want to do." Except maybe hurt other people, but I kept that to myself.

"Okay," he agreed, but from the misery on his face, it was easy to see that he wasn't convinced.

"You've got money," I offered.

"Big deal."

"It is if you don't have it."

"Right." That didn't help either.

"You have brains and education." He nodded. "How many people your age, any age, are as educated as you are?" He didn't answer. I couldn't imagine what he wanted to hear, so I said the only other thing I could think of. I thought it was a compliment. "If I've left anything out, all you have to do is look in the mirror."

"Bingo," he said, but in a way that left no doubt that of all the things I could've named, this was not a good one.

I looked at him, baffled. "What? I don't understand."

"Forget it, Maggie."

"I won't forget it," I objected. "You're upset about something and I want to know what it is. Is it something I did?"

"You?" He snuffed. "No, you didn't do anything."

"But what I said bothered you. Why?"

"You really don't get it, do you?"

I shook my head, totally at a loss.

"Look at me and tell me what you see."

I already was looking at him, and what I was seeing was the thing that always made my heart pound and my body turn to pudding. It wasn't his intellect or his money. His family was fascinating, but they weren't here, and I didn't spend much time thinking about them anymore. It wasn't even the way he brought Jennifer out of her shell. It was just him, the way he looked and the way he looked at me. The way he moved. The way he talked. The way he touched me. For the life of me, I couldn't figure out why this was a problem.

"You see?" he said. "That's all that really matters, isn't it?"

I couldn't speak. I felt ashamed, but didn't know why, and looked away to the play area, where Jennifer was busily climbing the jungle bars. Had I missed something all these months? Had my preoccupation with him and the way it had complicated my life prevented me from seeing signs of self-doubt or depression? Of course not. I was trained to pick up on things like that. He had never once let on that he was anything less than totally secure in himself and his life. Why now?

I felt a clutch at my arm and jumped. It was Jennifer telling me she was ready to go home. I looked toward Rick and saw that he'd rolled onto his back, one arm flung over his eyes. Jennifer must have thought he was asleep, and for a long moment, I thought maybe I had been too, that I had been dreaming. Then he dragged himself up, and I knew I hadn't been and let Jennifer pull me to my feet.

Rick and I looked at each other. "Let's go," he said, and Jennifer dashed away toward the exit path. I hung back for a moment, and he grabbed my hand.

"Why did you say what you did?" I asked, my eyes tearing up.

"Just in case," he answered softly.

"In case what?"

"In case you were beginning to think I'm something I'm not."

"The only thing I care about is what you are to Jennifer and me."

"There's a lot more I want to be, Maggie."

"Maybe you already are those things and you can't see it."

"Maybe I need to know that other people see it."

We walked the path in silence. When we reached the sidewalk, I didn't immediately see Jennifer and scanned the street in a minor panic until I spotted her swinging herself around a streetlight post. She saw us and came running.

"Come on. The light is green," I said and started to move forward. Rick pulled me back.

"Wait, Maggie." I turned to him. "Look, I don't know what happened to me in there," he said apologetically. "Too much sun or too much work or too much—I don't know."

The jolt of not seeing Jennifer right off had separated me from him for a moment. Finding her had calmed me down. "It's okay," I lied. "Just let's not talk about it anymore."

He smiled and was Rick again. "It's part of my life. I can't just pretend—"

"I know you can't. But it frightened me. Really."

"Why?"

"I don't know. You weren't like yourself. It was like you were someone I didn't know." *Wasn't that who he was anyway?* "I just want you to be you. I don't care about anything else."

He looked at me, and his eyes were sad. "Okay," he sighed. "We won't talk about it anymore."

We each took one of Jennifer's hands and crossed the street. On the way back to the apartment, we stopped at a little grocery a block from our building and picked up a few things for supper. It's what we always did on the way home from the park on Saturdays, but this time it was different. The routine was the same, but the fun, the togetherness, had gone out of it, replaced by a feeling of distance.

Jennifer went to bed soon after her supper, and we were left to ourselves. Rick read in the living room while I prepared our meal. It was all part of our Saturday evening ritual, but tonight it felt totally alien. As we ate, I thought, *It's true. He's still a stranger. I don't know him. I'll never know him. But still I sleep with him next to me. Still, I let him inside me.*

I went to bed early too, but couldn't sleep. Rick stayed up, working in the living room. I kept thinking about what he had said and what his mother had said, about how childish he'd been when his parents were around, and about the man he would be when he came into my bed.

That was it, wasn't it? That was the bottom line. It didn't matter who he was or what he said or did; I would let him in whenever he wanted me to.

I didn't have to read it anymore, Steve's letter. I knew it by heart. I'd read it over and over until I knew it would be ingrained in my memory forever. For a long time, I would sit very still after reading it and imagine how we would read it together every year on June 16, our wedding anniversary, in celebration of our gratitude for having won the prize he'd written about. I did this so often that I actually convinced myself it would happen. It was this letter, out of the dozens of others I'd received from Steve during the five months he'd been gone, that pulled me up out of the deep hammock of my despair, got me through my nursing courses, and took me to Chicago. This was the letter that allowed me to believe in the future, and I held on to it as tightly as I would a branch in a swamp. Today is May 13, 1973, and I haven't looked at any of Steve's letters since—when?—January. I can still remember Lt. Munson handing me the last one at my mother's house on September 14, 1966:

5/66

Dear Maggie,

I'm lying here in my hooch and thinking about you. I bet you'd be surprised if you knew how much I do this. It's freakin' hot, about 10 times as hot as Clearyville in July, and I don't have to tell you anything about that. I keep seeing you in my mind–the way you looked when we used to go to the lake or on a picnic at Mill Grove or on the Fourth of July, when you'd be helping out getting the tables ready. One of the things I always loved about you is how serious and efficient you were when you were doing things like that. When I think of the lake and Mill Grove, I remember how wonderful you are to be with, just so sweet and calm and, well, just such a special, beautiful girl. Sometimes, I feel terrible about all the years we lost because we ended up in different classes in school and had *different friends and just never looked away from our own lives long enough to actually* ***see*** *each other. Remember what Humphrey Bogart said in that old movie we watched on television the night we got rained out at the softball game? "Well," he said, "we'll always have kindergarten." Of course, he didn't say kindergarten, he said something like "Paris." You know, we could have Paris (and more) someday when I get through school and am* ***THE*** *foremost American architect.*

Speaking of jobs, how's school coming along? My mother wrote me that your mother told her she was "pleased as punch" that you finally came to your senses about nursing, but was disappointed that you didn't stay AT LEAST (your mother's words) part-time at the Christian College. I can hear what you're thinking right now, Mags—that she wouldn't be satisfied with you no matter what you did. Well, I'd be happy with you even if you didn't do anything, but then that wouldn't be you, would it?

I recently had a little disagreement with a guy in my unit who's from somewhere in the South about women working. He kept saying every woman's job was to have children and then stay home and raise them. His argument was that men, being so much smarter than women, are the only ones qualified to work. We went back and forth about this for a while until I gave up. Some of these guys are very small-minded, which makes me think that our country must have a lot of Clearyvilles scattered around.

Seriously though, Maggie. Sometimes I look around me and have to ask myself what I'm doing here. I know I wasn't given a choice, and you know, too, that I was not unhappy to go. But some things look different to me now. I don't want to worry you with details of what's going on here, but you think you have a pretty good handle on how it's going to be, but you don't. You just can't imagine it.

Well, I don't want to get you all depressed and scared. We've only got 7 months, 20 days, and probably a few hours to miss each other before my hitch is up, so keep your eyes on the prize, baby.

I love you more than I will probably ever be able to say out loud. But as soon as I get home, hopefully by New Year's, I'm sure going to give it a try!

All my love and devotion,
Steve

I read the letter in my head, and I couldn't cry. All I could feel was a wistful sadness. The vision I saw in my head looked like two cardboard figures sitting at a table with candles that could never be lit. And all I could say to myself was, *Please, Steve, send me a sign, anything, to tell me that you understand . . . that you understand what I'm doing.*

All my life, my tendency had been to take whatever came along, get through it as best I could, and then carry on without looking back. I never could see the use of going on about things you have no control over. Certainly, the few months after I'd learned that Steve was missing were an exception, but everyone in town had been stunned by the news. Eventually I'd found a way to deal with it, as I knew I would, and had gone on to make a life for Jennifer and myself.

When Rick Simon came along, he was something I had never expected either. Charismatic and enigmatic, he was the most interesting person I'd ever met, and I was overwhelmed by an inexplicable need to learn everything there was to know about him and his life. In the end, what he revealed about himself was disappointing and confusing, and I wanted him back the way I had thought he was, the way I wanted him to be. Even more, I wanted me back the way I'd been before I'd met him. It was impossible. A normally reasonable woman, I was steadily becoming more and more unreasonable. Maybe what my mother used to say was true: "Never wish for things you have no business having. You might get them."

As the fire I'd felt for Rick seemed to be cooling, I was suddenly developing an acute resentment about small things, trivial things, things I'd never even noticed before. Like his never taking Jennifer and me anywhere but to the park or the neighborhood McDonald's, or his not having insisted that I go to dinner with him and his parents. Why had it been his parents and not him who had invited me in the first place? There were times when I even found myself blaming him for taking Steve away from me.

It didn't take Kathy long to pick up on what she called my "broodiness" and less time for her to bluntly express her view that it had to do with Rick. I retorted defensively that she was wrong. She said, "Uh-huh," but didn't harp on it, for which I was grateful. I didn't want any more ill feeling between us. She had never brought up her discovery of the shaving kit, and I had decided that if she hadn't mentioned it to anybody by then, more than six weeks later, she wasn't going to. It was clear to both of us that we were growing apart, and once or twice I caught her searching my face with a kind of wounded expression I took to mean, "Don't leave it like this. Say something."

But we were not people who talked much about feelings, so whatever might have been said never was. Maybe that was the problem with Rick's few confidences. They were more personal than I had expected, perhaps more personal than I could handle. But he had shared them with me, and some things could not be ignored.

Sometimes I felt like a rubber ball, bouncing from one mood to another, from mindless happiness to misery and confusion, and for the first time since Rick and I had been together, I was beginning to wonder if the happiness was worth the misery. But then in the blissful warm time between lovemaking and sleep, when I lay drugged and drowsy against his smooth, humid body, I knew without doubt that it was. He had such a gift for tenderness, for making me believe that I was someone special and irreplaceable. Even the times when we did nothing more than curl up against each other and lie in the safety and warmth of total stillness, his presence, his aliveness, was all that mattered. It was only later, after he'd left my bed, that the night terrors would surface, and I would once again be seized by resentment and fear. This couldn't go on forever, but when I told myself to hold on, I wondered what I was holding on for. What was almost unbearably fulfilling in the darkness was no longer enough in the daylight.

Toward the end of the month, Rick received a letter from California, congratulating him on being chosen to participate in a prestigious workshop at which many of the country's top print and media journalists would be speaking or conducting seminars. His advisor, who had submitted his name, urged him to take advantage of this honor. It would only delay his work by six months, and it would be a dynamite addition to his resume. Rick admitted to being torn. He knew that to pass it up would be unwise from not only an educational standpoint but a professional one as well, Still, he was anxious to be done with school, having had seventeen straight years of it, and besides, his dissertation was really rolling, and he didn't want to break the momentum. I knew in my heart he should and probably would go, but when it came right down to the reality of his actually leaving, I had mixed feelings, in spite of my off-and-on ambivalence about our relationship. Even though I was both anxious and afraid to hear what his decision would be, I asked him every couple of days if he'd made up his mind yet. Each time he said he hadn't.

My mother and I generally spoke to each other on Thursday nights. These conversations were not exactly gabfests. Usually I gave her brief updates on Jennifer and my workweek, and she filled me in on what was happening at church and occasionally passed along a little town gossip. This week, however, she had a new item on her agenda, and she wasted no time in bringing it up.

"Kathy tells me you've been 'seeing' that young man we met at your apartment on Christmas Eve."

My stomach quaked. How could I have been so naïve as to take for granted that flighty Kathy would keep it to herself. I sighed. "What does she say she means by 'seeing'?"

"She didn't say, but I couldn't help feeling you're doing something, Grace, that you may regret later."

"Mother, please. I'm thirty-two years old. I don't need to be told how to conduct with my life."

"That may be so," she said in the stern voice I associated with the naughty moments of my childhood, "but don't forget you have a responsibility to your family: your father, me, Jennifer, especially Jennifer, and don't you forget the McLeans either. How do you think they'll feel when they hear you've taken up with some young fellow?"

I wanted to ask, "And how would they find that out, Mother?" but instead, steeling myself for a lecture on respect when addressing grown-ups, said, "They'd probably think I've finally gotten it through my head that Steve is not going to come back and that I have the rest of my life, and Jennifer's, to think about."

There was a momentary silence, during which my mother was probably trying to come to terms with my impudence. "Don't be impudent, young lady," was a warning that would forever be imprinted on my memory. I took advantage of the lapse to make things worse.

"Anyway, what business is it of theirs who I take up with? Or yours either, Mother?"

I heard a sharp intake of breath on her end of the line. "Mary Grace!" she exclaimed.

"Yes, I know. What on earth has gotten into me?" But what *had* gotten into me? Just because I had been spoken to as if I were a naughty little girl didn't mean I had to behave like one. *Repent, Mary Grace*, I told myself, but I just couldn't. I was so tired of her domineering ways.

"Mother, I'm sorry. I don't mean to be disrespectful, but I am capable of taking care of myself and Jennifer without anyone's help. I've been doing it for years. Believe whatever you want, from Kathy or anyone else. I don't care. Just let me take care of my life my own way. It's my life."

This was a side of me my mother had never seen. I'm not so sure I was very familiar with it myself. She obviously didn't know how to handle it and, as usual, she was doing her best to control the conversation.

"All right, Mary Grace," she shot back angrily. "Just don't you come crying to us when you get yourself into a corner and can't get out. If you disgrace yourself, you disgrace us, and you will have to live with that." She hung up.

My head swam as the disconnect signal buzzed in my ear. *What was happening? How had I come to this?* In no time at all, it seemed, I had distanced myself from my sister, alienated my mother, become a distracted, insensitive woman I didn't recognize. This had to stop.

At supper on Thursday night, Rick was uncharacteristically short-tempered and sharp with both Jennifer and me, and I suggested that he slow down and not drive himself so hard. This triggered an outburst of temper, with him barking at me that he had things to do, he couldn't waste time, and would I get off his case. Jennifer stared at him, bewildered and a little scared, much the same way she had the morning Kathy found his shaving kit. Since I had never known him to be concerned with time or the future, I couldn't understand why he was putting all this pressure on himself, but I said nothing more because his anger made Jennifer anxious. He left shortly after the meal and didn't return until sometime during the night. He did not awaken me, and his lingering scent was my only tangible clue that he'd been there.

We didn't see him on Friday at all.

Late Saturday morning, he stopped by and said, somewhat distantly, that he would be spending most of the weekend in the university library. Actually he'd been working more at his place than at mine for the past week because, as he'd explained, he'd accumulated too much stuff to drag back and forth. This was no surprise. Several times over the past months, I had run down the hall to bring him lunch or dinner and found him buried beneath a mountain of paper and reference materials. This was the first time, however, that I wondered if his absence meant he had made his decision and was weaning himself away from us before he left for California.

It must have been after midnight on Saturday night when he came to bed. I was on the edge of sleep and only dimly aware of his presence. He didn't try to wake me. On Sunday morning, Jennifer begged me to let her go down to his apartment, and I gave in, guessing she needed to see him to make sure he was still our friend. He didn't answer the door.

The memory of the pneumonia at Christmastime crossed my mind, but I was sure it was nothing like that. Jennifer was really missing him, and I tried to explain that he was busy with schoolwork. Though he was often immersed in books and papers when she saw him, it was difficult for her to reconcile the idea of a grown man with the idea of the crayon-and-chalk kinds of things that meant school to her.

When he showed up around midnight Sunday, I was in bed with an open book on my lap. He came into the room noiselessly, as he always did late at night. "Hi," he said, as if he'd been coming and going as usual all weekend.

"Jennifer's been missing you," I said, although I was feeling a little put off by his not saying why we'd hardly seen him for the past few days.

"Only Jennifer?" he asked.

"No, of course not," I said lightly.

Without another word, he proceeded to strip down to his Jockey shorts. Then he sat down on the bed beside me and looked into my face, into me in that way he had. I tried to keep my eyes off his body, tried to ignore his scent.

"You okay, Maggie?" The husky softness of his voice simply wilted any annoyance I was harboring.

"Rick, I was hoping we could talk about your trip."

"Not right now." He put my hand to his mouth and bit my knuckle gently, turned my hand over, then circled my palm with the tip of his tongue, cupped it around his face, and kissed it. My skin tingled at the fine-sandpaper texture of stubble as he caressed his cheek with my hand.

I pulled away. "I know you're tired, but it won't take long."

"Can't it wait until tomorrow? I've been working for two days straight and my head's about to explode." He closed his eyes, turned his face to the side, took my hand, and again stroked the roughness of his cheek.

I saw that he had dark rings under his eyes. "If we could just get it out of the way tonight . . ."

He nodded wearily. "Okay. What's up?"

"I've been wondering what you're going to do."

He lifted his lashes and peered at me with a puzzled expression. "What I always do. Get into bed, make love to you, then go to sleep until I have to leave."

"That's not what I mean."

"Then what?"

"The seminar in California."

He groaned, dropped my hand, rubbed his own over his face. "Do you realize that this is about the tenth time you've asked me that? Why does it matter to you if I go or stay?"

He has to ask? "Because I've been under the impression that we have a . . . relationship, Rick."

"Yeah, I guess we do," he conceded after a slight hesitation.

"Isn't the possibility of being apart for six months the kind of thing people in a relationship share with each other?"

He seemed to think about it for a minute. "I suppose so . . . depending on the kind of relationship they have."

"What do you mean?"

He yawned. "Look, I have a dissertation advisor. I agree to do the work and he agrees to help me through the process. I need his expertise and he needs my money. It's like we make a deal with each other. And because of that, I let him know when I can't do my part and he does the same with me. On the other hand, if I signed up for, I don't know, six free dancing lessons in a class and couldn't make it for one of them, I wouldn't feel obligated to let the teacher know I wasn't coming. There's no commitment there. Neither of us depends on the other for anything, so it doesn't matter whether I'm there or not."

I nodded. "All right. But what does that have to do with the seminar?"

"That's the point I'm making. We don't have a commitment, Maggie. What we have is an arrangement. We haven't made any promises to each other. All we have is an agreement, a tacit agreement, that I'll stay overnight and leave before Jenny wakes up. Right?"

Right. "I guess," I said slowly. I hadn't thought about it that way. "So you're saying that you could just leave my apartment at four some morning and get on your bike and go to California or New York or Canada without a word to us?"

"You really think I'd *do* that to you and Jenny?" he asked indignantly.

"Not really," I fibbed.

"Then relax. I haven't made up my mind yet, but if I do decide to leave, you'll know it before I go. Okay?" He sounded so reasonable and reassuring that I felt just awful. How stupid and childish I'd been to make a big thing out of this.

He lifted my chin and did the eye thing again. "Besides," he added with a shrugging admission, "it's been proven that I don't do commitment very well, anyway."

The girl in the photo skittered through my mind's eye.

He leaned forward and kissed me gently on the lips. "Can I go to sleep now? I'm about to pass out." He climbed over me to the other side of the bed and settled himself under the thin summer blanket.

I didn't know what I had expected from him, but a sudden wave of sadness came over me. It was a warm June night, sticky. I turned off the lamp, lay listening to him breathe. I wanted to touch him, but I couldn't. I waited for him to move toward me, but he didn't. I thought again of what his mother had said: "Don't ask for more than he can give."

"I don't know, Maggie, I just don't know," I heard him whisper a few minutes later, the muffled hoarseness of his voice seeming to come through a thick fog rather than from the darkness of the bedroom.

I lay still, waiting hopefully, but he said nothing more, and soon I heard the even breathing that signified he was asleep. I finally fell into an uneasy sleep, but it was short-lived. When I sprang awake, the clock read four thirty-five.

He was already gone.

June 11, 1973

The next day, Monday, began badly. At seven thirty, my supervisor called to remind me that I had agreed a month earlier to work a later shift that day. I had forgotten and was about to put on my uniform but instead threw on an old pair of jeans and a shirt and sat with Jennifer while she had her breakfast. At eight fifteen, I drove her to school, then came home and, overjoyed at being able to grab a few hours of extra sleep, reset the alarm for eleven, and got back into bed. After tossing around for an hour, however, I gave it up, made the bed, drank a cup of tea, and wrote out a shopping list. I also called Kathy at her office and arranged for her to stay with Jennifer that evening in case Rick wasn't able to be there. She had a date with Todd but promised me she would be here if necessary, and by the way, she added defiantly, she would be bringing Todd with her. I said that was fine with me. She wanted to prolong the conversation, but I was restless and told her I had a lot to get done before noon, which was true; only I didn't do any of it—no straightening, ironing, or bed making. What I did do was to make a fresh pot of tea and, all the while intermittently checking the clock, spend the next hour at the kitchen table poring over scrapbooks of my courtship and marriage. If I thought this would get my mind off Rick, I was mistaken. All it did was give me a headache and reinforce the fact that Steve was no longer a presence in my life. Finally, totally disgusted with myself, I gulped a couple of aspirin and headed for the grocery store.

The humidity of the past week had broken, and the weather was pleasantly hot and sunny. The air felt wonderful after a weekend indoors and I took my time getting where was going. Nevertheless, by the time I reached the store, my mind had gone blank. I had forgotten what I'd come for, and after discovering that I'd left my shopping list on the kitchen table, I spent the next fifteen minutes aimlessly wandering the aisles, picking up a few things at random. Once outdoors again, I decided that I wasn't ready to return to the apartment and drifted over to the park to sit on a bench for a while. But this place that had favored me with so many happy hours also brought to mind troubling ones, and before long, I went home, put away the few groceries I'd picked up. While I was dressing for work, I remembered Rick telling me that the deadline for the seminar application was June fifteen, four days from today. Had he told me the truth about his decision when we'd discussed last night? *And if he hadn't, were there other things he hadn't been truthful about?* I made up my mind to get a straight answer from him when I got home from work tonight. I didn't know how I would do it, but I had to know if he was going to go

For no particular reason, Carol popped into my head while I was on my way to the hospital. I hadn't seen or spoken to her since that night she and Jerry were over in—could it really have been February, four whole months ago? I dialed her office, but it was closed. The answering service said she would be back the next day. Did I want to leave a message? No, I said; I'll try her again. Tomorrow for sure, I told myself.

I got to the hospital at two forty-five, determined that the next eight hours would give me the strength to confront Rick once and for all about the seminar. It wouldn't be the first time I'd gotten an energy boost at work on days I'd been drooping. It was a moderately busy day, and eventually the rhythm and familiarity of the routine soothed me. Though I didn't feel quite up to par, I was in better spirits by the time dinner break came, and I kept working. I wondered who was having dinner with Jennifer, Rick or Kathy. Kathy would have told him at the station that I was working a later shift. Which of them would be there when I got home?

Just after dinner, the level of activity increased significantly with the admission of four new patients in a row. As often happened when we got busy, I became immersed in what I was doing and shut out everything else, which isn't hard to do when you don't have a minute to think.

Some of the patients in our unit have been with us for a protracted length of time, and I've established good rapport with one or two of them. They frequently asked for me if I wasn't there when they expected me to be and, in particular, when I was. It wasn't always possible to be available to them, but I tried. Sometimes when it's hectic on the floor, it's as if we're each juggling a dozen balls at a time.

It was somewhere around eight when I was able to take a breather and sit down at the desk for a few minutes, but as soon as I did, reality reasserted itself in a big way; suddenly there were what seemed like ten-pound butterflies in my stomach, and my breathing became short and shallow. I'd never had an honest-to-goodness panic attack, but I had a feeling this was close. One of the other nurses noticed and asked if anything was wrong. I shook my head and went into the bathroom, doused my face with cold water until I got hold of myself, and went back to work. Again I was able to fall back into the routine quickly enough, but I was still watching the clock and by now couldn't even pass the nurses' station without glancing across the corridor at the digital numbers over the new time-punch machine.

We had a small lull around nine forty-five. I took the desk again and immediately lapsed into a state of total abstraction. Rick would be working on his dissertation now, and I pictured him surrounded by a debris of typing paper, lined pads covered with scribbled notes, large hardcover reference books, piles of magazines. His metal-framed reading glasses would be sitting on the end of his nose, the sleeves of his faded denim shirt rolled partway up his arms. I could see him taking the glasses off, rubbing his eyes, leaning against the back of the chair in his apartment—or the couch in mine—and yawning. He would rummage around for his coffee mug, find it empty, check the pot on its warmer, and find it empty too. Then he would just put the glasses back on and go back to work. Never once had he asked me to bring him another pot. He could work for hours at a time, totally absorbed in what he was doing, and when he was done, he would pack it in and relax, devoting himself to relaxing as completely as he had to working, shifting gears as easily as if the work had never existed. We were somewhat alike in this area. I, too, had always gone about my work single-mindedly, never letting anything interfere with what I was doing. Until tonight. No matter how often I reminded myself that I had already decided it would be better if he left Chicago, or how many times I told myself I didn't care, I couldn't get my mind off him.

"Maggie, you're a million miles away. Anything wrong?"

"No."

"Well, 4011 has been ringing you for five minutes. Didn't you see the light?"

I glanced nervously at the clock. "Do me a favor, will you, Phyl? I have to leave right at eleven."

"I've been in there twice already. She wants you."

"The lady in 4011 was one of my special patients. She counted on me. But it was seven minutes to eleven, and there was no way I would be able to explain to her that I had to leave in five minutes. "Okay. I just hope it's nothing important. I've got to leave on time."

The crisis was minor. She was a very nice, slightly addled elderly woman who needed one thing and then another, but they had to be from me because according to her I was the only nurse on the floor who really cared about her. She'd felt neglected all weekend, and I hadn't been there this morning when I was supposed to be, and though I'd looked in on her six times this evening, she had one more important thing she had to tell me. I shifted from one foot to the other as she recounted the familiar story of a long ago time. She babbled and I squirmed. Just let me out of here, I prayed. It's eleven o'clock. As though Rick would turn into a pumpkin if I was fifteen minutes late. Finally I found a moment to break in and tell her, cheerfully and politely, that I would see her bright and early in the morning, but right now I had to get home to my little girl. But she craved the attention and chattered on as if I hadn't said a word. So I stood beside the bed, fidgeting, waiting for the moment she would run down and I could depart without hurting her feelings. When I finally got away, it was ten after eleven, and the extra minutes had devastated what was left of my self-control. I punched out and, too impatient to wait for the elevator, literally careened down five flights of steps to the emergency room in the basement, where there was a shortcut to the parking lot.

My heart was pounding when I reached the bottom, and I stopped for a second to catch my breath before proceeding through the stairway door and on across the emergency area to the street door. It registered somewhere on the edge of my consciousness that it was quiet tonight, that even the desk area, usually a frenzy of activity, had only a handful of staff standing around chatting. Someone happened to look up at me as I passed, and I couldn't resist asking what was going on.

"They're all at the party in room 3" she said. I nodded, though I had no idea what she was talking about, and rushed on to the revolving street door. Just as I was about to enter it, I thought I heard someone call my name. Turning reflexively, I saw a nurse waving at me. I had once worked with her and had dropped her off at her bus stop every night until she transferred down here. It had been years since I had seen her.

"Maggie, hold up a minute!"

In a frantic rush of words, I began to explain that I couldn't stop now, had to get home, but she silenced me with her hand and ran toward me.

"Glad I caught you," she said, breathing hard. "Maybe you can help us. They just brought this kid in. Accident out in the country. Nothing on him but his license." She held a little card toward me. Though it just as easily could've belonged to some twenty-year-old caught in a threshing machine or a teenager who'd dived fifteen feet into a shallow pool, I didn't need to look at the card; I knew. I came away from the door and went toward her, suddenly moving in what seemed like a surrealistic dream where she and I were the only people in the room.

It was Rick's license of course; I could see that clearly enough, but the rest of me seemed to be on hold.

"I thought I remembered your address being the same as his," she said, but I was having trouble making sense out of what she was saying. Rick was supposed to be home working. Drinking his coffee, scribbling his notes, taking off his glasses, waiting for me.

I found myself sitting on a bench, though I couldn't remember having walked over to it, and the woman I used to drive to the bus stop was peering at me, still talking.

"The matter? . . . Look so funny." Her voice came in waves, the way a car radio does when it starts getting too far from the broadcast area. She started shaking me. "Maggie, Maggie, are you okay?"

"Yes," I heard myself say, as if I was in a tunnel. "Yes. I'm sorry. That's never happened to me before. I—"

Right now, she wasn't concerned about me. "We really need your help, Maggie. Do you know this kid?"

This kid. Rick. I wished my head would clear. I looked again at the license, tentatively, not really wanting to see it.

"Yes. I know him. He's a neighbor."

"Thank God. All we have on him is this address. No phone, no relatives, nothing."

"There is no one else in Chicago." For the life of me, I couldn't remember this woman's name. I faded a little but snapped back. "What happened?"

"Totaled his motorcycle somewhere out in the country. No one saw it happen. Just some guy came along, saw the bike in the road, and called the police from the nearest phone. That's all they know."

"Is he bad?" I am a nurse, I said to myself. I'd seen terrible things during my training, things done to people by people, even things people did to themselves. No reason I can't handle this if I just hold on.

She took my hand. Did she sense that I was more than just a casual acquaintance of Rick's? Why else would she be making body contact and putting on her comforting nurse voice? Why can't I think of her name? "What? I'm sorry. I didn't hear what you said."

"I said I don't think he's too good. It's pretty quiet tonight, so half the staff is in there with him." She glanced around to the desk where the clerk was talking with a man in uniform. "Look, the police are trying to find out what they can about him. Will you talk with them?"

"Can I see him? Rick? Where is he?"

"Why don't you talk with the policeman first? The boy is going right up to surgery. You can see him when he comes out."

"What happened to him? What are the injuries?"

"I don't really know. I'll try to find out while you're talking with the officer."

She helped me up onto my unsteady legs and guided me to the desk, introduced me to the young policeman as a neighbor of the accident victim, who might be able to answer some questions about him. She suggested we sit on one of the couches in a cubicle to our left, and as we did so, I realized we were directly opposite room 3. I strained to see into the room, but the view was obstructed by a huddle of backs in white jackets.

The questions were routine: name, age, address, phone number (which I didn't know, since I'd never had to call him), occupation, place of employment, which school of the university he attended. I interrupted to ask the officer about the accident. He answered that he was not at liberty to release any details. This hardly seemed fair when I was sharing much more personal information about Rick with him. All I could get him to say was that it had been a one-vehicle smashup on some highway maybe forty-five minutes earlier. Nobody else involved in any way, no determination yet on the cause of the crash, and did I know the names of other friends of the victim and did the victim ride the motorcycle frequently. Could I tell him where the victim ate supper tonight or who the victim had been with. The victim. Rick. I answered whatever I could, but the voice I heard didn't sound like mine, and no matter how I tried to focus, my eyes kept wandering toward the door of room 3. I was desperate for some sign of what was happening in there.

"Mrs. McLean?" I tried to fix my attention on the policeman. "Just a few more questions and we'll be finished. Okay?"

I nodded.

"Do you know where we can get in touch with local relatives? Does he have any family?"

"Oh," I said, abruptly standing up. "I have to call home." It had suddenly occurred to me that Kathy would be worried. My watch read eleven forty; I should have been home by now. I was struck by another realization also. Forty-five minutes ago, I had been anxiously fussing over a senile old lady, while Rick had been splattering his insides across a rural highway, alone in the dark. I had been frantic to get home to him, and he hadn't even been there at all.

"Mrs. McLean, please," the young man said, "just one minute more. Please. Do you know if he has any relatives we could contact?"

"There isn't anyone in Chicago. They're somewhere in New York. Long Island, I think."

"Do you know his father's name? So we can get the number from information?"

"Yes." No. Wait. "It's . . . um . . ."

"Don't get excited. Take your time," he said.

"Richard. Richard Simon. But I don't know the name of the town."

"We'll find it."

I didn't wait to find out if he was finished with me. I simply walked away. By now the buzz of normal hospital activity had resumed, and the area was alive again with the coming and going of scores of people. At the desk, various staff members went about their usual business in the brilliant fluorescent light. I had never noticed before how much dimmer it was over by the doors than in the work area. I heard a telephone ring, saw it picked up by the clerk. Down the hall, doctors conferred with nurses and families. Housekeeping swished past with brooms, while people in other cubicles absently leafed through magazines.

I ran to the desk and, without asking, snatched a phone and dialed out. Kathy answered on the first ring. "Maggie, it's almost midnight. Where are you?"

I didn't want to alarm her, but I also didn't want to get stuck on the phone with nit-picking details. I lied. "One of my patients is in crisis. I probably won't be home for a while. How's Jennifer? Is everything all right?"

"Yes, but—"

"Sleep on the couch, okay? I'll explain later."

"Maggie?" she cried, frantically trying to hold me before I disconnected. "Rick was supposed to be here at nine o'clock and he never showed up. Todd and I were—"

My heart thudded wildly; I could feel it in my head. "Don't worry about it. Everything's going to be all right. I'll call you later."

"What's going on? Wait! Maggie?"

I hung up. I looked back at the cubicle, but the policeman I had been talking to was no longer there. I saw him instead in front of room 3, talking quietly with another officer. My attention was drawn to a roundish white object in the hand of the second man, and I realized with a shock that it was Rick's helmet and that one side of it was smashed in.

Oh my God, my God, his helmet is smashed and he is in that room with a dozen doctors and look at me, I am standing here not ten feet away and I can't move.

The policeman had asked me when I had last seen Rick. What did I tell him? Did I say that he had come to my bed last night but I couldn't reach him? That I had wanted him so badly but he was too far away. That I was afraid to try, afraid of pushing him further? Had I said that? Had I said that I had left him alone, the way he had been alone on that dark country road, with his life dripping away? the way he is now lying in that room ten feet from me, and all that might be left of him is in that policeman's hand?

My eyes blurred for an instant, then snapped back into focus, and somehow—I'll never understand it—I literally snapped too, snapped out of it, the fog, the dream, the shock, whatever it was that had overcome me the moment Ruth (Ruth!) had called my name. It was like your ear pinging clear after it's been plugged up from swimming, or the way it feels when your sinuses open up during a bad cold. Suddenly the only thing I could think of was getting into the ominous room 3 and seeing for myself what had happened to Rick. I was myself, and I was not about to lose it.

But I didn't have a chance even to march the ten feet across the hall, because at that moment, the doors of the holding room crashed wide, and the gurney came charging through, guided by three attendants. This was always a fascinating sight. Every type of sophisticated monitoring equipment was in full function. Red, green, beep, buzz. A small army of interns, residents, and nurses followed quickly along toward the service elevator, clipboards hugged tightly to white coats, murmurs of intensely serious conference barely audible as the group rushed past me to the gaping elevator doors. I could not see Rick. His body was covered with blankets, his face obscured by machinery, and they were moving fast. I stood, helpless, as the elevator doors slid shut. Someone tapped my shoulder, and I jumped. It was Ruth.

"Are you feeling any better?" she asked, genuinely concerned.

"What's happening now? Are they taking him to the OR?"

"Yes. Were you able to give the police any information?"

"I think so. Did you find out anything?"

She put her arm around me. "Let's go sit down." *Oh Lord. It must be bad.* My heart started pounding again. She led me to the couch where I had been interviewed a few minutes earlier and handed me a yellow chart sheet. I read it slowly, more carefully than I really needed to. Then I read it again. Several fractures, some simple, some compound, it said: ribs, arm, clavicle, jaw. Multiple facial injuries. "What do they mean spinal cord damage? How bad?"

"They won't know until they finish the exploratory. Maggie, you know this kid well?"

I nodded.

"I'm really sorry. I hope he makes it."

I looked at her, unbelieving. "Is there a chance he won't?"

She shrugged. "Let's just concentrate on the surgery now, okay? If he gets through that, it's one battle won . . . Look, this is going to take a while. Let me see you home."

"Thanks, but you go on. I'll be okay. I'm fine."

"There's really no point in hanging around. They won't know anything for hours."

"It's all right, Ruth. I can make it home by myself." *When I'm ready to leave.*

"You're sure?"

"Yes. Thanks."

For no particular reason, I walked with her until we were back where we had started. I left her at the revolving door, same place where she had found me a half-hour earlier.

This is different than with Steve. I'm older now, more experienced, and, despite my recent self-doubt, stronger. And I'm totally on my own. When the army notified me of Steve's capture, I simply sank into the cushion of family, friends, doctors, and medication. There will be none of that now; my mother served that notice on me the last time we talked. I'll no longer be able to conveniently give my daughter over to whoever is handy, while I lie in a stupor week after week, avoiding the painful realities. Nothing to do this time but face it. Is it that I love Rick less than I did Steve, that the feeling of loss is not as deep? I don't think so. Love has never figured in my fascination with Rick. Need *is the term I would use. I need Rick; I love Steve. And when Steve went away, any love I had to give went with him. Even now, I don't consider Rick a substitute for Steve. What I have with him is different. The only thing not different is that I am faced with a loss again, and whether the loss is due to death or to separation, whether it's someone I love or someone I need, makes no difference. It has to be faced.*

I call Kathy from a pay phone across from the visitors' elevators and tell her what happened. I wait patiently while she works her way through silent shock, then minor hysterics, and finally the questions, most of which I can't answer. By the time I insert the second quarter, she's calmed down and promised to help in any way she can. I tell her to try to get Mr. Wagner to let her into Rick's apartment so she can get his address book from his desk. She calls me back at the pay phone ten minutes later and gives me the number of his parents' home in a town called Roslyn Harbor. By that time, the police will have contacted the Simons, but I think it might be comforting for them to know that their son is not alone, that someone he knows will be with him until they arrive. I expect they'll try to get on the first flight out to Chicago.

A teenaged boy answers their phone. As I tell him who I am and that I'm calling from the hospital where Rick has been taken, it occurs to me that maybe the police haven't gotten through for some reason and that this is the first they're hearing about the accident. He identifies himself as Rick's brother Andy and says his parents are already on the way to the airport. I'm relieved to hear it. I thank him and begin to say that I will see them when they get here, but he interrupts.

"The police said Ricky is pretty bad and my parents should get there as soon as they could. Have you seen him? Is he going to be okay?"

I try to remember what Rick said about Andy, if he's twenty or twelve. How much do you tell a kid? Do you tell him anything at all? I've always believed that that's a job for a family member. "I haven't seen him, Andy, so I really can't tell you anything you don't already know."

"They said he was going to have an operation right away. What kind of operation? How bad is he hurt?" He sounds panicky, and my heart aches as it always does for the members of the families. Though years of training and experience have not taught me to hurt less, I have found a way to detach myself from the pain and deal with people from my head instead of from my heart. Still, there have been times when my heart has snuck in and I have had to get tough with myself. But this is Rick and his brother, and it's not so easy to put my feelings aside.

"Most likely, it's an exploratory to determine the extent of the injuries." I pause, trying to put myself in Andy's place, a thousand miles away, with nothing to do but worry and wonder. "I do know he's broken some bones."

A sigh of relief. "Oh," Andy breathed. "It sounded like it was a lot worse." A little lie of omission has given him hope, but it's false hope. Would I want false hope? I don't know.

"I'm sure your parents will call you as soon as they have something to report. Why don't you try to get some sleep until you hear from them?"

"Sleep," he echoed. "Yeah, well, if you see them, tell them to be sure and call us. It's hard not knowing what's going on."

"I know it is. Just hang on, Andy, and try not to worry."

"Right." He snuffed. "Well, thanks for calling."

I stand in the booth with the receiver in my hand. It's hard for me too, and I'm here.

How did I end up so involved in the pain of people I barely know?

It's the waiting that's the worst part, the aloneness and helplessness. I sit stiffly, trying to come to grips with the fact that I am not an observer this time; I am involved. I am not peering briefly into this room, casting sympathetic glances toward the families, the friends, the survivors; I am in the room and I am in it by myself.

The waiting room is dim, grim, and grimy. It hasn't yet undergone the remodeling process that has modernized the parts of the hospital that are more familiar to me. The out-of-date magazines hold no refuge, and so I spend the long hours reliving the past, the immediate past, starting with the moment Ruth called my name at the emergency room door. Everything before that is lost, no longer meaningful. The Simons have not arrived yet, and the time drags at an intolerably slow pace. People pass occasionally, peek in, move on. Housekeeping comes through once, emptying baskets, rearranging magazines, interrupting the otherwise absolute stillness in the room. Yet all the while, only a few yards down the hall, there is the frantic activity of a team of people whose only goal is to keep Rick Simon's life from slipping through their fingers. Those few yards of corridor stretch like a universe. *I need you, Rick. How did it turn out like this?*

The sky outside the window will begin to lighten soon. If Rick could wake up and sneak off that table just as he awoke each morning and snuck out of my bed . . .

There was no waiting with Steve. One day there was a letter from him, the next a telegram from the army. No wishing, no wondering. By the time we were informed of his capture, it had been over for him for a long while. It was up to us to accept the truth. I chose not to.

Now I have no decisions to make. I think of Rick's brother Andy, the troubled young voice on the telephone.

Each of us, Rick, Andy, and I, alone in the dark.

I have no idea what time it is when the doctor comes into the waiting room. I can hear birds, and gray light slits through the blinds. He's in a bloody scrub suit with his mask drooping on his neck. He peels off his silly blue hat as he walks over to me, then slumps beside me on the couch, yawns, stretches his long legs in front of him.

By now, every part of me is numb with fatigue except for my brain, which instantly launches into a hysterical exercise in rationalization: he would not just sit down here to unwind like this if Rick had died on the table; he would be in here to tell me. Or he thinks I'm just an interested bystander, a friend holding down the fort until the family arrives, doing them a favor because I'm a nurse here, but how does he know I'm a nurse here? Oh! I'm still wearing my uniform. Or it was a tough operation, and there isn't much hope, and he knows I'm here because I'm more than an interested bystander, and he's looking for an easy way to tell me. *No, not that. We all know there's no easy way; you just say it.* Or maybe he's so tired he's just resting and isn't about to tell me anything at all. But wouldn't he have gone to the doctor's lounge to unwind? *Talk to me*, I plead silently. *Just tell me what's happening.*

He hauls himself to a sitting position. "You Mrs. McLean, waiting on the Simon kid?" he asks.

I nod.

"They told me you were in here and that you might want to see him. He's in the recovery room."

"I'm a friend of the family," I explain. "They're on their way from New York."

He smiles wearily. "You can see him if you want, but he won't be awake for a few hours."

I know that. Just tell me.

He stretches again and then stares at my uniform for a long time. Perhaps he's wondering whether the fact that I am a nurse here is enough to permit him to discuss the case with me; that's usually reserved for the family. "That was one hell of a session," he says. Obviously he's decided it is enough.

"How is he?"

"Critical."

"What did you find?"

Again he seems to be considering my position and his responsibility. He gets up from the couch and my spirits sink. Then he says, "Come have a cup of coffee with me."

I am unsure about leaving the floor.

"The girl at the desk can call down if the family shows," he assures me.

Still I waver. I don't want to leave Rick here alone.

"Come on. The kid is sleeping. You can't talk to him yet."

I yield. At this point, a cup of tea sounds like a cup of heaven. My muscles scream at me when I stand up. When we get on the elevator, he introduces himself as the neurosurgeon who was called in by the doctors that were on duty in the emergency room when Rick was brought in. I already know who he is and that he has an excellent reputation at the hospital. In the elevator's bright lighting, I see him clearly for the first time—in his forties, moderately tall, stocky, and with a very tired face that for some reason reminds me of Snoopy, Jennifer's favorite animal character. He has a soft, faintly Southern accent.

We take our drinks to a corner of the large fluorescent-lit cafeteria. We're the only ones down here.

"Poor kid," he says once we we're settled at the table.

I tell him I've read the emergency room sheet. I know about the fractures.

"Fortunately, Jake Wyman"—who I also know is an excellent orthopedist—"was on tonight. There's a fair amount of internal damage. Motorcycle, was it?"

I nod.

"That'll do it . . . What I heard before we took him upstairs was that there was nothing else in the vicinity when he crashed. Some guy came along and saw the bike lying in the road, got out of his car with a flashlight, found the kid several yards away . . . Evidently got thrown thirty feet into a tree. From the looks of the injuries, whatever happened, he hit that tree with tremendous force."

"You don't think there's injury to his brain, do you?" I ask, instantly wishing I hadn't. I'm terrified of the answer.

"It'll be a while before we know about that, but it's certainly a possibility. One of the interns told me his helmet was badly smashed."

"I saw it," I say, not adding that I doubt I'll ever forget the sight of it. "It seemed to be just one side though."

"Which makes sense. It's consistent with almost all of the bodily damage."

We sit for a few minutes without speaking. I know from the chart there's more, but I'm not sure it would be appropriate for me to ask. He's already told me more than I ethically have the right to know, not being on the case. I feel ready to explode, but wait him out, hoping. Some of them become oblivious to the tragedy and waste they have to deal with from the endless parade of highway accidents. Until the one that's one too many. Maybe Rick is that one for this surgeon. His beagle face has sorrow written all over it. He drains his cup and goes to the machine for a refill. Mine is still half full. When he comes back, he says, "Too bad about his face. That might be difficult to—"

My cup clatters to the table. I right it quickly and wipe at the puddle with my napkin. "Sorry," I mumble. I should have been prepared for this; it was on the chart.

He hands me his napkin and goes on. "Really devastated the right side. That'll need a good plastic, the best we can find. The teeth are okay though." He smiles, shakes his head. "You never can figure it, can you? Jaw busted, cheek shattered. But the teeth are fine."

Does he notice that I'm trembling? I shove my hands onto my lap as he plunges ahead. He's hot now. Once you get some of them started, they really love—or need—to talk about the bad ones.

"Pretty severe nerve damage. No response in the lower extremities."

Paralysis. "Temporary?" I ask hopefully.

"Right now it doesn't look good. It'll take more surgery to be sure. We couldn't keep him under any longer than we did and there was just so much we could do. Had to remove the spleen, for one thing."

I am feeling a little faint and know I'd better get some fresh air if I don't want to pass out. "I think I've heard enough," I hear myself whisper. "If it's all right, maybe I can see him now." He checks his watch. I look toward the clock on the opposite wall; it's almost seven. *Where are Rick's parents?*

"Sure," he says. "He should be coming out of it pretty soon." He picks up both cups, and we leave the table. He tells me he's going to grab a nap in the doctor's lounge, would I tell the desk to let him know when the parents arrive so he can speak with them. Then he looks at me curiously for a moment. "Are you okay?"

"Yes," I answer, though I'm really not. "Thank you for talking to me."

He saunters off toward the elevators, and I walk up a flight and let myself out an emergency exit just to feel the morning air on my face. The sun is bright, and everything looks so normal that for just an instant I have an overwhelming desire to walk away from the hospital and not look back. But I know I won't get far. This is where Rick is. I take a deep breath, pull myself together, and take the next elevator up to the recovery room.

The blue gowns hang on hooks outside the recovery room door. I put one on and go in. Nobody questions my presence; they just figure I have a right to be there. Rick isn't hard to locate. There are only a few patients on the ward, and their beds are scattered. Two LPNs and a very young RN hover silently around his bed amid a battery of busy machines and monitors. All three turn to me as I approach.

His pulse is being taken, and I hold back in order not to disturb the nurse's concentration, but then I look more closely and see that what she is really doing is holding his hand. *What right does this girl have to be holding Rick's hand? I'm the one who should be comforting him and I've been waiting for hours.* I am consumed with anger over this injustice. No, I'm not. What I really am is not ready for this. The doctor should have understood about us, should have warned me. Just because I'm wearing the uniform, he shouldn't have assumed I could walk in here and handle it like any other case. It isn't any other case. It's Rick, and more than nine years of nursing training and experience have not prepared me for this. The doctor should have seen that. Somebody should see it. But these three women aren't seeing anything but their patient.

Rick is flat on his back. He looks as if he's being held together with tape and wire and hanging on by a network of tubing. Everything is humming, beeping, buzzing, flashing at once, like in the emergency room; only now it's intensified by the dimly lit stillness surrounding this little island of activity. At first he seems literally mummified in dazzling white bandages, but when my initial shock subsides, I see that above the light modesty sheet that covers the lower part of his body, it's only his rib section that is taped and his right arm, which is in a cast and a sling and is lying across his chest. A large bandage covers nearly all of the right side of his face. The eye on that side is swollen and purple and ugly. He looks grotesque, but this is mostly because the left side is basically undamaged. I move forward. The left eye is closed, but the lid is moving faintly, and one of the girls says, "He's doing it again."

Another looks over at me. "He's been on the verge of waking up for half an hour now. He just can't seem to pull himself out of it."

And the third adds, "I think he's going to make it this time."

I push my way through the little group, forcing the young nurse to let go of Rick's hand and drop back. "We're friends," I announce to no one in particular, then think, *Lord, that sounds dumb*. Nobody says anything for a minute.

Then the young one says, "Oh, I thought you worked here," and sounds stupider than I do, but then nothing is making sense right now.

"I do work here," I answer curtly, "but we're still friends." The conversation doesn't seem to have anywhere else to go, and the others drop back a little. I am finally beside Rick, and that's the only thing that matters. I lean over the bed and say his name.

"Don't bother," someone says. "He isn't going to respond."

The good eye is moving rapidly beneath the lid, but he can't seem to open it. The right one is hopeless, so I concentrate on the left, trying not to look at the rest of him; the bareness of the exposed shoulder, arm, and chest makes them look so vulnerable. I don't know how long I coax and coo and whisper at him, minutes maybe, seconds probably. The others don't interfere, and at last his eye flutters open and, after wandering a bit, focuses on me. I am mute with joy and relief. It's a miracle to me that he has come out of it and that I am the one who brought him around. He seems to be trying to speak but can't, and I look at the nurses questioningly.

"His jaw," one explains, "it's wired." Of course. I am embarrassed because the wiring is so obvious.

And then he does an amazing thing. He lifts his hand and touches my face, and I think I will cry if I let myself go. But holding on is easier now. Rick is alive and moving, my fear is dissolving, and I feel more in control. His eye swivels from me to the ceiling, from one side to the other. At one point he focuses on the three nurses down near the foot of the bed. He doesn't actually move his head, he probably can't, so his vision is limited, and his gaze eventually comes back to me. His mouth moves as the wiring permits, which is barely, and he utters a distinctly three-part sound, which I unconsciously decide means "hospital."

I nod my head. "Yes."

The bewilderment on his broken face says clearly that he has no idea of what's happened. He feels around for my hand. I take his instead and hold it against my face, prepare myself to read his questions. But he has no questions, just lies there watching me, each breath deeper and more labored from fright and confusion. The three nurses stare. I lower his arm, arrange it on the sheet, but hold tight to his hand. After a few tense minutes, I say, "Rick, listen. I need to know what happened. Can you blink your eye?"

He doesn't answer.

"Try, okay? Just blink once to say yes or twice to say no, okay? Please try. It's important. Can you hear me?"

He just stares at me. I squeeze his hand. "Rick, can you hear me?"

He blinks once. I let out a lungful of breath I didn't know I was holding in.

"That's good . . . The motorcycle, Rick, what happened? Did somebody hit you?"

Nothing.

"Did you hit someone else?"

Nothing again. He seems not to know what I'm talking about, and his good eye narrows in a frown. The effect is bizarre.

The nurses remain rooted in their places, and I grow more anxious at Rick's lack of response. I remember the bashed-in helmet. Did the doctor say anything about brain damage? No, I wouldn't have forgotten that. But maybe he didn't tell me everything. Why should he have? I force my attention back to Rick and see that he's trying to speak. The other girls close in, and as if we're in an old hospital movie, I lean forward, as close as I can get.

"Legs," he says suddenly, this time definitely making the sounds.

"You're fine, Rick. Your legs are fine." He'll find out soon enough.

Though nothing else appears to be moving, what's left of his face creases with exertion. "Shit," he croaks, and I watch helplessly as his expression changes from bewilderment to terror.

I look away for a moment, and when I turn back to him, his good eye is closed and his face is a mask.

"Rick?" I jiggle his hand. "Rick." I glance at the monitors, find immense relief in the continuing bedlam of light and noise. He seems to have gone under again. But I know what he's doing. He realizes the truth of his situation now and is dealing with it in his own way.

Hiding.

"Don't do it this way, Rick. Please don't do this." It's no use. Crazy as it sounds, he's not going to come back out until he's good and ready, and when he does come out, he's not going to be an easy patient. That's my guess. What I know, though, is that he will come out of it.

Rick Simon is not going to die.

Part 2

I glance at my watch as I hang up the phone—7:20 a.m. I've just checked in with Kathy, who assures me that she has already left a message for her boss that she'll be in late. She tells me that she'll be taking Jennifer to school in half an hour. Everything is under control, and there is no need for me to rush home. She sounds fine, not at all melodramatic as I'd been expecting her to be. According to a recovery nurse I spoke to earlier, Rick is scheduled to be moved to ICU "anytime now." She'd heard that his parents had arrived sometime in the middle of the night, had immediately gone in with the doctors on duty, and then had left for their hotel to register and get some rest. I promise myself that as soon as Rick has been transferred, I'll go home and try to do the same. For now, however, I stand across from the elevators, bone-tired and emotionally wiped out but unable to leave.

I need to decide what I'm going to do now. The sensible thing would be to go home and take a nap, come back later when Rick's parents get here, and maybe even see Rick myself. But I can't make myself leave until I know he's been moved to intensive care and I know for sure that his parents have arrived. I can't leave him here alone.

Someone's left a gray molded bucket chair near the elevators. I lower myself onto its hard surface, lean back, and close my eyes, only to bolt right back up when I suddenly remember that I have to report that I won't be working today. A long moment passes as I struggle over whether to go now or wait until Rick has been moved. Then I see a gurney coming toward me at a trot. I stand up as the attendants load it onto the service elevator, and get a glimpse of Rick, immobile, with good eye closed, exactly as he was when I last saw him hours ago. I wait until the elevator doors have shut behind them, then push the down button, but am too impatient to wait for it to return and hurry to the stairs.

Sharon, my supervisor, is not happy with me. My shift has already started and she is struggling to find a replacement. She is still annoyed after I've explained the situation. I don't blame her. I could've left a message during those long, empty hours in the waiting room. But I'm too wrung out right now to feel irresponsible, and I sling my purse over my shoulder and head back to the stairwell. I only get as far as the next landing before I am seized by a sudden headache and a wave of nausea. I lean against the wall and close my eyes until the nausea has passed. As I turn to continue on down, I notice the big "3" painted on the door opposite me. The third floor houses the ICU, where Chris, who worked upstairs with me until last summer, is now a senior nurse on the unit and might be willing to give me an update on Rick. On impulse, I pass through the door and head for the desk. As it happens, Chris is off today, but the ward secretary tells me that until further notice, no visitors are allowed to see Rick, except for family, who, if I would like to talk with them, are in the waiting room.

Rick's father and a young blonde woman, probably one of Rick's sisters, sit quietly on a couch in the waiting room. When Mr. Simon sees me at the door, he rises and comes toward me, grabs my hand with both of his, and pats it as he says, "Maggie, we thought you had gone home."

"I hoped I could see you first."

"It took us a lot longer to get here than we expected, and then we were in conference for an hour with a couple of doctors." He guides me toward the couch. "My daughter Susan," he informs me as we approach. "Honey, this is Mrs. McLean, Ricky's neighbor, whom we met when we were here in April."

"Rick has spoken about you often," I say feebly, unable to recall a single thing he might have said about her.

She looks up at me with a sad smile, extends her hand, and says, "I'm happy to meet you, Mrs. McLean." Her eyes are pink and watery.

Mr. Simon seats me in an adjacent chair and asks if I've seen Rick yet.

"Just for a few minutes in the recovery room. Have you?"

"His mother is with him now. They're only allowing one person in at a time."

"Mrs. McLean," Susan ventures fearfully, "is it really as bad as the doctor said? He told us to be prepared."

As if you could prepare yourself to see someone you love in the condition Rick is in.

"He is seriously hurt," I answer, "and he doesn't look very good right now, but that will eventually get better."

Except don't expect him ever to look the way he did when he mounted that motorcycle last night. And don't expect that your life will return to normal anytime soon. It only takes that one split second of impact to change the lives of everyone close to the victim. These words literally spring, loudly and intrusively, into my consciousness, and I pray to God I didn't say them out loud, but my head is throbbing like a bass drum, and I can't tell whether I'm talking or just thinking.

Mr. Simon gets up and starts pacing around the room, stopping once or twice to look out a window. The morning sun is brilliant, and I try to avoid it. Between the light and the headache, I am not at my best right now. I lean back and gingerly lay my neck on the top of the overstuffed chair.

"Are you okay?" Susan asks, her brow furrowed.

"Just a little headache," I answer dismissively, trying to deflect her attention.

She insists on giving me something for it and roots around in her voluminous bag, finally coming up with a bottle of Tylenol, which she hands to me before striding to the watercooler in the far corner of the lounge.

Her father drops back down on the couch. He is clearly exhausted, but his eyes burn with anger and energy, reminding me of Rick the morning Kathy found the shaving kit.

"How did this happen?" he asks angrily. "What the hell was he doing?"

The fury in his voice awakens memories of guilt and fear from my own childhood, and another wave of nausea spirals toward my throat.

"I don't know any more about this than you do," I whisper weakly and explain about Ruth and the addresses.

Somewhat defused, but with no less anger, he says, "We begged him to drive his car out here, but no, he had to have that damned motorcycle. Lenore knew it would be trouble and this time she was right."

"Oh, Dad, he's been riding it for years and he's never gotten a scratch. Mother would worry if he was riding an armored tank." Susan is back with one of those little conical paper cups, and I accept it gratefully and choke down the pills. "And it doesn't change things to be angry about that now anyway," she adds.

Her father concedes with a disconsolate shrug.

She slumps onto the couch beside him and looks at me closely. "Do you feel any better?"

"It'll take a little time."

She laughs. "That was dumb. I don't even know what I'm saying." She checks her watch against the wall clock, then takes the watch off and resets it to Chicago time. "Did Ricky say anything to you? Did he recognize you?"

"Not really. He opened his eyes and looked around. He wouldn't have been able to say much anyway with his jaw wired."

She glances wildly around the room. "I wish Mother would hurry up," she complains impatiently. "She's been in there for ages."

"It's only been a few minutes," her father says gently, then turns to me. "Maggie, could he have any idea of his injuries or is he too sedated?"

"He implied he couldn't feel his legs," I admit.

"Then he did speak to you," Susan says hopefully.

"Not exactly. His jaw is wired, but he uttered a syllable which I think was 'legs.' I have seen people come out of whatever they're in for a second or two"—*I momentarily relive the feel of his hand on my cheek*—"but then they usually go right back under, which is what your brother did."

"And you didn't tell him," her father says.

"I didn't know whether he could hear or understand me, but I assured him everything was okay. Besides, it wasn't really up to me to tell him the truth."

"How do we tell him the truth anyway?" he mutters.

"Then he closed his eyes and tried to turn his face to the wall."

"Are you saying that the reason he's in a coma is that he doesn't want to face the truth?" Susan asks.

"It would pretty much support what they told us, though they were clear about not calling it a coma," her father says. "So far, there's been no discernible brain damage and they haven't been able to find any other reason for him not to be responding. The anesthesia hasn't completely worn off, though, so maybe—"

He stops abruptly and stands up as Rick's mother enters the room. She looks ill—gray and worn and rumpled. I've been so blinded by my headache that I've barely been able to think about their needs, but the Tylenol is beginning to kick in, and I am remembering my role in all this.

"Maggie, I'm so glad you're here," she says, hugging me. I know from their visit in April that she tends to be an anxious person, and even though her eyes look as if a dam is about to burst behind them, there is something about her just now that suggests that she is a strong one too. She walks to where her husband sits, touches his hair, says softly, "Go on, Rich." He nods his head and rises slowly, then squeezes her hand. They look at each other for just a second before he turns and follows the waiting nurse out of the room and down the hall.

Mrs. Simon collapses on the couch where her husband had been sitting. "Dear God," she says quietly, "Why did Ricky do this to himself?"

What on earth would make her think he did this terrible thing on purpose, I wonder, then instantly flash to that conversation Rick and I had in the park weeks ago. Could there be anything in what she's implying? Too much has happened in the last nine hours and I can't think about this now.

It doesn't seem as if two minutes have passed before Mr. Simon returns, explaining that a team of technicians was rolling testing equipment into the cubicle when he got there and he was asked to leave. He doesn't appear disappointed about this, just sad and resigned. He suggests we take the opportunity to get some breakfast, and I lead them to the cafeteria in the basement. He tries to persuade us to eat, but nobody feels much like it, and he ends up getting a cup of black coffee for himself and a couple of pots of tea for the women. Mrs. Simon describes what transpired during her time with Rick, which, of course, amounted to nothing but her watching him while he slept.

Their misery is palpable as they rehash their initial discussion with the doctors. Mrs. Simon seems on the verge of collapse, barely able to hold herself together, and Mr. Simon tries to keep her on an even keel by repeatedly reminding her of the doctors' assurances that there is no reason to feel hopeless. They mention that their bags have already been moved to wherever they are staying and that they have decided to remain at the hospital throughout the day unless Rick's visiting hours are suspended for some reason.

Susan contributes nothing to the conversation. She had confided to me on the way down here that she was upset because she had not yet been able to see her brother. She appears to be a sensible young woman with a kind of quiet strength. I like that.

I drink two cups of strong tea and say little, all the while calculating the toll this catastrophe has taken on the three of them. Just as I'm thinking that Rick's parents barely resemble the people I met in April, Mr. Simon turns to me and, as if he has read my mind, apologizes for his scruffy appearance. It had been after 2:00 a.m. when the call came from Chicago and they had had no time to do anything but make arrangements, dress, and pack before leaving. He hadn't shaved since seven yesterday morning.

At this, his wife surprisingly lifts herself out of her melancholy to say, in a teasing deadpan, "I don't see the difference."

His eyes, filled with affection, fix on her for just a moment as he puts his hand over hers on the table. They are trying hard, but the banter is forced, and it doesn't lift anybody's spirits. I've seen this sort of thing before among people who are under enormous emotional stress.

We sit for several minutes in talked-out silence, during which I seize the opportunity to take the empty cups and used plastic ware to the trash. I'm desperate for a hot shower and a clean bed, and more than ready to pick up my handbag and say good-bye. Before I can break away, however, Mr. Simon suggests that I let Susan drive me home. I decline, saying it isn't necessary, but Susan assures me that she's a good driver and that she'll have no trouble getting back to the hotel. Unable to muster the strength to protest further, I give in, and we all walk to the entrance to the parking garage. I offer to do whatever I can to make their time in Chicago easier, and we finally say good-bye.

Other than offering directions as we ride, I don't speak, and neither does Rick's sister.

I find things at my apartment as Kathy normally leaves them: dishes in the sink, sheets on the couch, Jennifer's clothes and toys on the floor. I make extravagant sounds of dismay, but Susan silences me, saying that she has no interest in housekeeping, so there's no need for me to apologize for mine. *This isn't mine. It's my sister's.* I offer her first use of the shower, but she prefers to wait until she gets back to the hotel.

She refuses to leave before I am "settled comfortably in bed" and follows me to the bathroom while asking for Kathy's office number so she can call to let her know I'm home now. I tell her it's on the refrigerator. Though I'm beginning to seethe with annoyance over her take-charge attitude, something inside me welcomes the nurturing.

The water obscures everything but the therapeutic warmth of its jets on my skin, and I take a long shower, reluctant to relinquish the tranquilizing effect of the gentle spray. Whatever Susan Simon wants to do, I decide, is okay with me. At last, swaddled in my robe and a towel turban, I leave the bathroom. Susan is in the living room now, waiting for a taxi to take her back to the hotel. I just want to go to sleep, so I don't argue when she follows me to my room where, acutely embarrassed, I crawl into bed in front of this girl who is a stranger. I am nearly overwhelmed by a pang of longing for Rick as I pull the sheet over me—as he pulled it over himself thirty hours earlier—and I wonder if his sister is imagining him here too; she must at least suspect we've been sharing this bed.

I can't deny it feels good to be cared for, to be on the receiving end for once. Nevertheless, I sigh in relief when I hear her cab honk and the door close behind her. She has pulled the shades, and the silence and the half-light envelop me, comforting me, lulling me to a blankness like the cocoon I had so carefully devised for Jennifer and me before Rick came into our lives. I am grateful to be home and alone.

My last thought before I fall asleep is that I can't remember my mother ever hugging me.

I have a bad dream, one of those in which you have to be somewhere for something important. I don't know what it is that's going on. I only know I have to be wherever it is. I can't seem to get there though: can't find the place, miss the bus, the car won't start. I try to call ahead to say I'll be late, but the phone doesn't work. It gets later and later, until I have just minutes, then seconds, to get to where I need to be. It isn't until my legs refuse to move that my subconscious has apparently had enough, and I wake up screaming—at least I think I'm screaming.

My eyes fly open, and I find myself sitting straight up in my bed, petrified and listening hard. But the room I wake to is quiet, with not even the echo of my shrieking voice, and it takes a few minutes for my pulse to slow as I separate the dream from reality. I rarely dream, or at least remember my dreams, so I don't have much experience in interpreting them, but it seems to me that in this dream, I am being depended on for something and that I am responsible for the outcome of whatever it is that is happening. But what is it that's happening, and why would I be responsible for anyone but Jennifer and myself? Even Kathy's pretty self-sufficient now.

"Oh, hi," Kathy says as she comes into the room, sounding as if she is surprised to find me in my own bed.

"What are you doing here, Kath? I thought you went in to work."

"Left work early to come by and clean up. I didn't think you'd be up to it. I hope I didn't wake you. What time did you get home?"

"Around nine, I think."

She stares at me for a moment. "Are you feeling okay? You look a little weird."

"I had a bad dream. Thought I woke up screaming."

"I didn't hear anything." She sits down on the side of the bed. "Maggie, you should've—"

"What time is it?"

"Around three."

"Has anyone called?"

"No—oh, yeah. Carol Hauser called. She said to call her when you have time. I didn't mention anything about Rick."

I'm glad of that; I'm not ready to go into it with anyone else just yet. I ask how Jennifer is and if she wanted to know why I didn't come home last night.

"I told her you had to work extra time and that you'd be here when she came home from school today. She just nodded her head and went off to watch TV."

"Good. And what about you?"

"I was just going to tell you. It was really grim at work this morning. I went right in after I dropped Jenny at school. Everyone was talking about it. Nobody could believe Rick was in such a bad accident. I mean, he just doesn't seem like the kind of guy something like this would happen to. All day people kept coming to me asking about him, I guess because he rides me in to work sometimes, but it's not like I knew anything."

"Well, you know now, so you can give them all the gory details tomorrow," I tell her, "though I doubt Rick would appreciate your doing that."

"I don't know anything about what's happened since last night," she points out.

My head is beginning to ache again, and I massage my temples. "Maybe later, Kath. I'm not even sure I'm awake yet."

"That's not fair, Maggie," she protests. "I wouldn't have to ask you if I could've gone up to the hospital myself."

Which is of course true. I give up and describe what took place in the intensive care unit, tell her about being in the waiting room with Rick's family, and about how his sister insisted on driving me home and putting me to bed. I can't help noticing her resentful expression when I get to the last part. Though I pretty much feel the same way about Susan's high-handedness, the Simons have been nice to me, so I defend her. "I think she just saw how tired I was and did it to thank me for staying with her brother until they got there."

"I would've come down if I'd been able to," she says plaintively.

"It was not by choice, Kathy. Mr. Simon suggested it as we were leaving the cafeteria, and I was too exhausted to argue."

She shrugs indifferently, but I can tell Susan Simon is not going to make it into her good graces.

I push the covers aside, swing my legs over the edge of the bed, and stand up. The dream is still flitting around the edges of my mind, competing with Rick's omnipresence.

He'll never again be able to do what I just did—sit up, put his feet on the floor, get up off my bed.

Kathy follows me into the bathroom. I wash my face, brush my teeth, run a comb through my hair, all the while avoiding myself in the mirror. I am only slightly less uncomfortable with her sitting there scrutinizing me as I was with Rick's sister putting me to bed. At the same time, I'm glad she's here. Now that I'm up and somewhat rested, I don't want to be alone.

"What are you going to do now?" Kathy asks.

"I'm thinking I might go back to the hospital, if you don't mind taking care of Jennifer for a little while longer."

She looks at me for a long moment. "No, I don't mind."

As we settle on the couch, I realize that the living room is neat as a pin. "Thank you so much for helping me through this, Kathy. You've been a lifesaver." I put my hand on her arm. "I know Rick means a lot to you too, and this isn't easy for you either."

"Yeah, well, you know, I still like Rick, but now that Todd's around, I'm not that hung up on him anymore, so . . ." Her voice peters out; then she straightens up and stretches over to the easy chair for her handbag, from which she extracts a small square of newsprint. "I almost forgot. This was in the morning paper."

I unfold the sheet and skim it quickly. In the middle of the left-hand column is a small article, like you see in newspapers all the time. Someone wrecked a vehicle, was hurt, was taken to the hospital. Name, age, address. Extent of injuries. Period. As if the story ends there. You never hear about all the other people whose lives are touched.

Kathy notes anxiously, "It says he's in critical condition."

"They say that about most people in intensive care. As far as I know, he's not in a life-threatening situation, if you're worried about that."

"So many of his bones were broken!"

"True, but they'll mend. The worst thing I know about is the spinal injury, but not all spinal damage is permanent," I tell her. "It doesn't have to mean he'll never walk again." I can't bring myself to talk about the facial injuries.

"Is that what the doctors are saying?" she asks.

"That's what they told the family."

"Has anybody found out what happened, what caused the accident?"

"Not last I heard."

"I guess Rick didn't say anything."

"He was totally out of it, Kath. I told you that. He just barely knew he was in the hospital." I don't like the crankiness I hear in my voice.

"I know that," she retorts. "I just thought . . . because you said no one else was involved, so I'm just wondering what happened. Could there have been something in the road that made him swerve? Rick is a good driver. I was never nervous when I rode with him."

I turn toward her. "You know what's funny? After his mother saw him, she said, 'Why did he do that to himself?'"

"Oh no, Maggie!" Kathy says vehemently. "I knew Rick better than you think I did. He was a really together person. He never acted like he had any hang-ups or anything. I know he was kind of quiet and all, not talking about himself much, but it was like that's the way he was. Like he was in super control of himself."

An icicle slides down my spine. "Stop, Kathy," I interrupt. "We haven't lost Rick yet. We can still talk about him in the present tense."

She blushes. "I only meant I can't believe he'd do a dumb thing like crack himself up. Not when he had . . . has those dynamite looks going for him . . .

Correction: that's probably the one time in this conversation you can use the past tense.

". . . and that doesn't make sense."

What Rick said in the park suddenly snaps into perfect focus as Kathy zeroes in on the thing he despises about himself. In doing so, she validates what he believes is true, that most people see him the way she does. And I'm one of them. Of all his injuries, I can't get my mind off what's happened to his face. Maybe this isn't a figment of his imagination. Could what he said that day in the park actually have had something to do with him breathing through tubes in a death-smelling cubicle instead of being on his way home from work right now? We all have things we can't speak about to anyone, and that day in the park is one of mine. The one time he finally opened up to me, all I could think about were his sexy eyes.

It's a little after five, more than seven hours since I left the hospital, way too long for me not to know what's going on there. Kathy leaves to pick Jennifer up at day care and I dress quickly and head back to Wohlsein, wondering on the way if I'll be welcome. Maybe I should back off a little. The Simons have been kind and appreciative of my being there for Rick until they arrived, but I'm not one of the family, and now that things are well in hand, they'll most likely feel I've outlived my usefulness and will thank me and send me on my way. I have to be realistic and expect this. Yet, much as I wish I'd never become involved, I can't bear the thought of being excluded.

Chris happens to be working the evening shift, and I find her in the meds closet, but she has nothing to tell me. Rick's signs are the same, and he is still unconscious. His parents are expected back shortly for yet another conference with the doctors, who are considering a second exploratory of his spine. His brain function is being monitored closely.

Susan is sitting forlornly in the otherwise empty waiting room. "Were you able to get any sleep?" she asks.

"Yes, thank you. How about you?"

"Not really. I tried for a while when I got back to the hotel, but I was so wired, I couldn't even lie still long enough to calm down. Most of the time my mother and I sat together passing the tissue box back and forth and trying to keep each other from getting hysterical."

"How is she doing?"

"Okay, I guess. Keeping it together. She's called home every hour since one, with silly excuses like, 'Did Jody get home from school okay?' and 'Did you remember to defrost the meat for supper?' Like our housekeeper needs this? I told her she shouldn't call anymore. Every time the phone rings at home, they probably think Ricky's gotten worse or something."

"She's a mother, Susan," I offer. "It's her way of keeping it together."

"I guess."

"And your father?"

She smiles, and I notice that her eyes are shaped just like Rick's; only hers are blue. "He's hanging in too," she answers, "by doing what he does best. Calling people, getting information. He's probably run up the most monumental phone bill in the history of Illinois, attempting to contact every world-renown surgeon from coast to coast."

"That isn't necessary. We have some of the country's finest doctors right on our staff."

"I know you do. The doctors we talked to this morning told us."

"In fact," I went on, "this hospital happens to specialize in spinal cord and nervous system injuries and has a first-rate rehabilitation unit. This is probably the reason the paramedics brought him here instead of somewhere else."

"They told us that too."

"Then why's your dad shopping?"

"Thoroughness is my father's middle name."

I can't tell whether she's being sarcastic or just stating a fact. I often have trouble knowing how to take things Rick says too. These people are different from the simpler, more predictable folks I've known all my life. It's nothing I can put my finger on; they're just harder to read.

"My mother and I also talked last night about things people do to keep themselves together when something terrible happens," Susan continues. "She has to feel indispensable from a thousand miles away. My father has to maintain some kind of control with his endless contacts, and I guess I have my own ways." She averts her eyes. "I know I was awfully heavy this morning, but you looked like you'd been through so much, and nobody else was even noticing it. So, well—"

"You were just fine," I fib. "You made me feel better. I wouldn't have let myself rest and wouldn't have been good for anything if you hadn't taken over."

"I still came on a little strong and I'm really sorry," she insists. "I could tell that your sister was definitely pissed at me for insisting on bringing you home."

"Kathy likes Rick a lot. She's upset. Look, if it'll make you feel easier about it, I'm a little concerned about what I said to your brother Andy on the phone." Actually I'm hoping to relax her with "misery loves company." I hadn't given a thought to that call since I hung up from it.

"Andy," she repeats, puzzled, then recalls. "Oh, right. He told us you called. But it was so nice of you to take the trouble."

"At the time, I didn't know whether your parents had been notified about Rick. As it turned out, the police had already been in touch and you were on your way to the airport."

"So what was wrong about that?"

"I don't know how old Andy is. I wouldn't tell a thirteen-year-old certain things I might tell a twenty-year-old."

Susan smiles. "Don't worry about it. Andy's eighteen, but he's definitely the most mature of us oldest kids. He can take it. Besides, if it were me, I'd want to know everything. Ricky and I are pretty close." A short silence falls and is broken when she says, "I saw him today."

I am surprised she has waited this long to mention it. I try to gauge from her face what she's going to say, but her features are devoid of expression.

"What did you think?" I asked.

She considers for a moment before responding. "Nothing. Absolutely nothing." Then she adds uneasily, "I can't explain it."

"It's understandable. It's a big shock, the way he looks right now."

Her eyes mist; droplets stand in the corners. She blinks them away. "He's my brother," she says softly, all reserve falling away. "I love him."

How good it must feel to release the pain, to allow yourself to let it out.

"I know you do," I tell her, taking her hand protectively. "You know, Susan, I reacted exactly the same way when I found out my husband had been taken prisoner of war. With a numbness, a kind of limbo."

"Yes," she agrees. "That's exactly how I feel. Does it take a long time to get over it?"

"That depends. You'll probably stabilize when you know exactly what to expect of your brother's condition. I took a long time because I didn't know whether my husband was dead or alive . . . I still don't."

"Oh no," she says tenderly. "I'm so sorry. When did this happen?"

"Seven years ago."

"How horrible. How have you gotten through it?"

I can't help warming to this sweet, caring girl. "My daughter needs a functioning mother, for one thing . . . and your brother's friendship has helped a lot."

I don't know whether this is the honest truth, but I'm glad I said it because Susan reacts with a teary grin and whispers, "Thank you for telling me that. He's pretty terrific, isn't he?" Then she looks at me with that same curious x-ray stare that her father and brother have, and says, "You love him too."

Without meaning to, I gasp and pull back from her. "I—"

Her eyes widen, and she steeples her hands over her mouth. "I don't know why I said that! It's none of my business. I just . . . Oh, Maggie . . . Mrs. McLean . . . please don't be mad at me. I'm just so scared." The tears are flowing freely now, and she is trembling. I move closer to her and put my arm around her shoulders.

"It's all right, Susan. Really."

"This is the worst thing that's ever happened to me. I don't think I can get through it."

"You will," I assured her. "You really don't have a choice. Your brother's going to need all the support he can get."

And by the way, this didn't happen to you. It happened to him.

The results of Rick's scans, grams, and x-rays have been studied, and the indications are positive. His vital signs are good. There doesn't appear to be any organic reason for him to be in this state, and everyone agrees that he simply prefers avoiding his condition to facing it. This is not a healthy situation for him, and it is important that we do everything we can to get him awake, aware, and emotionally stabilized so that we can go on to the next phase of treatment. They want to give him forty-eight hours to come out of it by himself before they move forward. Their suggestion is that we try to reach him with constant communication. Maybe someone will strike the chord that registers. It has been known to happen. They believe it will be more effective if familiar voices—relatives, close friends—rather than hospital personnel, do the talking.

So now I am once again with the Simons in the cafeteria. This latest conference has given them some hope, and they seem less weary than they were earlier in the day. I listen to them discussing the option over a dinner of sandwiches and salads, and when they ask me for my opinion, I tell them I've seen this tactic work, and I urge them to try it for two days. What do they have to lose? It doesn't take much to persuade them. Now that the shock of Rick's accident is wearing off, they're realizing how little time is left before they have to leave Chicago. Mr. Simon is scheduled to appear in court on Thursday for a case he's been preparing for months. Susan has to be in Mexico on Friday to start her summer job, and I have to be at work by eight tomorrow morning. The importance of the plan's success only adds to the stress they are already under, but they decide to try it.

We spend some time making out a schedule of who will be with Rick when. We figure we can fill about twenty hours a day among the four of us. Mr. and Mrs. Simon will do tonight, and Susan will do most of tomorrow. I am on day shift tomorrow, so I can come right down and do a few hours when I get off work. Susan offers, simply and nonassertively, to sit with Jennifer if Kathy can't. I'm not sure that Kathy will be so quick to help now that Todd's in the picture, but I'll ask her.

I am allowed in to see Rick before I leave. On my way into the small cubicle, I notice that his monitors are registering his signs loud and strong, each blip a signal of hope. His body and neck braces are in place, but some of the paraphernalia has been removed, and the scene is less forbidding than in the recovery room. I sit down beside the bed. It could be my imagination, but the swelling in his face seems to have gone down some. I know he's not in mortal danger, but I am still uneasy. He's so perfectly still, so alarmingly peaceful. I have no idea how I will fill the long hours of my duty with this inert and unfamiliar figure. What will I find to say? The others share history, experiences, and relatives with Rick. My history with him is so short. What on earth will I find to talk about, and how many times will I have to say the same things over and over? I could read to him, maybe ask his family if they recall any books he has liked in the past. But looking at him now, so far from us, the task seems impossible.

And maybe it is impossible. Rick is content now. Why would he want to give up this self-imposed state of oblivion? Is it so different from what I concocted for myself after I lost Steve? I would have welcomed a state of unconsciousness. It's hard to face the day when what lies ahead is too frightening to contemplate.

I long to hold him, to kiss his face, to lie next to him. I'm unable even to touch his arm. I want to begin talking to him now, but I can't find the words. He looks almost like a wax figure, and I keep checking the monitors every few minutes to assure myself that he is still alive. He seems so very far away that I am engulfed by a terrible emptiness, as if I will never see him, the real him, again. It takes a deliberate effort for me to take my eyes from the flashing screens and walk from the room.

I leave without even speaking his name.

While I dither around distractedly, trying to pull together some kind of dinner, Jennifer sits at the table, coloring with crayons and blithely humming in her quiet, tuneless way. Every now and then she interrupts herself to murmur a few words, but she doesn't appear to be addressing her remarks to me, so I don't respond. I'm having a hard enough time as it is, keeping my mind in the kitchen and off the hospital. I feel guilty that I've neglected Jennifer for the past two days; I've been gone more than I've been home since Sunday. As attached as she is to Rick, she must've have noticed his absence and sensed Kathy's distress on Monday and Tuesday, but if she has, she hasn't said anything to either of us. That worries me a bit.

I realize that she's stopped humming, and when I turn to see if she's still in the room, I am surprised to find her staring at me intently, as if she's been willing me to turn around. She waits until she has my full attention before asking, "Mommy, Rick went away, didn't he?"

Thank you, Lord.

"What makes you ask that?"

"Because he isn't sleeping at our house anymore."

I gasp and sit down quickly. "Jennifer, you knew that Rick was staying here?"

She averts her eyes, but not before I see that she is close to tears. "Why didn't he say good-bye to me?"

I didn't expect this and don't answer immediately. This is a little girl who knows she had a father and lost him, and then had a father figure, whom she'll be losing too because no matter how things go for Rick, it's clear to me that he'll never come back to this house or even remain in Chicago. *I want to do this right.*

"Mommy?" she prods.

I sit down and pull her onto my lap. "You know Rick would never leave us without saying good-bye to you, if he could. The truth is, he didn't exactly go away, Jennifer. He had an accident on his motorcycle."

She seems neither shocked nor upset by this. Instead her face comes alive with interest. "When?"

"Late Monday night."

"Did he die?"

"No. He's in the hospital. He was hurt."

"Your hospital where you work?"

"Yes. He was hurt pretty badly."

"Did he bleed a lot?"

"I don't know. I didn't see that part. But some of his bones got broken."

"Which ones?"

"His arm, his collarbone—"

"What's a collarbone? Things you wear don't have bones."

I'm finding this conversation to be exceedingly strange. "It's here, around where you wear your collar." I pick up her hand and place it on my collarbone. With her other hand, she finds her own collarbone and nods in recognition.

"He banged up his face a little bit too," I add, instantly wondering why I feel compelled to mention this when I can't even bear to think about it.

"You mean like he got a black eye and stuff?"

"Uh-huh."

All these questions she's asking . . . is it normal for a six-year-old to behave so calmly and analytically when someone she cares about gets hurt? Probably, but it reminds me of something unpleasant I once experienced but can't remember, and I don't have a good feeling about the way she's reacting to this news.

She fidgets around on my lap as if something is making her uncomfortable too. She searches my face. "Mommy, is Rick going to die?" she asks in a small voice.

My stomach lurches, but I reply calmly, "I don't think so, but why don't we pray he gets better very soon?"

After a pause, she murmurs, "Does it hurt to be dead?"

"No, I don't think it does."

"Does Rick hurt a lot now?"

"Yes, but the doctors are giving him medicine so he won't feel it so much."

"But if he dies, he won't hurt at all anymore."

"True, he won't. But we will hurt because we'll miss him."

"Like Daddy?"

"Yes."

She shrugs noncommittally, is again silent for a few moments as she thinks about this. "I'll be sadder than Jody if Rick dies," she says finally, sounding more competitive than sad.

"Oh, I don't think so, Jennifer," I say. "Jody is Rick's brother."

"I know," she says, "but he has a lot of other people."

"You have me," I remind her, wrapping her in my arms and holding her against me, which makes me feel safer.

"I know, but it's better when there's a lot of people."

I hug her tighter. She is quiet for several minutes, maybe absorbing what I have just told her, maybe absorbing what I have just told her, maybe thinking about Rick. I hope she feels comforted. I wish I did.

For years I've heard women in the city talk about consciousness-raising. I've always associated it with Women's Lib and all those "personal agendas" and "issues" that Carol is into with a vengeance and Kathy makes jokes about, and which just turn me off. But right now I feel as if my consciousness has just gone through the roof. How can I know so little about my own child? How, with her limited exposure to the realities of life, does she perceive death? What is her concept of time? Does she really understand why she doesn't have a daddy, and what does she think when she looks at the picture of Steve that has always sat on her lamp table? I've put so much energy into keeping him alive for her. Why? Her grandparents never mention him; according to my mother, the very thought of him sends Mrs. McLean into a deep depression that can last for weeks. My parents, of course, refuse to talk about such things as death, unless it's the death of Jesus.

Having heard nothing to the contrary, I lived for six years under the delusion that Steve would come back one day. For Jennifer's sake, the least I should've done was face the possibility that he might never return. The worst of it is that I can't get into any of it right now, not until our future with Rick or without him has been resolved.

Oh, for heaven's sake—! I flinch, suddenly remembering that I've had a pot of rice cooking since before all this started. Jennifer slides off my lap onto her feet, exclaiming accusingly, "I almost fell off you, Mommy!"

"Sorry," I mumble. "I forgot all about supper and the rice is probably ruined. Why don't you go wash your hands and set the table while I see what's happening here?" I gingerly pull the lid off the pot, and I'm relieved to see that it's only on the verge of cooking out, and in fact, it looks to be ready. I check the oven, where the chicken is just about done and, grabbing a box of green beans from the freezer, quickly put some water on to boil. Jennifer comes back in and holds out her hands for plates, then returns for silverware. She asks if she can have Coke with her supper, and when I nod, she goes to the refrigerator, hauls out the big bottle, and adds it to the table. I bring her a glass just as the oven timer dings. A few minutes for the beans and supper will be ready.

We don't talk much during the meal. Jennifer seems to have withdrawn back into herself. "What happened in school today?" I ask.

"Nothing."

"Would you like to spend the weekend with Grandmother Hill?"

"Is Granddaddy going to be there too?"

"Of course."

"Okay." She helps some gravy onto her spoon with her index finger.

"Would you like a piece of bread for that?"

"Uh-uh."

End of conversation.

I hadn't planned to go to Clearyville this weekend, since we'll be there in less than three weeks for our annual Fourth of July visit, and I am not in the mood to see my mother either, but maybe I can talk Kathy into driving Jennifer there on Saturday and picking her up on Sunday—in my car, of course. Or maybe I can persuade her to get Todd to take them in his. If Jennifer is away, I'll be able to spend more time with Rick.

My mind wanders back to the hospital and what I'm going to do to pass the time with Rick during my turn. I wish I could stifle this compulsion to spend as much time with him as I can while his family is here. *What can I do to help?* But as Jerry always used to say, "You never know from one minute to the next what will happen, which is why you can't give up hope."

After Jennifer has fallen asleep, I call the ICU and speak with Chris, who reports no change, which I consider good news under the circumstances. Then I call Kathy and propose my Clearyville idea. She says she'll think it over. I suggest she convince Todd to go with her so she can introduce him to the family. She had already planned to do that on the Fourth of July, but I remind her how chaotic the town picnic always turns out to be. She repeats that she will think it over. After this I take a hot bath, get into my robe, and settle on the couch. It's been a long time since I've had a quiet night alone in the apartment, and though I appreciate the solitude and silence of it, I'm restless and don't know what to do with myself. Rick's absence is like a presence in the room, looming over me as I flip through the newspaper, pick up the new *Redbook* from the end table, and read two paragraphs of the serial novel, before laying it back down. I've been meaning to call Carol for weeks. This is as good a time as any.

"Maggie!" Carol says warmly. "I'm so glad you called. I've been thinking of you on and off for months, but just never get around to picking up the phone. What's happening?"

"Same as always. Nothing very much."

Carol explains that Sarah, their two-year-old, has been sick, that her mother had surgery, and that she and Jerry went to a medical convention in Hawaii and ended up staying for two weeks. I alternately commiserate and enthuse with her as she talks.

"Now tell me about you and Jenny. How're you doing?"

"You know how it is with us," I reply breezily. "Nothing ever changes," and add that we are starting to think about summer as the end of the school year is almost upon us. My stomach turns queasy as I suddenly flash on Rick in his hospital bed. I know in my heart that I called Carol tonight because I need to talk about him, but now that she's on the phone, I'm afraid that I won't be able to mention his name, even casually. If she so much as suspects we're involved, she'll pick at me until I divulge every detail. *What on earth possessed me to call her?* I frantically search for a way to end the conversation before that happens.

"So," she says, "how's your neighbor?"

"Neighbor?"

"You know, Maggie. The gorgeous invalid who was sleeping in Jenny's room when we had dinner at your house a few months ago?"

I blew it. "You mean Rick?"

"Yes, dear. I mean Rick. He still around?"

"He . . . hasn't been over in a while. You know, he's . . . working and studying and . . . whatever else he needs to do."

"So it's over?"

"What's over?"

"Oh, my mistake!" she exclaims pointedly. "I must have misread the situation. Do forgive me." An uncomfortable silence that follows is broken when she says casually, "Maggie, I have an idea. Why don't you and I meet for dinner some night this week? We haven't done that in ages."

Don't, I warn myself. *Make one wrong move and she'll have you blurting out everything that's on your mind. Do you really want that? No! Still, if I don't talk to someone soon, I'll burst.* So I tell Carol I'd like that. We make arrangements to meet for dinner on Friday at five, then hang up.

I curl up on the couch again and open the magazine to the novel that I began earlier. It's not very good, and I quickly doze off, though I don't realize it until after the doorbell startles me awake. Springing up as if I've been shot from a cannon, I move toward the door, managing a quick squint at the kitchen clock—10:05—on the way. A wary peek through the peephole reveals Susan Simon. I unlock the door and invite her in. She appears tired, but not in distress, and immediately assures me there has been no change in Rick's condition.

"Coffee or tea?" I ask automatically.

"Coffee, black. It's going to be a long night." A tea drinker, I rarely had coffee in the house, until Rick brought over a jar of instant, which he left here for himself. I take it down from the cupboard and stand staring numbly at it, seeing only the image of him in his bed at the hospital, the tubes and bandages, the grotesque purple swelling. I have to shake myself hard to make the pictures in my head go away.

Dropping into Jennifer's chair at the kitchen table, Susan begins relating her day as companionably as someone would who is accustomed to stopping here frequently for coffee and a chat. She describes the visit that she and her parents made to the apartment rental office late this afternoon in hopes of coming to terms over Rick's lease. Though it was two months short of expiration, the agency was kind enough to break it without hassle because of the circumstances. They then rented a station wagon so they could pack up his things to be sent home. I realize as she speaks that as early as the end of next week, someone else might be occupying the little efficiency at the end of the other wing, and I hold back a shiver at the thought. Apparently the agents are as confident about a quick rental as I am. They asked that Rick's things be removed at once, and Susan is here now to start the packing. Since she doesn't want to bother the super this time of night, she has come to get the key from me.

I tell her I don't have a key to her brother's apartment. "I've only been in there a few times—when he was sick," I explain.

"Oh," she says, appearing surprised. "I thought—"

I cut in before she can tell me what she thought. "Susan, what your brother and I had was an . . . arrangement." *Because he isn't sleeping at our house anymore.* "He babysat for me when I worked the late shift. I'd have him to dinner. Sometimes on the weekends he took my daughter to the park. Other times the three of us went. None of it involved his apartment."

"I see," she says, but she looks skeptical.

I suggest she get the key from Mr. Wagner after all, and she gulps down what's left of her coffee and starts for the door. "I'll be back later to pick up anything Rick left down here, okay?" The door closes before I can tell her I plan to be in bed and sound asleep in twenty minutes and prefer not to be awakened.

Ironically, the only thing Rick has left here is his shaving kit. The incident with Kathy a few months ago left me more worried than ever about our being found out, and I asked him to be extra careful about not leaving his things here. He was—until Sunday night when I tried to pin him down about his plans. Maybe my insistence distracted him, and he forgot to take his bag with him when he left. I don't know, but whatever the reason, I have it now, and I intend to hold on to it until he's ready to use it again. Or do I just want to keep it myself for the memories, gold initials, and soap smell to remind me of sunny days in the park (the good ones anyway), of him laughing and dancing in the rain with Jennifer standing on his sneakers, of him poring over his books in my living room, of him sleeping beside me in my bed. *Because he isn't sleeping at our house anymore . . .*

When Steve's image, unbelievably, began to fade, I had to open a scrapbook or sit with a photograph just to bring his face back to me. Some of the other MIA wives, those who were veterans when I was just beginning, had warned me that would happen, that I would forget his face. Many of them considered it a symptom of recovery from grief, but I didn't want to recover, not if it meant giving up on him, and so I sat, night after night, with my pictures and my pages, just to keep him alive as I remembered him. I have no such mementos of Rick. In all the months we've known each other, not one picture has been taken. All I have of him is the black leather bag with his initials, and I want it, just to help me conjure up his face, his real face, someday.

On the couch, the magazine is still open to the boring serial, but I close it and shove it aside. I still don't feel like sleeping or reading, so I turn on the television, find an old, blurry black-and-white movie, and gaze at it blankly for a while, neither seeing nor hearing it. I quickly doze off, only to be awakened by the doorbell again.

This time Susan apologizes for waking me, though I swear to her that I haven't been asleep. It's just that their schedule is so uncertain, she says, and she wants to get everything into boxes and bags tonight, no matter how long it takes. Who knows what might happen tomorrow to prevent her from returning? She accepts my offer of another cup of coffee. We sit for a while without talking until Susan asks if there is anything of Rick's that I would like to have. Instantly an overwhelming desire to cry rises up, envelops me, warms my face. I catch hold of myself, though, and reply without a quiver, "No, Susan, but thank you and, by the way, there's nothing here of Rick's that I can give you."

She looks at me curiously, then pretends to concentrate on her coffee. I am again intrigued by her resemblance to Rick. I hadn't noticed how strong it is, probably because their coloring is so different. It's as if one is in positive and the other in negative. Even the creases under their eyes and the shallow dent in their chins are the same. I lower my face to my cup so she won't catch me staring at her, and when I look up again, her head is cocked to one side and resting on her hand, and she is looking at me with a serious expression.

"You know, Maggie," she says, "I really envy you."

"Why?"

"You've seen this a lot, haven't you? I mean, like what's happening with Ricky."

"Well, I've never handled a spinal cord injury before, but of course I've seen serious illness and suffering families. I've had a lot of experience with that."

"You're lucky."

"How do you mean?"

"You can handle it so well. You're so strong."

This is not the first time I've been told that since I started nursing, but I never thought I'd be hearing it now. Many people tend, at least at first, to perceive nurses as infallibly competent, which is a stereotype I'd be proud to fit. But after spending the past few days with me, she must see that I don't fit it, at least not in this situation. I'm dumbfounded.

"What makes you think that?"

"I've been watching you, the way you deal with everything and—I hope I'm not being too personal again—but you said yourself that you and my brother became good friends because of your daughter, so you must have some kind of emotional investment in Ricky. Yet you're able to cope with everything so, I don't know, so normally, while we're going to pieces."

I don't understand how anybody can see me as strong when my entire foundation has been cracking apart for months. I feel ashamed, as if I'm playing a bad joke on Rick's family. "You think I'm taking this well?"

"We all do. Think about it. We're laying everything on you while my mother and I sit around popping Valium. It really isn't fair. You're juggling your schedule and your babysitters and offering us your car and everything, helping with Ricky even after you've put in a day's work, and consoling us on top of it. Believe me, Maggie, we'd be a lot worse off if you weren't here to get us through this."

I never get over how people will grasp at even the weakest of straws in times of crisis. Compared to the Simons, I am barely involved in this crisis, but they perceive me as a crutch and an anchor, whichever they want or need me to be, because I'm a nurse, and that's how nurses are supposed to be. Well, I don't like them needing me to be what I'm not, which at the moment, is strong. As peripheral as I am, I'm still too "invested" in Rick not to let my feelings get the better of me. Six months ago I might've been able to fulfill their expectations, but the rate of inflation on my emotions has gone up drastically since then. Besides, I'm angry, and while I'm so busy being Joan of Arc and Florence Nightingale all rolled into one, where am I supposed to find the energy to suppress the anger, this anger that I've been holding in since I spoke with the neurosurgeon on Monday night? Susan is right: it isn't fair. That man never even stopped to ask how close I was to Rick; he just assumed that because I was wearing a uniform, I could cope with the gravity of Rick's situation. Good Lord, my hands were shaking so hard in the cafeteria, I dropped my cup. Couldn't he see . . . ?

Oh well. There's already enough to deal with without adding my anxieties to hers. "Nurses are people too," I say mildly, quoting a bumper sticker I saw recently in the hospital parking lot. "I'm not what you think, Susan. It isn't easy even for professionals to get through these things when they can't leave them in the hospital at the end of the day. We're only human."

I don't think she even heard me. "We'll never be able to repay you for everything you're doing," she replies earnestly. I don't think she even heard me.

Don't owe me anything. Let's just work together to get Rick on the road to recovery. Then you can pick up your pieces and go home and get on with your lives. Of course, after we've got Rick back on track and all your pieces have been picked up, I'll just be starting on mine and Jennifer's. And where will the grateful Simon family be then?

"Your family owes me nothing, Susan. Nothing at all," I tell her.

She leaves soon after, and I breathe a sigh of relief.

"Mommy, Rick went away, didn't he?"

"What makes you ask that?"

"Because he isn't sleeping at our house anymore."

Dear Lord, what am I going to do?

And so the vigil begins. The three Simons, of course, bear the brunt, doing their time singly or in combination during the day and again from ten to two at night, sleeping in their off hours. I cancel my Friday dinner appointment with Carol, and Kathy and I begin to alternate early evenings.

The nurses take over from two to seven in the morning. It's grueling for all of us. Being part of this crisis is for me like looking through both ends of a telescope at the same time. On the one hand, each hour since the accident has seemed like a day; on the other, how can it already be Wednesday a week later?

On the ninth day, I sense excitement in the air as soon as I enter the ICU on my way up to work. During the night, the blips on Rick's monitor screens began registering some positive activity, and at this moment, a knot of staffers is crowded around the console, arguing the implications of this sudden movement. I try to take a peek, but nobody makes room, and I give it up and slip across to Rick's cube. The family is between shifts and he is alone.

He's been moved from his bed to a Stryker frame, a flat-bed, canvas-sling contraption designed to avert bedsores by making it possible for the staff to turn him over every two hours without compromising his need for immobility. Right now he's on his back, and his eyes are closed. I gently rest my hand on his forehead for a few seconds, and I'm pleased to note that he feels normal. Good; at least the elevated temp was a transitory thing.

"Rick, wake up," I command sharply, as I do each time I come. "It's time to wake up."

I don't really expect him to respond and he doesn't, but his eyelids are fluttering rapidly, the way they did that first night, just before he awakened and recognized me. It's easier to look at him now that the swelling has gone down quite a bit and the dressings are smaller, and I stare at him intently, waiting for something more to happen, praying it will be encouraging when it does. As I watch, I become aware of a slight distortion of his features, as if the left side of his face has shifted slightly, upsetting the symmetry. My imagination, I'm sure, but troubling nonetheless.

"Eric Simon, open your eyes," I order sternly, feeling as silly as I used to when Jennifer was a baby and I would catch myself talking to her. Ignore the self-consciousness, the neurologist told us. Just keep it going. You never know what he might connect with. "It's Thursday, Rick. The sun is shining. Susan will be here in a few minutes and she has something she wants to discuss with you. She . . . she needs your advice. Come on now, get up and get dressed and have your breakfast so you'll be ready for her when she comes. Let's go." I babble on like this for a few minutes, then give it up. I can't get past feeling like an idiot.

Through it all, Rick lies motionless, except for the brief stretches of eye movement and a twitch of his mouth which, though it was probably reflexive, sent a ripple of nervous excitement through me.

One of his assigned nurses, Ginger Crockett, a comfortable-looking middle-aged woman with gray-streaked, faded red hair, comes into the cube and greets me by name. In as large a hospital as this one, you generally know the staff from the floor or floors you've worked on in the past, maybe from car pools or committees. Many other people you recognize by sight from the elevator or the cafeteria but will probably never know them by name. In the last two days, I've come to know almost everyone in the ICU. It's funny how your personal connection with a patient elsewhere in the house can sometimes make his case personal to everyone you work with as well. Because of Rick, the girls in my unit have suddenly become unbelievably friendly and solicitous, urging me to take a longer coffee break, to go down and look in on my friend. They've offered to cover for me if I need a few minutes to be with his family. And if there is any change in his status while I'm on shift, I can rely on the grapevine to let me know about it almost immediately.

"I guess you heard. Nights were all excited," Ginger says. "They think he's on his way out of it. Did you take a look at the monitors?"

"Couldn't get near enough," I answer. "But I heard someone say there was increased activity."

"Very encouraging. His folks are going to be ecstatic. I'm anxious to hear what the doctors have to say. In the meantime, we all have our fingers crossed . . . Incidentally, did you notice he's registering a temp?"

It didn't seem like it a few minutes ago, but I touch Rick's forehead again. This time, the gesture flashes me back to Christmas Eve, when he came to my apartment, flushed with fever, after the news broadcast. He does not appear flushed now, but maybe he does feel slightly warmer than he should. I. "You think it's an infection?"

"I have no idea, but I hope not."

"Me too," I agree, trying not to sound concerned. I turn back to him. Except for the occasional eye movement, I can't see any change in him at all. Some people are prone to fevers. This is his second in six months.

"Well," Ginger says, glancing at him one more time, "he's young and strong. He'll be just fine," which in nurse-talk is often a less threatening way of saying, "Poor kid. This is the last thing he needs right now."

I sit watching Rick's eyelids for another minute or so, then pull myself up. "I have to go, Rick," I tell the inert body on the bed. "Susan will be here in a few minutes. How about surprising her by waking up?"

Ginger shrugs, smiles reassuringly. But I know that smile. It means nothing. I've used it myself hundreds of times when I was not about to reveal what I was thinking.

I am in the meds closet making up pill trays when I hear the loudspeaker page my name to the ICU. I freeze for a moment, then take a deep breath, and carry the unfinished tray to the nurses' station. My supervisor happens to be talking on the telephone at the desk and, with a resigned look, waves me on.

The slight trepidation I was beginning to feel on my way down to the unit evaporates immediately when I see Susan lounging against the wall outside Rick's cubicle. She looks up as I approach and, grinning from ear to ear, announces ecstatically, "Ricky's up!" She throws her arms around me and hugs me, as if I've had something to do with his awakening. "Isn't it fantastic?" she bubbles.

"It sure is," I agree. "When did this happen?"

"I don't know, about ten minutes ago, I guess. I was reading to him and his eyes were, you know, fluttering around under the lids like they've been doing, and he was moving his head from side to side every now and then. I just kept on reading, lifting my eyes occasionally. It must've been the tenth or twelfth time, when I looked up at him and his eyes were open and *he* was watching *me*. I almost went into cardiac arrest!"

If I ever doubted you, Lord, I apologize with all my heart. All I can think of to say is, "Oh my! I can't believe it."

"He didn't make a sound," she goes on as if she didn't hear me, "but he kind of smiled at me as if he knew me . . . God, his face is such a mess. Anyway, I was too surprised to say anything either, so I just sat there looking at him. Finally, he tried to talk, but it kind of got stuck in his throat. I forgot about the nurse's button and I didn't want to take my eyes off him, so I started shouting, 'Nurse! Help!' and in about a minute, everything just kind of erupted around me. I can't believe he's awake. It's incredible!" At this point, a nurse hurries out of Rick's room with an armful of bedding,

"Is anyone else in there with him?" I ask Susan.

"A doctor, that nurse that just went by, and a few technicians with a lot of equipment came when I called for help. They kicked me out and I took the opportunity to use the ladies' room, so the nurse is the only one I've seen leave." I glance over my shoulder, but the curtains behind the window are drawn.

"Where are your parents?"

"They went downstairs to get some coffee. They were here most of the night. I called them from the nurse's desk when I was done in the ladies' room. I had just gotten back here when you came, so they should be back any minute."

"Just out of curiosity, Susan, what was it you were reading to Rick?"

"Oh," she says, digging into her large bag and coming up with a medium-sized book bound in plain gray paper. "It's called *Fear of Flying* and it's by Erica Jong."

"I don't think I've ever heard of it."

"You wouldn't have," she tells me. "It won't come out till the fall. A friend of mine's father is an editor at Henry Holt and she was able to get a bootleg galley. She loaned it to me."

"Oh. Well, I was just wondering whether Rick could somehow have connected with whatever you were reading to him."

"I don't know," she says. "It's a novel about female sexuality."

"Mmm," I comment. Having no interest in feminism myself, I don't know how else to respond.

"But now that I think of it," she continues, "I was reading him one of the really explicit parts when he woke up. Knowing my brother, you might be onto something."

The elevator door opens, and Mr. and Mrs. Simon step out.

Susan furtively winks at me and quickly stuffs the book back in her bag.

I head for the stairs to return to my floor. At the first landing, I lean back against the wall, shut my eyes, and whisper, "Thank you, Lord."

Susan

My earliest memory of my brother is when we were at the beach—I think I was maybe two or three? Anyway, my dad had shown me how to build a sand castle with my red shovel and a pail of water, and I was working hard at making a fancy one, when some older kid came along and stomped all over it. I started crying, and then Ricky was there—he seemed so big to me—and told me he'd fix it; and he sat down with me, and we built what I thought was this fantastically beautiful structure that our parents pretended was the best there ever was.

Another time I recall—and I don't know why I remember this particular day, except that it might have been my first time walking instead of riding in the double stroller—is Ricky and me holding hands walking down our street in the city. Our parents were behind us, pushing Andrew in the carriage, and I remember that my dad called out, "Ricky, stop at the corner and don't let go of Susie's hand!" We got to the corner, and the cars were whizzing past us in the street, and I was scared that Ricky would let go of my hand, but he didn't. When our parents caught up with us, my dad said, "Good boy!" to Ricky and picked me up and carried me across the street.

I always felt sorry for my best friend Ronnie, next door, whose two older brothers were mean to her, calling her names and playing tricks on her all the time. I don't remember Ricky ever doing anything like that to me. He was mischievous though. I also remember clearly how, before the men came to get our furniture and things, the day we moved to Long Island, my mother told each of us to pick out two toys to keep with us, because the rest of our things were going to be put in boxes to go to the new house. Ricky and I had to sit on the couch in the living room so we wouldn't be in the way. After a little while, Mom came in to check on us, and Ricky, who was restless, said he had to go to the bathroom. When Mom came again, he still hadn't come back, so she went to the bathroom to see if he was all right, but he wasn't there. She called and looked everywhere, but neither she nor Dad could find him. The front door was open, but there were big packing boxes blocking it, so they knew he couldn't have gotten out. Mom, who was pretty close to having Matthew, was really upset, and Dad kept telling her to please sit down and not worry; he'd take care of it. At last he found Ricky in their bedroom, scrunched down inside their big armoire, which was standing behind a stack of cartons. He snatched him up, carried him into the living room, and threw him down in the big chair so hard that he bounced. I started to giggle. Then he said to him in a very low, angry voice that I'd never heard before, "Eric, don't push your luck. If you don't stay right where you are until we're finished here, we will send you to your grandmother for the summer." I stopped giggling. Our grandmother was not a very warm person, and we hated going to her house. I'd never seen Dad look so angry, and it was weird to hear him call Ricky Eric. Anyway, Ricky took the hint and stayed where he was, but we made faces at each other across the room until it was time for us to go.

Ricky must not have taken the threat that seriously, though, because he hid again later in the summer up at our house on Cape Cod. We have this big house on the ocean that belongs to all of the Simon families. Though more than one family is usually there at the same time, that summer we were the only ones who went up at the end of July. One night, Ricky disappeared soon after supper, and again Mom and Dad and then some of the neighbors called and looked, but no Ricky. When it started getting dark—and this I recall vividly—Mom decided he had sneaked down to the beach and drowned in the ocean, so Dad called the police. A couple of cars showed up, and once they turned on their big lights, it took no time to flush Ricky out of the tall dune grass, where he was hiding. This time, Dad was so angry he smacked Ricky hard on the backside and sentenced him to two days in his room. Ricky couldn't have cared less about the punishment; he was too interested in the lights from the police cars and all the excitement he'd caused. Dad felt really bad about hitting him, but he didn't change his mind about the two days. That was the only time I remember Dad ever lifting a hand to any of us. Ricky could be really stubborn and bratty when he felt like it, but even when he was being a brat, I adored him. We were very close.

Ricky did junior high in one school year, so when he started ninth grade, he was just turning twelve. He was great with academics, and though I wasn't exactly stupid, there were times when I needed help, especially with math, and he was a whiz. He never gave me the answers, but he showed me what to do and how to do it to get the right answer. I think he would make a terrific teacher, but that's not what he wants to do. I don't know what he does want to do.

When he started high school, we began to have what we called "meetings" down at the end of the backyard, where the creek is. We would just sit on the bank and talk about a lot of things. Even now, there's no one I'd rather discuss stuff with. He was so smart about everything and so easy to be with. I'm sure if I wasn't his sister, I'd have had an immense crush on him. All the girls did. My friend Ronnie was insanely crazy about him, but Ricky never seemed to realize it.

Eventually, well, during the last two years of high school, when he'd started staying out late and doing whatever he was doing, he'd come into my room when he got home. Everyone was usually asleep by the time he got in, and he would wake me up, sit on my bed, and talk about, you know, how he felt about stuff in his life, like school and when he went out at night. And I could tell him anything too. I really felt close to him, even closer than I did to Ronnie. But there was the . . . it's hard for me to say . . . the drinking. I knew that was a bad thing, but he made me promise not to tell our parents or Carly. Most of the time, I knew he'd been drinking because he'd be chewing gum when he came to my room, and he didn't like gum, and I could smell the alcohol anyway. He was such a good kid, but it was like he'd somehow gotten kind of . . . I don't know, confused. Like he'd . . . like he'd lost his way somehow. I didn't understand much at the time, but when I got older, I sort of came to the conclusion that it might have had to do with what happened to him toward the end of the summer before he went into tenth grade. Even though so many years have gone by since that summer, I still think about it every now and then, no matter how hard I try not to. It was so horrible . . .

Ricky had gotten his swimming and lifesaving certificates the year before. Our family belonged, and still do, to this golf and country club called The Beeches. We've known the people there most of our lives. So when they needed an assistant lifeguard that year, they thought of Ricky. They knew he was young, but he had the credentials; and he always came on like a responsible kid, so they hired him. It was less than a half mile through our woods to the Beeches swimming pool.

About the woods: I guess I shouldn't say that it's our woods. Actually, only part of it is our property, and part of it belongs to the club. A long time ago, my dad and the club's board jointly agreed to put in a brick path through the woods for members in our neighborhood to use as a shortcut instead of driving the long way around to the parking lot in front of the main building. Since it starts practically in our side yard and comes out at the club pool, we and our friends have always used it, but the other members just go around the regular way to the club parking lot. It's always been kind of understood that it's our private path.

Anyway, I think it was in August when it happened. There was this ugly skinny woman from Germany or Austria, some place in Europe, who was new at the club. She was old, like maybe forty, and I think she was married to a man who was a lot older than she was. Ronnie and I saw her hanging around the pool a lot during the summer, but we never saw her go in the water.

So . . . God, this is so stupid. I'm twenty-one years old, I have a degree in psychology, and I still have trouble talking about what happened. I mean, it's 1973, not the Dark Ages, you know, and it's been a year since George Carlin said those seven dirty words in public. But Ricky was just a kid . . . just a boy in jean shorts walking home with a towel around his shoulders . . . Was it his fault he was physically mature for his age? Or that she did that to him on our path . . . ?

Mom and Carly had gone grocery shopping with Andy and Matt, and I was sitting on the sunporch floor finishing a Chutes and Ladders game with Kerry and Brian, when I saw Ricky come running out of the woods. He bombed into the house and up the stairs, like someone was chasing him and he was scared. I got a bad feeling, and I ran up after him to find out what had happened. He wasn't in his room. I looked out the back window to see if I could see him down by the creek, but I couldn't, so I went to my room, and there he was, sitting on my bed with his head down.

"Ricky?" I sat down next to him. He was shaking and breathing hard, and he had goose bumps, like he was ice-cold. "Are you okay?" He didn't answer. "You look like something terrible happened."

He kept his eyes on his hands, which were clasped real tight in his lap. I knew right away that whatever it was, it was something I wasn't equipped to handle, but my mother wasn't there and my dad was out of town, and Ricky probably wouldn't have told them anyway.

"Did you do something bad?" I asked, willing him to turn so I could see his face.

He shrugged, but he still didn't look at me. I didn't know what to do or say, so I just waited; and after a while, the shaking and the breathing got a little better, and he asked in a quiet voice, "Have you ever seen that weird woman that hangs around the pool? She never talks to anybody. She's old, like mom's age, and real skinny . . . ?"

I knew who he meant. "And she has this husband who's bald and kind of fat and he wears a big gold ring on his little finger?"

"Yeah, I think so." He sighed and let his head drop even lower.

"Did they have something to do with it?" I prodded.

"Not them. Her."

I waited for about two minutes, but he didn't say anything else, which was kind of annoying. "Ricky, if you're not going to tell me what happened, I'm going back downstairs. I'm supposed to be watching Brian and Kerry."

"Okay," he mumbled, "if you swear to me you won't tell anybody—"

"You always make me swear that and I've never told yet and I never will. I swear!"

Finally he looked around at me. "I know I can trust you, Susie. This is just so bad."

I was so frightened by now that my heart began beating hard, but I didn't say anything, and then he started talking in a voice that I could hardly hear.

"I was coming home from the pool and that woman was sitting on the bench that's about halfway along the path. I smiled and said hi as I passed by. She didn't say anything and I kept going. Suddenly I felt a cold hand on my back and this low voice said something that sounded like 'leepshin.' It almost scared me to death, and I spun around. It was her. She was wearing a big hat and these big sunglasses, so I couldn't see much of her face, and she was so creepy. I tried to run, but she grabbed hold of my shoulders. I tried to pull away, but she dug her fingernails into my arms, and she was strong. And she kept saying that 'leepshin' word over and over. I never heard it before. I don't know what it means."

"It might be a German word. I think they're from Germany." He began to breathe so hard and fast, his chest was going in and out.

"And before I could get her off me, she . . ." He shook his head frantically.

"You're scaring me, Ricky. You can't not tell somebody if it's that bad. I already know she did something awful to you. I told you I'm not going to talk, so tell me."

"Yeah." He nodded his head and took a couple of deep breaths, then said quickly, "Okay, she . . . ran her hand down my front and inside my jeans and pulled me off the path and into the woods. It happened so fast. She was holding on to my pants so tight, and it was like she was as strong as a man! She pushed me down on the ground, and I was so scared, all I could do was lie there and concentrate on this branch that I landed on when I fell. The end of it was sticking into my back, and it hurt like crazy. And then . . ."

My brain was spinning. I was right; I wasn't the one who should be hearing this. I was twelve years old, and okay, my mother had already given me "the talk," and yes, my friends and I discussed sex a lot when we got together, so I wasn't totally ignorant of what I suspected was coming, but I thought that it was only men who did it to women. I never imagined a woman could do it to a boy.

His voice dropped to a whisper. "She unzipped my jeans and pulled away my suit and started . . . doing things to me. I . . . felt like . . . she was moaning and saying a lot of those weird words I never heard before . . . It hurt." He started to cry. "Why, Susie? Why did she have to do this to me? All I ever said to her was hi." His chest was heaving now, and he put his hands over his face.

I wasn't much more than a child. What could I say to him, except that he *had* to tell Dad, but he said he thought the woman must be a very sick person, and he didn't want to get her in trouble. I wondered what my mom would do if she was here instead of me and guessed she would just hold him, so that's what I did. I held him, patted his back, felt the deep scratches from the branch and the fingernail marks, brushed the bark and stuff off him, and cried with him.

After a while, he sort of calmed down, and I told him that was the worst thing I had ever heard that somebody did to another person.

He pulled away from me. I'd never really seen him cry like that before, with his face blotchy and his eyes red and brimming.

"That wasn't the only worst part," he said, snuffling. "You want to hear the other really worst part?"

No, my mind protested. *Tell it to a grown-up who knows what to do.* I thought about telling someone myself, but I knew I wouldn't. I'd sworn not to. Ricky trusted me; I would never break a promise to him. He stared at me for a minute, then said, "I can't explain it, but some of it—not the part that hurt so much, but some of the other things . . . Some of it made me feel weird all over, but good at the same time."

My brain started whirling again. That couldn't be right, I thought. He said she hurt him. She couldn't hurt him and make him feel good, could she?

His face turned dark again. "I know it's not right for me to be doing that, you know, liking it, and that scares me more than anything. I think there must be something terrible that's wrong with me. How could I even think it wasn't all bad? It's like I must be some kind of a sex freak."

The way he said that made me want to giggle, but I could feel the terror radiating from his body and was instantly ashamed of myself. All I could think of to say was, "I don't care if she's sick or not. You need to tell Dad about this."

He just shook his head and said, "Never," and that he was going to take a shower. In the doorway, he turned back to me.

"I shouldn't have laid this on you, Susie, but you're the only one I could tell it to. You're the only one I can trust not to talk about me behind my back."

Then he was gone, and I heard the bathroom door close and the shower come on. I just sat where I was, thinking about my brother. I knew Dad had given him the boys' version of "the talk," and I knew that Ricky had already messed around with a few girls, but you know, junior high kinds of stuff—kissing, a little fumbling. I couldn't have articulated it then, but he definitely wasn't prepared for what had happened that day . . . the violence of what that woman did to him. And I certainly wasn't equipped to be his confidante. Maybe I knew a little bit about sex, but nobody had ever told me about violation, so there was nothing I could say that would make him feel better, and for a long time I was sure that I'd failed him.

Ricky didn't eat for a week. Mom made him go to the pediatrician, who gave him a cursory examination, which obviously didn't include looking where the real evidence was. He believed Ricky when he told him that he'd tripped and fallen backward in the woods and that I had dug my fingernails into him while we were horsing around. To this day, the name for what was done to him has never been spoken.

It took months for Ricky to begin to get over what happened on the path. He went through the fall and most of the winter pale and subdued. He just wasn't himself. For the first time, he didn't make the honor roll. But then he gradually began to perk up, and finally, by spring he was more like he used to be.

Ricky was very popular, and though he never said it, I soon got the idea that what he really wanted was to be left alone a lot of the time. I liked that he was popular because I enjoyed attention, and all I had to do to be popular was to be his sister. But some part of my brother had definitely been lost that day in the woods, and I was the only one who knew how. Though he tried to hide it at school, he became more moody than he'd ever been, and people noticed.

Until this day, I've never told anyone about what happened, not even Ronnie.

There was one thing in Ricky's senior year that I think described my brother in a nutshell. One day, while the yearbooks were being put together, the kids who were working on the senior class section were playing around with the thumbnail descriptions under the pictures. After school, a few of the girls who Ricky had only dated once made a kind of crude mock-up of his entry by pasting his picture on a piece of paper and writing under it:

Eric "Ricky" Simon

Hung up, Hung over, and Hung

I don't remember what they actually wrote in the yearbook, but they made a copy of the phony page. Ronnie and I were with Ricky when they presented it to him. It was pretty nasty, and we were embarrassed for him. But he just laughed and thanked them. Then as we walked away, he rolled his eyes, shook his head, and, with a grimace, muttered, "Sore losers."

It was vintage Ricky, and I remember it as the moment when I realized he'd finally come back from what had been, at that point, the most traumatic experience in his life.

Mr. Simon has invited Jennifer, Kathy, and me to join their family at an excellent restaurant in honor of their son's rebirth. It turns out that we are going to Grendel's, the only fancy restaurant I have ever eaten at in my life. Ironically, it is the place where Steve and I toasted to our future when he proposed to me. "Oh, look," I whisper to Jennifer as we walk from the cab, "this is where I had dinner with Daddy before we got married." She shrugs, says nothing.

My first sight of the dining room immediately sends my memory into overdrive. The décor, the lighting, and the subdued noise level come back to me as if it were yesterday. The maitre d' seats us at a roomy round table off to the side of the room—Mr. Simon, Jennifer, and me toward the wall; his wife, Susan, and Kathy toward the room. As soon as we've been seated, the wine waiter fills our glasses with champagne from a bottle that has been resting in a bucket of ice, and we toast to Rick twice, first to his being alive and alert—*thank the Lord*—and then to his continuing recovery. From where I sit, I can see the table Steve and I sat at, in a corner and a little away from the other diners. Candles, flowers, champagne—I loved the romantic in him. I can't get over being here in this particular restaurant. Apparently, neither can Kathy. She momentarily appeared spellbound by the room when we first entered, and when I glance at her now, I see her eyes darting from side to side in awe of its elegance.

Our parents don't go to restaurants; never have. In their eyes, it's a waste of money. Mother is a good shopper and a good cook, and they consider going elsewhere for a meal just short of wicked. To the Hills, eating out means a picnic in the backyard. The Simons probably find Kathy and me pretty boring. Well, we are, and knowing that eating in places like this is a commonplace experience for them makes me nervous, as if I'm going to commit an unpardonable social error every time I lift my fork.

Jennifer, who's never been in a real restaurant—unless you count McDonald's and a little neighborhood deli Rick once took us to—is enthralled by the waiters. She watches them intently as they move quickly among the tables with their heavy trays.

"—decided, madam?"

I look up and see the waiter patiently standing next to me, waiting for my order. I haven't even opened my menu yet, and I flush with embarrassment.

Mr. Simon, who is sitting on the other side of Jennifer, says, "Jenny and I were just discussing which appetizers she might like, but she hasn't quite made up her mind either."

"Mommy," Jennifer says, "Uncle Richard is Rick's daddy and Jody's daddy."

Uncle Richard? "He is," I confirm, glancing quizzically at Mr. Simon, who cocks his head and smiles in the same sweet, playful way that Rick does. "Jennifer, do you know what you want yet? The waiter will be back soon to take our orders, and we'll have to be ready."

"But we didn't make up our mind yet," she protests.

Uncle Richard leans toward her and says, "Don't worry. I've got it covered," then glances over her at me.

"How about you, Maggie?"

Nothing looks familiar from the last time I was here. "I can't decide either." I'm not even 100 percent sure what some of the dishes are.

He picks up his menu. "If you'll let me, I'll order for you. I think you'll like what I have in mind."

The wine waiter returns and offers us our choice of red wine or white. I know nothing about wine, so I choose white because it's what Steve ordered for me. Mr. Simon looks at me for a moment, then gives the waiter a name for the wine. Another man fills our water glasses, and a third, our food waiter, returns for our menu choices. Kathy, who's been whispering with Susan, picks something I never heard of before. When he gets to our half of the table, Mr. Simon quietly confers with him for a minute. The waiter leaves, and conversation resumes.

By now, I'm hopelessly sidetracked by memories—Steve, that special night, and the three years we had together. It must be the wine, which is light and tastes a bit like fruit. Mr. Simon seems to be captivated by Jennifer and has no end of questions to ask her. Lenore is deep in discussion with Susan and Kathy, and snatches of what they're saying float toward me. I'm content just to sit back and watch what's going on around me.

After a while, the waiter comes back with a child-sized wineglass of what might be white grape juice for Jennifer and an enormous platter filled with a multitude of small stuffed rolls, crackers with toppings, and I don't know what all else. He sets a small plate in front of each of us and wishes us "bon appétit."

"Finger food," Uncle Richard says, choosing a stuffed pastry thing and handing it to Jennifer. "Just the right size for little fingers." He looks over at me. "Help yourself, Maggie. We have meat, cheese, vegetable, um, seafood, all kinds of good stuff."

"I got a hot dog," Jennifer informs us happily.

What is it about these people that brings her out of her shell? Why can't I do that?

It's not till I've drunk some more of the fruity wine and Kathy has escorted Jennifer to the ladies' room that I work up the courage to ask Mr.

Simon about this mysterious ability he and his son have to get my daughter to open up to them.

He looks puzzled. "I don't know what you mean."

"Well, Jennifer's only just met you and already she's talking like she's known you all her life."

"Nothing mysterious about it. She's an open, friendly little girl."

"No, she isn't. Normally, she's shy and withdrawn. But whenever she's with a male from your family, she's like a different child."

He smiles. "Do we really have that effect on women? That's very flattering. But, the truth is, by the time you spend twenty-plus years knee-deep in kids who probably represent a fairly good cross section of children in general, you pretty much have a handle on how to get through to them. Some are harder to connect with than others, but you just keep trying because it's worth the effort. Watching them grow and learn and develop their individuality is the most rewarding thing any parent can experience . . . at least, until they go off to college and the first time they come home, you see right away that they've changed. They act as if it's a chore to even talk to you, as if they've outgrown you." He smiles again. "I don't know what happens after that. I haven't quite reached that point yet." He looks across the table with a wistful expression to where his wife and daughter are sitting. Maybe he's thinking about Rick and that except for that one split-second less than two weeks ago, he would be here now. A moment later, however, he snaps back as Jennifer and Kathy approach the table. He stands up to swing Jennifer over to her chair, then grabs an hors d'oeuvre for her. I notice he has taken off his tie and opened his collar.

Kathy gushes, "Oh, Mr. Simon. This is the best party I've ever been to"—giggle—"and I'm having a really great time! Thank you, Mr. Simon."

He bows. "You're wery velcome, Kathy." She giggles again and flounces off to her seat.

I could cry with embarrassment. "I'm so sorry," I blurt, trying to neutralize what must be a bad impression of us. "She's not used to alcohol. I'll go tell her she's had enough."

I make a move, but he puts a hand on my arm. "Don't bother. Lenore will tell her. She doesn't drink either and she has a good sense of when people are getting ahead of themselves."

I settle back in, and we eat in silence for a few minutes.

One nice thing I remember about this restaurant is that the entrees weren't so big that you couldn't possibly finish them after you'd had an appetizer. To me, leaving food uneaten is like insulting the chef, even though our appetizer tonight was big enough to feed all of us for the next three days.

When the staff starts collecting the plates from the table, I ask Jennifer what she wants for dessert.

"'Nice cream soda!" she replies instantly. "A pink one. And I'm not going to spill anything on my dress, because the lady in the bathroom said my dress is pretty."

"The lady in the bathroom? Where was Kathy?" My mother always cautioned us against using public restrooms.

"She was going to the bathroom behind the door."

Mr. Simon makes a small choking sound, spears another hors d'oeuvre, and stuffs it in his mouth.

"Who was the lady?" I ask.

"She's the one Kathy gave the money to when she came out . . . Can we get dessert now?"

"The attendant," Mr. Simon clarifies, then signals the waiter. We linger over coffee and dessert, talking as a group. I would never have imagined Kathy and I could find so much to talk about with eastern city people. Susan says she has regained some anticipation for her job in Mexico in July and August now that Rick is showing signs of improvement. Mr. Simon will be able to attend to his court case with an easier mind. Even Mrs. Simon—Lenore—might be able to consider the possibility of leaving for New York now that she knows her son is in good and caring hands.

I watch and listen as the family begins to pick up their lives. It's hard to believe what Susan said about the Valium and their inability to cope, that they were falling apart. Though I still believe they're special, tonight they acted like ordinary folks. They're not like the people I grew up with, but the way I imagine people should be. Susan had it twisted. They are the strong ones, not me.

At last the extraordinary night comes to an end. We toast to Rick one final time, and Mr. Simon settles the bill. I notice that Jennifer, who has been leaning against me for some time, has fallen asleep, and he offers to carry her to the taxi. We are all in high spirits as we wait on the sidewalk for the taxis to pick us up.

"Ricky won't be alone," Susan says, evidently continuing a conversation she and her mother were having on the way out of the restaurant. "Maggie's here."

"Let's not take Maggie for granted," Mr. Simon says quietly. "She has a family of her own. She's been very generous these last couple of weeks, but she must be anxious to get back to her own life."

"Oh, I don't mind," I say. "I'll already be at the hospital anyway." Instantly I regret that I said that. I should have thought before I spoke. I have to remember that it's not just me involved here, but Kathy and Jennifer. For the past eleven days, their worlds have been turned upside down too.

"I just wish we could take him home." Lenore sighs. "It would be so much less complicated."

"That won't be possible for a while," I tell her. "He won't be ready to move for some time."

"Just wishful thinking," she murmurs sadly.

Two taxis finally pull up to the curb, and I take Jennifer back from Mr. Simon and thank the family for this wonderful treat. Our good nights are brief; I guess we're all exhausted. It's been a very long day.

Kathy has decided to stay over. I lay Jennifer on her bed beneath a light summer blanket and go help Kathy make up the sofa. She appears to have sobered up pretty much.

"You and Susan seem to have hit it off pretty well," I comment.

"She is so cool. You know, she's going to Mexico next week to work with poor people, teaching them things like how to take better care of their kids and how to know when water is too dirty for drinking. She went to a really good school in New York that only has women students. If I were going to go to college, I'd rather go to a school that has men and women, but I guess she's more serious about education than I am."

"Her whole family is. It must be one of those things that gets passed down from generation to generation."

We've made the bed, and we're sitting side by side on the edge of it. Kathy looks sidewise at me and says, "You were thinking about Steve while we were there, weren't you?"

"How did you know?"

"I heard you tell Jenny that he once took you there."

"It's where he proposed to me."

"Maggie, do you still believe he's coming home?"

"I don't know what I believe anymore."

We sit in silence for a time, and it's only now that I realize how emotional the evening has been, how really drained I am.

Kathy speaks first. "I'm sorry for what I said that day when I found Rick's kit in your bathroom."

"I forgave you. Sometimes I think it would've been better if I'd taken what you said to heart and stopped the whole thing. I was so worried about Jennifer discovering us."

"Well, she never said anything to me, and I know she never said anything to Mother."

I nod. "Jennifer knew, Kath. She told me."

"Maggie, do you love Rick?"

I've never had such an intimate conversation with anyone in my family, and I don't know how I'm feeling about this. "Honestly, Kathy, I don't know. I love being with him, but I can't say why. He's just . . . smarter and funnier . . . more interesting than anyone I've ever met. Besides, I don't see how any woman can love two men at the same time."

"Oh, I can see it. There's all different kinds of love, so I think it is possible."

I suddenly feel as if there's some role reversal going on here. I'm supposed to be the wise one in this relationship, and Kathy is behaving a lot less than the flighty, immature little sister I've always known. A sudden yawn surprises me, and I take it as my cue to struggle up from the sofa bed and head for my bedroom. "I don't know, Kathy," I mumble through another yawn. "Maybe you're right about that, but I need to get to bed."

She smiles brightly, and I wonder whether if it's because she's totally unused to hearing me approve of anything she says.

I awake on Monday eager to get to the hospital, since I haven't seen Rick since Saturday. I spent most of yesterday with Jennifer and Kathy, catching up on chores that I'd neglected. Later, we all went out for a movie and ice cream. Now I quickly dress for work, get Jennifer to the sitter, and arrive at the hospital with enough time to do no more than just look in on my unofficial patient.

It will be two weeks tonight since the accident, and the devastated right side of Rick's face actually looks as if it is under control. There is a narrow strap from the broken jaw up over the top of his head, probably to keep the fractured cheekbone in place, and the eye is still pretty swollen, which makes me think that the orbit was also smashed, though I don't remember the doctor mentioning it. I gently rest my hand on his forehead for a few seconds and am pleased to see that he feels normal. Good; at least the elevated temp was a transitory thing. I want to take his hand, but I'm afraid I'll wake him.

Chris comes through the door with an armful of clean bedding. I'm glad she's working the shift; she's a lot friendlier and more forthcoming than Ginger. "Hi, Maggie," she calls cheerfully as she deposits the linens in the closet adjacent to the window. "I was hoping you'd stop in this morning." She comes over to the bed and checks Rick's pulse. He doesn't stir. "Rick just had a nice little sponge bath," she continues, "and now he's napping until his physical therapy starts in"—she consults her watch again—"five minutes. I heard you didn't come in yesterday."

"I took the opportunity to do the chores that I've neglected all week, then spent the rest of the day with my daughter and my sister."

"Who're also feeling neglected, I bet. This sort of thing is so hard on families and friends."

"I'm sure the Simons were here, so at least the patient hasn't been neglected," I say.

"They were here most of the weekend. Rick's been much more alert and really trying to communicate with them, but he doesn't have a lot of staying power just yet. They're more hopeful though. Did you hear they found a plastic surgeon from Las Vegas who's flying in for a consult tomorrow?"

"I thought Mr. Simon was leaving tonight on the red-eye."

"He was, but he got a continuance—is that what they call it?—'til Thursday."

I nod. "Have they said anything about taking Rick home in the near future?"

Chris looks at me as if I've just bitten the head off a chicken. "Home? You can't be serious. He can't even lift his head!"

"Just asking," I say quickly and a bit too defensively. "They seem to be able to do anything they want."

"Isn't that the truth," she agrees. "But then, if our families' law firms have been contributing to this hospital forever, I guess we'd be special cases too . . ."

I can't have looked as dumbfounded as I felt. "How's that?"

"Rick's great-grandfather was a German immigrant who ended up in Chicago and got his law degree at the university years before this hospital was built. Out of gratitude to the university, he set up a perpetual endowment fund, which somewhere along the way must've been diverted to the hospital."

"I wonder why they haven't named a wing for them if they're such generous givers," I laughed.

"Because it's stipulated in the endowment that they can't. No name recognition allowed. Evidently, they don't like public attention."

"How do you know all this?"

"The sister. She came in around midnight on Saturday and it was like a tomb on the unit, so I sat watch with her during my break. Have you ever wondered why the name of this place is Wohlsein? She told me about that too. It mean good health or well-being" in German."

I shake my head in wonder. "Doesn't it strike you as ironic that the paramedics brought Rick to this very hospital?"

"Not so ironic," Chris remarks. "They found a card in Rick's wallet: 'In case of injury, transport to Wohlsein Medical Center without delay.'"

How the other half lives . . .

At lunchtime, I go back down to the unit in hopes Rick will be awake. The family is with him, and I'm not sure whether to intrude, but Ginger happens to be passing by and without breaking stride, she says quietly, "Don't stand on ceremony, honey. The more the merrier." So I knock on the viewing window, and Mrs. Simon—I mean Lenore (we're on a first-name basis now)—who is on the far side of the bed, looks up, smiles, and motions me to come in. Her husband stands up as I approach, but Susan, who is at the window, doesn't turn around. I sense tension in the air.

Rick seems to be sleeping again, and Mr. Simon gestures for me to take his chair at the right of the bed. Nodding toward Rick, he remarks, "The patient has just 'mainlined' his lunch and is sleeping it off."

While seating myself, I search Rick's face for evidence of movement but see none. Even his breathing is shallow. Rick looks more peaceful and not as beat-up as he did a few days ago. "The nurses told me he's doing a lot better today," I remark.

"He is," Lenore agrees, "except that they've decreased his medication and he's in more pain than he was. If you can stay just a little longer, he might wake up before you have to go back."

I turn, looking through the viewing window at the clock over the nurses' station. I still have thirty-five minutes. As I note that the jaw-fixation device looks like an instrument of torture that can in no way be comfortable, Mr. Simon, as if reading my mind, murmurs that he looks as if the Marquis de Sade himself had wired his jaws. I am fighting the impulse to touch Rick, but it's a losing battle, and I almost involuntarily reach out and lay my fingers on his arm . . . *And then he does an amazing thing. He lifts his hand and touches my face and I know I will cry if I don't hold on to myself . . .* Instant déjà vu. My face—my whole body—flames at the memory of this moment in the recovery room a week ago, and I look at the Simons furtively, fearful that they saw my momentary emotional tremor and interpreted it as what it was: that simple three-letter word, the mere thought of which leaves me feeling shameful and guilty. Actually, nobody seems to have noticed anything at all, and Susan hasn't budged from the window.

I turn back to Rick and find him watching me. He brings his good hand to his face and draws his forefinger from the corner of his mouth to his cheek—a smile.

"Hi, Rick," I say softly and squeeze his arm. "How are you feeling?"

He points to me and holds out his hand. I'm not sure what he wants, so I put mine in his. He blinks once, then turns my hand palm down and with his finger proceeds to write on the back of my hand, NEVER BETTER. I cock my head at him, and he shrugs his good shoulder and makes the smile gesture again.

"Wait a minute." I always keep a small pad of paper and a pencil in the pocket of my uniform smock, and now I take them out and look around frantically for something Rick can lean on. The Simons have been watching this pantomime with what looks like amusement. Mr. Simon strides out of the room and a moment later reappears with an empty clipboard, to which I attach the paper. Rick makes a sound in his throat, and I look at him. He points to himself, pretends to write, then points to his bad arm.

"Right-handed!" his father interprets. He and his wife are beaming as if their son has just uttered his first words. I've never seen two happier parents.

"Not anymore," I announce, shoving the pencil into his left hand and holding the clipboard up so he can reach it. "Now. Are you feeling better?"

His good eye glares at me. I glare back. "Write," I repeat.

He starts to scribble on the pad slowly and carefully, but it's a struggle, probably because he's loopy and tired from his medication. After a minute or so, he drops the pencil and grunts again. I look at the pad. He's written,

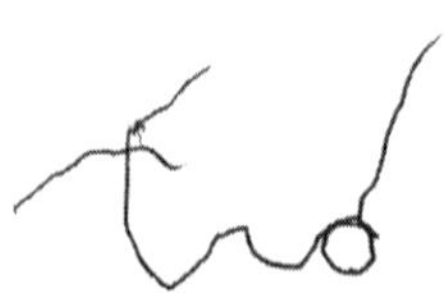

His parents hurry over to look. “Erd? What does that mean?” his father asks.

“Blink once for yes, twice for no,” I instruct Rick. He winks twice.

“No! End,” guesses his mother. Two more winks.

“Susan, could you drag yourself away from the stunning view of the parking lot down there and see if you can figure this out?” Mr. Simon asks with a tinge of sarcasm in his voice.

Rick’s left eye flutters a couple of times. He’s ready to doze off again. The door to the cubicle opens, and a nurse pokes her head in to remind us that it’s time for him to be turned and we’ll all have to leave for a while.

Susan, who barely comes up to my shoulder, cranes her head around my left arm and looks at the clipboard. “Tired,” she says. “He’s tired.” Rick opens his eye halfway and slowly winks once. “And I’m going to the cafeteria for a cup of coffee.” He lifts his arm toward her, and she squeezes his hand. “Hang in there, Ricky,” she whispers. “It can only get better.”

I say good-bye, and though I still have ten minutes left, it’s too late for lunch, and I decide to go back to work. Lenore follows me out of the cubicle. “It was good of you to come down on your lunch hour,” she says.

“It’s no trouble at all. Rick’s been a good friend to us. I care what happens to him.”

She nods rapidly. “Maggie, join us for dinner at the hotel tonight.”

Somehow I’m not surprised she’s suggesting this. “Oh, thank you for the invitation, Lenore, really, but I need to be home with my daughter tonight. We didn’t have much time together last week.”

“Our fault.” She sighs. “But of course Jenny’s included in the invitation.”

“You’re very generous, and it wasn’t your fault. I had a choice and I made it. However—”

Lenore Simon, who makes her petite daughter look like a giant, looks up at me. “Please,” she says quietly. “We’ve been under so much pressure and we’re beginning to get on each other’s nerves. Besides, I need advice on a new issue. I thought we could talk privately for a while after we eat.”

My guess for “new issue” is the plastic surgery. This might explain the tension in the air when I first entered the cubicle. “Well—”

“Tonight, Susan’s meeting a college friend who lives up Lake Shore Drive and Richie will be over in the suite working on some business papers he received this morning. It will be just the three of us. I’m in a quandary, Maggie, and I don’t know where else to turn. I promise it won’t run late because I want to come back here and spend the rest of the evening with Ricky."

I frankly don't relish the idea of another restaurant meal, and being out means that Jennifer will get to bed late. Still, after a little more discussion, we agree that she will come to my apartment—provided that I let her supply the meal.

It was about the plastic surgery. Over the weekend, Mr. Simon contacted a surgeon from Las Vegas who had been recommended to him by two or three people he knows in New York. The man arrived this morning to consult with Rick's parents and doctors, after which he studied the case for a couple of hours, made his decision, and returned to Nevada.

Right now Lenore and I are sitting at my dining room table amid empty paper bags, Styrofoam cartons, and a large flat box containing a cheese pizza with one slice missing. Jennifer, having filled herself up with this all-time favorite, has disappeared to her room to draw and color. Lenore and I are just finishing our sandwiches and side orders of coleslaw and potato salad. I had phoned the orders in, but when the food arrived, she insisted on paying for it and tipping the deliverymen. In addition, she has brought a large bag of doughnuts for dessert, as well as a book and a toy for Jennifer. I protest that none of this is necessary. I reminded her that Rick has been very good to us.

Lenore scans the hodgepodge of containers set out on the table and reflects on the time when her children were young and ordering dinner in was a rare occasion. They never could agree on just one meal for the whole family, she recalls, and it was commonplace for them to have food sent in from as many as three different restaurants in order to please everyone. I can't begin to imagine such extravagance, or them even giving in to kids like that.

While we eat, we chat about small everyday things, my job, her four kids still at home. She asks about my family and what it was like for me growing up in a small town.

I've been asked this before—by Carol, one slow night at the clinic when I first moved to Chicago. I can't remember what I told her, but I tell Lenore, "Very different from the way Jennifer is growing up. As kids, we were so much freer. No matter where we went in the town, everyone knew us, so we couldn't get lost even if we wanted to. My mother is a nurse and she worked for one of the two doctors in town, but my grandmother lived down the street and two of my aunts were only a block away. So I always had a place to go to after school. Our lives—my family, I mean—our lives revolved around our church, and we spent most of our free time there. Clearyville's big event was the carnival that came to the outskirts of town once every summer for two or three weeks. One year, I pretended I was staying overnight with a friend and we went by ourselves. We had looked forward to that one night for months."

Lenore smiles. "Believe it or not, Maggie, my experience is a lot like yours in some respects. I grew up in the Queens part of New York City in a neighborhood that sounds much like your small town. We lived in the upstairs flat in the house we shared with my grandmother and her bachelor brother. As in your town, the storeowners knew all the neighborhood kids. So, as long as I didn't have to cross the street, my mother could send me to the store for her when I was four or five years old without having to worry about me. I didn't even have to carry money."

"It was the same in Clearyville," I interrupted. "They just put it on our account."

She nodded and continued, "Like Kathy, I had an older sister, Audrey, nine years older than I am. Both of my parents worked every day, so it was my grandmother who took care of me during the week. When she got sick, my mother relied on me to come right home from school and stay there until she got home. I did. Then when I was thirteen, our parents died within six months of each other, and I went to live with Audrey and her husband and little girl in their small apartment in another part of Queens."

I am fascinated by her story. I could never have imagined Clearyville having anything in common with New York City. Walt Disney was right. It's a small world after all.

We are nibbling on doughnuts and pondering these similarities when she asks whether I've had any recent news about Steve, but it's been so long since I've sought information about my missing husband that there is nothing to tell. Only months ago, I wouldn't have been able to admit that to anybody for fear I'd be judged a terrible, callous person. But I've gotten to know Lenore in the last weeks, and I can't imagine her reacting in such a way if I confessed it to her. She had been so kind and accepting of me in April when I'd blurted out the truth about Rick and me. I decide to take the chance.

"It's an awful thing to admit, Lenore, but for the first five years, I called Amnesty International and the MIA wives organization every three months, even though I knew I'd be notified if any word of Steve came to them. But then . . ."

She smiles, leans across the table, and puts her hand on mine. "But, if I remember my math, then my son came along and, shall we say, diverted your attention?"

It's at this moment that I realize how good a job I've done all these months of hiding from myself the guilt over this additional betrayal of Steve. Now it strikes with the force of a migraine headache.

Lenore is quick to recognize this and squeezes my hand. "Actually, Maggie, I think you're looking at it the wrong way. From my point of view, it's not bad. It's good," she says calmly. "Of course they would've let you know, and yes, it would have given you some closure. But would your grieving process to this point have been any less painful had you not had other things to think about? Having a new relationship"—*as if Rick and I were the most natural thing in the world*—"doesn't mean you have to forget what you had before. It just shows that after all these years, you're finally able to move on. Don't you consider that a positive move?"

I shake my head uncertainly. "I want to. It's just that after five years of being so sure he was going to come back, it's hard for me to truly accept that he's gone forever."

"Yes," she said sympathetically. "I remember when my husband's brother was killed in Korea, how incomprehensible it was that we would never see him, never hear his voice again. I was heartbroken. It's been twenty years and my heart still aches for him. But there always comes a time when you have to get around it. Maybe this is your time." She smiles wistfully, gives my hand a firm pat, and looks at her watch. "Would you mind if I call home? It's getting late and it's even later in New York."

While Lenore calls—collect—I peek in on Jennifer, who is sitting at her little round table beneath the window. The table is littered with paper and crayons, and she is engrossed in both coloring and watching her small color television set. She seems to know instinctively when it's time for her favorite programs, which Kathy calls the Big Three: *Mr. Rogers' Neighborhood, Sesame Street*, and *The Electric Company*. It was only a couple of weeks ago that I noticed she was reciting and singing along with the songs and lessons.

"You know something, Jennifer?" I start. "I've been wanting to tell you how happy it makes me to hear you sing and talk along with your programs. I bet you know all the songs by now."

She turns her face to me as if she's been aware of my being in her room all along, and totally ignoring what I just said, she holds up the picture she's been working on. "Does this look like Lady Abbalin?" she asks.

"I don't know," I answer, coming over to the table and peering at her artwork. "Who is Lady Abbalin?"

"Mom, everyone in school knows who Lady Abbalin is, even the kindagarden kids," she replies with a hint of contempt.

"Well, I'm sorry to say I don't know her. Does she live around here?"

"'Course not. Everybody knows she lives in Mr. Rogers's neighborhood, even Aunt Kathy." She pointedly picks up a purple crayon, bends over her picture, and goes back to work.

Suddenly I feel weary and depressed. "Well then, maybe Kathy's the person you should ask." Again she doesn't bother to respond. I breathe in, breathe out. "Okay . . . well, Mrs. Simon is waiting for me in the kitchen. We can talk more about this tomorrow. You tell me all about Lady Abbalin and then I'll know too. Okay?" Nothing. "I'll be back to get you ready for bed."

"I can do it myself, Mom."

"Of course you can. Then I'll be back in a while to tuck you in."

She shrugs and again turns back to her drawing.

Lenore has cleared the table and stacked everything neatly on the kitchen counter for washing. "You don't have a dishwasher," she notes.

"No."

"Well, you wash and I'll dry. It'll go faster that way and we can talk while we get the dishes done."

It's beginning to occur to me that there's no point in trying to dissuade Rick's mother from doing what she wants to do any more than there is in trying to refuse his sister. I hand her a clean towel. "You said you needed to talk with me."

"Yes . . . I don't know about you, Maggie, but this last week seemed to last forever. I'm so exhausted and confused, I can't think straight anymore."

I nod. "It's been a very intense time. Traumatic injuries are like that. An ICU nurse I know says a serious trauma case just sucks the marrow out of her bones." I wash a couple of utensils and stand them in the drainer cup.

"That's an understatement."

"I'm in such a fog, I don't know what's the right thing to do anymore. Richard wants one thing, the doctors favor another, and my daughter is furious that no one is consulting Ricky, who can't even speak for himself! I thought, with your experience, you might be able to give me some guidance—but first, could I trouble you for a cup of tea?"

"Oh, of course! I'm so sorry!" I exclaim. "I meant to serve tea with the doughnuts." I quickly fill the teapot and get it started on the stove. "In my town, there's a saying for when people feel like their lives are out of control," I tell her. "They say they're on a runaway horse and they need to get out of the saddle."

Lenore laughs and lowers herself onto a chair. "I have to remember that. It describes my week perfectly."

I place another dish in the drainer, turn off the faucet, and wipe my hands on a towel. I sit down across from her and hand her a napkin from the dispenser. "Did you meet with the surgeon from out of town?"

"Yesterday afternoon. Actually, the result was encouraging—pretty much. He said that the jaw and cheek have compound fractures, so it'll take time and care for them to heal properly. Ricky's eye itself is fine, but the orbit is slightly damaged. His deepest cut is above his eyebrow. All the cuts will leave scars, but he said they can fix those to look as if they were never there. If the symmetry of his face is compromised, it can be corrected. He thinks that ultimately, the permanent damage will be minimal, considering the extent of his injuries." She pauses and sighs. "I think that's everything."

"Sounds like good news."

"Except that he's not going to do the surgery himself unless we can give him a lot of notice, which of course we can't do because it's too early. He highly recommended a local person, but I don't know. He made a very good impression on us, and we'd rather he did it, even if we have to take Ricky to Nevada."

"Is that your only concern?"

"No . . . I just don't know whether the cosmetic repair is worth it or even necessary. From what the doctors say, Ricky already has two or three spine operations to look forward to." She shakes her head, picks up the towel, takes a plate from the drainer. "Why are we even thinking about cosmetics? Isn't it enough that our son survived?"

Because of things Rick has said to me about his face, I have to wonder what he would want in this situation. "As long as that surgeon won't be operating, why don't you put the issue on hold for a while? The worst thing that can happen with the damage at this stage is infection, and that's unlikely to occur in the ICU."

"I'd be happy to put it off, but Richard believes that all that can be done should be done, and the sooner the better. If not this week, then next week. He wants to get Ricky out of here and back to New York as soon as possible."

The words are like a sudden sharp cramp, but I say evenly, "I don't think that's a possibility right now."

She laughs softly, and admits, "Richard is a wonderful, smart, kind, and loving man, but he's always had difficulty with the concept of 'not right now.'"

"It's been my experience that reality has a way of winning those arguments. Maybe he's just on edge."

"We're all getting on each other's nerves. We had an argument in Ricky's room just before you came in yesterday morning. We had the presence of mind not to raise our voices, of course, but Susan was, as I said, furious with us, because we were arguing in front of him. She's also angry because we don't bring him in on anything. We make decisions about him without asking his opinion. His opinion! He's only been conscious for a few days . . . Honestly, Maggie, I'm at my wits' end."

I sit silently for several minutes, wondering how I can say what I am thinking without upsetting her even further. I'm tired, Jennifer has to go to bed soon, and Lenore herself wants to get back to the hospital. Why draw it out? "You came here for advice," I say, looking straight at her.

"Yes." She picks up her napkin and twists it around her fingers.

I shift nervously in my chair. "Then here's what I think. You need to get off the horse—now. Rick has a great team of doctors. They are all respected in the medical community here. Let them do what they need to do, Lenore. Go home to the rest of your family. They need you more than Rick does at this point. When the time comes, the doctors will let you know, and you can contact the surgeon who was recommended by the doctor from Nevada. In a little while, when Rick is able to function again, he'll know when he wants to go home. This is a fine hospital with good nurses and an excellent care record."

"It's hard to leave him like this," she says disconsolately.

"I know that. But it's important for you and your family to get back to normal before he does go home. He's only been awake since Friday. He's still in intensive care. He hasn't even begun recovery treatment. You'll feel much better about it when things start happening for him here."

"Will you keep in touch with us? Let us know what's going on?"

"Of course," I assure her. "I'd be happy to do that."

"It's a blessing that you happen to be working at this hospital, Maggie. A mitzvah."

I'm not familiar with the word she has just used, but it occurs to me that it's something Jewish people might say. Carol will know. Before I say anything more, I pray that a simple thank-you will be an appropriate response.

Before the Simons left for New York on Thursday, they sent me a huge floral arrangement with a lovely card of appreciation, which also renewed their wish that I keep in touch. I stopped in at the ICU Thursday morning and afternoon, but Rick's curtain was closed both times. Yesterday I worked from three to eleven, so my visiting hours were different, but he was asleep at both ends of my shift. Ginger, who was on duty both days, told me Rick was doing very well. Chris was on last night and said he was lethargic, depressed, and retreating again, so I don't know what I'll find this morning when I try once more.

Lenore

Ricky is our first child. He was born in September 1950, three years after Richie and I were married. Having spent my teen years with my sister and her small children, I had had a lot of experience with babies, and I thought I knew everything there was to know about child raising. But this little guy was full of surprises. Though he was slightly below average size at birth, he managed to gain 19 lbs. and grow 8½″ in his first year. This prompted Richie's youngest brother, Danny, who was thirteen, to call him Rick, which he insisted was manlier than the "sissy" name we had given him: Eric. Somehow the name stuck, and our Eric has been Ricky—or Rick—ever since.

He was a beautiful little boy, with the same dark features and mop of thick black hair that Richie had inherited from his mother's Portuguese-Sephardic side of the family. He had a good disposition too—easygoing, even tempered, and self-sufficient. He was a joy. But easy can't last forever, and as always happens, complications set in before Ricky was two years old.

In the first six months of 1952, three changes occurred in our lives: Susan was born, the "conflict" in Korea became a full-blown war, and Richie shipped out for the Far East.

Susan was cranky and demanding, the total opposite of her brother, who by now was a lively, inquisitive toddler who never napped, stayed active from morning till night, and made it clear that he wasn't happy to have a tiny noisy invader on his turf. By summer he was prematurely into the terrible twos with a vengeance, and suddenly I wasn't the organized, tireless mommy I'd expected to be.

The summer, however, brought Danny to live with us temporarily. He was a very sweet, very unhappy kid whose parents neither understood him nor had the patience to deal with his problems, and he'd been asking if he could stay with us during school vacation. With Richie away, Dan could take charge of Ricky, who already adoringly followed him around everywhere when they were together, and I'd be free to take a brief nap during the day, which would help me be better able to cope with Susan's nightly fitfulness and wailing. We lived in a spacious apartment on the Upper West Side of Manhattan, so we had plenty of room for Danny. It seemed to be a good solution for all of us, and it was.

In September, Danny went back to Long Island, and Ricky turned two. Surprisingly, the behavior he should have been exhibiting at this age had already passed, and he had calmed down considerably. Now he was a sweet, loving little boy, affectionate and protective toward his baby sister, whom he had decided was not so bad to have around after all. I suspect the fact that Susan had also calmed down and was demanding less attention had something to do with his new attitude. He seemed to be intuitive at times, if that's possible in a two-year-old; sometimes I felt as if he sensed I was unhappy. I was. I missed Richie so much, I could hardly bear it.

Around Christmastime that year, Richie's middle brother, Mitchell, who had preceded him into the service, was killed in action in Korea, and Richie came home on three weeks' bereavement leave. Six weeks after he went back, I learned I was pregnant again. I was in a panic, unable to imagine how I would manage alone with three babies, but the war ended in June, and Richie was home for good by the time Andrew was born in October.

I remember that after Richie had fallen asleep the first night he was home, I lay in bed taking stock: The war is over. Richie is home. Two boys and a girl make a perfect-sized family. We live in a beautiful large apartment in a great area of the city, and Richie can finally go back to work at the firm. What more could we want? Nothing. But "nothing" doesn't matter to rabbits, and we got more anyway. Matthew was born in June '56, a month after we left our beloved city neighborhood and moved into a big old white house on the north shore of Long Island.

Suburbia was a culture shock for both Ricky and me. I'd lived my entire life in apartments, always dreaming, like the little girl in *Miracle on 34th Street*, that one day I'd have a real house of my own. For the kids, Roslyn Harbor was a whole new world. No longer stuck within the confines of a city playground, free of exhaust fumes that made Ricky wheeze, they now had a big yard of their own to play in and children next door to play with.

Ricky had had half a year of kindergarten in the city, and was reading on a second grade level when I brought him to his new school for a placement evaluation. Though he wasn't yet six, they decided that his size, independent attitude, and reading ability equaled maturity, and put him into first grade. I had reservations about rushing him into real school, but surprising us again, he did well.

Our twins were born prematurely when Ricky was seven and a half. Kerry, the older by ten minutes, was healthy, but Brian had a few problems that required special care for a while. Through a domestic agency, we hired Carly O'Hara, a recently arrived Irish girl with rudimentary nurse's training, to help out with the care of the babies. She had a way with the kids, and they were crazy about her—so crazy that they begged us to let her stay after we thought we no longer needed her. I'd never imagined having daytime help, but with six children under the age of eight, Richie thought it would be a good idea to have someone to help out. So stay she did and ultimately became our live-in housekeeper. There's no denying that with the ever-calm and organized Carly around, everything to this day has gone more smoothly than it would have without her, and I'll be the first to admit it. If Richie is the backbone of the family and I am the nurturer, Carly is the metronome that keeps the rhythm of the household ticking along steadily.

In junior high and high school, Ricky was busy with activities—band, sports, and the school newspaper, among other things. He barely had time to do his homework. Still, he made honor roll every semester but one. Throughout his school years, he was a healthy, happy, good-looking kid who was liked by everybody, especially females of all ages. He graduated with honors when he was sixteen and was eager to leave for Amherst College. I'm not saying we didn't have our ups and downs with Ricky. He could be frighteningly mischievous when he was young, and there were periods during his teen years—one in particular that lasted for several months—when he was constantly moody or angry or difficult. Two of the big issues that stand out in my mind involved his repeatedly jumping curfew and his sullen embarrassment about my pregnancy with our youngest during his senior year of high school. But he was a teenager. He was good in so many ways that he seemed no different from any of the other busy teenagers we knew. He never rebelled against helping with the younger kids and actually ended up adoring Jody, even though he'd been so upset about the pregnancy.

We always knew that he and Susan had a special bond. As very young children, they made up some kind of manual language that only they understood, and as they grew older, they did seem to be unusually close. I've always assumed that they confided in each other and shared secrets, but if Ricky ever said anything that might have troubled Susan, she never mentioned it to us.

Might Ricky have had serious underlying problems growing up? If he did, we didn't know about them. Between Carly and me, the children received a lot of attention, often more than they wanted, and it's hard for me to imagine how we could've missed anything important that was going on with him. He was a smart kid, though, and I suppose if there was something he didn't want us to know about, he could've made sure we didn't find it out.

Despite his broken engagement, we've been very proud of Ricky, as we are of all of our kids. As a mother, I'd be devastated to learn that there were things we should have known about and didn't. But outside of the normal everyday problems of a large household, there was nothing that raised any alarms for us, and believe me, we've been grateful for that every day of our lives.

I drop Jennifer off at Kathy's at nine fifteen as arranged and continue on to the hospital. As I enter the ICU, I am, as always, struck by the lack of noise. My regular floor, which is one of the medicine units, is often noisy with complainers, ranters, and wanderers. It's a grab bag of diseases and disorders and somehow always has its share of difficult and lonely patients. The times when I fill in for someone, it's usually in OB, where there is a steady influx of jubilant family members and friends during visiting hours. At times, it can be a little chaotic when you factor in the shrieks and screams coming coming out of the labor rooms and the jittery daddies-to-be. A lot of men prefer not to stay with their wives during labor, and occasionally someone will bring a deck of cards to pass the time. When that happens, it's like boys' night out in the fathers' waiting room.

The ICU is a self-contained and not very large area, with eight small cubicles built in a horseshoe around the nurses' station, which is not more than ten or twelve feet away. In terms of ambience, it has more in common with the subdued and orderly little chapel on the first floor. The wall of cubicles facing the desk is mostly glass so that the nurses at the desk can see each bed. The patients in the cubicles are in various critical conditions and hooked up to machines whose readings are visible on consoles at the desk. A patient has only to do little more than blink and the console alerts the staff with a flashing light, a buzz, or a strident beep. There is no way to hide from the staff and only one way to defy their efforts, and that's by passive resistance. It hasn't taken Rick long to figure this out.

I check in at the desk and am told I can go right in. Rick's signs are good; he's had breakfast, morning therapy, and his bath. He's free until ten fifteen, when he's due to be flipped. Without even glancing through the window, I enter, pull a chair over to the bed, and sit down. His eyes are closed. "Hi, Rick. How're you doing?" I ask brightly. He doesn't respond, and I assume he's dozing. I give his arm a squeeze, and he still doesn't open his eyes—*sitting with him hour after hour when he was in what wasn't a coma*—but the desk nurse just assured me everything is fine. I recall what Chris said last night: lethargic, depressed, and retreating. I lean over and kiss his forehead, but he might as well be made of stone. I don't expect him to turn his head; the neck brace makes that difficult. But he could acknowledge my presence. I am annoyed. Whenever Rick was frustrated or angry, he used a word that I've never spoken in my life, nor did I ever hear Steve say it, or my parents. Right now it seems like the perfect word to express the way I am feeling. I utter it softly and furtively, but it still comes out sounding fierce: "Shit!"

During the weekend, I can't stop thinking about Rick. After Jennifer has gone to bed on Saturday, I turn his behavior over and over in my mind. It would be foolish and insensitive to expect him not to be depressed. All that lies ahead for him are grueling physical therapy sessions, needles, examinations, chronic pain, and, probably, more surgery. Unfamiliar things like suction and catheters will become a way of life for him, interrupted by endless hours of immobility and monotony. He's a prisoner in his body for now, trapped there by a random split second on a deserted highway. Nothing will ever be as it was. He's scheduled for a psych evaluation tomorrow morning. Jerry and Carol both have good connections with psych people, and I call them twice during the day, but it's Sunday, and they don't answer. I'll try them again on Monday.

My thoughts turn to the accident itself. I've hardly had a moment to think about it since it happened. It's now seventeen days later, the Simons have gone home, and I'm sitting listlessly on the couch with plenty of time to go over the events since it took place. I don't know what the Simons learned in the two weeks they were here. All I do know is what I was told that first night: no witnesses, no evidence of another vehicle or a pedestrian or an animal or even a rock. Nothing. I'm sure that once the Simons recover from this initial ordeal, their interest in the circumstances surrounding the crash will be revived, and I begin to think about calling the police myself. Knowing doesn't change anything, of course; it just makes things neater somehow. So I'll call them Monday also, to see if they've picked up any new information.

Sunday evening.The living room is quiet and dim, with only the light of one low lamp. For the first time since the dreadful hours in the waiting room, I relive the weeks preceding the accident. It all seems so far away now, so removed. Was it really necessary for me to know what would have transpired between Rick and me that night; what solutions would have been reached in the talk we never had? It's finished now, that part of our lives . . . of my life. There are new problems to face. Yet, if he hadn't had the accident, would he be in California now attending that seminar, or would he still be with us, working in my living room? No matter how I try, I can't let go of my curiosity of wanting to know what was on his mind that night. Whatever he decided then no longer applies, but maybe, when he's better, we can discuss it, dispose of it, put a clear and definite finish to the episode. I need to have closure, which is probably why it's been so hard for me to accept Steve's death; we never had a chance to say good-bye.

Rick is intelligent, sensible, and basically stable. Once he gets past the spinal shock and the depression, it won't take long for him to pull himself together. In the months that I've known him, he's been driven by the things he has to do, and those things will still need to be done. I have to believe that with the help and encouragement of the people around him, he'll come to his senses and begin to fight his way back.

Neither of the calls I make at lunchtime on Monday are successful. Jerry is attending a convention in Minneapolis and won't be back until tomorrow. Carol has patients straight through till six. The police have nothing new to report. All they can say is that Rick was thrown from the motorcycle into a tree some distance from the road. His body traveled at considerable speed, judging from the force with which he hit the tree. He is damn lucky to be alive. As to the cause of the accident, they have no idea; it was just one of those freak things. Any further information will probably have to come from the victim himself. If I'm a friend and I'm really interested, why don't I just ask him? I inform the officer that that is impossible due to his critical condition. He informs me that they have no evidence to prove that anybody else was involved or that the vehicle had been tampered with, so, as far as they are concerned, the case is closed. At first I am disappointed in their lack of interest, then decide it's just as well. It won't change things to know the answers, so why beat a dead horse? Still, it seems as though the police would want to get to the bottom of it, in case there was some contributing factor, like someone having run Rick off the road. This is the first time I've dealt with the police, and I'm appalled to discover that they couldn't care less.

I spend the remainder of my break at Social Services on the first floor. The clerk pulls out Rick's file, which lists his admitting diagnosis as "multiple trauma." I give her my name and identify myself as a friend of the family, who live in New York. I ask that her office keep the family up-to-date through me in my capacity as their surrogate, which I am if you count Lenore's request that I keep them informed. As usual these days, my uniform is my credential; she assumes that I am representing the Simons and doesn't even check to see if I actually am who I claim to be. So much for medical confidentiality. As it is, all the clerk can do is tell me what I already know—that is that one of their counselors will be up to meet with Mr. Simon later on today.

I have just enough time left on my forty-five-minute break to either look in on Rick or grab a sandwich. I head for the coffee shop in the lobby. As I stand in line, my mind picks up where it left off last night, when I spent hours going over the situation, trying to decide what would be the most helpful way to pull him out of his depression. By the time I dragged myself to bed, I had a headache.

When I visit the ICU on my way home at five, Chris is at the nurses' station, and after peeking through the observation window, I stop to ask her how Rick is doing.

"Just great, according to the monitors," she replies. "Stronger every day and healing real well."

"I just looked in at him through the window," I tell her, "and he was lying pretty much as he was the first time I saw him. Not moving, just staring at the ceiling. He doesn't sleep with his eyes open . . ." *Careful, Maggie!* "Uh, does he? Anything going on with him?"

"No," she says, "he's just doing what he does best: looking for bunny rabbits on the ceiling. He doesn't read or watch TV. All he wants to do is lie there."

"But only a few days ago he was trying to talk, blinking, and writing notes on a pad, Chris."

She shrugs. "Maybe he's depressed because Mom and Dad went home and left him here."

"Seems like he has more important things to be depressed about."

"Maybe not as many as you think, Maggie. Take a look at this." She rummages around the desktop till she finds some papers, which she hands to me. "Orders for more tests. Dr. Sabir told Rick this morning that they've decided his injury is incomplete instead of complete like they initially thought, so there's a good chance the damage isn't permanent after all. They're thinking about doing another exploratory."

I look over the doctor's notes and orders. "This does sound hopeful. I'm . . . let's say, cautiously excited."

"So am I, but that one"—she indicates Rick's cubicle with her chin—"didn't blink an eye when we gave him the good news."

I look through the glass once again. Rick hasn't moved an inch. "You know what I'm wondering? Maybe he needs a kick in the pants." She looks at me quizzically. "Have you tried getting tough with him? You know, like insisting that he behave himself?"

"That sounds more like something you'd say to a pediatric patient," she counters.

"He's acting like a peds patient. He's not a fool. He knows perfectly well how important his cooperation is to his recovery."

"Oh, he does what he's supposed to," she says. "Goes through the exercises and doesn't complain about being poked and prodded, fed through one tube, peeing through another. That's not the problem, Maggie. It's just when it comes to what he should be doing for himself, like keeping in touch with the world around him . . . after all, he's not comatose anymore and he has one good eye and two good ears. He's not even all that sedated now. It's like he just doesn't want anything to do with reality."

This does not sound like a person who's getting ready to fight. I glance through the window again. "All the more reason he shouldn't be left to vegetate. You know he's a doctoral candidate at the university."

She nods. "I heard."

"I'm wondering if maybe, when one of the girls has time, she could read to him. Start with the newspaper. He used to read three or four a day."

"We tried it," she says patiently. "We talked with his parents even before he woke up and asked them what they thought would stimulate his interest, in case he was depressed when he came out of it. We never expected this."

"I know . . . I know, but maybe if you just keep at it, push him a little bit . . ."

"This is intensive care, Maggie. Babysitting is not in our job description." She smoothes the notes and fits them back into their folder. "But . . . he'll be leaving us soon anyway. He was ready to be moved on Friday, but we've had to wait for a private bed to open up. He'll probably rally up there. From what I hear, you gals up on the floors don't coddle anybody either."

"That depends on who you're—" The telephone jangles loudly, startling both of us; we've gone an unusually long time without being interrupted by a call. Chris picks up the receiver, and I take the opportunity to break away and head for Rick.

I touch his hand; he doesn't respond. Say his name, brush his fingers with my lips; nothing. He blinks, and out of nowhere, I feel a burning redness in my face and a seething rage in my stomach. It's suddenly so clear that Rick has manipulated me for nine months. Now he's manipulating all of us. In the time I've known him, I've become angry more often than I ever have in my life, and I just don't want to be a party to it anymore. I know I should walk away from here right now and never come back, but I can't. I promised his mother that I would see them through this, and I can't let them down. And besides, I . . . I what? I have to get home, for one thing. I need to think over these past months and sort out my feelings. Also, I'm late picking up Jennifer. "Have a good evening," I call out to Chris as I dash past the desk.

Looks like it's going to be another long, hard night.

Though I try my best to leave it at the hospital, my anger toward Rick persists in following me home and occupying my mind during dinner. It isn't until Jennifer asks in a small wary voice, "Are you mad at me, Mommy?" that I become aware of the scowl on my face that has probably been there since I stood at Rick's bedside. It's the kind of revelation that makes me feel like a tarnished penny in a bag of brand-new silver dollars, as my father used to say.

"Oh no, Jennifer. It has nothing to do with you. A patient made me angry just before I left work. I'm sorry I brought my bad feelings home with me."

"Grandmom says that getting mad is a sin and God won't like it if you do a sin."

Every child in our church has been taught this from the time we threw our first tantrums. For years our parents held it over us at every opportunity, as if it was a way for them to control what we thought and did. At some point I must have made an unconscious decision not to get angry when my mother was around and simply quit fearing God's wrath coming down on me because something rubbed me the wrong way. Hearing this, to me, dubious Biblical interpretation coming from my daughter's mouth, I am momentarily infuriated, but I already have enough anger to deal with tonight. "Well, that's something we can talk about later," I tell her. "Okay?"

She nods her head and goes off to do her own thing. My thing is cleaning up after dinner, all the while stewing about Rick's in-and-out games and the possibility that I'm reading him wrong and my anger is unjustified. The last thing I want is for God's wrath toward me to be warranted. I'm just about finished in the kitchen when the phone rings.

"Mommy, it's Aunt Carol!" Jennifer calls. It strikes me that this is the first time she has ever answered the telephone.

Bad timing for me. Carol picks up on every nuance, and I do not want to talk about this. "Hi, Carol," I say cheerfully. "I've been thinking about you."

"The receptionist told me you called. Things have been hectic for the past couple of weeks. I'm sorry I couldn't get back to you."

"It's been a while."

"The last time we spoke was a few weeks ago, when you called to cancel our dinner appointment. I think it had to do with Rick. You never followed up. Is everything okay?"

"Oh, yes, I remember. The doctors thought if one of the family was there as much as possible, talking to him, he might wake up sooner. I offered to help out, and my first shift was that Friday night. They were pinning their hopes on this, and I didn't want to let them down right off the bat."

"Did it work?"

I catch Jennifer pass the doorway slowly, as if she's planning to linger just out of sight so she can hear my conversation. "Carol? Listen, I can't talk at the moment. I'll get back to you. Okay?"

"Just tell me how—"

"We're all fine here. I'll talk to you in the next day or two."

"Great. I'll—"

"Oh, wait! Before you go, I have to ask you something."

"Okay."

"Are you familiar with the word 'mitzvah'? I think it's a Jewish word."

"It is. It means 'good deed.' Why?"

"I'll tell you when I see you. Thanks. I'll call you. Promise."

I hang up before she can insist on details and go looking for Jennifer. She's in her room, playing with her Slinky on a staircase made of blocks. She was probably just on her way to the bathroom. I feel like an idiot, a paranoid idiot.

My driver's ed teacher in high school always warned us never to ruminate while we're driving. I was never quite sure what he meant, but I was too timid to ask.

On my way to the sitter's house, I think back over my conversation with Chris, wonder what she makes of my attentiveness to Rick, and whether she suspects we're more than just friends. Did the slip I made about him not sleeping with his eyes open open her eyes? I mean, how would I know that if we weren't involved? Does she see me as just another lonely single mother having a fling with a younger man? The thought disturbs and embarrasses me until I ask myself what difference it makes what anyone thinks. What does it matter if the story travels through the grapevine until it's suddenly displaced by a fresh new piece of gossip?

Oh, dear God . . . !

I don't realize I've been on overdrive until I slam on my brakes to avoid running through a red light. I'd thought that only cows ruminate and that the driving teacher was being funny. I see now he wasn't, and I determine that bovine or human, I will never again ruminate on, over, or about anyone. Besides, life is too short to go home to another long, depressing evening on the couch. I decide on the spot that tonight will be girls' night out and that the girls will be Jennifer and me.

"What do you want for dinner tonight?" I ask Jennifer on the way home.

"Pizza," she says enthusiastically.

"Didn't we have pizza the other night when Mrs. Simon came over for dinner?"

"I like pizza."

"I do too, but if we have it too often, we'll get tired of it."

"I won't," she argues.

"If we try something new, we can eat it in the restaurant instead of bringing it home. Want to do that?"

She thinks it over for a minute. "Can we go to that restaurant we went to with Mr. and Mrs. Simon and Aunt Kathy and their sister?"

"No, that's only for very special occasions. But I saw a nice cozy little place not far from here. I think we can get all kinds of food there. Want to try it?"

I glance over at her, smile at her skeptical expression. "Mmm, I . . . okay. I'll try it."

"If you don't like it, we won't go back. If you do like it, we'll put it on our list. Fair?"

"What list?"

"The one we're going to start keeping about all the things we like to do."

"Okay." She settles back in her seat.

The restaurant, which is named Our Kitchen Table, is homey, with sturdy wood tables and chairs and gingham place mats. It offers special attractions for children, such as low counters full of little colorful, nonbreakable knickknacks and toys for them to look at while waiting for the meal to arrive. Coloring books and crayons appear with the table settings, and there is a special children's menu of universal favorites. I order a sandwich and a cup of coffee. Jennifer chooses a hot dog. She finishes almost everything on her plate, and then, without so much as a glance at me, gets up and walks tentatively to a toy shelf. I watch as she studies each of the objects and finally takes a chance on picking one up. She holds it in her palm for a minute or two, then wraps her fingers around it and brings it over to me.

"Look, Mommy. She's just like you." She opens her hand, and I see it's a beautifully painted miniature wooden doll in an old-fashioned nurse's uniform. I look up at Jennifer, and she's smiling and genuinely happy. "Can I take her home with me?"

"I don't know, Jen, but we can ask when the waitress comes back. Do you want dessert?"

"You know what, Mommy? They have doughnuts with pink icing."

"That sounds good."

"But I don't want one. I want chocolate ice cream in a cone like that boy over there."

I glance over my shoulder and follow her sight line straight to a kid with a "satisfied customer" expression on his face. The waitress appears, and I order a chocolate ice cream cone for Jennifer and a coffee refill and a pink doughnut for myself. When she returns with dessert, I ask her if the toys are for sale.

"Only the plastic ones. We buy them by the lot. This one's wood, so I'll have to ask the manager."

Jennifer frowns and bites her lip nervously as her eyes track the waitress back through the swinging door. I can't bear for her to be disappointed tonight; it's been so perfect. She puts a clean napkin over the doll to keep it safe from her ice cream cone, which is beginning to drip a little, then licks off the drips and starts eating. As I sip my coffee, I notice our waitress talking animatedly with a middle-aged couple just this side of the kitchen door. I look away; I don't want to see her boss giving her the wrong answer. Jennifer finishes her cone, wipes her hands, and picks up the napkin with the doll in it. She looks at me sadly, then gets out of her chair and returns the tiny nurse to the shelf. I want to cry.

I am draining my coffee cup and eating the last of my doughnut when the waitress gives me the check, then takes from her pocket a small box, which she hands to Jennifer. Jennifer's mouth opens in an *O* when she lifts the lid. She looks up at the girl.

"Thank you very much," she says shyly. Then she adds, "My mom is a nurse too." I hear pride in her voice and can't think when I've been as happy, genuinely happy, as I am at this moment.

On the way home, I realize with a start that I forgot to call Chris about Rick's psych intake. Anxious as I am to know how it went, I have to admit that its slipping my mind has given me a glimmer of hope that there will be life after Rick Simon.

I manage to get a good night's sleep for the first time in almost three weeks and wake up early, alert, and full of resolve. I don't have to be at work until three today, and with Jennifer in school, I am free to do whatever I want to. First on my list is finding a solution to my on-and-off anger with Rick. Second, it occurred to me last night that Wednesday is July 4 and that we will have to go to Clearyville, as we've done every year since I moved to Chicago. I want to concentrate on healing the breach with my self-righteous and unforgiving mother, and going home might give me a chance to start. I know from experience how much patience and emotional energy it takes to reach my mother, and I can't begin to try until I am comfortable knowing Rick is truly emotionally stable.

July 3-4, 1973

I get to intensive care at two, only to learn that Rick has been moved to the seventh-floor medical unit and that Chris won't be in until Thursday. I ask a nurse at the station for his room number.

"Are you Mrs. McLean?" I nod. "7A32. Chris, the nurse in ICU, left this for you."

I thank her, tear open an envelope, and read the note quickly. "According to Social Services, the intake could not be completed today, 7/2/73, because of the patient's limited ability to participate. Recommendation: Reschedule in two weeks. Sorry we couldn't meet. Chris." I make a mental note to stop down to see Chris in the next few days, then head purposefully toward Rick's room.

The door is ajar. I step across the sill and stop to admire his new surroundings. He's been moved to a VIP corner room that is larger than any other two-bed I've seen. It has two adjacent windows with muted floor-length drapes, a sofa, and wooden bedroom furniture. Of course, there is a hospital bed, which is to the right of the door. The day is cloudy, and the silvery light coming through the windows gives the room a grayish cast. The soft light from a table lamp at one end of the sofa along the left wall does nothing to brighten the dimness. The only thing in here that is familiar is Rick, who, as usual, appears to be sleeping and totally unaware of the change in his surroundings. Or is he sleeping? This is the thing that maddens me, the possibility that he's playing. I stand at the side of the bed, surveying his inert form and how pale, thin, and defenseless he looks, and I waver. But only for a moment. I suddenly remember the times he acted like a spoiled child, and how it was just a few days ago that he was alert enough to interact with his family. "Rick, do you hear me?" I encircle his wrist with my fingers. His pulse appears normal. "Rick?" I pull a small chair over to the side of the bed, in front of a night table, on which somebody has had the foresight to leave a pencil and a clipboard with lined paper. I sit down and lean toward him. A cart rolls by in the hall behind me, the sound reminding me that someone might come into the room at any time, and it would not be a good thing for me to be caught with my hands on a patient who isn't mine. Besides, I don't have much more time before I have to go on shift.

"Rick, it has to stop, you know," I begin. "You can't keep doing this. Today is Tuesday, two weeks since you had your accident. You were in a coma for nine days. Your family left on Thursday. Do you remember? The day before they went home, you tried to smile and talk. I gave you a pad and pencil and you wrote what you wanted to say. They felt so encouraged. We all did. But now, the doctors and nurses have done everything they can for you up to this point. They can't go any further without your help."

Rick hasn't budged, but I'm determined to say as much as I can before I have to go upstairs. Besides, the more I talk, the madder I get. I take a deep breath and continue.

"Listen to me carefully, Rick. I'm talking to you now as a nurse and I'm only going to do this once. The overall opinion is that there is no sign of neurological impairment and all of the fractures are healing properly. When I spoke to your ICU nurse this morning, she said that the neurosurgeon now believes that your spine injury is not as serious as the doctors thought at the beginning, which means you'll probably get back a high percentage of function. You have to be relieved about that." *Small constriction of his throat. A swallow? How much longer can he keep up this mannequin act?* "So why aren't you responding? The only things left are anger and depression, which are understandable under the circumstances. But the fact is that you're off the critical list, out of intensive care, and your overall prognosis is positive. I can tell you, Rick, that that better mean something to you, because if you don't pull yourself together and start helping the rehabilitation process, you'll be a cripple for the rest of your life." Again I check his pulse, which if I'm not mistaken, is now racing. Am I on the right track? Every professional instinct I have says yes, and I feel my own pulse quicken.

I get up and walk to the window. No view of the parking area here. Instead the room looks down on the small grassy area at the back of the building. A few benches, a couple of picnic tables. These are used in good weather, mostly by staff on their lunch hours. Sometimes visitors take their young children out there to run around. It's not a particularly pretty spot, but neither is it a parking lot. A glance at my watch tells me I have only ten minutes left. I return to Rick to say what I spent last night planning out. I'm not sure if I should say it at all, but if he's not listening, it won't make any difference. If he is listening, maybe it will.

"I have something else to say, Rick," I continue, a bit uncertainly, "and now I'm speaking as a—well, now I'm no longer sure exactly what our relationship is, so I'll just say as a friend. Before the accident, you were trying to decide whether to go to California or stay in Chicago. I kept trying to pin you down on your decision before you got hurt, but you kept putting me off. It was clear that Jennifer and I weren't a factor in whatever you decided to do and it was hurtful that you could even think of just walking away from us like that." *A muscle in his good jaw twitches. I know he hears me.* "I didn't expect you to stay because of us, but the least you could've done was let me know what you were thinking, so I could prepare Jennifer. She's deeply attached to you, I think more than to anybody else. I realize now that your presence in our lives has made a big difference in her. I didn't know how to tell her about the accident, but she brought it up herself. She asked me why you weren't sleeping at our house anymore." *His jaw tightens.* "I almost jumped out of my skin. I explained the situation to her and she asked all kinds of questions about your injuries and if you were going to be okay. I've never seen her so . . . so interested in anything. Rick, she loves you. You're almost like a father figure to her. She keeps asking when you're coming home and why can't I bring her to see you. I'd like to, now that you're not in the ICU anymore, but what's the point if you're just going to ignore her? It would only upset her. So please stop this . . . hiding. You will get better if you give us a chance to help you, if you help yourself." *Another twitch—I have to wrap this up.* "I know you can hear me, Rick, so think about what I've said. I have to go now. I'll see you later." I bend over him, touch my lips to his forehead, then put the chair back where it belongs. I'm moving toward the door when I hear a sound behind me, a guttural sound from Rick. I stop, unable to decide what to do. Another sound, something like a person who is gagged. I turn back. He is looking right at me. He tries a third time to speak and mimes writing, as he did when his parents were here. I know I'm going to get called down for being late for my shift, but I have to go back to him. I stand the clipboard on his stomach and hold it while he writes. He watches me intently as I read the note, which very clearly says,

"I don't want you here, Maggie.
Leave me alone."

He pushes the pad aside, turns his face away, and fixes his eyes once more on that distant place that only he can see.

I leave the room on shaky legs, my heart pounding, and as close to hyperventilation as I've ever been. By the time I come out of the ladies' room, where I flee to patch myself together, I am almost twenty minutes late for work. My supervisor passes as I am getting off the elevator, but she doesn't say a thing to me, just scowls and continues on her way. Four hours into my shift, I still feel like a zombie, trying hard to function, but basically just going through the motions and praying I don't do anything clumsy. And all the while wondering how I ever let myself get into this situation.

The last time I leaned on anybody was after we received the telegram about Steve's capture, and then I didn't have to ask. My needs were anticipated, and everyone—even my stoic mother was, to some extent, supportive and solicitous. It has occurred to me since that if I had only had the chance to work it through myself then, I might now fit the wonder-nurse image that the Simons have of me. Right now I am in a black hole for the second time in three weeks. At the beginning, at least I could submerge myself in trying to fill the needs of Rick's family. Tonight I'm the one who feels muddled, helpless, and alone. Kathy will be at my apartment when I get there, but since she and Todd have become a couple, she's been so wrapped up in her own life, we hardly talk anymore. If it weren't for the babysitting, I doubt we would see much of her these days.

It's almost eleven thirty when I let myself into the apartment. Kathy and Todd are playing Scrabble in the dining room. "Everything okay?" I ask as I pass through to the kitchen.

"No. Todd's winning again," she complains.

I put water on for tea. "Anybody want anything to drink?"

"No, thanks," they answer in unison, followed immediately by an anguished little shriek from my sister.

"What happened?" I ask, rushing in.

"Todd just put a *z* on a triple square. I might as well quit right now."

"Might as well," Todd agrees. "I have to get home anyway." He begins tossing letter tiles in a bag. "Have to get up early tomorrow."

"So do we." Kathy stands up and stretches, looks in my direction. "What time are we leaving?"

"Leaving?"

"For Clearyville," she reminds me. "Knock, knock, Maggie. Tomorrow's the Fourth."

I groan. "Oh, I forgot. It's been a busy day."

"How's Rick doing?"

"Moved to a private room on the seventh floor."

"Great!" she exclaims as they move toward the door. "Now we can visit him. Jenny makes a wish every night that she can go see him."

Kathy's not telling me anything I don't already know, and I don't want to talk about it. In fact, I don't feel like saying anything except "good night," which I do as the door closes behind them. The teakettle whistles, and I hurry into the kitchen to turn off the heat. After I've poured my tea, I stand in the middle of the living room and listen to the little ticks as I rotate my head in a circular motion, trying to work the stiffness out of my neck and shoulders. I am literally aching from the tension caused by that single moment in Rick's room. I check on Jennifer, who is sleeping soundly in a tangle of sheets, get into my nightgown, return to the kitchen to fetch my cup. On my way through the dining room, I step on a stray Scrabble tile and put it aside for Kathy. Kathy . . . Clearyville. I've forgotten about the salads I'm expected to bring tomorrow. I'll have to pick something up at the deli in the morning. I also forgot to ask her what time she wants to leave, but I can call her before I go for the food. Thank the Lord it's only a forty-mile drive, and the weather's supposed to be good. At the latest, we'll be back around ten or eleven p.m. Going home for the Fourth has always been fun and probably will be this year too, except for one thing: I don't want to go.

I get into bed and will myself to fall asleep immediately, but it doesn't work. The prospect of having to face my mother has distracted me somewhat from Rick's rejection, which is good. I'll have too much to deal with in Clearyville to be dwelling on it. Kathy told me about Mother's reaction to the news of Rick's accident; how she smirked and said she wasn't surprised, how she could tell at Christmas that he was "a bad sort" and would end up causing me some kind of trouble, how she gloated that maybe now Mary Grace has finally come to her senses and realizes what a "laughingstock" she's made of herself by getting mixed up with someone like that. I've always had a good reputation in town, and I'm not worried about losing it. I can be sure that no one else will ever hear about Mary Grace McLean's outrageous behavior, because my mother would rather die than let it be known that her daughter has lost her senses. I wouldn't have expected otherwise from her, but mulling it over now only reinforces my feeling of having no one to turn to. This is my last thought before I finally drop off.

I awake at seven thirty, surprisingly rested and knowing exactly what I need to do. I make a pot of coffee and call Kathy to tell her that I've decided to leave later, and probably won't get to Clearyville until twelve or one o'clock.

"What?" she squawks incredulously, as if I had told her I'd decided to become a Democrat. "Mother always expects us to be there by ten to help set up!"

"I have a few things to take care of before I go."

"You mean you're going up to see Rick first, right?"

"No. I'm skipping him today."

"Then why? Nothing's open today."

"There's something I have to do first. It's personal."

"What's your problem, Maggie? You're acting so weird lately. It's like—"

"Here's what I need you to do," I interrupt. "Todd was going to pick you up and bring you here, wasn't he? I'll have Jennifer ready when you get here, and then you all can drive on to Clearyville. I'll be along later and I'll take the cleanup detail."

"I thought we were going to go together, like we always do."

"Well, we're not today."

"Maybe Todd will decide not to go after all," she says petulantly.

"Of course he'll go. You know Roger and Marion think the world of him and are bursting to show him off to the neighbors."

"Roger and Ma—! What on earth has gotten into you?" After the ensuing short silence, she adds huffily, "Well, you just go on and do what you want. We'll be by for Jenny at nine." She clicks off before I have a chance to wish to her a "happy face" day.

In some way, the conversation reminds me of the shaving kit incident, but when I think of how upset I was at that time and how little fazed am right now, I am unable to suppress a tiny smirk of triumph. Maybe losing your senses once in a while can be the beginning of personal growth.

But I don't have time to work that out, because sometime during the night, I realized that I'm not alone after all. As I dial Carol's number, I say a prayer that she'll still be in town and able to meet with me.

She answers on the sixth ring. "Don't you usually spend the Fourth in your hometown?" she asks as soon as she hears my voice.

"Kathy and her boyfriend are picking up Jennifer in a few minutes. I'm going later by myself. How are you spending the holiday?"

"We're heading up to Glencoe around noon. Jerry's parents are having a family barbecue. "Is everything okay, Maggie?" Carol's never been one for small talk.

"Actually, I was wondering if there's a chance we could meet this morning for an hour or so."

"Well, let's see. It's eight twenty-five now. Jerry's spending the morning at the office catching up on stuff that accumulated while he was away. Where would you want to meet?"

"I was thinking of that little coffee shop near your house at around nine thirty?"

"I'll have to bring Sarah with me. Will that be a problem?"

"No, not at all. I haven't seen her in ages. I really do appreciate this, Carol. There's—"

"We'll talk about it at the coffee shop," she says quickly. "I'll see you there at nine thirty."

For once I don't wonder if I'm doing the wrong thing by consulting Carol. I don't know where to go from here, and I need to talk to someone who is not judgmental or involved.

The coffee shop two blocks from Carol and Jerry's house has a counter and six or eight tables. It's about as sterile and uninviting as a hospital cafeteria. When I get there, Carol has just arrived and is settling Sarah into a booster seat. She puts a few crayons and some blank paper on the table, and Sarah grabs for them immediately. As soon as I sit down opposite them, the waitress appears with menus. I ask for a pot of tea. Carol orders a couple of bagels and a cup of coffee, then waits for the waitress to leave before asking about Jennifer. I describe the sudden and exciting, though inexplicable, personality change I've seen in my daughter over the past month. Since she has occasionally expressed concern about Jennifer's lack of interest in other people and the world around her, her face lights up in a huge grin. "I like what I'm hearing," she says.

Sarah looks up from her scribbles and says, "Me too." I give her chubby little arm a squeeze, and Carol rolls her eyes.

After the waitress brings our order, Carol takes a sip of her coffee and asks, "So what's up?"

The usual wave of reticence and regret sweeps over me, but only for a moment. "Do you remember the last time we talked?"

Carol nods. "About a month ago."

"Well, 'what's up' now had already begun, but I couldn't bring myself to talk to you about it then. Remember how we made plans to meet for dinner a couple of nights later—"

"On the Friday, but—"

"I cancelled."

"Uh-huh. Can you talk about it now?"

"I think so."

"I'm listening."

"Okay." And before I can get my thoughts in order, I'm pouring out the whole story: the night I worked late and Rick sat for Jennifer, which led to our first physical encounter; our "arrangement"; his parents' visit; the revelations in the park, everything, even what he said in the bedroom about commitment the night before the accident. Through the whole thing, Carol never takes her eyes off me, not when she quiets Sarah's fidgeting or shushes her babbling or when the waitress comes to refill the coffee cups. It isn't until I get to the part about Rick's accident that her concentration falters. Stunned, she closes her eyes and whispers, "Oh my God, my God."

Finally, I go through the night of the crash, the emergency room, the police, the waiting during the initial surgery, the week with his family. I admit that I felt guilty at first because of having pressured him about California, but she assures me that it's highly doubtful that I had that much power over him, so I can let go of that notion. Whether he subconsciously caused the crash will be his problem, not mine. Period. She reaches across the table, grasps my hand, and confesses that she feels partly responsible for my having gotten into the relationship to begin with.

"We should never have encouraged you to get involved with him," she says ruefully, "but we had no idea it would turn into such a . . . a thing. All we were thinking was that you needed to get out of your shell and live a little."

"I never thought it would go anywhere at first either," I say around a sip of lukewarm tea. "But I just couldn't help myself. Steve kept drifting further and further away, and Rick was so gentle and sweet. Even when his mother warned me that he could be, well, difficult"—Carol's eyebrows shoot up when I mention this—"I didn't pull away. Instead, I thought she was trying to keep him away from me, not the other way around."

"It sounds to me like he was getting the better of the bargain."

"I don't think there was any bargain. That's the whole problem, Carol. I guess we just didn't put the same importance on whatever we were doing."

"I don't know exactly what he was doing, but what you were doing was falling in love with him."

"No!" I say quickly. "I never thought I loved him."

"Okay, then call it falling in lust," she says patiently, "whatever label you want to put on it. My point is that if you weren't in such a deep emotional turmoil over him, would you have been so hurt when you perceived he was rejecting you?"

"Why do you say 'perceived'? He wrote a note to me saying, 'Leave me alone. I don't want you here.' Sure sounds clear enough to me. I thought I had perfect control of my emotions and where I was going from here, but now my mind is muddled again and my deep emotional state is getting deeper. I don't know what to do, Carol. I promised his mother I'd keep an eye on him and keep them posted on his progress. I can't just drop him, can I?"

She ponders this for a moment. "Under the current circumstances, I have to say no. Wait until he gets his head on straight. Since I only met Rick once, it's basically unethical for me to give you any professional advice. But as your friend, I can give you my gut feeling."

"Which is?"

"The truth?"

I nod yes, but inside I'm shaking.

"Everything you've told me about him makes me suspicious that he was—no, let me set it up for you. He's depressed and in pain, so he goes to a place inside himself where he doesn't have to deal with the reality of his life or anybody in it. But he can't stay there forever and it's beginning to get monotonous. That note he wrote you yesterday, I'll bet it made him feel good to do it. Not to use hurtful words, but to physically pick up the pencil and write the words. I just have a feeling he didn't mean it as a rejection of you. He's angry and frightened about what's happened to him, and there you were, handy at the bedside, and he just took it all out on you. Maggie, my guess is that he used you to vent those bad feelings the only way he could at that moment. Subconsciously, he might even want to come out of that safe place, but he's afraid. He has to be one confused guy right now."

I shake my head at this. "There were people at the bedside all week. Why wasn't he angry with his parents or his sister? Why not the nurses or the doctors? Patients do this to us all the time."

"Maybe he knew he could trust you to understand without all the family history influencing your response," she replies. "Maybe he chose you because he thought he could hurt you and be forgiven. You know, just because his mother has good insight into his negative behavior doesn't mean she can forgive him for it." I want to believe what Carol is saying, but I have to think about it for a while. "I know how traumatized you were when you lost Steve, and how unnerving this Rick thing has been for you since you met him, but if you have fallen in love with him, it's happened.

You can deny it all you want and it won't take away the fact that you have, right?"

"If."

"And you can just as easily fall out of love with him. So admit it to yourself and work from there."

"How, Carol? Where do I go with it?"

"Hang on a sec," she mumbles and gingerly lifts Sarah out of the booster and into the stroller, which has been sitting next to her chair. I've barely registered that Sarah has been sleeping for some time. Now she whimpers as Carol arranges her under a light blanket to counteract the blasting cold of the air-conditioning system, but quiets when Carol starts moving the stroller back and forth. The waitress suddenly pops up to refill our cups, then retreats without saying a word. Turning back to me, Carol asks, "So what's your next move going to be?"

She might be right on the mark about Rick's not meaning what he said, but how do I know that? I don't want to put myself in the position of being dismissed again. "Am I wrong not to chance visiting him again?"

"Not really after he lashed out at you. It's your choice. I just think it would be a good idea to give him a chance. He needs you more than you need him right now. You've seen this kind of reaction a hundred times in your work."

"That's true, but it's not so easy when you're personally involved with the patient."

"Of course, it isn't. And if you weren't in the middle of it, you'd have been the first one to have seen it for what it really is. Think about it objectively, if you can. Go back in there tomorrow morning and pretend it never happened. Who knows? Maybe he'll even apologize."

That would be the day. "Right, and maybe he'll have been so doped up, he won't even remember he said anything," I reply cynically.

Carol laughs. "If that's the case, what have you lost?"

Nothing, because I know I don't love him.

It's eleven thirty, and I'm on my way to Clearyville. Do I feel better for having met with Carol? I don't know. But I know I don't feel worse either. She's so good at putting things in perspective, but also so definite about her suggestions. I'm going to have to spend some serious time thinking about our talk before I proceed. For today, however, I have to concentrate on dealing with my mother.

The next fifty-five minutes pass quickly, and then I see the familiar

Welcome to Clearyville, Illinois
Home of Cleary Manufacturing, Inc.

sign, and I'm there. I park in the municipal car park and walk over to the center of town, which in Clearyville does not mean the three-block business area but the town common. I have plenty of company on the way, mostly parade stragglers—families and men and women singly or together—who are cheerfully making their way to the common, calling out friendly greetings as they go. Even children sprinting past us on skates or on foot manage to wave or breathe a preoccupied hi. As it does every year, a sense of excitement and expectation fills the air; I can already hear the sound of the commotion on the green.

I take my time. Kathy said they'd be at the gazebo watching the band set up at twelve forty-five, and it's only just past twelve thirty. I hope Jennifer is with her and Todd and not back at the house. I know I should have stopped there first, but I can't be sure my mother's already at the church tent, and I'm not ready to face her sternness just yet. I stop a moment to watch the activity before I cross the cordoned-off street beside the common. Fourth of July has always been my favorite holiday, and until this year, the thought of missing it has never so much as nipped at the edges of my mind. Now that I'm here, I'm glad that I decided to come.

Being in Clearyville on this particular day is like suddenly finding yourself in one of those old Technicolor movies of what life in Middle America is supposed to be. Everything is green and yellow and clean and sweet. The center of town has been closed to automobile traffic in preparation for the festivities. People wander around the common to stop and chat and watch the band assemble in the bunting-draped gazebo. The air is thick with anticipation of the fireworks display, always the climax of the evening. Today is the one day of the year when children can race around waving miniature flags and get in everybody's way, without anyone scolding them or telling them to behave. I used to be one of those children and have often regretted that Jennifer never will be.

The parade has just ended when I cross the street. The weather is warm and fine, and from what I can see, Clearyville is outdoing itself in patriotic pageantry. I find Kathy, Todd, and Bobby McLean sitting under a big elm tree, sipping cola through straws. For the first time, I notice what a nice-looking couple Kathy and Todd make. Kathy is wearing a cap-sleeved white shirt with a modest scoop neck and a blue and white candy-stripe wraparound skirt that I've never seen before. Her sandals are lying on the grass next to a big straw hat she must also have bought recently. She looks cool, comfortable, and pretty. She glances up and sees me.

"Hey, Maggie, come on over. We saved you a place."

"Hi," I call, striding toward them. "How'd you manage to find a nice shady spot in the middle of all this chaos? Bobby! I haven't seen you since Christmas. How've you been?" I tuck my Indian madras skirt beneath me and settle in beside my sister.

"It's Rob now," my brother-in-law answers. "I'm fine. How 'bout you?"

Rob? He was Bobby at Christmas. What is this?

"Bob—I mean, Rob's engaged, Maggie. Isn't that *fabulous*?"

"Congratulations," I say. "A local girl?"

"Rockford. We met at a Bible seminar in March."

"Is she here today? I'd love to meet her."

"No. Her family is having their yearly family circle get-together in Elgin. I'll probably go on up there a little later."

"Well, I'm happy for you, B—uh, Rob. And how's your mother?"

"Same. Try to find time to say hello. I know she'd like to see you, Maggie."

"I will, after I pick up Jennifer."

Bobby is a shy man, but no conversation with him has ever been as . . . stiff . . . as this one. I guess he finally gave up on Kathy, which might be the reason she seems to be a lot more excited about his engagement than he is. We sit in awkward silence, until Kathy gets to her feet and announces that she's ready to take a walk across the green and see what people over in the food area are up to. Todd jumps up, but Bobby says he's waiting for some friends of his to show up. I decide to wander around with Kathy and Todd before I go to the house and pick up Jennifer. Dad likes to wait until later in the afternoon before he heads for the green, and she loves to be with her granddaddy no matter where they are.

The red, white, and blue tents are up, and the long tables are exactly where they've been every year for as far back as I can remember. I don't have to take a look inside the tents to know that spigoted watercooler-size bottles of homemade lemonade and big buckets of pop on ice line the walls, that the prep tables are crowded with casserole dishes—the perennial favorite being macaroni salad with ham, from our church's secret recipe—and plates and plates of deviled eggs. There are always huge bowls of different slaws and potato salads, baked beans, rolls, condiments, and early corn on the cob from surrounding farms. I quickly set down my puny store-bought contribution behind a large bowl. My mouth waters at the thought of the ranks of pies made with every kind of seasonal fruit. Year after year, apple pie and peach cobbler are the first to run out.

The grills are behind the tents. Traditionally, the grilling is done by the men's clubs at the churches. When I was little and my father used to help with the grilling, I never wanted to go behind the tents. No matter how hot the day was, it always felt ten degrees hotter back there. Besides, the men always looked dirty and sweaty, and that didn't appeal to me, even when I was six or seven years old. Mother would never let Dad in the house after he'd been grilling until he'd cleaned up at the spigot behind the garage.

Right now it looks as if the whole town is out here, and I'm mindful that my mother, who always works behind the scenes, can appear at any moment. It's time for me to walk over to the house. Before I do that, however, I make a detour to the McLeans', which is six blocks from here, but in the opposite direction from our house.

My mother-in-law's name is Margaret. Though I've known her most of my life, I've never called her anything but Mrs. McLean. When I get to the house, she is alone and depressed, the way she's been since the day we got the news about Steve. As always, though, she does seem happy, in her subdued way, to see me.

"I just met Bobby on the green and heard about his engagement," I say when she returns from the kitchen with a plate of cookies, a pitcher of lemonade, and one glass. "Have you met her?"

Her mouth curves in a smile. "Oh yes," she answers quietly. "She's a sweet girl."

"Are you happy about it?"

"She's a good girl. She'll make him a good wife." She fills the glass and offers it to me. There's no point in suggesting that Margaret, who is thin as a rail, eat or drink with me. I don't mention the "Rob" thing either. To her he'll always be Bobby, and she's had enough changes in her family already.

But back to the engagement. "I didn't get her name."

"Bernadine Clemons."

"And they met at a Bible seminar."

"Yes." Clearly she has nothing more to say about it.

I understand that holidays are agony for my mother-in-law, particularly Fourth of July and Christmas, which were Steve's favorites. We get a Christmas card from her every year, and she has come to Jennifer's birthday parties in August when she's felt up to it, but I can tell that her heart is never in it. I once heard my mother say that she's never really recovered from the loss of her husband many years ago, but I don't remember her being this removed from the world when he died. Today, it seems to me that even the reminiscences are not as many as usual, and before long, we fall silent.

"Jennifer is staying here for a week, you know," I finally mention in hopes of reviving the conversation. "I hope you'll be able to spend some time with her."

She nods. "I'll try, dear. She is doing well?"

"Oh yes. Growing up so fast. She's going into second grade in September. Shall I ask Dad to bring her over?"

She nods again but says nothing. She was always a quiet woman, but it's as if she's lost any capacity that she might have had for joy. It's a painful thought.

I finish my lemonade and stand up. She walks me to the door, thanks me for stopping by. I impulsively give her a peck on the cheek and open the screen door. As she draws back, she looks me in the eye and says in a half whisper, "He's gone, you know."

What? I stare at her. "Did they—"

"No," she anticipates. "I've heard nothing from the army. But I know. I feel it. Steven will not be coming back."

A dozen thoughts flash through my mind like minute lightning strikes, but I can't catch hold of even one. I can only stand there like a statue.

She reaches past me and opens the screen door further. "Go on with your life, Grace dear. Don't wait any longer. Do tell Roger to bring Jenny over, and thank you for coming to see me today." She closes the door behind me.

If I'm dreaming, Lord, wake me up. If I'm not, please help me take my mother-in-law's advice. I have nowhere else to go now, so I go on home.

My parents live in a very ordinary two-bedroom, one-bathroom white frame house with black shutters on the front windows and four steps leading up to the gray front door. Below the windows is a hedge that stays green all winter. The concrete path from the sidewalk to the steps is straight. The grass on the front lawn is healthy and green. Dad waters it almost every evening during the summer and is scrupulous about keeping the hedges neatly trimmed. He keeps the path and concrete driveway to the left of the house swept clean. The house looks exactly as it looked on the day they moved into it in 1938, three years after they were married and two years before I was born. I know this because one of the few family pictures we have is of them standing in front of the house that first day. I suspect the real estate agent took the picture; though they rarely used it, my parents did have a camera when I was small. The inside of the house is Mother's domain, of course, and she is as finicky about neatness and uniformity as Dad is.

The front door is open when I arrive, but that doesn't mean that someone is home. People in Clearyville still keep their doors open in the daytime and unlocked at night. The house is cool and dark inside and feels empty.

"Dad? Jennifer?" I call. No answer. "It's me. Mary Grace. Hello?" Again no answer. They might have gone downtown already by a different route than I took coming. Dad would've taken Jennifer early if she'd asked him to. The window over the sink looks out on the side yard, and I walk through Mother's spotless kitchen to take a peek. The two of them are nestled in the hammock, reading a book. As I start for the back door, I am reminded of the kind black lieutenant, Steve's friend, who scared me half to death when he appeared behind me in the yard, but turned out to be a blessing. I can't stop thinking about what Steve's mother said: *He's gone. Go on with your life, Grace. Don't wait any longer.* Have I been blessed again? I purposely let the back door slam as I go out. In honor of the lieutenant.

"Hi, Mommy!" shouts my daughter, my former shrinking violet, who slithers out of the hammock and runs to me. "Granddaddy's reading me a story about Jonah, who got stuck in a big whale." I wave at my father.

"Why aren't you at the green with Kathy and Todd?"

"'Cause Granddaddy wanted to come home for lunch after the parade, and I came with him. There's too many people there."

"Where's your grandmother?"

"She went to help make sandwiches with the ladies from church. I wanted to stay here with Granddaddy."

"Well, maybe we can get Granddaddy to come with us when we go back later."

"We'll see," she says tentatively.

By this time, Dad is standing behind Jennifer with his hands on her shoulders. "Good to see you, Grace," he says with the smile he seems to reserve for the younger women in his life. He's not much more physically affectionate than my mother is, but there's never been a question in my mind that he is a loving person.

"How are you, Dad?" I ask.

"Just fine, now that my three princesses are nearby."

"Who are your three princesses?" asks Jennifer. "Me, Kathy, and my mom?"

"Yup."

"What about Grandmom? Oh, I know. She's the queen, right?"

Dad clears his throat impressively.

"Jennifer," I say, "would you go into the house and bring us three glasses of water? Put them on the big tray. You know where Grandmom keeps it. Just call us when you're ready to come out and we'll come and hold the door open for you. Okay?"

"Yup," she says.

As soon as she disappears into the house, I turn to Dad. "I need to talk to you before I go back tonight. Can we take a walk or something later?"

He looks at me with a serious expression. "I won't speak against your mother, Grace," he warns.

I feel my resolve sink a notch. "I know that, but I need your advice about how I can approach her to talk about why she's angry at me."

"You know why. You're having an affair"—I flinch involuntarily—"with a man you hardly know, who's younger than you are. Oh, I know what you're thinking. No, neither Kathy nor Jenny has said a word to us about it. We saw it coming at Christmas."

"At Christmas! I barely knew his name then."

It's as if I haven't spoken. "What's more, he isn't even Christian," my father continues.

"None of those things matter," I retort defensively.

"I guess they don't. If they did, you would have found a more suitable man to run after."

Oh Lord. "I won't even dignify that comment with an answer, Dad. The important thing is that Jennifer has formed a strong attachment to Rick. I believe she sees him as a substitute father. Can't you see how different she is since he came into our lives?"

"Now, now. She's just shy," he says in an exaggeratedly reasonable tone, as if I was a child he was soothing after I'd dropped my lollipop in the dirt. "She would've come out of her shell, given time. You were the same way—"

"And I never really came out of myself until I met Steve. I was a scared mouse."

"No, you were not. You were just . . . quiet."

"Actually, how I was as a child has nothing to do with this. The point is, you seem to forget I've been a widow for six years!"

His eyebrows shot up. "A widow? Are you saying that Steve has been declared dead? Margaret never mentioned that to us."

"Of course not. The army can't declare him dead, because they haven't found him. But I think it's quite obvious after all this time." *I really don't want to talk about Steve.* "Dad, I just feel it in my heart. And I have to get on with my life, if not for myself, for my daughter."

My father nods sadly and sighs a deep sigh. "Yes, I know. I just don't—"

"Somebody come open the door! It's ready!"

"On my way!" I call back. It suddenly occurs to me that Jennifer's taken a long time to get a couple of glasses of water, but I find it unlikely that she's gotten into any kind of mischief while she's been indoors. Through the screen I see her standing with a large tray on which are three cups of water and a plate of cookies. *Oh, Jennifer.* My heart does a handspring at the sight of the happily excited expression on her face.

"We're having a tea party," she explains, "except I'm not supposed to turn on the stove, so it's really water."

"That's a lovely idea, Jennifer, and I see you've put ice cubes in the water. Just the thing to do on a hot summer day." She beams. "How about you get the door and I'll take the tray. It looks kind of heavy. Okay?"

"Yup." She holds the door for me, then rushes down the steps, leaving the door to smack me in the rear end, a perfect way to put an end to a horrific conversation that did nothing but upset both my father and me. The tea party lasts until the cookies are gone, which is about fifteen minutes. I take the party things into the house, clean up, and return to the yard. Jennifer and Granddaddy are having a quiet moment, but it is soon broken when my father declares, "I'm ready to go down to the celebration. How about you princesses?"

We pretty much have the streets to ourselves now, and I smile as Jennifer skips on ahead of us. Just as I expected, we don't resume our conversation, and I know we never will.

At the common, we stop to watch the pie-eating contest. Jennifer is rapt at the sight of men sloshing and dripping and slurping and wolfing down whole pies one after the other. Did I mention dripping? When she's had enough of the stains and the mess, she turns to us, makes a disgusted face, and says simply, "Yuck."

Mother, finished with her job now, is sitting in the refreshment area with Kathy and Todd. She definitely approves of Todd, and they are chatting and eating the macaroni and ham salad that she had put aside for them. Jennifer makes a beeline for Mother and hops up into her lap. I can tell by the big smile on Mother's face that she is delighted. I can also tell, when the smile magically disappears, that she sees me walking toward the table with Dad. "Grace?" she says cordially.

"Mother," I respond neutrally.

And so it goes.

We stay until the final firework has been exploded and the last hamburger, marshmallow, and baked bean have been consumed. By that time, it's going on ten p.m., and Jennifer can hardly keep her head up. Mother, as always, takes her place with the cleanup committee. The rest of us, Todd with Jennifer on his shoulders, start back to the house. I don't feel like cleaning up, and head back to the house with Kathy, Dad, and Todd, who is carrying Jennifer on his shoulders. It usually takes the committee more than an hour to get done, and I expect to be on my way back to Chicago by the time Mother gets home. Kathy and Todd decide to wait for her to get back, but I am anxious to be on my way so I can be alone to reflect on the day as I drive.

I have mixed emotions. From a nostalgic point of view, it was a good day. It's when I confront the schism between myself and my parents that I feel miserably unhappy. I'm disappointed that I didn't have a chance to talk with my mother seems to be no possible solution to our differences, no way even to approach either of them. Even so, whether I like them or not, my parents are my parents no matter what. I just want to stop feeling wrong.

Nevertheless, I am satisfied that I did well with Mrs. McLean, managed to disguise my increasing emotional remoteness from her lost son and the life he and I once shared. At Christmas, my preoccupation with Rick was overshadowed by Steve's presence, but today it's Rick who is constantly with me, and my memories of Steve are all just that: memories. It scares me to think I might have become like Margaret McLean if Rick—and she—had not come along to show me the way.

This visit to Clearyville catapults me into a disturbing bout of introspection, much as the visit in December did. I love Clearyville, the laziness of it, the simplicity, but I know for certain that I no longer belong there.

Maybe it's over with Rick; maybe it isn't. I am apprehensive about how he will treat me when I see him—ignore me, insult me, tell me he never wants to see me again—but I have to risk it. I need to be near him.

The last time I looked at the clock beside my bed, it read 3:45 a.m. Luckily I'm able to give myself a little extra time in bed because Jennifer is still in Clearyville. She always stays a few days longer before my father brings her back to the city. She is her grandparents' pride and joy, and every visit with them is an event in her life. I've long since given up trying to figure out how my mother, so cold and non-nurturing with me, can be such a warm, loving grandmother to my daughter.

Rick's door is closed, but there is no Privacy Requested sign on it, so I knock lightly and go on in. Just like I expected, nothing has changed. He's basically as I left him on Tuesday. I realize that deep inside me I've been praying that some part of what I said to him on Monday actually penetrated his consciousness and things will be different today. As I advance toward the bed, a sigh of frustration and disappointment manages to escape me in spite of my effort to stifle it. At the sound, Rick's head swivels in my direction, and my heart skips a couple of beats.

"Good morning," I announce with a nursely chirp. "How are you feeling today?" I touch his arm as I usually do at the beginning of a visit. He stiffens but doesn't turn away from me, a small sign of progress since the day before yesterday. The strap has been removed from the right side of his face, and the damaged eye is looking much better, allowing him to glare at me angrily with both eyes.

He reaches out and snatches the clipboard from the bedside table. Someone has mercifully attached the pencil to it, so that now he can just somehow position it against the cast on his other arm and begin to vent without having to depend on someone to set it up and hold it for him.

why not come yesterday

He catches me totally off guard. "I . . . I meant to leave a note for you with the nurse," I stammer. Of course, I never meant to leave him a note. Why would I try to communicate with someone who refuses to acknowledge my existence? I didn't think he would care whether I was there or I wasn't. "We went to Clearyville for the holiday," I explain, taking pains to keep my voice even. "The town has a big party every Fourth of July and my parents always expect Jennifer, Kathy, and me to come home for it." Though he gives no indication that my words register, I feel compelled to continue. "I've been so focused on you, I didn't even remember it until Kathy reminded me the other night."

He turns toward me. After a moment, he stiffens. "Rick, are you in pain?" I ask.

He glares at me, and I am intoxicated by his responsiveness, even his anger, which I deliberately ignore. "How are your exercises going?"

He shrugs his good shoulder in indifference, but the tiniest hint of a smile in his eyes betrays him. I remember that I'm not going to let him manipulate me anymore.

"Chris—she was your nurse in the ICU—"

know who Chris is His pencil attacks the pad, and his face clearly spells disgust and impatience.

"She mentioned on Friday that you were having pains in your legs. Do you still?"

Better now

"Have they given you something for the pain?"

don't know what they give me, don't care

This is what a lot of patients say when they start to accept the reality of their situation, though they usually experience a change of heart during rehab, when they finally see some progress and don't feel so hopeless. Until then, it's a hard attitude to change and a worse one to work with.

I move nearer to the bed. "Rick, I know you're depressed and frightened but, as I told you on Monday, you're the person who determines the rest of your life. Either you work with what you have or you don't have a life at all."

He covers his eyes with the heel of his palm for a minute, then lets out a big breath and picks up the pencil.

you've been there

"Yes, until you came along and made me see what I was doing to Jennifer and myself." He nods. "Now it's your turn. At least, try. Read a newspaper, watch the news—"

He drops the clipboard on the bed and turns his head away. I sense that he's worn out. So am I—emotionally exhausted, frustrated, and discouraged. I've gone as far as I can go for now.

"Okay. I've said all I can say. Just one more thing. Promise me you won't give up."

He raises his hand, presses it against my face. I hold it there for a quiet moment, then draw away, return the clipboard to the nightstand, and go to work.

Rick is sleeping when I stop by on my way home, and I take a couple of minutes to get acquainted with Patty, the nurse who I was told is in charge of his case. She looks to be in her thirties and is familiar to me from the elevator and cafeteria, though until now we've never had occasion to meet. She's soft-spoken and low-key. I doubt she will be as good a source of information as Chris has been. But then this is just a stopping point on the way to the rehab unit. Rick probably won't be in this area in the hospital complex much longer. I've been trying not to think about the move, and get an anxious, prickly feeling whenever it sneaks into my mind. I keep telling myself there is still the "meanwhile"; he won't leave here until the doctors say he's physically and psychologically ready. As it stands, his physical progress is pretty much on target now, but let's face it, trying to rehabilitate a withdrawn, recalcitrant patient has about as much chance for success as trying to milk a steer.

I probably should be ashamed to admit that I've always looked forward to the few times a year when Jennifer stays in Clearyville after I come back to the city. It's not that she's ever been difficult or demanding; Lord no. It's my job that's demanding, often hard to walk away from at the end of the day. Getting away from it for even two days of solitude has always been enough to restore my energy and equilibrium. Tonight, though, the apartment feels empty, lonely, and I'm wishing that Jennifer had come home with me this time. All of a sudden she seems so different, and the change is a little frightening. Or am I imagining things? Can she actually have undergone such a transformation in less than a month? Her seventh birthday is not even two weeks away. Can the difference between six and seven be this striking? Lately there have been times that I've felt as if I'm meeting her for the first time, as if there's another little girl—a Jenny that Rick and Kathy know but that I never knew existed—and I have an uneasy feeling that I'm wasting precious time being away from her. It's very strange.

It's nine o'clock now. I should call the Simons with an update, but what is there to tell them? I'm no longer on the inside. Besides, I'm sure they're keeping in close touch with the doctors themselves. Or maybe Rick has convinced them that he's making wonderful progress, though judging by what his mother said to me in April, I suspect he can't con her as easily as he does everybody else. Still, I did agree to call them regularly, and I was raised to keep my promises. I glance at the clock. It's 9:07 in Chicago now, 10:07 in New York. Too late. I'll call them tomorrow.

The Wohlsein Rehabilitation Center is housed in a large one-story building connected to the main hospital by outdoor paths and an underground tunnel. Built about fifteen years ago, it was specifically designed to provide treatment for victims of spinal cord injury. It seems like an incredible freak of fate that of all the serious injuries Rick might have sustained, it was the one that would be most likely to send him to the hospital of which his grandfather had been a founder, rather than to one of the numerous others in the Chicago area.

The rehab is filled with paraplegics, quadriplegics, and people with traumatic brain injuries. Not all were victims of the road. Some were hurt in falls, some in athletic mishaps; others have tumors or were victims of violent crimes. A few have tumors. Many will never walk again, while some will recover completely within a few months. Still others cannot know for sure what the future holds for them. The one thing all of these people have in common is that his or her body will never be the same as it was before whatever it was that brought them here.

The fact that Rick has made it to this stage of treatment reminds me of the days following the accident, when his doctors did their best to explain his condition to us but couldn't say much about how things would go later on down the road. All they could do was suggest that we just hope for the best. The situation was complicated and there would be a great many decisions to make along the way. During the initial surgical intervention, they had removed bone chips, studied the site of the injury, and eventually arrived at a working diagnosis. What it came down to was that certain vertebrae had been crushed and certain nerve roots damaged, causing paralysis and loss of sensation in the organs and limbs below the waist.

Mrs. Simon had laughed tearfully. "It took me eighteen months to train him and it was a struggle from beginning to end. Now it all has to be done again."

The situation had looked pretty grim. More tests had been scheduled, resulting in the possibility of further surgery. By that time, Rick should have been wide awake and coming to grips with himself, but he wasn't, so the neurologists took precedence for a little while. Only one, Dr. Sabir, was optimistic.

After the Simons had returned home, they called the doctors every couple of days. Lenore also called me frequently for my input on how Rick was progressing on a personal level. What I saw and what Chris told me didn't amount to much in the way of offering the family hope, and the phone calls from New York stopped. As of today, I haven't spoken to Rick's parents in two weeks.

Last Wednesday, however, Dr. Sabir's hopeful prognosis was at last confirmed by his colleagues; there was a good chance of fiber regeneration and restoration of some muscle control. Nobody cared to say what constituted the odds of a good chance exactly, but it sure sounded better than being told Rick definitely would never walk again. We were all greatly encouraged, except for Rick, who still preferred hibernation. By the time he became borderline responsive, they had decided that surgery was out; physical therapy and retraining were in.

Now it's time to start the next phase of treatment: rehabilitation. From now on, Rick's future is up to him. It's also time for us to accept the fact that there is nothing more we can do for him. The speed of his recovery, his will to succeed, and how hard he's willing to fight to regain some semblance of his previous function are dependent upon his motivation. It's also time for us to accept the fact that there is nothing more we can do for him. He's finally back in charge of his life.

This is how things stand on Thursday, July 12, when Rick is transferred to his new quarters.

It's a long walk from the main building to where Rick is, which means I won't be seeing him nearly as often as I did. The good news is that visiting hours are much less strict at the rehab unit, and patients who are perambulatory or ambulatory are not confined to their rooms. We are hoping this increased freedom will revive Rick's sunken spirits.

Except for me, Kathy was the first person to visit, but she came home disappointed at his lack of response and said she wouldn't go back until he's in better shape. After a couple of information calls following the accident, no one at the television station showed much interest in Rick's condition, until this week, when Jack Ryan, accompanied by somebody else from the newsroom, came around. Apparently all those eager young girls whose attention embarrassed and annoyed Rick in the company cafeteria have moved on to more attainable pastures. The other day, Rick's dissertation advisor stopped by. He's a very nice older gentleman, who told Patti that

Rick is one of the most promising candidates he's ever had, and he will not give up on him.

The rehab unit presents some difficulty for me. I don't know anybody working over there, and my uniform doesn't seem to cut any ice with the nurses. It's more obvious than ever that my days of privilege are over, and it strikes me as ironic that as far as my relationship with the Simons is concerned, the shoe is now on the other foot. It isn't that I need to be in the middle of their drama; I just find coping easier when I know exactly what I have to cope with. I don't like having to settle for the usual noncommittal information given out by the staff to those who are not closely related to the patient, but I can't imagine myself calling the Simons long-distance two or three times a week to find out what's happening almost under my nose.

And so it's goes. A week, two weeks. True, Rick has recovered sufficiently to be fitted for a body cast, and he's been moved from the frame to a regular hospital bed. He's gotten that far physically, but emotionally he remains unchanged—distant, detached. I speak to a nurse in his wing, and she smiles at me, the meaningless nurse-smile that thanks you for your concern while tacitly telling you that it's really none of your business. "He is depressed," she says.

"I know that," I snap. "But he's never going to be able to get anywhere if he doesn't come out of it. Don't you do anything over here to help these guys with depression?"

"We're doing everything we can," she assures me placidly, in a soothing-syrup tone that makes visions of violence dance in my head. It's all I can do to get my mind under control again. "His social worker and his occupational therapist and, of course, his physical therapist have all been seeing him regularly, so you can be sure he's getting the best of care. You just keep coming and talking to him and making him feel he's important to you. That's the best thing you can do for him."

"He is important to me!"

"Of course he is," she cooed. "And he needs your support." The level of violence in my mental images is escalating rapidly. Florence Nightingale herself would have surrendered her cap in shame if she'd had my thoughts.

I arrange to meet with Rick's social worker and occupational therapist. They admit he's a difficult case, that he doesn't seem to be trying very hard. "He's depressed," they say, "but we're working with him. We've seen it all before. Don't be discouraged." How many times have I said those very words to worried families in the same practiced way they're being said to me? I do not like being on this end of a medical situation.

The physical therapist that Rick has been assigned to points out that at least he is submitting to the exercises.

"Submitting? What does that mean?"

"Well, let's just say that he isn't fighting me . . . but then, that's the best part of working with hostile paraplegics. However ticked they are about their situation, they can't kick you, no matter how much they want to." At the moment, I am too frustrated to appreciate first-year med student humor, and he, unexpectedly sensitive to this, immediately becomes serious. He assures me that in time, the patient's outlook will improve and progress will be made. He has plenty of experience with stubborn cases, he says, and he can already see what he's up against with Rick. He—his name is Curt—seems to be genuinely caring. I like him and pray he will be able to crack Rick's shell.

He adds casually, as I am leaving the office, that he suspects that Rick's mother's visit over the coming weekend will have a good influence on his attitude and that by next week, they'll all know better how to deal with him.

"His mother is coming?" I ask with a pang.

"Didn't he tell you?"

"Does he know?"

"I was in the room when he got the letter."

"Oh," I say lamely, feeling as though someone had stuck me in a tender area with a hypodermic needle, even though I know that it's only an acute sting of exclusion. Rick's parents are coming, and though an almost complete stranger knows about it, Rick hasn't seen fit to mention it to me. If I have to choose one moment when I know my relationship with him is over, it is this one.

"I bet they'll be able to turn him around," he continues. "It's tough, being away from everybody who really cares about you when you're in a bad situation like this."

As I look back on today, I know that what the therapist said is not true—I'm here for Rick—but I wish it was. I want to wake up tomorrow morning not caring anymore. I want my old life back, the cocoon, the vacuum, the limbo, with Rick only a distant memory as Steve is now. I don't want to have to spend another six or seven years rebuilding, remolding, regretting. I want it now, complete control of myself, mind and body. I want no longer to need Rick as he no longer needs me. I've served my purpose in his life, whatever it was, and

I don't begrudge him having used me. I was raised to a life of service to others, and I understand the pitfalls. I just can't bear being left behind anymore. In all these years, I haven't learned a thing. I've found no foolproof method for escaping the horror of losing someone I care about. I haven't discovered a single survival technique. My instincts for self-preservation are no sharper than they've ever been. No matter what people in Clearyville think about me, I feel I am the same Mary Grace McLean I was six years ago, when I first came to Chicago. I haven't done anything for myself. If I've changed, it's Rick who is responsible.

And now it's over.

July 27, 1973

When the phone rings at seven thirty Friday evening, I am in the middle of dealing with two tasks I have assigned myself for tonight, one of which I have been putting off for months, and another, which is probably doomed to fail no matter how hard I work at it. The first consists of getting rid of several piles of magazines, paperbacks, newspapers, and junk mail that have been accumulating for months. I suspect that one will get done in the usual way: keeping most of the books, half the magazines, and not even glancing at the junk mail before I dump it in the incinerator. The second will be much harder to accomplish: exorcising Rick from my life. I am working on both at the same time. I expect the call is from Kathy to remind me that Jennifer and I are meeting her tomorrow morning to apartment-hunt. She's outgrown her shabby little studio with the pocket kitchen. I take this as a sign of maturity and am pleased that she's asked me to go along. The voice on the other end of the line, however, is not Kathy's. It's Lenore Simon's, and she is calling from her hotel room downtown. She arrived in Chicago around five and has spent the past two and a half hours with Rick. Could I meet with her tomorrow morning?

I don't know what to do. Meeting with her could weaken my resolve and I don't think I should risk it right now. Yet I can't say no; I promised to be here for the family, and I can't back down on that. "Yes of course," I agree and invite her to come at eleven.

I return to the small circle I've cleared amid the stacks and think about why she wants to talk to me. Maybe she'll tell me that they've finally persuaded Rick to have his physical therapy in New York, so she is here to make arrangements for transporting him. She might have come just to spend a little time with him. It could be anything, and I finally give up second-guessing. *Just go with it, Maggie*, I tell myself. Now that he can travel, there's really no reason for him to be a thousand miles away from home. I get done around eleven fifteen, drink a cup of tea, and lie awake wondering whether tomorrow will be the day I'll be jerked back into the life I was so fervently wishing for this morning.

Kathy comes over at about nine on Saturday to take Jennifer to the Shedd Aquarium, but when she hears I've invited Mrs. Simon for tea and cookies, she talks Jennifer into baking cookies with her first. As I do a quick cleanup in the living room, I hear them laughing and singing in the kitchen. The sound of them warms my heart. When the cookies are done, Kathy puts a half dozen in a baggie and she and Jennifer take off downstairs to wait for Todd and start their day.

Mr. Simon is involved in a "legal battle" in New York, so Rick's mother—I keep forgetting, I'm supposed to call her Lenore—has come to Chicago by herself. Well, not really by herself. She is with a girl whose short curly black hair and hazel eyes lead me to assume she is Rick's other sister, Kerry. She isn't. Her name is Ronnie Taylor. She and her family have lived next door to the Simons since she and Rick were children. I ask Ronnie if she is in school, and she answers that she is studying library science at a college near her home. She shifts uncomfortably in her chair. I offer coffee, but they both decline. Lenore sits patiently during my attempts at being a proper hostess, but I can sense her own eagerness to get on with whatever she is here for, so after a brief silence, I suggest she tell me why she wanted to see me.

She starts with a quick recap of Rick's situation to make sure we're both agreed on his status. "He's still on soft food because he says his cheek hurts too much when he chews," she begins.

"His jaw wires will be coming off in a few days," I remind her, "and it will be easier for him to eat."

She nods, then continues. "He cooperates passively with physical therapy and he's responsive only when it's absolutely necessary. He stares at the ceiling for hours at a time, exhibiting no interest in the outside world. Is that true, Maggie?"

"Yes." I want to add "he behaves like a child," "manipulates everyone," and "why don't we just get to the point?" but I hold my tongue.

Lenore, however, does get right to the point. "We didn't realize how hard Ricky's been fighting recovery." I detect in her voice what I can only describe as a weary sadness. It is painful to hear.

"I have told you several times how depressed he is," I remind her gently. "Haven't the doctors said anything about it?"

"I guess we've been in denial." She sighs. "This just can't be happening." Ronnie puts a supportive arm around her shoulder.

"As soon as you left, he withdrew into himself," I say, repeating what I'd already told her on the phone. "No one's been able to reach him." They say nothing. "Then you stopped calling me. I assumed you'd been speaking with the doctors as often as you needed to, so I . . ." *So I what? Reneged on my promise to keep in touch?*

"The doctors are only rarely available," Lenore continues, "and I don't trust what the nurses say. They often try to put a better face on the situation than it deserves, and the doctors—since Ricky's been at the rehab—we don't know them and they don't know us. I sometimes get the feeling that they haven't really seen him. They're just reading words from a chart."

"It's true there are now other professionals on the case," I assure her, "people who know more about various therapies than the orthopedists and the neurologists do, but I know for a fact that Dr. Sabir is continuing to oversee Rick's case. Rick is still his patient, and Dr. Sabir is very conscientious."

Lenore bites her lip, appears to lapse into deep thought for a moment, then says, "I think the only thing we can do is take him home. I can't leave him here like this any longer."

I look down at my hands, not wanting them to see my stricken face. *I was right. It's official now. It's over.*

Lenore turns to Ronnie. "I'll speak to Dr. Burden tomorrow about the best place for Ricky in the city or on the Island."

Ronnie nods.

Lenore draws herself up straight and leans forward to touch my hand. "Maggie, there is nothing else you could have done. There's no way we can tell you how much we appreciate your help."

"Thank you," I whisper, my words as faint as hers are suddenly decisive and forthright, as if she's suddenly done a 180° turn.

It's twelve thirty Sunday. Jennifer and I have just finished lunch. As I clean up, I try to think of something we can do this afternoon. This is a new challenge for me now that Rick and his weekly outings to the park, the movies, and the lake are gone. Though she mentions Rick only occasionally, I am convinced that his absence has left an empty place in her life, and I am trying to fill the gap.

The phone rings, and once again I find myself talking to Lenore. I didn't expect to hear from her so soon. She says it is urgent that she speak with me. My first impulse is to explain that the afternoon is promised to my daughter, but she sounds distraught, and I tell her to come over. I'm instantly concerned about Rick, but my gut tells me not to get involved anymore. He's going home. I'll never see him again.

The bell rings within a half hour. "I hope I'm not interfering with your plans," Lenore says hastily.

"Well, as a matter of fact, I usually try to spend the whole day with Jennifer on Sundays. We were planning to go out for a while." I realize immediately how rude that sounded and wish I hadn't said it. I try to cover by asking if the girl she brought with her has gone back to New York.

"No, she's still with Ricky and then she'll go back to the hotel to meet a friend . . . Maggie, I wish you had mentioned your plans on the phone. You have little enough time to spend with your daughter. I'm sure my little problem will work out just fine. I just thought . . ." She picks up her handbag and turns toward the door.

I feel like an insensitive fool. "Please, Lenore. Don't go," I insist. "I can take Jennifer over to the park a little later instead. It's something Rick used to do with her a lot"—*pang in my stomach*—"and she's very happy being there."

"Then why don't we get her things and take her now? We can talk just as easily there."

I protest—she doesn't seem like the park-sitting type to me—but inside of fifteen minutes, we have collected Jennifer, the fruit, the thermos, and a bag of park toys, and we're rushing across the boulevard.

The sky is bright and blue, with a tier of thick white, purple-edged clouds hovering on the horizon, the kind of clouds that have a habit of suddenly rushing forward, blocking the sun, and turning everything gray. A vision rises in my mind's eye of Rick dancing home from the park in the rain, Jennifer perched on his sneakers and, for a moment, I feel as dismal as the park looks when clouds move in and obliterate the sunlight.

"I'll bet Ricky liked it here," Lenore remarks. The past tense upsets me. "He's always loved being outdoors. Whenever spring came and it was time for the kids to line up their summer jobs, if he had a choice between indoors or out, he'd always go for the outside one. He was a lifeguard at the club for, oh, his last three years in high school, and one year during college, he even worked on a construction crew. He'd come home dirty, sweaty, aching all over. He certainly didn't need to do hard labor and I thought he was crazy, but that's what he wanted. In fact, he once told me he liked that job the best of any he'd ever had." She smiles sadly into the distance, maybe at the memory of her high-class college-boy day laborer.

"He did like it here. We used to come a lot."

We seat ourselves on an empty bench under a tree on the perimeter of the playground. I glance around the concrete area to see where Jennifer has disappeared to and spot her in one of her favorite places, the sandbox. There are several other children in there, all some years younger than she is, and she has removed herself from them and into the particular corner she always claims when it's empty. Sometimes a younger kid will try to usurp her territory, and she always gives it up willingly, not wishing to fight for it. If no other spot is available, she will quietly pick up her things and climb out of the large concrete box. Another image of Rick fleetingly crosses my mind: he is sitting on the edge of the sandbox in his jeans and faded shirt with his bare feet in the box, idly sifting sand through his fingers or playing some silly game with Jennifer. I want to describe this to his mother, but I can't say the words. I miss him being here so much . . .

Lenore accepts an apple, and we sit, munching, for a while. She seems to need an indication that I am ready to listen, so I prompt, "You have something you want to talk to me about?"

"Yes." She nods. "First, I want to apologize for being so abrupt yesterday, I mean about my decision. I know it upset you. I wasn't very . . . tactful, and I'm truly sorry."

I'm grateful for her sensitivity, of course, but she could have done this on the telephone. There has to be something else. "I'm usually more successful at hiding my feelings," I respond, actually somewhat embarrassed.

"I suppose you have to be." She takes a tissue from her handbag, wraps her apple core inside it, and looks around for a trash can. There's one at the end of the next bench, and she strides quickly to it, tosses the apple, and comes just as quickly back. The day is warm, but with a brisk breeze that ruffles her carefully arranged hair and flutters the jacket of her summer pantsuit. She doesn't look like Rick's mother should look. Susan's maybe, or Jody's, but not Rick's. She is the most pleasantly ordinary of short plump women, and I think again of Rick in the sandbox, his blue-black hair tumbled by the wind, his teeth dazzling as he laughs with Jennifer, the grayish sand white against his olive skin, and the mothers, those young mothers, their attention torn between him and their babies. I wonder at how the most ordinary people can produce the most extraordinary children.

Seated again, she looks in my eyes for a long, disquieting moment. "I've made a terrible mistake," she says at last. "I didn't know until last night how much Ricky means to you. That probably sounds very dense of me but, as you say, you know how to hide your feelings."

"After I lost my husband, I had to learn to be independent. Being emotionally strong is a very important part of being independent."

"Yes," she agrees. "I can understand now how hard this thing with Ricky has been for you. We've been so unfair to you."

"No, you haven't. I took it on myself—"

"I wonder if you remember a few months ago, the first time we came to see Ricky in Chicago—"

"You gave me a warning. You told me I should be careful."

"Yes, I think that's what I said."

"That's why I say I've taken this on myself. I remember exactly what you told me."

"I still don't know if I was wrong to speak out like that. Richie, my husband, was angry with me for interfering. He said it was none of my business, that you and Ricky were both adults and capable of managing your own lives—"

"I didn't think you were interfering."

"But he was right. The thing you should know is that I didn't say it just for your sake, which is how I think it sounded. I did it out of my own need too. There were things I felt guilty about, and that's what made my husband mad."

"Lenore, you don't have to explain."

"I do if I want you to understand about the rest."

I have no idea what she is referring to, but she obviously needs to talk about it, and with Jennifer right in my line of sight, I'm willing to listen.

"I don't know if Ricky ever told you about this girl he was engaged to at Amherst."

"He mentioned her once." *But what has that have to do with anything?*

"And that he jilted her?"

"He said they broke up after he graduated. It was a bad time in his life."

"His life!" she hoots. "It was terrible for everybody. Did he mention that she was the daughter of a professor who had taken him in as though he were a son? They thought so highly of him. He practically lived at their home for a year. I don't know. Maybe he thought he could repay them by marrying their daughter, but it certainly wasn't necessary. She's a lovely girl.

Well, to make a long story short, after graduation, he arranged for Devon and her parents to come to visit us for a weekend. We'd met briefly at his graduation a few weeks before and, at that time, he'd told us that he had asked her to marry him. We told him we thought he was too young, but he said his mind was made up, and though they wouldn't be married for a while, at least not until he'd gotten his master's and had a good job, he had asked her and she had accepted, and he wanted us all to get to know each other. Ricky had gone with one girl after another for years, so Richie and I decided he must know what he was doing, and anyway, he'd always had a mind of his own, so there wasn't much we could say about it.

So Devon and her family came down from Massachusetts on a Saturday. All our kids were there. That night, we had a big fancy dinner at the club, made the formal announcement, and did all the things that are done on such occasions. The professor and his wife were so thrilled to have such a smart, accomplished young man in their family and we thought, and still do, that Devon was one of the loveliest girls we'd ever met. We all liked her immediately. Anyway, the next day, with the leftovers still in the icebox, Ricky took Devon for a walk on the golf course and told her very simply that he had made a mistake and he just couldn't go through with it. He wasn't ready. Needless to say, the world turned upside down. Though Devon and her parents behaved much better than we deserved, it was horrible. Instead of returning to Smith in the fall, she went to England, their original home, and as far as I know, has been there ever since."

While Lenore's been talking, I've noticed Jennifer glancing over at us every few minutes. I wonder if she needs to use the bathroom, but don't feel I can interrupt Lenore to go and find out. Toward the end of the story, she comes running over and settles herself on my lap, at which point Lenore stops speaking entirely, though I have the sense that there is more she wants to say. I send Jennifer back to the playground with an apple, watching her as she ambles obediently toward the swings.

"Is she always so well behaved?"

I smile and nod, and Lenore comments, somewhat distractedly, "The only time my children have ever listened to me was when I was speaking to someone else."

"Sorry for the interruption," I say, hoping she'll continue with what she was saying. I want to hear the end of the story; maybe then I can figure out the point of her telling it to me.

I don't have to wait. As soon as Jennifer is beyond earshot, Lenore says, "I don't talk about that to many people, as you might imagine. We weren't proud of Ricky and what he did to Devon. Nor am I terribly proud of myself as a mother. Like most mothers, I feel responsible for my children's conduct. I don't know how I fail when I do, but I feel it nevertheless." She smiles. "My husband, on the other hand, has a totally different perspective. He believes he's done his best raising the kids, and that's that. Ricky was twenty then. Old enough, Richie thought, to take responsibility for his actions, if not for getting married. He was furious and disappointed with him. I doubt he'll ever completely forgive him for showing so little character. I guess he's right—I don't know—but his attitude only made me more protective. I didn't give Ricky the chance to feel guilty. I felt it for him. I know that now, and I've been determined not to let him hurt anybody else. I persuaded him to live at home during the year he was at Columbia getting his master's. I was wrong to do that. It only pushed him further from us, out of our reach. And then, I tried to prevent him from getting involved with you, not through him—I was afraid to approach him—but through you. I know now that what guided me mainly was my own guilt. I've been wrong about everything, but I didn't know it until I saw your face yesterday and then spoke to Dr. Burden and Barbara Perez, today."

"The social worker."

"Yes."

I'm still no nearer to figuring out why I am hearing all of this or what I even think about it. I feel as uncomfortable as I did the day Rick unloaded his problems on me. Don't these people know that shrinks go to school for years to learn to help people deal with problems like this? That old sense of "what am I doing here?" returns. How did I get so involved with this family? I always thought "arrangements" like Rick's and mine were supposed to be casual. I feel bad for this woman; I can't imagine that she deserves the heavy load she's placed on herself, but I have no background in psychology, and being basically a nonjudgmental person, I have no opinion of my own about her feelings of responsibility for her son's behavior, any more than I know whether I deserve to hold myself responsible for his driving the motorcycle off the road. Yet in the same way she punishes herself, so do I punish myself. I don't like much of what she's told me so far. I'm not even sure I'm someone who should be hearing it.

The clouds are moving closer, are nearly overhead, and the park is beginning to take on a silvery sheen. The air remains warm. I look around for Jennifer and find her this time near the rocking horses, patiently waiting her turn. We've already been here for almost an hour, and I don't know how much longer she'll hold out. Lately she doesn't have the staying power she used to have. I mark it up to her associating the park with Rick, and his not being here anymore.

Lenore notes my distraction and says quickly, “I’m taking a long time to tell you what Barbara and the doctor told me in fifteen minutes. I’ll try to get it over with so you can take Jennifer home.”

“Oh, she’s okay,” I respond defensively. “She’ll let me know when she wants to go.”

“Well, if you think . . . ,” she concedes with hesitation, clasping her hands tightly in her lap.

Her misery hurts me—how could it not?—but it also makes me feel stronger. In some mysterious way, it allows me to distance myself from her situation and be more objective, and I sense myself becoming a professional again. It feels like control, and I am comfortable with that. “Tell me what Dr. Burden said,” I urge gently and hear my voice sounding like that Sympathetic Nurse Doll I find so irritating in my coworkers.

She doesn’t speak again right away, seems almost to be organizing her thoughts, maybe choosing her words with particular care. I concentrate on Jennifer swinging happily to the push of some other child’s mother. When was the last time I pushed my little girl on a swing? I wonder sadly.

“I was lucky to catch him on his rounds this morning,” I heard Lenore say. “You can’t imagine how hard it’s been connecting with any of these people on the telephone from New York, especially Burden. The man never returns calls, even collect, and I feel as if I’ve spent my life on long-distance these last few months. Anyway, when I got here, I left messages all over the hospital for him to find me. I said that we were leaving tomorrow morning.”

“Are you? Leaving tomorrow?”

“We have early reservations. That’s the reason I’ve been so insistent. Saturday is such a bad day to reach a doctor. I didn’t really expect to see him, but believe it or not, he walked into Ricky’s room while Ronnie and I were there. After a quick look at his patient, he started to rush away, but stopped and forced himself to give me a few minutes.

She becomes more and more relaxed as she relates the meeting, which took place in the hall outside Rick’s door. At first, Burden had been pleasant, actually had made an attempt to appear unhurried. She expressed her surprise that the family had not been informed of Rick’s emotional condition, and he explained smoothly that he deliberately had not told them in order to avert their rushing right out to Chicago. Puzzled, she asked him why he felt that she and her husband should not be involved. With that, the tone of the meeting changed; the doctor’s charm vanished, and whatever rapport she had felt was instantly gone. This was clearly a man who did not like his authority to be challenged.

"That's nothing new to me," she says. "The men in my husband's family tend toward overinflated opinions of themselves, though Richie has somehow escaped that, at least in his personal life. Of course, being familiar with ego trips doesn't make them easier to deal with when your son's life is at stake."

I say sympathetically, "I've never worked with Dr. Burden personally, but I have heard that he does tend to be rather . . . matter-of-fact . . . with his patients' families. Still, I've never heard anybody dispute the fact that he's an excellent doctor, and in the end, that's what counts."

They'd never thought they were interfering, Lenore had protested. "We only meant to offer support. We've always been a close family, always available to each other. All the children know that and expect it."

The only help Rick needs now, Burden had countered bluntly, is his own. He has a long and difficult road ahead of him and if your son is going to make it, it will have to be on his own two feet and not on the backs of his family.

I know in my heart Burden is right. I know that families need to hear what he said to Lenore. I just wish he could've been kinder about it, but that's not his style.

"He told me—us—to go home and stay home. Let 'the boy' pick up his own pieces. Said we can support and encourage all we want, so long as we do it from a distance."

I can't help myself from taking her hands in mine. "I'm so sorry you had to go through that," I say.

She laughs. "Oh, don't be. I didn't expect to be spoken to so callously and it hurt, but I did pull myself together enough before he hurried on, to tell him that there was no way I was going to leave my son here any longer. I told him we wanted Ricky moved to the best rehab center we could find in our area and the sooner the better. I said, 'Thank you very much, Doctor, but we feel it's important for him to be in a place where people really care about him as a person, not a case.'"

I almost do a double take. "You said that to Dr. Burden?"

She smiles sheepishly. "I did, but I have to confess that I never would've been able to if I hadn't lived with the Simons for twenty-five years. It's true what they say, Maggie. The rich and successful *are* different. When I first came into the family, I was like the Little Match Girl, the perfect embodiment of a poor, downtrodden little waif. Lucky for me, it didn't take long to learn that that was like committing marital suicide. The Simons do not respect weakness. It took several years, a lot of conscious effort, and a little bit of acting to get tough, but I've done it. The only problem is that it's never become second nature, so the assertiveness usually takes a little time to kick in."

It is at this moment that I realize that I have come to feel comfortable with Rick's mother, odd couple though we may be. I want to ask her more about her life as a Simon wife, but I spot my daughter coming toward us. "Here comes Jennifer," I say quickly. "I can tell she's ready to go home. We can talk on the way, if you don't mind."

"Of course not," she assures me with a smile. "We might even beat the rain too."

I notice now that the clouds are crowding the treetops, the sky has gone dark gray, and we are the only people left in the park. As we start up the exit path, Jennifer sprints past us, her sand pail bobbing back and forth at her side, reminding me of a day in the spring when she scraped her knee painfully and Rick, trying to divert her, wore her pail on his head with the handle as a chinstrap all the way home. Jennifer thought it was hilarious and forgot about her knee. Rick was like that sometimes. He would let you think that he existed in near-total self-absorption, and then suddenly he would dance in the rain or grab your face and kiss it gently or wear a pail on his head to cheer you up. I want to tell his mother about this too, but I don't. I can't, because these memories are all I have left of him, and I just can't share them.

I give Jennifer milk and cookies to take to her room while she watches her little television set. She considers this a rare treat; I consider it bribery. I shut her door and join Lenore in the living room. She accepts my offer of tea and follows me into the kitchen. As I am filling the pot, I remember what it is she hasn't talked about.

"So your meeting with the social worker went better than the one with Dr. Burden," I coax as we wait for the water to boil.

"Yes. When I had spoken with her earlier, she'd sounded so young that I thought, 'Oh no. Not someone else I can't have confidence in.' I made up my mind that as soon we were finished talking, I'd look up air transport companies for information about moving Ricky back east. But when she told me she'd meet me in her office in the hospital today, Sunday, I decided I'd give her a chance. I told her everything. The phone calls Ricky never accepts or returns, the letters he doesn't answer, my anger about us not being informed of everything that's going on here. I told her how shocked I was by his condition and about the talk with Dr. Burden, how upsetting it was. She listened to everything I had to say, afterward conceding that Burden is not known for his sterling bedside manner. She said she wished she'd been able to speak with me first.

"It turns out that she's been seeing Ricky for his twice-a-week scheduled appointments since he entered the rehab five weeks ago and, because he's a challenge, has also taken to dropping by his room whenever she's in his area." I breathed a sigh of relief as soon as she told me this; just knowing that somebody is taking an interest in him made me feel better. But that didn't last long. Right away she confessed that at this point, she's tried everything she can think of to reach him, and he hasn't bought any of it. The kettle shrills, and I jump up to turn it off and fill the cups as she continues.

"He stubbornly refuses to acknowledge anything any of his therapists say or try to do with him, to the point where his physical therapist is concerned that unless he begins immediately to get his muscles back in shape and his impaired organs retrained, he'll wind up spending the rest of his life in a home for the disabled somewhere, lying on his bed staring at the ceiling the way he's been doing, while his body shrinks and shrivels."

Tears threaten Lenore's eyes as she relates this, and a lump rises in my throat as bleak images flash past my mind's eye. I can't think of anything to say in response to what she has told me, and we drink our tea in silence.

Eventually Lenore looks at her watch and sighs. "I really do have to go and let you two have some time to yourselves." She pulls herself to her feet. "May I use your phone to call a taxi?"

"What time is it?" I ask, surprised the afternoon has gone by so quickly.

"Almost four."

It's been less than three hours since she knocked at our door, maybe a long-enough time for her to have unburdened herself but not for me to feel that I've heard everything about Rick's situation. I still have a strong suspicion that there is something more she wants to tell me. I don't know where this idea comes from, but I can't seem to shake it.

"Of course you can use the phone. It's on the little table in the dining room."

When she's done, I ask if she's still planning to leave tomorrow.

"Yes," she answers, returning to her seat, "on a 9:10 flight. I still have four children at home. My husband is buried in complicated litigation, which means he's spending long hours in the office. Though our housekeeper is entirely competent to take over and the kids love her, I'm the one who should be with them while they're worried and upset about their brother."

I'm tired and wrung out, but sometimes I feel as if I've been tired and wrung out since I met Rick. Yet I can't be feeling as downhearted and miserable as his mother. "Where are you going now?"

"I suppose it's an exercise in futility, but I'm going to see Ricky, if I can. I'm at the end of my rope with this situation, and we simply can't let it go on. But who knows? Maybe I'll hit on the magic word that gets him to pull himself together." She lowers her head and laughs. "I'm getting punchy. Sorry."

"And now?"

"Back to the hotel to pack."

"And Ronnie will be at the hotel?"

She looks up with a forlorn smile. "No, she's spending the night north of here with a college friend. We're going to meet at the airport in the morning. Thanks again, Maggie, for letting me impose on you and Jennifer. Unfortunately for you, our cousins in Kenilworth have been on an extended vacation in Europe. Otherwise, they'd be bearing the brunt of my visits."

This is new to me. "I didn't know you had family in the area. Rick never mentioned it."

"Oh yes. They run the firm's Chicago office. Rick has visited with them a few times since he came out here. They had just left for their long-awaited trip when Rick was hurt, but their kids must have told them about it. They've sent cards and flowers and have called several times to find out . . . Oh! Did I just hear the cab? Already?"

I stride to the living room window, which overlooks the front of the building, and see the waiting taxi just below. "It's here."

She takes up her handbag, and I accompany her to the door. As I open it for her, I am almost overcome by a powerful rush of emotion—a mixture, I think, of sympathy and warmth for this woman. I don't want her to have to spend the evening alone in her hotel room.

"Lenore," I blurt, "come back here after you've seen Rick. Please."

"No, it's enough, Maggie. I'm not going to—" The taxi driver honks impatiently. "The cab's waiting—"

"Please. I would like very much for you to come back."

Again, we hear the blare of the horn. Lenore takes a harried breath. "I'll let you know after I've left him." She dashes out the door toward the staircase. I run to the window and watch her disappear into the cab and watch the cab turn the corner into the late afternoon traffic on the boulevard.

I've been sitting at the dining room table for a half hour trying to decide what to do about Jennifer's birthday on August 8, ten days from now. Every year I take vacation time the week of her birthday and we drive to Clearyville for a family dinner followed by a party with my parents and Kathy, Steve's mother, and Bobby. My mother makes the birthday cake from scratch, always a yellow one, decorated with pink icing and tiny edible shapes made of sugar. It never varies; only the number of candles changes. I supply the hats and noisemakers. Jennifer wears her best summer dress and shoes. We sing the "Happy Birthday" song and the three of us stay overnight. This year will be no exception.

Whatever possessed me to so impulsively ask Lenore Simon to come back later? I'm bone tired from all the talk in the park and here. I'm exhausted from all the confessions, the regrets, the stories, the emotion. All Rick and I were supposed to be were casual lovers. How did it get to be my drama too? The other thing I can't figure out is why she is telling all of this to ***me****. Maybe I'm safe for her because once Rick goes home, we'll never see each other again. Maybe because she can't keep the fear and frustration inside herself and I'm handy. I don't know why she trusts me, but I'll listen as long as she needs me to, no matter how it wears me out. Lenore Simon is a warm, caring, humble person, and I feel close to her. She's the woman, and especially the mother, I would like to be someday.*

I hate this unsettled feeling, yet I dread the thought of going back to the way we used to be, the lack of activity, the dreary, boring repetition of everything in our lives. Eleven months ago, we were living in a different universe, one in which we'd never heard of a Rick Simon. Until he came, we rarely went to the park across the boulevard. Jennifer had never even eaten fast food or been to the Aquarium. I'm ashamed of how I limited her world, of how I forced her to share my desolation. It's time now for us to start over.

But, dear Lord, how do I begin to do that?

I clock out for lunch at noon the next day and hurry down to the cafeteria to meet Lenore. She called yesterday at around six to say that when she'd gotten to Rick's room, she'd found him, to her amazement, against a slant board reading the *New York Times* and so much like himself that she decided to stay an extra day. She wondered if she could come over to the hospital today and have lunch with me. I told her I'd meet her in the cafeteria at noon.

We settle at a table in a back corner. I have less than an hour, and I don't know where to start, so I pick up my tuna salad sandwich, take a bite, and wait for her to speak. She doesn't, and I ask her if everything is okay at home. We talk for a few minutes about the family. Finally I prompt her to tell me about her time with Rick this morning.

She shakes her head slowly. "It's so sudden, Maggie," she says with a quiet smile. "I haven't got it straight in my mind yet. I . . . just—"

"You saw him this morning?"

"Yes'. He had twenty minutes between physical therapy and occupational therapy."

"And he was like he was last night?"

She took a deep breath. "No! I was scared to death I'd find him the way he's been for all these weeks, but no." She says this with—how do I describe it?—wonder. Wonder, as if she's just witnessed a miracle. "It was almost as if he'd never been away. How can this be?"

"I'm not sure he ever was away," I confess.

"You think he's been faking it?" Her tone is incredulous, and as so often happens, I instantly wish I hadn't said it.

"No, not faking," I amend quickly, as if I haven't had my suspicions. "More like hiding."

She sips her tea slowly while she considers this. "Maybe . . . ," she murmurs, then switches subjects. "He couldn't get over the date, and said that the last he remembered, it was June 11, which, of course, was the day of the accident."

I experience a sharp twinge of excitement. "And?"

"And nothing." She shrugs regretfully. "Said he has no idea what happened. Can't believe six weeks have passed. He has no memory of knowing, right after the initial surgery, that he was in the hospital, and when I asked him if he was aware of anything at all those first weeks, he said he had no sense of time, so he can't say what was happening when. He could feel himself slipping in and out of awareness but, though he tried, he couldn't seem to stay awake. It was if he'd been drugged. He has no idea how long that went on." She shakes her head again. "He does vaguely remember us being here during a more lucid time and that he tried to write on a piece of paper, but he has no idea what he actually wrote. When I told him that we had no idea either, he laughed. He thinks it was around then that his lucid times began to be longer and more frequent. He knows that at some point he wrote notes to you too, and talked to you, but he's forgotten what you and he talked about. The only thing he remembers clearly is that he was angry with you for nagging him." She lifts an eyebrow at this and smiles. "When was that?"

"When he was still in the private room. I gave him a pep talk and I guess I overdid it a little. He wrote me a nasty note."

Her smile widens.

"Lenore, do you have any idea why he . . . happened . . . to . . . surface . . . last night?"

"I asked and he said he's confused right now, but that the doctor told him that it's possible everything will eventually come clear. He asked about you and Jennifer."

To my dismay, I flush.

"He said that he doesn't really know if he was even thinking most of the time," she continues. "It was as if he were in the middle of a dense cloud, dimly aware of movement and sound around the edges, but unable to grasp what was happening or being said."

I glance at my watch—fifteen minutes left—and finish my sandwich.

"What do you think, Maggie? What does this mean? I'm so afraid to get my hopes up. I'm so scared that one day you'll call us to tell us he's gone under again, that this was just an aberration."

"I'm not sure, Lenore, but I don't think that's something you have to worry about. It looks to me as if he's coming out for good. He may never remember what he did on June 11 or who visited him in the hospital, but that's not important. I truly believe it's time for a new start. The doctors I've spoken to are encouraged, so you can go home with a lighter heart than you came with. You know he's in good hands."

"Yes," she murmurs, "thank God for that." She takes a moment to drain her cup, then looks at me. "This brings me to something I must talk to you about before I leave."

I sneak a look at my watch again. Ten minutes. "Can we—my time is getting short," I say apologetically.

"Call your supervisor, Maggie," she says, uncharacteristically firmly. "Tell her you're with me and we're in the middle of resolving something. It will be okay. I promise."

Whatever it is sounds ominous, as if I'm in some kind of trouble and Lenore Simon knows about it. But what could it possibly be? Without a word, I walk quickly to the house phone on the back wall of the cafeteria and do as she ordered. And it was an order, not a suggestion.

My supervisor responds pleasantly. "Take as much time as you need, Maggie. I understand the situation."

Is this the same Sergeant Sharon who I've known for six and a half years? Personality transplants must have become available while I had my back turned.

"What is it?" I ask curiously when I get back to the table.

"I'll explain," she replies, "but please just listen to everything I have to say before you ask a question or make a decision. Okay?"

I settle back with a mixture of mild trepidation and some expectation.

"I'll make it as short as I can," Lenore begins. "Last night I asked Ricky once again to come home to recuperate, and once again, he refused. I told him he would have all the goods, services, and support he needs, and that we believe he'll be better off with his family, instead of a thousand miles away. He replied that he basically has all the family he needs in Chicago right now and if he's at home, he'll be waited on and catered to and treated like an invalid, and he might get to like it. And anyway, he'll be home as soon as he has his degree, and he has no intention of leaving Chicago without it." She looked away and slowly moved her head from side to side, a gesture of hopelessness.

"I'm sorry, I—"

She sighed. "I already knew how he would respond, but I just had to try again. At least, we'll have the option of talking to him on the phone once in a while. But listen . . . Richie and I have discussed this from every direction and have come up with an idea that we think will hasten Ricky's recovery and lessen the anxiety we've been under for the past two and a half months. We've taken the liberty of researching the pros and cons, and"—What on earth does this have to do with me? It sounds like a business deal—"and what it comes down to is this: we're wondering whether you would be interested in doing private duty with him. From the beginning, we've been struck by your tenacity, patience, and common sense. We believe he needs to be surrounded by these qualities more than ever now. We know he has many frustrating and difficult days ahead of him, and we think you're just the right person to get him through them . . . So, Maggie . . . do you think you could consider staying on with him here?"

Think? I can't think. I'm stunned out of my mind. How could I—how could they even think I would give up my job, my patients, my routine?

"Don't answer right away. Think about it. It wouldn't be a really hard job. Actually, you'll be more of a companion than a nurse as time goes on. He'll stay here in rehab, of course, the regular nurses would handle some of the—well, more unpleasant jobs."

Say something, Mary Grace. Speak. "But—"

"If you're concerned about your current job and what will happen when Ricky is ready to leave, don't worry. You'll get your job back, if you want it."

"How? I don't understand."

"The hospital has agreed to give you an extended leave without pay. For however many months he'll need you, you'll be working for us. It's been assured and you'll have it in writing."

In writing? Good Lord, it *is* a business deal. Is this something their law firm is involved in? What will happen if I say no?

"You can have it any way you want it. We're thinking of a thirty-to thirty-five-hour week. You choose your own hours. The pay will be somewhere around one and a half times to twice what you're getting now, depending on the shift, and we'll pay for a sitter for Jennifer so that Kathy doesn't have to make herself available if she has something else to do." She watches my face quietly for a minute or two, obviously trying to gauge my reaction. I have none; my mind is a blank . . .

"I know this comes as kind of a surprise to you," she continues, "but perhaps you can at least tell me if you'll consider the offer. I promise we'll understand if you say no, and there'll be no hard feelings."

Except . . ."Does Rick know about this?"

"This morning. He said it was fine with him."

My heart is beating rapidly. "Uh," I squeak. "When do you need to know?"

Lenore smiles hopefully. "A week or two? Would that be enough time to look at it from every angle? We know it will probably play havoc with your routine for a while, but we honestly believe it would be a good move for all of us. If we didn't think so, we'd never have asked you." She stands, picks up our cups and my plate, glances at the wall clock. "I think you need to go back to work now. Please apologize to Mrs. Vincent"—Sharon—"for me for keeping you this long."

I pick up my bag and meet her at the exit. "I don't know what to say, Lenore. This is totally overwhelming."

"Everyone deserves a break at least once in life, Maggie, and you've more than earned this one. Call me when you've decided. Maybe, if all goes well, I won't have to come out again for a while."

We exchange hugs, and she starts toward the tunnel to rehab.

"Lenore?" She turns. "I'm totally overwhelmed. Thanks again."

"Call me when you decide and don't worry. You haven't seen the last of us yet." She smiles as she moves down the hall.

"Thanks," I call. "Have a good trip home."

I return to my floor, head spinning, almost breathless with the excitement and anxiety triggered by the Simons' offer. Sergeant Sharon, filling in for the desk nurse, watches with just the tiniest hint of a smile as I come out of the elevator. I can feel her eyes on me as I punch back in. She knows about this; I'm sure of it. She knows, and she's wondering what I'm going to do.

That makes two of us.

I've gotten to hate having to make decisions.

Life used to be simple. Come home from work, make supper, get Jennifer into bed. Sit on the sofa reading a book or watch a program on television. Go to sleep so I can wake up the next morning and do it all over again. In those days, it was just Jennifer and me, a doorbell that was almost never used, and a telephone that seldom rang.

Then one night, Rick Simon came to dinner, and everything changed, for the better in many ways, but with an anguished uncertainty in my heart that has left me confused, distracted, and tired. And I see now that all the hours I've spent trying to figure out why it's been this way have been for nothing.

In the beginning, I blamed Kathy for starting the whole thing, but that was clearly ridiculous; all she did was bring a guy she liked to my apartment. Then I blamed Rick for my predicament. But that was stupid too; it takes two to have a relationship. So I went higher up on the power chain, to fate, to life, even to God. Nothing fits. It's only now that I realize what should have been obvious to me from the beginning. It's all been a matter of choices—my choices. From the beginning, I could have said no instead of yes.

It's not as if I don't know how to make decisions. Hospital nurses have to make them all the time and often in a split second. As worn out as I might be on a rough night shift, I still know without having to think twice what needs to be done and how to do it. So how can I honestly blame extreme fatigue or Rick himself for my giving in the night we had sex for the first time? In spite of my guilt over knowingly betraying Steve, I said yes. And I could go back over all the other dilemmas that have disoriented me this year—whether to go the restaurant with the Simons in April, whether to confess to Lenore about her son and me, whether to pressure Rick about his plans in June, and so on and on—and it would still be me who bears the responsibility for my inner turmoil. And it is me who is in charge of my life and the road I will have to travel to get to where Jennifer and I need to go.

The simple fact that I can even consider renouncing all those years that I lived in total denial and self-deception about Steve astonishes and excites me. This sudden surge of determination is like a charge through my body—electrifying. Spiritual. I will take advantage of Lenore's offer and not because of the money or the hours. While they'll make life easier for me, I've managed for six years without those luxuries. And though I'm certainly grateful for the opportunity, I'm not doing it to help bring Rick out of his own personal black hole. Here, I even allow myself to admit the truth—I wanted to accept the opportunity the moment Lenore offered it to me. If I did have any real qualms about giving up a familiar, comfortable job in which I've had six happy years, to spend eight hours a day with someone whom I am inexplicably drawn to, but who scares the living daylights out of me, they're gone now. None of those things are as important as my need to be with Rick. I can't explain it, but right now—*God forgive me*—I just have to be with him.

So in the end, this one's for me. Just for me.

I was still feeling pretty rocky emotionally when I came to Chicago and went to work for Carol and Jerry as the receptionist at their clinic. One night, not long after I was hired, Carol came down to drive Jerry home. He was in the middle of minor surgery and was going to be a while, so she decided to wait for him. We began talking. It was then that I told her that I had lost my husband and that I couldn't understand why I was still unable to come to terms with the loss even though it was almost eight months since we'd gotten the news. Carol explained to me the seven stages of bereavement: shock or disbelief, denial, anger, bargaining, AND SO ON . . . *She told me that I was in the denial phase and would eventually pass out of that one and through another, maybe even a couple of others, before I reached acceptance. I had never heard of this before, so she wrote down the stages and gave them to me. Having the list actually helped me; at least I could define what I was feeling.*

Steve had liberated me from certain ingrained aspects of my life that I had never really felt comfortable with since I was a teenager. Despite the fact that we came from the same background, he was much more open, much freer than I was. In the short time we had together, he taught me to be the person I was instead of the person I was expected to be. When he disappeared, it was as if my real self vanished with him. I had nowhere to go but back to my parents, and it didn't take long for me, in my grief, to regress completely. I retreated from the world into what I picture in my mind as a small dark cave, and except for the hospital, I hid there for six years until Rick forced me to emerge and be the person I wanted to be. It's like Rick simply continued what Steve had started.

Lying in bed later and savoring the headiness of the day, I realize that because of my vacation, I will not have the couple of weeks to wean myself away from my patients that I thought I would have—but, in reality, will have only four days. For a moment I can't imagine actually being able to leave my patients flat like that. But only for a moment.

August 3-9, 1973

Friday, my last day at my job, is nowhere near as difficult as I thought it would be. None of the patients I had when I first met Rick are on the floor anymore, and though I haven't been aware of it till now, I've been distancing myself from my new patients in the last few months, something I'm not proud of. The staff knows I'm going to the rehab unit, but only a couple have put two and two together and ask if I'm going to be taking care of "that kid who was in the accident a couple of months ago." I nod, but I don't elaborate. The way gossip flies around this place, I don't know why they even have to ask.

At a quarter to five, I make my final rounds and tell each of my patients that I'm leaving for a new job. At five o'clock, I walk out of the main hospital door without looking back.

During the afternoon, I had called the babysitting agency Lenore had chosen. I explained that I would need someone to begin on Monday, the thirteenth, that the hours of service might vary, and that the ending date was uncertain. I named the hourly wage that Lenore had mentioned. The coordinator asked when I could meet to talk with the three people she would be pleased to send over for my approval. I told her that we would be out of town for a few days but I could do it on Friday.

"That's cutting it pretty close," she said with a tinge of reproach, "though I do have a couple of very competent girls who will be ending their current situations tomorrow."

Our leaving Clearyville on Friday instead of on Sunday isn't going to make Mother very happy with me; she's never been able to tolerate sudden changes unless she's the one doing the changing. "We'll be back by Friday noon," I assured the woman. We settled on a time, and I gave her our address and directions, then hung up, smiling smugly about the shorter amount of time that I will be spending in Clearyville. I also congratulate myself for having the nerve to bring Jennifer back to the city with me. It will be the first time I haven't given in to my mother's insistence that I leave her with them for another week or two.

The evening is spent wrapping Jennifer's birthday gifts, packing, and steeling myself for being back home. If only next week will go as well as today has. It might. All I really have to do to make that happen is stay out of Mother's way, speak when spoken to, and take no initiative.

I go to bed with a feeling of calm and self-confidence. The hard decision is behind me, my job has ended, and now I can put all my energy into getting ready for my new position. I fall asleep immediately.

After I graduated from high school, I got a job in the office of the Christian college in Waynesburg, a few miles from Clearyville. One day, after I'd been there about a year and a half, Steve McLean came into the office, handed me an envelope, and asked me to make sure it went to the registrar. Of course, I knew who he was. We'd been in the same class until third grade, when he was sent to a different school, and though his family had stayed in our church, he hadn't gone to our Sunday school. By the time we were both attending the regional high school, we only recognized each other in passing. Now he was standing at my desk, staring at me blankly.

"You're Mary Grace Hill," he said finally. "We were in the same graduating class."

I nodded. "And you're Steve McLean."

He held out his right hand. "Good to see you again, Mary Grace. Are you a student here?"

"No, I just work in the office."

"Ahhh, okay . . . Well, I'll see you around then." He was already backing toward the door.

"See you around, Steve," I echoed. "Tell your folks I said hello."

"I will." He disappeared into the hall, and the door closed after him.

A month later, he came in again. This time he asked me out. We had a really good time, and I began fantasizing about him. I went to church every Sunday and found it puzzling that he was never at services with his parents. The first several times he took me out, he didn't say anything about religion, and I was too timid to ask him about it, maybe because I was afraid I wouldn't like the answer. It may sound weird that I was harping on it, but religion had always been such a major part of my life that I couldn't imagine myself with someone who didn't believe. After we'd been dating for a while, though, he brought up the subject himself, explaining that although he did and always would believe in God, he no longer felt comfortable with many of the tenets of our families' church. He'd found a church in the next town that was more tolerant of their congregants' right to worship in whatever way was comfortable for them. When he had discussed the change with his parents during his senior year in high school, they had grudgingly accepted it. Now I understood why my mother's enthusiasm for Steve as a viable marriage prospect was somewhat less than I had expected.

As Steve and I grew closer, we often talked about the religion issue, and I began to realize that not being totally devoted to our church did not mean I had totally forsaken God. I found myself, for the first time, admitting that I resented our church's sanctimonious rigidity. Nevertheless, I continued to attend services with my parents until after our wedding. Steve and I moved to a small apartment in Waynesburg, where we were both working, while he saved up for drafting courses and, ultimately, a degree in architecture. It didn't take any urging from Steve for me to decide to switch to his church. He reminded me I was a married woman now, and though my parents might make a fuss, this didn't make me a sinner, and my parents couldn't get me into hell if they had an "in" with Satan. The transition was much easier than I thought it would be.

Then Steve was drafted. He left for boot camp on November 15, came home for Christmas, was sent to Vietnam in January. Maybe it was denial, but I, then in my second year of nurse's training, didn't realize I was pregnant until early March. I was terrified. I gave up our apartment and moved back to my parents' house. I didn't write Steve about the baby until late in April. A month later, he was declared missing, and three months after that, our baby girl was born. I was in complete conflict about God, who had given me Steve's baby but taken Steve away, even whether God had anything to do with any of it in the first place. I agonized for months, each day bargaining with Him that if He couldn't bring Steve back, could he please show me the way out of this maze of grief and confusion? God didn't answer. Mother did it for him. "Pull yourself together, Mary Grace," she ordered. "You're not the only woman to have lost a husband. You have a child to raise. Do you expect me to raise her for you?"

No, I didn't expect that, and I pulled myself together. By Thanksgiving, I had enrolled in the second semester at a university nursing school in Chicago. Mother, who had decreed years before that I was to be a nurse—"and no argument about it, miss"—relented since she had enough time coming to her from work to take a year off to keep Jennifer while I completed my training. I would take my daughter back when I had a job and had made arrangements. So all by myself and scared to death to be alone and on my own, I found an apartment, got an evening job at Jerry's clinic, and finished my courses.

I went home every weekend that year to see my daughter and try to put up with Mother's jibes about my ability to manage once I took Jennifer to Chicago. I made a vow that as soon as Jennifer and I were settled in the city, I would never again be dependent on anybody for anything. I brought her to Chicago on a cold, blustery day the following January and I did build a life for us. Maybe it wasn't a very satisfactory life, but it was secure and safe. I thought I was happy. And I will be happy again, no matter what it takes.

Kathy and Todd are over for dinner. Yesterday when I told Kathy about Lenore's offer, she said right out that she thought it would be a mistake for me to take the job. I told her that if it turned out she was right, I'd let her know.

"What was wrong with the way things were?" she now asks peevishly.

"Nothing," I answer. "I just think it's time for a change."

"But—," she starts, then cuts herself short as her confused expression turns into a knowing smirk. "Oh, I get it. Now you're working for rich people. We're not good enough for you anymore."

"Good Lord, Kathy, besides sounding like an old black-and-white movie," I retort while trying to swallow my anger, "that was insulting."

"Well, everything was fine until you got mixed up with those people."

"You brought Rick to my house, remember?"

Todd, who has been listening to us with the same level of interest he might lavish on a hockey game, now decides to jump into the fray. He turns to Kathy. "You mean, you were dating that guy too?"

"No!" Kathy barks defensively. "We worked in the same building. He was new there and I invited him to Maggie's for dinner."

"Just being a Good Samaritan, huh?"

I get up, quickly gather the empty plates, and hustle them out to the kitchen, from which I can hear them talking heatedly, but too low for me to make out what they're saying. I set a peach pie on a plate and grab a pint of vanilla ice cream from the freezer. By the time I get back to the dining room, they've come to terms with each other and are holding hands. As I slice the pie onto their dessert plates, Kathy says quietly, "I'm sorry, Maggie, I didn't mean to insult you."

"Never mind, Kath. It's okay. I just don't ever want you to think like that about me. I'll be making good money and I'll have more time for Jennifer. Besides, it's only temporary. As soon as Rick gets back on his feet, he'll go home and I'll get my old job back."

"I sure hope so," she says, but she doesn't sound very hopeful it will happen.

I haven't seen Rick in almost a week. During his first two weeks in rehab, I went over a few times, but he was distant and apathetic, and it wasn't worth the trek. This only supports my sense that the relationship is over, and I'm a little concerned that it won't be Rick who will be my biggest challenge on this job but my ability to treat him as objectively as another nurse would. In retrospect, I think the weekend with Lenore has been good for me. She has more confidence in me than I've had in myself for a long time, and I intend to justify that confidence.

I'm supposed to meet Kathy and Todd this afternoon to take Jennifer to see *Tom Sawyer* and go to the Pizza Hut afterward, but I call Kathy around ten to say I have to go to the rehab unit for an orientation. This is not true, but I don't want to get into another hassle with her if I tell her I'm going to visit Rick.

"Why do you have to do that today? It's Saturday," she complains.

"Because we're going to be in Clearyville all next week and I need to get this over with before I start the new job. It's not a big deal, Kath. You can go without me."

There is a short pause, then Kathy, brazen as brass, says, "To be honest, Maggie, I don't believe there is any orientation. You'd just rather spend the day with Rick instead of us is all."

I gasp—more, I think, at her audacity than her frankness. Shades of the shaving kit incident in the spring flood my brain as I come face-to-face with the reality that where Rick is concerned, there will always be conflict with my family. I don't want that, but I did lie, and guilt is already setting in. "You never used to challenge everything I say!" I retort with the anger of the defensive.

"And you never used to lie to me!" she declares with the calm of the righteous.

"Okay," I sigh. "I'll make a deal with you. If you stand by me next week when Mother starts in on me about Rick, I'll"—*only to save face, Lord, I swear*—"skip the orientation and go to the movie. But I have things to do before we leave for Clearyville, so I really can't go for pizza."

The silence is longer this time, but finally she relents, grudgingly. "Fine. We'll take Jenny back to my apartment. You can pick her up later."

"Thank you."

Click.

Saving face doesn't come free, though. It's the same face I'll have to put between my sister and me whenever we meet from now on.

It's three thirty when I get to the hospital. Rick is propped up in bed, surrounded by books and writing furiously on a long yellow legal pad. His arm cast has been replaced by a much smaller, lighter one, and he's wearing his glasses. In general, he looks much more like he used to, and I feel as if I'm getting my first glimpse of the light at the end of the tunnel.

He looks up when I enter the room, but doesn't say anything. Just gives me a blank stare. *Oh Lord. Lenore made it sound like he was back to normal. Am I going to have to put up with this every day? Well, if there's anything I've learned from Rick, it's the withering sound of sarcasm. Though I'm not officially working here yet, I think I will give the moody Mr. Simon a dose of his own medicine.*

"Are you talking to me today or should I turn right around and leave?" *It doesn't sound withering though. Too much like my regular tone. Oh well, withering is just not my style.*

Rick blinks, then smiles apologetically. "Sorry, I was concentrating. I guess I have to relearn the art of rapid mode-switching." His voice is mild and friendly.

"I didn't know you were working again. It's good news." *Good? It's wonderful.*

"I haven't been sleeping much at night since I got here, so to fill the hours constructively, I've been forcing myself to get back into the dissertation. All it's done for me, though, is put me to sleep." He says this with a straight face, but it's been so long since we've had a coherent conversation, I have to wonder if he's joking.

"Maybe you've been sleeping too much during the day," I suggest.

"I don't have time to sleep during the day," he counters.

"Well, I mean between therapies and bed care."

"I'd never do that," he protests. "You think I want to miss my soap operas?"

I stare at him. "You watch soap operas?"

"And you're forgetting I'm Mike Douglas's biggest fan."

I squint suspiciously. "Tell me you're kidding me, Rick."

"I'm kidding you, Mary Grace," he says earnestly.

"Well, that's . . . that's good." I smile approvingly, though I'm not 100 percent sure I believe him. "Because if I have to sit here every afternoon and watch those soap operas, you'll have to find yourself another nurse."

"So you're going to go through with it," he says, in a kind of offhand way.

"With the job? Of course. Why?" *Didn't Lenore say he'd agreed to the arrangement?* A queasy uh-oh feeling starts in my stomach. "Your mother told me you said it was okay with you."

"That part is fine, Maggie. If someone has to be here, I'm glad it's you." He gathers up the pad, pencil, and newspapers, sets them on the tray table, and pushes the table out of the way. "I just wonder if you thought the whole thing through before you said yes. You do realize that you might not get your job back when this is over. We have clout in this place, but even we don't have the authority to create a position for somebody just because his private contract expired."

"I know that, Rick. And believe me, I didn't accept the offer on a whim. I couldn't afford to turn down your parents' terms. With this job, I can build a nest egg. Maybe even have a little home someday. And there's so much more. A babysitter when I need one, flexible hours, things I never dreamed of having. Somehow they got the hospital to call it a leave of absence so that when you go home, they'll have another place for me. This will be so good for Jennifer and me." *And you're alive and healing, Rick, and some of the old sparkle has returned to your eyes . . . Dear Lord, thank You for bringing him back.* "Your folks have been so worried about you. Your mother's been nearly out of her mind."

"I know that, Maggie. That's why I was afraid you'd let them buy you."

Buy me? How could he even think such a thing about his parents? I sit down on the side of the bed and lay my hand on his. "They didn't buy me. I want to do this. Jennifer and I care about you, you know."

It's as if a cloud crosses his face, and he looks away. I glimpse the nasty gash near his ear from the rim of his helmet when he hit the tree.

Remembering how it looked that first night makes me wince, even though it's healing nicely now and is mostly covered by his overgrown hair. I suspect it will be high on the list if he ever goes through with the plastic surgery. He says in a low, muffled voice, "Forget it, Maggie. I'm a losing proposition. Why don't you get your doctor friends to introduce you to somebody who can make you happy?"

"I don't want somebody who can make me happy. I like being with you." It seems like a logical answer to me—it's the truth—but just like that, the cloud disappears, and Rick bursts out laughing . . . and laughing . . .

"Oh God, Maggie," he finally manages to sputter, "don't do that. I just had physical therapy and every working part of me is sore." He rubs his diaphragm and dissolves into another helpless fit of hysterics.

"I wasn't trying to make you laugh," I protested. "What did I say that was so funny?" *Remember me? The nurse without a sense of humor?*

All I can do is stand by as he holds his good hand firm over his mouth, tries to stifle the laughter and pull himself together. I caution myself not to place too much importance on his way-out-of-proportion reaction to whatever it was I said; likely it's just some kind of autonomic response. Eventually he runs down and is able to catch his breath. Wiping his eyes with the back of his hand, he, not surprisingly, tilts his head back in exhaustion. I lean over the bed, rearrange the pillows so he can place his head more comfortably. "How's that, Rick?"

"Good," he answers and looks up into my face with that penetrating stare of his, that *look* that turns my legs to jelly and sends thoughts of Italy, a country I'll never know and don't even want to, whirling around in my head, while certain sensations, which I don't want either, course through my body.

I start to back away, but he reaches toward me with his good arm and touches my cheek. *No!* Unable to break away from his eyes, his hand, his aliveness, I do nothing to stop him from pulling me down to him. *Maggie! How can you let this happen? You are his nurse now, not his lover.* Whatever good sense I have managed to hold on to since that night in January vanishes the instant he kisses me. At first it's a gentle, tentative kind of kiss, almost as if he's uncertain or shy. But within seconds, it becomes deeper and then almost—I can't say passionate, because I don't feel passion coming from him—almost frantic. For someone whose ribs were aching five minutes ago, he's breathing hard without complaint. I try to say his name, try to pull away, but his mouth presses harder, and he holds on to my arm with a strength that, given his circumstances, both takes me by surprise and scares me. It can't be more than a minute, however, before he runs out of steam and I manage to break loose. He sinks back against the pillows with his eyes closed and his chest heaving. I immediately straighten up, horrified that I allowed this to happen, that I find myself in a hospital room in which both patient and nurse have racing pulses and flushed faces. This is something nursing school didn't prepare me for.

I hear a faint squeak behind me. "Excuse us . . . are we interrupting?" a female voice asks, and every nerve in my body springs to attention. I turn slowly, expecting to see a tech or a volunteer poking her head in. Instead I discover a man and a woman in their thirties, tan, well dressed, and bearing gifts. I take a quick look at Rick. His arm is over his eyes, and his chest is still moving, though a lot less violently than it was a minute ago. Oh no, he's laughing again.

Thanking the Lord I'm not in uniform, I get up and approach the visitors. "Can I help you?"

"Well, yes, we're here to see Rick, but maybe we should have called ahead," the woman explains. "I guess we came at a bad time."

"Oh, hi," Rick says a bit breathlessly. "I had a . . . a . . . spell and she was giving me some mouth-to-mouth resuscitation. But I'm better now. Come on in." He is leaning back on his elbows, smiling and obviously trying to keep down quiet little bursts of laughter. "Maggie," he says, "these are my—hun-hunph!—cousins, Joyce and Greg Green." I hurry over to help him sit up. "This is Maggie McLean, my—hun-hunph!—sorry, the nurse who's going to be babysitting me during the summer." He shines his grin on me. "Thanks, Maggie—hunph!—I'm fine now."

I, in turn, smile at the couple and, mumbling, "I'll get another chair," flee from the room. Since the chair will be for me, I take my time using the ladies' room and having a cup of coffee in the visitors' lounge, which is empty at the moment. When I return to Rick's room with a folding chair and a pitcher of ice water, Mrs. Green—Joyce—is speaking enthusiastically, probably about their trip, assuming these are the relatives from Kenilworth whom Lenore once mentioned briefly.

"—history was fascinating. They'd been invited—can you believe it?—*invited* to settle there in 1590, and they remained respected and prosperous citizens until just before World War II, when most of the town was almost decimated by both the Axis from the mountains and the Allies from the sea. Much as I like Modigliani's work, I don't think I ever knew that he was born there or that he's also—do you know Modigliani's work?" she asks Rick.

Even I've heard that name. Italian, I think, but an artist or an opera singer?

"Only if he's the one who does those long, skinny women."

"That's the one," she confirms.

Rick looks as if his eyes are about to glaze over as she continues her story. The nurse in me wants to tell them he's very tired and they'll have to leave soon. I've kicked family out of a patient's room more times than I can count, but for some reason, I am hesitant to do so with these people. Lucky for me, then, that Mr. Green touches his wife's arm. "Joy, don't forget what the nurse at the desk said."

His wife stops in midsentence. "Oh, I got carried away. Sorry, Ricky, the nurse at the desk told us we shouldn't stay too long and here I am babbling on about Italian art history. Besides, you were in Italy a couple of years ago, weren't you? It occurs to me that you might have done Livorno yourself."

Rick valiantly tries to stifle a yawn. "Uh, no, we didn't. Actually, we flew into Rome without any idea of where we were going from there, so we flipped a coin and south won." The laughing appears to have exhausted itself. How long was I gone? No wonder he's tired. "We ended up in Taormina. Also indescribably beautiful." He flicks his eyes toward me quickly and smiles. My heart quickens, and I flush—again. *In a manner of speaking, I've been there too, and yes, it was indescribably beautiful.*

The Greens don't notice. They're already on their feet and moving to the bed to give Rick the packages they brought. She kisses him on the cheek, and he shakes his hand. Rick thanks them for coming and bringing the presents, and invites them to come back soon with their vacation pictures. Then they nod politely to me. "Nice to meet you, Ms. McLean. Take good care of this guy. And, by the way, if you think he's a handful now, you should've known him twenty years ago." Rick smiles wanly.

"His mother may have mentioned that once or twice," I respond dutifully while I walk them to the door. "Perhaps we'll meet again the next time you visit."

After they've gone, I turn back to Rick, who is lying back with his eyes closed. "I'd better go too, Rick. I'm supposed to meet Kathy, Todd, and Jennifer at the Pizza Hut."

"Why didn't you stop me?" he groans, looking at me from beneath his lids.

"From what?"

"From saying what I said before they left."

"Don't you want them to come back?"

"Oh, sure. But without the pictures."

"They seem very nice," I tell him.

"They're fun, but travel pictures are boring as hell."

"Well, I suppose after you've had a near-death experience and spinal surgery, anything else would be boring."

"First, you're funny. Now you're ironic," he murmurs, yawning. "And you say you have no sense of humor." His voice is fading.

Now what did I say? I'll probably never know. I look around for my handbag and find it just where I'd left it, on a table across the room. While rummaging around in it for my keys, I say lightly, "Rick, I'm going to be away for a week. Jennifer, Kathy, and I are leaving for Clearyville on Monday and I have to pack and take care of a few things before we leave. But I'll be in on the Monday after to start working with you. Okay?"

Rick says nothing. He's already fallen asleep. Remembering the scene last month when I got back after the Fourth, I write him a note and leave it on the tray table.

It's eleven Monday morning, and I'm at the kitchen table drinking my fourth cup of coffee. Ever since I finished the newspaper two hours ago, I've been thinking about Margaret McLean and the last words she said to me last month. *Go on with your life. Do it now.* If only my mother could say that, but I can't get her to discuss anything with me, let alone the way my life has changed. I wish I could talk to Lenore Simon. She's so easy to confide in, and I know she'd understand. Carol is a good listener, but she's a professional, and I keep thinking she's hearing things I'm not saying or I'm not consciously aware of. And my father. I used to be able to talk to him about things that bothered me. Now it's as if my mother has set up a kind of war situation. Anyone who isn't on her side is the enemy. She has always had ways of punishing her enemies, and I've seen her use them. It doesn't surprise me that neither my father or Kathy want to get between my mother and me.

For the tenth time, Jennifer comes into the kitchen with the same questions: "When are we going to Grandaddy's? Why can't we leave now?" She's beginning to sound fretful.

Well, why can't we? We're packed. The birthday things are in the car already. Why can't we—no, why can't I—just pick up and go? This time I tell her, "Okay. I'm ready. Get your toy bag together while I get dressed. We'll go in about fifteen minutes. Okay?"

She dashes off.

The telephone rings, but I don't answer it. I know it's Dad wondering where we are. Let them think we're on our way; we will be in another twenty minutes. As we pull away from the curb, I utter a silent prayer, *Please, God, let this week at least be tolerable . . .*

The minute we get inside my parents' house, I know my prayer hasn't been answered. It's close to twelve thirty when we arrive, and Mother, who is on vacation, has had lunch on the table since noon sharp, which is the time we've always had lunch when she isn't working. Now she's on the warpath. Though she goes about her business in tight-lipped silence, it's not hard to tell she's more than just angry. She slams around until the meal is over. Dad gives Jennifer a kiss, me a nod, and Mother a look of total consternation, then goes back to the factory accounting office to finish his workday. I start clearing the table, but Mother barks, "That's my job, thank you," and grabs the plates out of my hands. I motion Jennifer out the back door to the yard, where, I notice, Dad has brought out our old croquet set and has put up the wickets. The chipped, color-striped mallets are in their stand nearby. My friend Marjorie and I used to play when we were kids, but I've forgotten the rules, and I don't see any instructions lying around. Maybe Dad remembers. I shrug and sit down on the grass, and Jennifer sits down next to me.

"Mommy, why is Grandmom so mad at us?"

"She's not mad at you, Jen. She's mad because we were late for lunch."

"Lots of times when I'm here and you go home, Granddaddy and I are late, and she doesn't get mad with us."

I give her a little smile.

She frowns and thinks for a minute. "Is Rick gonna be there when we get home?"

What on earth—? Jennifer hasn't asked about him in weeks. Why now? "He's not ready to come out of the hospital yet, but he's working on it," I answer calmly. "What made you think about him?"

"I don't know. I just want to see him. You never take me where he is."

"He hasn't wanted any visitors since—"

"His mom came to see him a lot."

"Well, moms and dads are always allowed. But Jody and the other kids in his family haven't seen him either."

"'Cept Susan."

"Right. But none of his younger brother or sisters. Rick needs time to be alone while all his hurts are healing."

"Oh," she says sadly. "I miss him."

"I don't think it'll be much longer until you can see him. He gets a little bit better every day."

She nods. "I don't like when Grandmom gets mad. She gets a scary face."

I think to myself, I've felt the same way most of my life, but I don't say anything. What can I say? Your grandmom is a totally unreasonable person who wants everything to be the way she wants it to be? Can I tell her her grandmom behaves like a manic-depressive? How can I explain these things to a child who isn't even seven years old?

Jennifer seems to be as deep in thought as I am, and I'd give anything to know what's in her mind right now. Happily, this new Jennifer doesn't make me wait.

"Remember last time when we came here for Fourth of July? In the morning when I woke up and went downstairs, Grandmom and Grandaddy were in the kitchen and I heard them talking and they said that Mary Grace has gone crazy . . ."

Uh-oh.

"And that Rick is one of them and he doesn't fit in her house . . ."

What does <u>that</u> mean?

"And he shouldn't be allowed near Jenny because he's dirty and a bad infulence. I went in the kitchen and I told Grandmom that that wasn't right. Rick isn't dirty and he's very nice and I like him a lot!"

"Jennifer? Wait—," I interrupt, but she doesn't hear.

A tear rolls down her cheek as she continues. "And I told her my mom is not crazy!" She starts to cry.

"It's okay, Jen. Don't cry. I'll fix it."

"Grandmom pretended she didn't know I was there, but I know she heard me because I said it really loud."

"What did Grandaddy say?" I ask.

"Nothing. He took his lunch box and went in the car to go to work."

He never fights back.

"Mommy, Grandmom shouldn't say those mean things."

"No, she shouldn't." *And you're the only one who's ever had the nerve to fight back.* "I'm proud of you for speaking up, Jennifer. Most of the time, it's rude for children to speak to grown-ups the way you spoke to Grandmom, but if you hear someone—even your Grandmom—saying mean things that are not true, then it's the right thing to do. I know that Rick would be proud of you too."

She smiles brightly. "Can I tell him when I see him?"

"Sure. He likes people who tell the truth."

She jumps up from the grass and brushes off the back of her shorts. "Can we walk to where the Fourth of July party was?"

"Okay. But you know that none of the party things are there anymore."

"I know, but I want to go there anyway."

"Go in and tell Grandmom that we're taking a walk and we'll be back later."

She takes a couple of steps, then turns back to me with an uncertain look on her face. "What if Grandmom is still in the kitchen and she heard me telling you about what happened. She'll be really, really mad at me."

"Don't worry about that. I'm here to protect you." *Which is sort of a joke if you think about it, since I've never even been able to protect myself against my mother.*

"What did Grandmom say?" I ask her as we start off hand in hand down the street toward the common.

"She said, 'Go.'"

"That's all?"

"Mommy? I don't think Grandmom likes me anymore."

"Grandmom loves you, Jennifer. It's just—well, she has some problems." I have to wonder if I know what those problems are. My parents are secretive people. There could easily be something they're not telling Kathy or me. Or at least me. For all my sister's outgoing, friendly ways, it wouldn't surprise me a bit if there are things she keeps from me. Now that I think about it, I'm probably a worse offender than any of them. The only difference is that somehow my secrets always get found out.

The common is rarely empty during the summer. There is always something going on. Frisbee games, touch football, knots of folks gathered on the periphery to rest or chat. The benches are back in place, and those under the trees offer readers respite on these hot days. Jennifer and I head for Village Drugs to get giant-sized ice-cream cones. Four people who knew me when I was growing up are still working in the store, and they all say hello to both of us by name as we pass them on our way to the fountain at the back. The air-conditioning feels so good that we decide to eat the cones here instead of outside, where half the ice cream will be lost to heat drip. There's just one other customer back here, and we smile as we pass her on the way to a booth. New housing has been built on the outskirts of Clearyville to accommodate the people hired when the mill expanded a few years ago, and lately I've been noticing how many strange faces I'm seeing. Nothing stays the same. It's kind of sad.

Jennifer and I are sitting in quiet companionship, lapping up our ice cream, when I become aware of the woman from the other booth heading our way. Dark blonde, thirtyish, wearing a checkered blouse, denim wraparound skirt, and Dr. Scholl's clogs. I assume she's one of the new people, until she stops at our table.

"I might be way offtrack, but aren't you Mary Grace Hill?"

"Yes," I say, trying to fit a name with her face. She smiles, and a faint bell goes off, but I still can't place her.

"I'm Marjorie Barr, Shipman now. You and I were friends when we were kids."

I feel my face get red from the embarrassment of not recognizing the girl who was my best friend for almost five years. "Marjorie? I can't believe it! You look so . . . so—"

"Different. I know it. I probably wouldn't have realized it was you, except that my aunt mentioned that Mrs. McLean said you were going to be here this week, and I've been hoping we'd run into each other."

"Can you sit down for a few minutes?"

Marjorie looks around. "I really can't. I promised I'd be back by eleven. Could we meet this evening perhaps?"

"I don't see why not. What time?"

"Six fifteen. I'll get my aunt's dinner ready for her and then I'll have a couple of hours free. How about Millie's?"

Millie's Diner is a Clearyville landmark on the western edge of town. "Is it still in business?"

"It is and it hasn't changed a bit. But we have, and we have a lot of territory to cover. Can you make it?"

"I'll be there."

"Great," she says. She flashes Jennifer a big smile, as if she's just seen her for the first time. "Your daughter?"

I nod. "Jennifer, this is Mrs. Shipman. We were good friends when we were children."

"I'm happy to meet you, Jennifer."

Jennifer says, "Hi," then glues her eyes on her drippy cone.

Marjorie looks back to me. "All right!" she says enthusiastically. "See you at Millie's at six fifteen."

The house is empty when we get back. Mother hasn't left a note, but most likely, she's gone to the grocery. The heat is really oppressive today, and I would love to be napping when she gets back. Maybe I should take Jennifer to see her Grandma McLean. No. Too hot to walk all the way back over there. As I peer out of the living room window to see if Mother is coming down the street, I recall Jennifer saying that sometimes she plays with the little girls at Mrs. Crowley's house, a small brick bungalow directly opposite us. Mrs. Crowley often watched Kathy when Mother was working. Now she sometimes sits for her two young granddaughters.

"Hey, Jen, why don't we go across to Mrs. Crowley's house and see if Debbie and Cindy are there today? Maybe they'd like to play for a while."

"Can I bring the puzzle that Grandmom got for me?" she says with enthusiasm.

"Oh? I didn't know she gave you a present. What's the picture?"

"Noah and the Ark. It's a story from the Bible."

"Of course," I murmur, rolling my eyes, "the Bible. Sure. Come on, I'll go with you." It could be worse. At least it's not hell and damnation.

As we go out the front door, the Crowley girls emerge from around the side of their house and stand in the front yard. Their grandmother follows a few steps behind. The three of them wave and watch as we cross the street. After exchanging a few friendly words with Mrs. Crowley, I tell Jennifer I'll be in Grandaddy's hammock if she wants me, and I leave her standing in the yard, looking shyly at the two other girls. The image of her on the living room floor with Jody Simon suddenly comes to mind, and I wonder fleetingly if she is any more responsive to these children than she was to him. But then I reassure myself. She's changed so much in the past four months, and these girls are not strangers to her. She'll be fine.

I'm excited about meeting Marjorie tonight. Maybe reliving the old days will take away some of the sourness I'm feeling about Clearyville. After all, my mother isn't the only person I know in town. As long as she doesn't spill her venom on Jennifer, I guess I can endure being here for a few more days.

Though I haven't been to Millie's since Steve and I were dating, I can see at a glance that I haven't missed anything. As Marjorie said, it hasn't changed a bit. Neither has Millie Norland, who has owned it for about fifty years. Dad once confessed he used to come here with his friends when he was in high school, then added, a little ruefully, that he never came back after he met Mother, who won't eat anywhere but at home. This, of course, doesn't stop Millie from knowing everything about the Hills, and she recognizes me the minute she sees me come through the door.

Marjorie is sitting in a booth looking over the menu, and Millie waits until I'm seated across from her before she comes over to chat. I suppose a lot of people get a warm, fuzzy, one-big-happy-family feeling when someone from their past proceeds to relate the customer's life story to them as if it was their own. I don't. I become uncomfortable. But I manage not to squirm too much, and eventually Millie takes our orders.

Reminiscing continues nonstop while Marjorie and I eat. I laugh as I haven't laughed in years. Nothing is sacred. Boys we liked, teachers we didn't. Nights we did homework together. Notes we passed in class.

"You were such a Goody Two-shoes," she says. "It wasn't easy for you to have fun, was it?"

I consider that for a moment. "I never thought of it that way, but no, I guess it wasn't. It always made me feel a little guilty because children were starving in Armenia, and here I was having a good time when I should be doing something else, like—"

"Praying or going to church, I bet. Your parents! I'm sorry, Maggie, but they were the strictest, most humorless people I've ever met."

I nod. "It's the way Mother interprets the teachings of the church. For her, work and worship are what God wants from us. Nowhere in the Bible is the word 'fun' mentioned and she takes the Bible literally. But we did manage to have some fun, didn't we? Do you remember the carnival?"

"Oh, do I! Us two 'fraidy cats on that ride, and then—"

"And then you went off with Carolyn Perry and her coven. The only reason I was on that ride was that she deigned to let me ride with them—and you."

"Oh yeah. I'd forgotten about that."

"I was devastated."

"Well, I came back. They were awful. So shallow, only interested in makeup and shopping. You and I were into *books*. We didn't give a damn about what we or anyone else was wearing. I felt ridiculous being their friend, but I loved being yours. And my mother was happier too."

"I liked your parents. They were so nice to me," I said with a touch of envy.

And so we talk for a while about our years in Clearyville, our families, who is living and who's gone. This progresses naturally into our adult lives. Marjorie is a stewardess, and her husband, Jeff, is an airline pilot. She lives near Phoenix, Arizona, and only gets to Clearyville once or twice a year. She has no children. I wonder about that, but don't ask. She says she loves her life and is a content woman. We talk about Steve and how wonderful our marriage was and how it ended . . . We have a good laugh when I tell her about the lieutenant and my mother's reaction to seeing him in her yard.

"If it had been my mother, she would've invited him in, given him supper, and insisted he stay overnight. God, my mother hated Clearyville with a passion. She couldn't wait to get out of here. My poor father. She drove him crazy, but he was a native of Clearyville and he was happy here. Besides, he had a good job with the factory and didn't want to start over until another good job came along. So here we were for five years."

Over dessert, she asks me about Chicago. "So how do you like living in the big city?"

"I'm not sure that you can call what I do 'living,'" I answer. "I go to work and I go home. I'm a hospital nurse and I like it. Jennifer is going into second grade and has a sitter after school. Remember my sister Kathy?"

"Only in terms of diapers and milk bottles."

I smile. "She's twenty now and living in Chicago, also. She's an office receptionist during the day and sometimes takes care of Jennifer when I have to work at night. She's got a nice boyfriend and seems happy with her life. I'm very glad she left here as soon as she graduated high school."

Marjorie looks searchingly at me, and I guess what the next question will be, "No man in your life?" *Right on the button.* While Jennifer was at the Crowleys', I had thought for a long time about how I'd handle this question if it came up. Given my mother's attitude toward him, I finally decided I didn't want Rick to be in Clearyville with me. Maybe I'll tell her about him the next time we get in touch, but not tonight.

"No," I answer. "It's only been in the last year that I've accepted that Steve is dead. I just couldn't let go of him, Marjorie. It was so painful."

She squeezes my hand sympathetically. "It must've been awful. He never saw Jennifer?"

"I had just sent him the letter that I was pregnant. I don't know if he'd had the chance to read it."

"For a girl who was afraid to go on a carnival ride, you've turned out to be pretty strong."

"I wasn't until Jennifer was born. After Steve left, I knew I had to pull myself together and make a life for us."

"I admire you," Marjorie says and opens her handbag. "My life has been too easy. Sometimes I take things for granted." She digs around in her wallet and drops a big bill on top of the check Millie had left on the table.

I reach for my wallet, but she stops me. "My treat and don't argue. It's been wonderful running into you, Maggie. I wish we lived closer together."

"So do I, and I've enjoyed this more than I can say. If you're ever in Chicago . . ." *I don't want to let her go.* "I have an idea. My mother is expecting us to stay till Sunday and I haven't told her yet, but Jennifer and I are interviewing babysitters, so we'll be going back to the city on Friday morning. If you have some time tomorrow, I could come over to your aunt's house for a little while. I'd like very much to see her again."

"Oh, Maggie, let's do that. I'm sure she'd love to see you after all these years. She naps at different times during the day, so call me first, and we'll work out the time."

"It's a deal."

Marjorie was the best part of my childhood, and I'm delighted we will have just a little more time together.

Though it's begun to get dark by the time I get back to the house, Mother and Jennifer are working together in Mother's flourishing vegetable garden. In my mind, I can almost hear Rick say, "Vegetables don't care who they grow for, do they?" Jennifer greets me warmly. Mother throws me a brief sideways glance, her lips pinched in disapproval.

"Remember my old school friend, Marjorie Barr?" I venture. "Jennifer and I ran into her at the drugstore this afternoon. I met her for supper at Millie's." Mother doesn't respond right away. "I left you a note saying I was going to be out."

"I saw it," she mutters acidly. "Heathens, that family. Nothing but heathens . . . Past time for your bath, Jennifer. Let's go!" She pulls herself up and stalks toward the house. Jennifer puts down her weeder and reaches for my hand.

"The lady at the drugstore was nice, wasn't she?"

"Very nice," I agree and reluctantly walk with her to the house.

"Why doesn't Grandmom like her?"

"I'm wondering the same thing, Jen. I wish I knew."

The next day, Tuesday, is again beautiful and hot. Mother has planned to take Jennifer shopping for school clothes, and I get myself a glass of iced tea and make two calls, one to the day care agency to confirm that they have lined up three women for Friday, and the other to Marjorie, who tells me to come at around eleven.

Marjorie's childhood home is an old house with a wide wraparound porch, a mossy brick path, and two huge maples in the front yard. It occurs to me that it was probably the aunt's house to begin with, since she was living in it when we were kids. Marjorie answers the bell, then ushers me past the dim living room, which is just as I remember it, and down a hall, through the kitchen, and out to the screened-in back porch, also shaded by tall leafy trees.

Her aunt, sitting in a wheelchair, squints at me and says, "It's Mary Grace, isn't it? Oh yes. I remember you well. You and Margie were such good friends." She holds out a hand. I go forward and clasp her hand loosely. Her fingers look painfully gnarled with arthritis.

"I'm happy to see you again, Miss Wilkinson," I say. I find myself recapturing some of the warmth I used to feel when I came here, and how I envied Marjorie her family. They were always friendly and welcoming to me even though they were not members of our church. I recall that in good weather, Ms. Wilkinson was often at an easel out on this porch, painting what I thought were beautiful pictures.

"Margaret mentioned to me that you were coming to visit this week. She often talks about you and your little girl. Janet, is it?"

"Jennifer. I visited with Margaret when I was here for the Fourth of July. My daughter wasn't with me at the time, and I'm counting on Margaret to join us tomorrow for Jennifer's birthday."

She smiles. "Oh, a birthday party! I'm sure she will."

The three of us chat for another hour or so before Miss Wilkinson begins to show signs of fatigue. I say I have to be going, and Marjorie walks me to the door.

"I remember sitting on your back porch watching your aunt paint," I tell her. "Do you remember that painting she did of sunflowers next to a window? I just loved that one. The colors were so beautiful."

"She would have liked to hear you say that," she comments wistfully.

"I didn't want to mention it for fear of making her sad about not being able to paint anymore."

"Oh, she adjusted to her situation years ago."

"I don't look forward to getting old," I confess. "It can't be much fun to lose the things that made you happy." Not that you have to be old to be unhappy, I amend to myself.

"Yes," she agrees sadly. "Painting made Aunt Ruth very happy. She's never really had anything else but us . . ." She takes a deep breath and perks herself up. "Well. It's just about time to settle her in for her afternoon nap, but I'll walk you to the corner first."

We are halfway down the street when she says, "I'm flying out tomorrow evening, Maggie. You'll be busy with Jennifer's party tomorrow, so I'll say good-bye now."

I suddenly feel deflated. "I wish we had more time. Wasn't it an amazing coincidence that we happened to be in the drugstore at the same time and that you recognized me after eighteen years?"

"It wasn't a coincidence. It was fate that brought us together," she declares, as if she possesses some kind of special knowledge about such things.

I nod noncommittally. "Well, let me have your address, so we can at least keep in touch." I take a pad and pencil out of my handbag and scribble the information for her, then hand the pad to her so she can do the same for me.

"We have a commitment, right?" she says brightly, then glances toward her house. "I have to get back now. Wish your daughter a happy birthday for me and don't forget to write."

"I won't. Have a good trip home."

We hug heartily and go our separate ways—she, back to her aunt, who is elderly and ailing, and I to my mother, who is icy cold and unyielding.

Jennifer's birthday party turns out to be a lot livelier than usual. At her request, we invite Mrs. Crowley and her granddaughters. Dad picks up Mrs. McLean. Of course, Kathy comes on the bus and grumbles for an hour about having to take the bus there and back because Todd can't get off work.

Jennifer is ecstatic as she opens her presents this year—twice as many as usual, including books, a Viewmaster, a game, and a couple of dresses. Grandmom ceremoniously presents her with a small gold cross necklace, which she personally puts around Jennifer's neck, while telling her that she must never take it off. Jennifer is so excited that she makes sure she is not more than an arm's length away from this treasure trove for as long as we are in Clearyville.

For the remainder of the visit, Mother devotes all her attention to Jennifer, leaving me to lie in the hammock most of the day with a couple of books I've wanted to read for years. I have to admit that I can only get through forty pages of *The Great Gatsby.* The arrogant rich, the seedy poor, and the sleazy gangsters are not people I want to spend my time with. It's just the opposite with *To Kill a Mockingbird*; I'm having trouble putting it down. The rest of the week passes uncomfortably but uneventfully, with no direct exchanges between Mother and me until Thursday night, when I tell her that we will be leaving for the city in the morning.

"What do you mean, 'we'?" she barks. "Surely, Jenny will be staying until Sunday."

"No, she has to come back with me," I say firmly, determined not to wilt in the face of her fury.

"Oh? I suppose her 'father figure' misses her and demanded that you bring her back."

Did I say wilt? I meant laugh. "Not quite, Mother. Her 'father figure' has been flat on his back in a hospital bed for the past two months. He's in no condition to demand anything from anyone. Kathy must have mentioned it to you."

"She did not," my mother retorts stiffly. "In any case, it's no business of mine. For your information," she huffs, "I resent you taking our granddaughter away so soon."

"We've been here for five days, Mother. It's not like we just arrived this morning."

She pins me with her steely eyes, then turns on her heel and stalks out of the kitchen, leaving me shaking my head at the futility of communicating with her. Frankly, at this moment, whoever this woman is, whatever my relationship is to her, I don't care if I never see her again.

Dad and I pack the car the next morning, stashing Jennifer's booty at her feet, as she has instructed us to do, so she can have ready access to it. But having gone to bed quite late last night, she falls asleep before we've driven ten miles.

Am I proud of how easy it's become for me to speak disrespectfully to my mother? No. But I'm not sorry either.

Marion

I cannot understand what Mary Grace is up to or why she has chosen to behave this way, but whatever the reason is, we are appalled. This boy she's taken up with and that high-society family of his . . . we don't have a thing in common with them, and they have nothing to do with us. I'm not a fool. I know that money is their God. Everyone knows that people like them have no moral values. If they did, they would never condone their son carrying on with a married woman, and Mary Grace McLean is a married woman. *We* happen to respect the sanctity of marriage and God's seventh commandment, which says, "Thou shalt not commit adultery." Has Steven been confirmed dead? No. Margaret, his poor mother, would certainly have told us if he had been, and until that happens, we must believe he is alive somewhere. Our family has always lived according to the Commandments, and what Mary Grace is doing with the boy and his people is just plain wrong, no two ways about it.

Of course, she hasn't admitted she's having an affair with him. Why should she? She's already informed us that in her mind Steven is dead, so for her purposes, it follows she is now a free woman. How lucky for her then that she has found someone to take his place, and she's as much as said so. "He's a father figure for Jennifer," she told Roger. Has she gone crazy? He's hardly older than Katherine. For heaven's sake, he's still in school!

I'm honestly beginning to doubt she's fit to raise the child. Has she put Jenny in Sunday school? Does she make any effort to teach her God's Word? The last few times Jenny's been here with us, I've had to remind her to say her prayers before she goes to bed. She used to say them automatically. It's clear to us that Grace has forsaken everything that we've taught her that is right and simply turned her back on God. They do that, you know—try to convert us over to their way. I'm sure the boy is very persuasive.

It's not hard to figure out how he seduced her into this illicit relationship. Both Roger and I could see at Christmas that there was something between them. He's a good-looking kid—I'll give him that—and I suppose he has a working brain if he's at the University of Chicago; it *is* supposed to be a good school.

And, of course, there's the money. Katherine tells me he's from a very wealthy family; as she put it, they're "super loaded." The Lord knows we've always lived modestly. Our discretionary money, when we have any, goes directly to feeding the poor or supporting our church's outreach and mission programs. We've never been interested in material things or, for that matter, worldly people. We're servants of our Lord, and that's what we raised our children to be.

Oh, I knew there'd be trouble when Grace moved to the city. I begged her not to go, but she didn't listen. Well, I was right, wasn't I? Look at her, bringing shame and disgrace on us with her sinful behavior. Haven't I had enough to worry about with Katherine? She was always less obedient than Grace, and I've been afraid for her ever since she moved to Chicago. The only reason we allowed her to go was that Grace promised to look after her and make sure she didn't do anything foolish. Now it's Katherine who is the sensible one. Just look at Todd. We've become very fond of him. He may not have been brought up in a home quite as devout as ours, but he's a good God-fearing man.

Another thing I can't understand is what this boy wants with Grace. She's never been a great beauty. Lord knows she's no mental giant. Oh, she reads a lot, always has, but now I wonder just what it was she was reading when she was young and forbidden any but church-approved books. I blame that little friend of hers from that godless family—what was her name? Marlene?—for introducing her to the wrong books.

At least Grace has always been a good worker. She put off going to nursing school after she graduated from the regional high school, but to her credit, she spent five years working in the registrar's office at the Waynesburg Christian College. That's where she met Steven. Like his brother Bobby, he's a fine, intelligent man, and quite nice looking in his own way. Roger and I brought up our daughters to be the kind of pure and decent Christian young women a young Christian man like Steven deserves.

But what she's doing now! I don't know what to think. If Margaret knew about this, it would kill her. What on earth has happened to Grace's conscience and compassion?

And what are Roger and I supposed to do? Pretend that she's still the daughter we raised? That she is behaving the way a wife and mother should? It's out of the question. To ignore this would mean compromising what we have believed in all our lives, Roger and me. Now if Grace were to come to us and say that she's seen the error of her ways and given up her boyfriend, if she were to beg forgiveness and pray to God to take her back, then maybe we could come to terms. Otherwise the only thing we can do is let her go her own way. Nothing less is acceptable. Well, it's up to her to make the first move. Until then, there's no point in us talking with her about it.

Only God can save a sinner . . .

The road back to Chicago is being repaired in several places, so with backups and reduced speed limits, we don't get back to the apartment until just after noon. We'd had breakfast at about 8:00 a.m., and Jennifer is hungry, so the first thing I do is put a thrown-together lunch on the table for both of us. The telephone rings as I sit down with her.

"Hello?"

"When did you get back?" It's Kathy.

"About five minutes ago."

"Oh. Well, I just wanted to tell you that Mother called me after you left. She was having fits because you didn't stay until Sunday like you said you would and you took Jenny back with you."

"I figured she'd be angry. I forgot to tell her at the beginning of the week that Jennifer and I had other plans for today."

"What are you doing today that's so important?"

"We're interviewing babysitters."

"What happened to Mrs. Fallon?"

"Nothing. I would rather have someone come here from now on."

"She's had Jenny since she was a year old. What did she say when you told her?"

"I haven't told her yet, but I don't think she'll be too upset. She takes care of four other children besides Jennifer."

A moment of silence ensues, then Kathy asks softly, "So does that mean I'm fired too?"

"No! For heaven's sake . . . you're kidding, aren't you?"

"I guess," she answers, sounding sulky.

I take a deep breath and move on. "Are you at your desk now?"

"I'm on my lunch break."

"Kath, did you say anything to Mother about my working for the Simons?"

"No. I thought you already had. Why?"

"No reason, except she didn't say a civil word to me all the time we were there. It was really unpleasant. The only saving grace was that I ran into a woman who was my best friend in junior high."

"Far out! Who was it?"

"Her name was Marjorie Barr, but you wouldn't know her. She moved away while you were a baby."

"I bet it was fun seeing her again."

"It was the only thing that made the week bearable."

"I'm glad you had that, at least. Sometimes I think there's something really, you know, wrong with Mother. I mean, you know, like she's sick in her soul or something."

"She's something all right, but I don't know what. I just wish she didn't take it out on me."

"Yeah, I know . . . Darn. I have to go. I'm past my break. Can we talk about this again?"

"I'd like to. Can you come over tonight? Maybe we can hash it all out and come to some kind of conclusion."

"I'll call you later and let you know what time. Okay?"

"Can you come without Todd? I'd feel better if we kept it in the family for now."

"Me too. Talk to you later."

During the week, one of the applicants decided she wanted definite hours. I couldn't promise her that, and she withdrew. This left us with two to choose from. The first one arrives at three, the other at four thirty. Both interviews go well.

As soon as the second woman leaves, I pour a cup of coffee for myself and a glass of cherry Kool-Aid for Jennifer, grab a bag of chocolate chip cookies, and take them into the living room. I haven't spoken with her about the new job, just explained that Kathy wouldn't be able to stay with her as much as she had been, and that we needed to find someone she liked who would take good care of her while I was at work. Now I call her in to talk about which woman she liked better. Both of them have good qualifications, but I already know which one I favor and fervently hope my newly spunky, opinionated daughter will agree. Otherwise we might have a problem.

"What did you think of those ladies?" I ask between cookie bites.

"Are they going to take turns taking care of me?"

"No, we have to pick one."

"Umm," she mused, "I don't know. I forgot their names."

"One was Mrs. Gillis and the other one was Ms. Moore."

"I like the one with the curly hair the best."

"That's Ms. Moore. Why do you like her better?"

"Because she didn't look like she was only pretending when she smiled. And because I think she really likes kids."

"You don't think Mrs. Gillis likes kids too?"

"She looked like she would get really, really mad if I spill something by mistake, even when I don't mean to. That's how Grandmom looks if I do something wrong."

"Good reason, Jen. Anything else?"

She shrugs her shoulder, breaks into a big smile. "She's the one I like. I could tell it when she smiled at me. Who did you like best?"

"Ms. Moore."

"Then she's the one who can take care of me?"

"Yes."

"Cool!" she exclaims, sounding like a true child of the '70s.

Erin Moore, the younger of the two women, is a twenty-nine-year-old doctoral candidate in early childhood education. All she needs is library time, she says; otherwise her work is portable. She's outgoing and—what's the word?—effervescent, I guess, and I had a good feeling about her five minutes into the interview. Thank God Jennifer had a good feeling too. I call the agency, tell them our choice, and the time I will expect Erin on Monday. They ask me to come in to sign some papers.

After dinner, I call Lenore and tell her how the interviews turned out and how pleased I am with the agency she chose. Rick had called her today, and we chat about him for a few minutes. I ask if she has plans to come out here, and she says she doesn't at the present time.

The telephone rings as soon as I replace the receiver in the cradle. It's Erin Moore, thanking us profusely for choosing her and assuring me that she will be here at seven thirty sharp on Monday morning. Ten minutes later, the phone rings again. This time it's Kathy, saying she can't make it tonight. Todd has a surprise for her. This is not bad news for me. All I really want to do is sit, quiet and alone, until Monday morning.

When the doorbell rings on Monday, Jennifer jumps up from her breakfast and runs to the door, but as soon as Erin enters the apartment, her eagerness turns to shyness, and suddenly she is again the Jennifer she was only a few months ago. I don't have time to deal with her now, so I welcome the new sitter with enthusiasm and then leave the two of them alone while I finish getting ready for my first day on the new job. Ten minutes later, I find them sitting on the couch, talking earnestly. I ask Erin if she has any questions, tell her where I will be, and that my work number is next to the telephone, along with other important numbers.

"Jennifer can show you where things are in the kitchen and how to get to the park a few blocks away. She knows her way around the neighborhood."

"Don't worry, Jenny and I will be fine."

"I know, but don't hesitate to call me if you need to."

I give Jennifer a kiss and go out the door, thinking that this girl is too good to be true, while praying to God that she isn't.

Why am I the only person who calls my daughter by her whole first name? Why, of all people, am I so formal with her? I've never thought about this before, but now that I have, it suddenly seems so cold to me. I decide to make an effort to call her by the name everyone else, even my inflexible mother, uses. She is, after all, my Jenny.

Part 3

It seems like forever since I've entered the rehab unit. So much has happened in the past couple of weeks that it's almost cathartic to be stepping through the door in my uniform with nothing on my mind except going to work. I go immediately to Rick's room, but he's sound asleep, so I backtrack to the main desk to introduce myself and remind them that I'm supposed to have an orientation meeting. The desk nurse directs me to the kitchen, where the person who is to show me the ropes is waiting for me. She is an attractive blonde woman, who smiles, offers me a cup of coffee, and says, "Welcome to the unit, Mary Grace. I'm Terry. I didn't know we were getting a new nurse."

"Please call me Maggie. Technically, you're not getting a new nurse. I'm here to do private duty for the patient in 107."

"Really? He didn't get off to a good start, but the last I saw of him, he was doing pretty well."

"His family is concerned about his mental state."

"It's a tough adjustment for these guys, but we do work hard for them," she says a tad defensively.

"Please don't think that they're not satisfied with what you're doing. They are. They're just awfully concerned about his emotional well-being, and feel that since he and I know each other—we were neighbors and friends for almost a year—I might be able to help out a bit with the moral support he needs. They know how busy you all are over here." It might sound lame to her, but I don't know what else to say.

She looks through my folder for my resume. "So you worked over at the hospital for . . . six years?"

I nod.

"You've had experience in a number of different types of medical situations. That's helpful. I'll just take you around and show you where everything you'll need is kept, and give you an idea of our routine. You'll also have a chance to watch the therapists at work. When we're done, you can go spend a while with your patient and acclimate yourself to the room. Meet me here for lunch, so we can talk more. Okay?"

"Sounds good to me."

"Super! Then let's get started. We can talk while we go. Don't hesitate to ask if you have any questions."

The tour takes about an hour and a half. Along the way, Terry introduces me to several of the women and men on the nursing staff. I don't worry about getting their names straight; I probably won't be seeing most of them. After that, we have another cup of coffee and talk more about the ins and outs of paraplegia. It's a little after 10:00 a.m. now, and I'm getting anxious to see Rick. I check his schedule on the clipboard Terry gives me and confirm that, as I recall, he has physical therapy from nine thirty to ten thirty. I decide to take that time to run over to the agency and sign the papers the woman mentioned. I just hope I won't run into Mrs. Gillis there.

Parking in the area around the agency is practically impossible. Even the lots and garages are full; waiting for a space adds a half hour to the trip. When I get back, Rick's door is open, and he is propped up in bed with his eyes closed. He looks like PT has literally sucked the marrow out of his bones.

I rap lightly as I enter. "PT wear you out?"

He smiles weakly. "Hi, Maggie. Just get here?"

"No." I make a brisk entrance into the room, looking around, checking it out from a professional standpoint for the first time. "I've been in orientation. I stuck my head in when I got here at eight, but you were sleeping. I didn't want to wake you."

We look at each other for a long moment, during which I note that his facial damage is pretty much healed, though the scars are still fresh. I am experiencing an almost painful desire to touch him, but I know that giving in to such impulses won't do my nurse's objectivity any good, so I force myself to distance from him emotionally, at least for the moment.

Rick asks, "How was Clearyville?"

"Same as usual. Except that I met a childhood friend I hadn't seen since I was fourteen years old."

"That must have been interesting," he comments, sounding as if he would like to add "for you."

I don't elaborate on the encounter but introduce a subject that I suspect does interest him. "How have *you* been?"

"Every day is the same here, Maggie. I sleep, I obediently endure torture twice, I eat so they won't nag me—"

"How's the food here?"

"Three and a half stars compared to a feeding tube."

"If you make out a daily menu for me, I'll bring you what you want for lunch and dinner. What time do they bring breakfast?"

"Between seven and seven thirty."

"You're on your own for that then. I can't get here until eight."

He shrugs. "Can you hand me the newspaper, please? Somebody left it over on that little table."

I hand it to him, and he checks out the front page, then, eyes still on the paper, says quietly, “How’s Jenny?” I am surprised to see him swallow the way people do when they are suddenly struck by emotion.

“She’s fine, Rick.”

He smiles. “She knows about the accident?”

“Of course.”

“Good. I don’t want her to think I just abandoned her.”

“She knows that. She asks about you constantly and when she can see you. She misses you terribly. In fact,” I manage to report with a straight face, “my mother has referred to you as Jennifer’s ‘father figure.’”

He laughs ruefully. “Some father figure.”

“No, Jennifer really cares about you. Is it okay for me to bring her here? I knew you wouldn’t want her to see you when you were all banged up.”

“Yeah, sure. The worst is over. I’d like her to come.”

“She will, but I have to warn you. She’s not the same little girl she was two months ago.

I proceed to tell him about the new sitter and how well and easily Jennif—Jenny—took to her. I describe how she has matured in just a couple of months and how much more responsive and self-confident she’s become.

Rick listens to me ramble on, with a smile that makes my heart act like a grandfather clock gonging the hour. It’s a battle to restrain myself from doing something inappropriate with him. It’s going to be hard to remember that he still has a lot of unresolved problems to deal with before he achieves some semblance of good health.

“And what about you, Mary Grace? How are you doing?”

“I’m fine. I’ve also—” A knock on the door interrupts me.

“Come in,” Rick calls unenthusiastically.

An aide carrying a bed tray steps into the room and cheerfully announces, “Lunchtime!” She lays the tray on the little table near the door and strides over to the bed, cranks it up a few notches, then straightens Rick’s pillows behind him for support, retrieves the tray, and settles it in front of him. He groans.

“Just leave it on the table, Nessa, okay? I’m not hungry right now.”

“Eat it anyway,” Nessa orders. “Children are starving all over the world and it’s a crime to waste good food.”

“This does not count as good food,” Rick informs her.

Nessa shakes her head and looks at me. “Are you the nurse who’s going to be taking care of this grump from now on?”

"Yes. Maggie McLean. Nice to meet you."

We shake hands. "On behalf of the dietary staff, let me welcome you with open arms. Good luck." She turns to leave, winks over her shoulder at Rick as she goes through the door.

I can see that Rick is irritated by the tray. "I'll take it away, if you want—"

"Oh, thanks," he says with a look of relief.

"But not until you've eaten five bites of everything on your plate."

"That's not funny, McLean. It's blackmail."

"So it is," I agree, standing up. "I'll be back after lunch and you'd better have cleaned your plate, mister." He is staring at me, speechless, when I leave to meet Terry in the lunchroom, wherever that is.

I don't even remember whether I should turn right or left after I go out the door. All I can think about is that beautiful smile . . .

Over lunch, Terry fills me in on the physical duties I will have with Rick. I'll be responsible for bathing him, washing his hair, changing his clothes, checking for bedsores, managing the catheter, cleaning out impactions, and administering meds. Nothing I haven't done before, including the intimate chores that are definitely not what Kathy would call "turn-ons," situations that might tempt us into the kind of intimacy we used to have. It isn't the kind of work that would inspire someone to be a nurse.

When I return to Rick's room after lunch, he is resting. I settle into the stuffed chair in the corner near the bathroom and take out the schedule. Physical therapy again at two thirty. Tomorrow he will have physical therapy only once, but he will have an occupational therapy session and psychotherapy. Each of those classes is an hour and a half in length. I don't know what I expected, but it looks as if I'm going to have some time on my hands, something I'm not used to on a job. I'm not sure I'm going to like that, but it's part of the package, so I can't complain. I take a *Redbook* from my bag and turn to the serialized book. I haven't done much reading since Rick came into my life, and I have six months of magazines to catch up on. About five minutes before his PT, I notice he has dropped off to sleep, so I shake him gently and tell him it's time for the therapist. While he's out, I start the story, but I'm not in the mood to read, and I close the magazine and return it to my tote. I walk over to the bed to snatch the newspaper, but I'm sidetracked by a paper grocery sack sitting on the bedside table. When I pick it up to move it out of the way, something flutters to my feet. A greeting card. In fact, the bag is full to the brim with cards, letters, and telegrams. Some of the envelopes have been opened, others not. I make up my mind that one day, while Rick's out of the room, I'll tape them up where he can see them. At least it will be something to do during the empty hours. Besides, this sterile, impersonal room could use some color. I put the bag behind the chair I'm sitting on. Something to look forward to, I guess. Well, it's only the first day. Things are bound to pick up.

By Friday, the end of my first week as Maggie McLean, private nurse, I've pretty much got Rick's schedule memorized. I've asked each of the nurses who handle his personal care if they will let me watch them do what they do so I'll have some idea of the way they operate. Nobody has a problem with that, and they all basically work the same way as I do, so I am already on my own with most of the functions I haven't performed in a while. Things have gone more smoothly than I expected they would.

Rick's endurance is still pretty low, and he's wiped out after the physical therapy sessions, but he's only been here a month, and I've been told that the exercise sessions are rigorous. He's admitted to frustration and discouragement a few times, but those times have been brief. I think the frustration is mostly due to the fact that he's too tired to work on his dissertation. I wish I could do something to help.

I never did call Jerry's office for the phone number at the lake, but as if there actually was such a thing as ESP, Carol called me on Wednesday evening. Before I could try to arrange a time that she and I can get together, she invited Jenny and me to her house for a barbecue on Sunday. I accepted on the condition that we find time for the two of us to talk alone. Her parents are visiting from Florida, and Jerry's parents will also be there, she said, so we'll be able to slip away for a while.

Socializing with strangers has always been difficult for me—I flash back to April and the day I couldn't bring myself to go to dinner with Rick's parents—but when I think about visiting with my own parents, I tell myself that an afternoon with the Hausers' families can't possibly be that bad.

The barbecue is in full swing when Jennifer and I get there. I hand Jerry the cake I bought for the occasion and thank him for the good driving directions. "This is a lovely neighborhood," I remark.

He smiles broadly. "Hey, Jenny. Do you remember me?"

Jennifer looks at me with a quizzical expression.

"This is Dr. Jerry. He's known you since you were a little baby."

She looks up at him shyly.

Jerry takes my arm and steers us through the dining room to the kitchen, where he deposits the cake box on the counter. We proceed to a door that opens into a large screened-in porch overlooking a nice-sized yard with a huge maple tree in the corner. Before we step out onto the porch, he stops. "So how's everything going, Maggie?"

"We're fine, thanks."

"How's Carol's 'crush' getting along?"

"Who?"

"Your former neighbor whose name I don't recall at the moment."

"Rick." He nods. "He started rehab three weeks ago. I think he's doing okay."

"You don't see him anymore?"

"I still see him."

He looks at me for a moment, then says, "Good. Tell him I said hello."

"I will."

He opens the door and ushers us onto the porch, where Carol and three older people are seated around a table filled with snacks. Carol jumps up. "You made it!"

"Thanks to Jerry's good directions. I've never been in this area before."

"Well, we're happy you're here now." She turns back to the others. "This is our good friend, Maggie McLean, and her daughter, Jenny. Maggie, my parents, Max and Florence Goodman, and Jerry's mother, Irene Hauser." After a minute's worth of nods and hellos ensue, Carol continues, "My father-in-law is in the backyard pushing Sarah on the swing."

From behind my shoulder, Jerry says, "Why don't I take Jenny out to see Sarah? How about it, Jen? It's like a playground in the backyard. Want to see it?"

Jennifer glances uncertainly in my direction.

"Great idea. Go with Dr. Jerry and have some fun with Sarah. I'll be right here if you want me."

She nods and dutifully follows Jerry toward an area at the left side of the house beyond my vision. Carol motions to an empty seat and passes me some iced tea in a tall glass. It's a hot sunny day, and I sip my tea, every now and then basking in the welcome breath of a cool breeze. *How lovely it would be to have a home like this. Nothing big or fancy, just a place with a porch and a backyard with a big shade tree.*

Mrs. Goodman says, “Jenny is a shy little girl, no?” She has a faint accent I don’t recognize offhand.

“A shy child from a shy mother. Not so unusual, Flo,” Mrs. Hauser responds, then turns to me. “So. Carol tells me you worked in the clinic.”

“Yes . . . yes, several years ago.”

Carol speaks up. “If you think Maggie is shy now, you should have known her when she came to work at the clinic.”

“So why did you leave?” Mrs. Goodman cuts in indignantly. “My son-in-law didn’t treat you good?”

A flush spreads over my face. “Oh no, of course he—”

“Of course he treated her right,” her husband says gently, reaching over and rubbing her shoulder protectively.

“Okay, okay. Don’t get excited. I’m only asking.”

Mrs. Hauser says quietly to me, “Carol mentioned you left to get a full-time job when you graduated nursing school.”

“Yes, I did.”

Carol stands up. “Irene, Max, would you mind if I take Maggie away for a few minutes to show her the house?”

Mrs. Hauser makes a small dismissive gesture with her fingers. “No, not at all, darling. Take your time, we’re not going anywhere.”

Carol leans down and gives her mother a peck on the cheek, then motions me to follow her into the kitchen, where she says in a half whisper, “I’m so sorry, Maggie. I forgot to tell you that my mother has suffered a few strokes.”

“Oh no, Carol. How terrible for all of you.”

“Sometimes she’s perfectly fine, just like she used to be, which was a pain in the ass a lot of the time, but she was basically a good person. I’m already beginning to miss who she used to be.”

Over the years, I’ve had more than a few patients with dementia or stroke damage. They can be quite difficult to deal with unless they’re far enough advanced that they don’t know what’s going on around them. For me, the hardest time is when there are still brief lucid moments that let us see the way the patient was before. It’s hard because the damage always reasserts itself and it’s very difficult to watch.

“Your father’s very patient and loving with her.”

“Yes, he’s devoted to her. It’s hardest for him.”

“Jerry’s mother is also good with her.”

“She is. Sam, Jerry’s father, doesn’t have the patience that Irene has, so he avoids being near my mother unless he has to be.” She smiles. “And now, let me show you the house. We did a lot of the work ourselves, so we're obnoxiously proud of it. Then we'll go out to the yard and see how the girls and the barbecue are getting along."

Carol and Jerry's two-floor house in Irving Park has a similar layout to my parents' house in Clearyville, but that's the only thing the two have in common. My mother, who Kathy calls a "neat freak," has always been obsessive about her house being immaculate at all times, and the two of us learned at an early age not to thwart her. As clean as an operating room and as neat as a military bunk bed, our house had, and still has, the Spartan sterility of the model houses Steve and I used to look at once in a while after Sunday dinner.

But this house is more than a house. It's a home that is obviously lived in. It is sloppy with the easygoing disorder of people who prefer comfort and contentment to the total lack of human warmth that defines my mother's idea of home decor. In Carol's home, I feel the family's presence in every room.

"Ahem," Carol says quietly, "sorry to interrupt your reverie, but we should be getting back to the festivities."

"You and Jerry have done a wonderful job with the house. I can feel you both in every room."

"Glad you like it. I'll give you our decorators' names."

What? "I thought you said you and Jerry did a lot of it yourselves."

"Then never mind. You already know their names." She puts her arm around my shoulders as we move toward the stairs.

The food is ready, and everyone is present. Suddenly Carol becomes someone I've never seen before, a hovering, fluttering housewife.

"Is it too hot out here? We can eat inside if it would be more comfortable.

"Wait, Jerry, I'm going to take everything off the table and we'll move closer to the tree. It's shadier there.

"Who wants iced tea? I also have water, juice, and Coke if anybody wants it.

"Maggie, mustard stains. Should I get a towel to protect Jenny's dress while she's eating?

"Should I—"

"No, no, no, and no!" Jerry says forcefully. "Just sit down and let Jerry the Barbecue Guy do his stuff, okay?"

While Jerry fills our plastic plates, Mr. Goodman says to his wife, "You hear your daughter, Flo? She's become a real *noodnick*."

To which Carol, on my left, says to me in an informative tone, "Noodnick: pain in the . . . neck."

The banter at the table reminds me of being with the Simons when they get together.

About halfway through the meal, Mrs. Goodman upsets her iced tea and gets herself in such a state that when her husband tries to help, she pushes his hand away and says sharply, "Get away from me. I don't know you." A look of fear mixed with grief passes between Carol and Jerry, and Carol gets up to help her father lead her mother into the house.

Mrs. Hauser starts to say something, but Jerry quickly shakes his head and says, "Not while the kids are here." We all continue with our meal as if nothing has happened. At last, a reaction I can identify with.

"You're not eating," I admonish Jenny, who is sitting still with her fork in her hand.

"Why did Sarah's grandma act like that?" Her voice is troubled and even smaller than usual.

"Because she didn't feel well. But we can talk about it later, if you want."

"Okay," she concedes. "Can I have another hot dog?"

"Coming right up," Jerry says and jumps up from his seat, as if eager to escape the suddenly subdued mood at the table.

Carol clatters out of the house with a large tray and resumes her place. "Grandma's okay. She's already fallen asleep and Grandpa's going to stay with her for a while. Who wants popsicles?"

The children eagerly lunge for their dessert and spend the next ten minutes licking and slurping until they and the table around them are a sticky mess. Jerry frees Sarah from her booster seat and, with Jenny following, takes her to the hose and washes them both clean. Sarah runs away from him, flops down on the grass, and begins playing energetically with her toys. I suggest to Jennifer that she ask Carol if she can go up to Sarah's room and find some other toys that she and Sarah could play with together. To my astonishment, she says okay. I watch her approach Carol cautiously, almost gingerly, and gently touch her arm. Carol swings around, listens for a moment, then escorts Jennifer into the house.

Mrs. Hauser starts clearing the table, and I get up to help her. The three men are now discussing President Nixon and the appointment of Henry Kissinger as secretary of state. As I lift away their plates, cups, and utensils, I can't help comparing them to the men in Clearyville, who usually sit around the green on July Fourth, discussing politics.

To say that the men of Clearyville argue about politics is not really accurate; after all, what is there to argue about when everyone is in accord? They don't exactly discuss the current situation. It's more like they exult loudly in their positive agreement of it. What they say sounds a lot different from what I heard from Rick one Sunday afternoon, when he painstakingly crystallized and analyzed American politics for me, to me, and at me. I realized halfway through his lecture that I didn't really know what he was talking about. All I can say for certain is that his opinions were the opposite of what I'd heard all my life. Now I know that what Rick said was right. Clearyville doesn't want to know that the president it unanimously helped to elect is a crook, a liar, and what Rick calls a "prick"—a term I'd never heard before but can guess what it means. Clearyville doesn't even begin to see the president that way. Rick believes the country is in critical condition, but Clearyville makes excuses for its leadership. Rick predicts that the senate hearings being conducted on television the last couple of months will culminate in impeachment of the president, yet in Clearyville, he's glorified as a hero and a victim. In the past, I would have gone out of my way to avoid boring topics like the government, the economy, the responsibility of leadership, and Steve would have approved, no more expecting me to be interested than my parents would have expected me to be interested in a course on comparative religions.

Now though, I sometimes have this fantasy of sitting and watching the hearings with Rick on the ceiling television in his hospital room. He'll be commenting wisely on the proceedings, and I'll be nodding in total agreement. It won't matter that I'm still not certain whose side I am on, his or Clearyville's. What will matter is that I will have finally gained entry into a vital area of his life. I will probably never know what Rick sees in me, a provincial, ignorant hayseed from Middle America. I just know that I don't want to be that person anymore. I want to learn, to be more than I am. *Dear Lord, at the very least, I want to have an opinion.*

Jerry, his father, and Carol's father talk in quiet voices, but there is a current of energy among them that is almost palpable. Jerry looks up at me. "Maggie, could you find out if the coffee's been made?"

"Sure. I'll be back out in a minute." I deposit the trash in a big plastic bag next to the porch and enter the kitchen, where Carol and her mother-in-law are discussing options available to Mrs. Goodman. It's a depressing subject, and they both seem to be in lower spirits than they were an hour ago.

"Jerry's looking for his coffee," I tell Carol with an apologetic look, and she points to the pot.

"I have a tray ready. Just put out the pot, the cups, and whatever they want."

"The table's clear. Can I help in any other way?"

"No, thanks. We're fine," Carol answers. Then she says, "You were surprised when Jenny came right over to me at the table."

"How did you know?"

"I saw the expression on your face. She's really making progress, isn't she?"

"Yes. I can hardly believe it. I'm even thinking of taking her up to see Ri—" *Not now. Later.* I clamp my mouth shut.

"Rick is a neighbor Maggie and Jenny have befriended," Carol quickly explains to Mrs. Hauser. "He's been hospitalized since he was in a terrible accident a couple of months ago, and Jenny's been anxious to see him."

"I'm sorry to hear about that. Will he be all right?"

I glance sideways at Carol, mentally send her a prayer to change the subject. She doesn't get it. "He's out of the danger zone and getting better little by little."

"Thank God," Mrs. Hauser says.

Carol picks up the loaded coffee tray and starts for the door. "Irene, will you bring out Maggie's fantastic-looking cake? You know where the cake knife is. And, Maggie, would you bring out a few more popsicles from the freezer in case the kids want more? Oh, and there are extra napkins on the table." She kicks open the porch door and holds it open for Mrs. Hauser and me.

While the others have a cup of coffee, Carol invites me to join her on a walk.

The air has cooled a bit, and clouds are beginning to roll in. I hope they're not bringing wet weather. At first we talk about Carol's mother. "The trouble with being a mental health professional," she says, "is that everyone expects you to handle the situation with perfect calm and strength. In fact, they *count* on you for that, because they can't do it themselves."

"It's the same with nurses," I say. When Rick first got hurt, his family turned to me like I was a human meds cart, loaded with all kinds of goodies that would take away the pain and ease their anxiety. I tried to explain to them that nurses have feelings too."

"Thank God for Irene and Sam. They seem to understand things in a way that my parents never would."

We walked for a few minutes in comfortable silence before Carol asked me why I was upset about her having mentioned Rick.

"It was silly, I guess, but you stepped in right away and covered my awkwardness. Thank—"

"Don't evade the question."

"Okay. I didn't want to get into it because there's something you don't know, and I didn't want that to slip out the same way."

"Isn't that the reason you asked if we could have some time together?"

"Yes. Here it is. I've left my job at the hospital. The Simons asked me to work private duty for Rick."

"And you thought this through thoroughly before you committed?"

"From every angle." I went on to explain the benefits.

She agreed that the terms were generous. "But what happens when he leaves Chicago?"

"It won't be a problem for me. His family has some kind of influence at the hospital. Evidently, his grandfather, I think it was, was a founder and was on the board for some time."

"I'm impressed, Maggie, but you do understand that they can't invent a position for you if none is available when Rick goes home."

"Rick said the same thing. But they assured me there will be a place when I need one."

"Do you have any idea how long he'll be here?"

"No, but he's beginning to make good progress. He's working hard now."

"And you're okay with this arrangement?"

"It was a very difficult decision to make, but once I did, I felt good about it. Sure, I get night terrors every once in a while, but I trust the family to do right by us. They're good people."

"So what do you have to do for Rick?"

I told her. Some of the chores made her blanch, but I expected that. "I agree that some of it is not very palatable, but I look at it as all in a day's work."

"And how does Rick feel about it?"

"He seems to be okay with it, though at first he asked why I had let his parents buy me. Doesn't that strike you as a strange thing for him to say?"

"Intellect doesn't equate with maturity. I don't know that much about him or his background, but my therapist's instinct tells me that he has issues with his parents, a lot of anger. It sounds to me like he has a lot of growing up to do."

"I . . . I'm not good at analyzing people. I think sometimes he wishes he came from a different family."

"I'm not asking you to analyze him. I just want your impressions of his level of maturity."

I don't know what to say. The truth is he does act like a spoiled little boy sometimes, like the time when his parents visited him and his mother came over to take Jody back. I was disgusted by Rick's reaction, but I'm embarrassed to talk to Carol about it. "He's very intelligent," I offer feebly. "He knows so much about so many things."

"I'm not interested in his intellectual or his sexual maturity. I'm talking about his behavior as an adult."

This is getting too close for comfort for me. There are still things I can't, won't discuss even with Carol. Besides, it's time for us to be getting back to the city, and I feel a headache coming on. "I'm sorry. I don't know what you want me to say."

As usual, Carol reads me like a book. "Okay." She sighs in frustration. "Look, I'd like us to meet in the city when we get back. I'll call you after Labor Day and we'll set up a lunch. I know you're having a hard time with a couple of difficult situations, Maggie, and that things might get harder. I want to help you deal with whatever happens, but I can't if I don't know what the truth is." She checks her watch under the next streetlight. "We should probably head back. I want to say good-bye to Sam and Irene before they leave for Glencoe, and you're ready to get home." We turn and head back to the house.

Jerry, his parents, and Mr. Goodman are in the living room continuing the spirited discussion about politics. Sarah's been put to bed, and Jennifer is drowsing in a big armchair. Good-byes are exchanged quickly and warmly.

Driving to the city, my mind wanders back over the day: the barbecue, the lovely house, Carol's and Jerry's parents, and Jennifer's ease with them. I think too of the similar good-natured camaraderie among Rick's family, and I feel sad that I'll never be able to provide my daughter with that kind of happy and loving environment. Somehow a weekend at the family homestead in Clearyville doesn't quite make it. I want what those people have. I want to know what they know and feel how they feel.

I want to be like them. I want change.

Carol

We opened the clinic in 1966. We had both earned our degrees in the early '60s,—Jerry, an MD in general medicine, and I a license in practical nursing and a masters in clinical social work—and we were totally antiestablishment long before it was fashionable. Jerry had done his residency at Cook County and was determined to commit himself to making health care possible for even the poorest people in the city. We even thought of moving to the country so farmers could barter with us for visits, but that was way far out for me. I'm a New Yorker and too much of a city person to live in the boonies. We had both come into small inheritances from family members, so we invested in an old two-story house in a relatively impoverished area on the South Side, which we and a few friends worked our asses off to get in some kind of shape. All of our equipment was secondhand when we started out, and Jerry's folks, who live in Glencoe, pretty much bankrolled us for the first year, while my parents in Brooklyn sent what they could to help. Somehow we managed to get ourselves entrenched in the community, and people began coming in. My therapy clients kept a roof over our heads and food in our stomachs.

I spent my nights helping out at the clinic, from answering phones to holding patients' hands during procedures. By the time a year had gone by, we were able to hire a retired registered nurse to come in during the day. On weekends, we or the part-time doctor who worked for us gratis opened up only for emergencies. We definitely needed someone who could assist with procedures and help with the paperwork, so we ran an ad in the paper. That's how we met Maggie.

Neither of us had ever met anyone like her. She was shy and sweet, the essence of guilelessness and vulnerability. At first I thought she was maybe nineteen and just off the farm. At the interview, she was quite composed and answered my questions in short straightforward sentences, with no extraneous information. She smiled twice, once when she came in and once when she said good-bye. There was something about her—I don't know what—that told me she was someone we'd be lucky to have in the clinic. That she'd had five years of secretarial work and was in her last semester of nursing school were definitely in her favor.

She started right in the first night, organizing and working out an efficient record system, and before she was there a month, Jerry had her helping him with patients, which meant that I didn't need to be at the clinic at night anymore. Maggie said very little to any of us, and we both sensed that she wouldn't appreciate our asking her for the story of her life. In fact, it was months before we learned anything about her, past or present.

The night that she finally opened up was miserable and rainy. I came in to pick Jerry up at closing, but he was doing some kind of a minor procedure on someone and wasn't ready to leave. I sat out in the reception area with Maggie—in complete silence. The magazines were all about six months old, and I was bored to tears. I've never been good at sitting around doing nothing, so I finally just came out with it and said, "Tell me about yourself, Maggie."

"What do you want to know?" she asked.

"Just about who you are and what your background is. If you tell me yours," I said slyly, "I'll tell you mine."

She smiled and started talking, timidly at first, but with more confidence as she went on. I heard about the jerkwater town she grew up in, how her family life revolved around the church, and how much she liked to read. I was surprised to hear that she had been married at the age of twenty-two and that she had a baby daughter, who was back in "Dullsville" staying with her parents until she was capped and had a steady nursing job. I asked about her husband and was shocked to learn that he had been declared missing in action while on a mission in Vietnam the previous summer. We would never have guessed that she had so recently suffered such a tragedy. The therapist in me immediately wanted to know if she needed help. As time went by, I learned that she was convinced that her husband would return, even though it seemed that that wasn't going to happen. I kept in touch with her in between the times I went to pick Jerry up after work, and we talked a little when we could. We went to her graduation and offered to take her out afterward, but her family was there, and we sensed that we would be intruding. So we just congratulated her, nodded to her family, and left.

A month later, Maggie took the job at the hospital and soon brought the baby to Chicago. I had offered to go shopping with her for a crib and a changing table and whatever else she needed, but she thanked me and said her father was going to bring her all the equipment they had at their house.

Jerry, who truly missed having Maggie in the clinic, made me promise I wouldn't give up on her, and I agreed not to unless she gave me a negative response. I wouldn't force myself on her. The next time I heard from her was about a month after she left. She invited us over to meet Jennifer, who was about a year old. She was a cute little thing, but to me, something seemed to be missing. Maggie said she was crawling, but when she put her down on the floor, Jenny just sat there with a plastic toy in her hand, staring into space. She didn't respond to any other of our attempts to play with her. It was strange. We didn't say anything to Maggie, but we discussed the baby at length, Jerry and I, on the ride home. He wondered if she might have a hearing problem.

After that day, months went by without a word from Maggie. We were quite busy with our lives, and I hardly had time to brush my teeth, let alone call her. The days just flew. Jerry was already on his third secretary since Maggie had left.

I finally made the effort, and invited Maggie for lunch in the neighborhood where she worked. She said Jenny was doing well at her sitter's house, and she had heard nothing about Steve but still knew in her heart that he would return. I tried to persuade her, very tactfully, to accept the *possibility* that he might not come back, but she was adamant. And so it went for the next few years. Four, then six months would go by before we talked again. I don't think she herself took the initiative more than a couple of times. But I was concerned enough about her state of mind and her empty lifestyle that I was determined not to lose touch with her completely. I continued calling her now and then, even though the calls had degenerated into mere politeness.

Maggie came over to our flat to deliver a gift after our daughter, Sarah, was born. She was just as reticent as she'd always been. It was frustrating, but I felt compelled to keep trying to get her to accept the probable reality of her husband's "disappearance." Let's just say she acted like she was listening, but nothing I said moved her.

And then one night last winter, February maybe, she called Jerry at the clinic and said she had a neighbor—a male!—who seemed to be quite ill but was refusing medical care. Jerry got excited, you know, that maybe Maggie was seeing someone. But he also knew that she recognized illness when she saw it. So he said we'd come for dinner if she got the guy over to her apartment. And that's how we met Rick, the sexy, adorable, and very sick twenty-two-year-old whom she had befriended. Maggie was flushed, distracted, and unwittingly giving a good imitation of—how can I put this politely?—a dog in heat.

While Jerry fixed Rick up as best he could, I encouraged her to continue the flirtation or whatever it was. Later I was sorry I did. Though Rick managed to turn her around in terms of her accepting that she no longer had a husband, she seemed to be having just as hard a time dealing with Rick in her life as she had dealing with Steve gone from it. The best thing to come out of that evening was that she began calling more often. We started meeting for lunch or dinner fairly regularly. She was much more forthcoming than she'd ever been, especially after Rick barely escaped with his life from what appeared to be an accident without a cause. In our most recent conversation, she said Rick was making good progress in rehab.

Maggie's once-boring, solitary life seems to be turning into a saga, and right now I'm waiting to see what's going to happen next.

August 27, 1973

My second week in the rehab unit went smoothly. Rick was in good spirits for the most part, and I found things to do when I wasn't ministering to him. By Friday I'd decorated two walls with get-well cards from all over the country, many of them from people with the last name of Simon; his extended family must be very big. One day, I decided to read the personal notes to him; but after the fifth or sixth, he said he appreciated the thought, but he really "wasn't into cards," and he retreated into his academic shell. I couldn't resist going through the rest myself. On Wednesday I brought in curtains I had bought for the triple-width window that overlooks the parking lot, but had left the tension rods on my dining room table, so I had to be content with reading magazines most of the afternoon. On Friday, when I nagged him once again about his not eating, he angrily accused me of neglecting to bring him his breakfast and lunch as I had promised. I told him I hadn't forgotten at all, that he had kept putting off telling me what he wanted. He glanced at me sheepishly, said "oops," and wrote out his preferences for next week on the spot, starting with lunch for the coming Monday, which is today.

Over the weekend, the city turned into a steam bath that the weatherman predicts will last at least ten days. Jerry and Carol had invited Jennifer and me to spend the weekend with them at their cottage on a lake about an hour north of the city. The weather was hot, sunny, and unbearably humid, only slightly cooler near the water, especially at twilight, when we barbecued. I hadn't spent a day at a lake in years, and Jenny was happy as a clam building sand castles at the water's edge. It was paradise. We all knew what we were in for when we went home, and Carol and Jerry moaned and groaned (or, according to Carol, "bellyached") all the way back. Needless to say, the fan in my bedroom is useless against the humidity, and I hardly slept last night.

As I'm driving to work at eight twenty this morning, I notice on a thermometer outside a bank that the temperature is already close to 90°. The air is so dense, it's hard to breathe. When I enter the rehab lobby, the receptionist informs me that the air-conditioning in our wing of the building broke down last night. I find Rick lying on his stomach on the bed, totally inert, with his arm dangling limply over the edge and his catheterization tube snaking out from beneath the thin sheet that covers the lower part of his body. He mumbles that he didn't sleep last night. I spend half the morning giving him alcohol rubs, running back and forth to the bathroom to soak towels for his forehead and neck, and refreshing the ice in his water pitcher. The only thing worse that can happen today is a water main break. At least PT is on the other side of the building where the air-conditioning evidently is still operating.

It's nine thirty now, and I'm sitting in the room, wretched, uncomfortable, and in a slightly grouchy mood. My nylon uniform is dampish and sticking to the plastic chair. My mind keeps going back to the lake—the sun-spangled tranquility of the water, the only sounds those of songbirds and our girls, and the long, narrow green lawn, which, shadowed by tall old shade trees, leads down to the Hausers' pier. Paradise.

But I am on duty here. "Rick?"

"Whuh."

"Don't you think you should have some breakfast before it gets too close to your PT session?"

"Too hot."

"I brought you some fruit salad with sour cream dressing and a croissant. Come on. I'll share it with you."

Slowly turning his face toward me, he singsongs listlessly, "Here is the airplane, here is the hangar—"

"What does that mean?"

"It means you're treating me like a baby," he replies a bit more forcefully. "I'm old enough to know when I want to eat and when I don't. When I do, I'll ask for it. Right now, I don't, but if you want to, then you eat. Just let me lie here—or die here. Whichever comes first."

And here we go. I sigh. I'm getting tired of him lecturing me when I say something that annoys him, but I refrain from telling him so. "Everyone's uncomfortable. This heat is fierce, but the air-conditioning is working on the other side, so you'll probably feel better once you get to PT. Just be thankful that your casts have been removed. Otherwise, you'd be in agony from the itching." I get up and drag myself to the window. Straight ahead, the sun's glare on the tops of the cars in the parking lot is blinding, and I turn my head toward the wing of the building that forms a right angle to us. "Oh, look at that! The air-conditioning repair truck is parked outside the maintenance door. Thank the Lord. I think we're being fixed!"

"Great idea, Mags," he drawls. "I'll be over to take a look as soon as I check under the bed for my slippers."

I spin around, realizing what I just said. "Oh . . . I didn't mean that literally."

"Maggie, I was joking," he informs me in the tone of voice I usually associate with rolling eyes. "Call me a cripple, call me half a man. Nothing you or anyone else says can bother me. I've got it all together now. So you don't have to walk on eggs or bring the Lord into it. He and I aren't on very good terms at the moment anyway. Now . . . could you forgive yourself long enough to help me turn over on my back?"

I'm pretty good at moving patients of normal size, but today presents difficulties. Rick and I are both sticky from the heat, and our skins chafe when I take hold of his arms. Fortunately he's gained strength in his upper body during the past month and a half and can now assist in moving himself. Nevertheless, the dead weight of his lower body makes it awkward for me to maneuver him onto his back. When we finally manage it, I start getting him ready for the day with a quick bed bath and a pair of jeans. As I raise the head of the bed and get him into a sitting position so he can put on a tee shirt, I notice for the first time that he looks like he hasn't shaved since Friday, and I wonder if he might be growing a beard. These days the magazines and newspapers are full of men sporting shoulder-length hair, sideburns, mustaches, and beards. Kathy thinks they look "sooo sexy" with all that hair. I can't say that I agreed with her when she first said so, but now I have to admit that a couple of days without shaving does make Rick look kind of, well, even more appealing, like when he had pneumonia last winter. I couldn't let myself acknowledge the thought then. Now I'm distracted by it.

The orderly arrives to take him to PT, and I watch carefully as he is maneuvered into the wheelchair. I haven't attempted this yet and won't until I've spoken to whoever has the time to teach me to do it. I'm strong for a female, but I'm not sure I'd be able to support Rick if he buckled during the transfer.

As soon as he's gone, I go into the kitchen to make a pitcher of lemonade from the can of frozen concentrate I'd bought with his lunch. I pick up his mail at the front desk, then return to the stifling room and set about hanging up the rest of the cards, including the two from today's mail. One is from R. Taylor in the town in New York where the Simons live, and the other is from Mr. and Mrs. Phillip Dana from Arizona. The out-of-state addresses fascinate me. How does he know all these people? There is also a packet from the registrar's office at the university. Rick's been back working on his dissertation for a couple of weeks now, and he's taking telephone calls, which, except from his family, he had been refusing to do until last week. He never says anything to me about the calls, and I don't believe it's my place to ask. In fact, the last time we talked about anything other than his physical condition was the night before the accident. Sometimes I feel as if I'm being shut out. But then . . . why should he talk with me about anything else? I'm here to help him stay focused on getting stronger and more independent. Nothing in my job description mentions involvement in any other area of his life.

Around eleven, I call Erin, but there's no answer. The apartment was so stuffy and unpleasant before I left it this morning that I suggested she take Jennifer to one of the city's public beaches to cool off. In her efficient way, she had a bathing suit in her bag and was more than happy to comply. I am determined not to spend the day worrying about Jenny's safety. She has always been timid around water, and all of the beaches are supervised. Besides, Erin is not a teenager with a roving eye, and I feel confident that she will keep both her eyes on my daughter the whole time.

I move the mail from the little table next to me to the bed tray, on the way noticing a postcard that must have fallen to the floor when I first came in today. Again I can't resist taking a peek at the handwritten message, which says only, "Expect a delivery by air." No signature, only a New York City return address on the front. I lay the card on the opened envelopes I left on top of the packet and go once more to the kitchen to get the breakfast Rick didn't want. Maybe he'll change his mind or eat the turkey club sandwich I bought for his lunch. I also bring my own ham and Swiss back with me and settle down as comfortably as I can with the food and a magazine.

Rick comes back from PT looking worse than he did when he left. Instead of the usual orderly, his primary therapist, Curt, has transported him, a sign that never bodes well. He helps Rick back onto the bed and motions me out of the room.

"Your patient had a little 'episode' today," he begins. My stomach lurches. "I'm telling you about it so you might be able to find out why it happened and if and how we can help him with it."

"What on earth—?"

"Rick's a very hard worker. He's always trying to do more, be better than he was at the previous session. Today, he took off like a firecracker. Started off great, worked harder than I've ever seen him work, made some real progress with his mobility. Then, about fifteen, twenty minutes before the end of the session, he seemed to fall apart, to crash."

"What do you mean, crashed? Collapsed? Got hurt?"

"Nothing like that. It was more of a mental thing. Granted, he was physically exhausted and having to put up with the horrendous heat in his room, but it was as if he suddenly gave up mentally. He was doing the parallel bars and he just kind of let go, dropped to the floor, and lay there between the bars. We rushed up and pulled him out of the way of the two guys coming along behind him. I got him over to the wall and propped him up, but he wasn't cooperating and he wouldn't talk to us. We tried to get through to him, but he just refused to respond."

This may not be a genuine *uh-oh,* but I don't like the sound of it. Things have been going relatively well. Why would he regress to those awful weeks after the accident? I open the door to his room and look in at him lying on his back on the bed. He appears to be asleep. Oh Lord. I can't think.

Curt stands quietly, watching, as I try not to make a mountain out of a molehill. "Can you think of any reason—"

"No," I interrupt, wanting him to leave so I can see if Rick is in a talking mood. "Maybe he just ran out of steam."

"I've seen him drop down before, but he always wants to get up again. I know he's temperamental, but if you can get anything out of him about this, please let me know. I was with him every minute, and I didn't see anything. We checked him and didn't see any sign of injury either."

"Okay," I sigh, glad he's wrapping it up. "I'll pass along anything he says."

"Great . . . What's your name again?"

"Maggie McLean."

"Thanks, Maggie," he says, shakes my hand briefly, and disappears down the hall.

I approach Rick's bed. His eyes are closed. No, this doesn't bode well at all. "Rick? Are you awake?"

His eyes open. "Yes."

"I just spoke to Curt for a few minutes. He's worried about you." He doesn't react to this. "Can you tell me what happened?"

"Yes, but I don't want to."

"If you don't tell me, you might end up having to talk about it to the social worker. Why don't you let me run interference for you?"

Deep sigh. "Why can't everybody leave me alone?"

"If we all leave you alone, you'll never walk again."

Slow blink, another sigh.

"Damn it, Maggie. Please just put a Don't Disturb sign on the door and go home."

"Not till I know what happened." I have a feeling that if I let him go to sleep before he tells me what took place, I'll lose him, I'll never find out, and I'll have failed at a very important part of my job.

"God, I'm tired. I'm so damn tired." He closes his eyes again.

"Curt said you work very hard in PT. He said this is the first time he saw you give up."

Rick swallows but doesn't say anything. It's all I can do not to give up myself. I'm tired too, of his moods, his inability or refusal to share his feelings. It's as if we've lost weeks of hard work.

I pick up his hand, kiss the back of it. Then I return to my chair to sit and wait—for what, I don't know. I just feel like I'm waiting for something.

Lunchtime comes and goes. I just sit. Rick hasn't moved, and I know he's too far inside himself for anyone to reach. He has OT at two and another PT session at three. Without saying anything, I leave the room and head for the nursing supervisor's office. The door is open, and she's at her desk, deep in paperwork. I knock lightly.

She looks up. "Hi, Maggie. I haven't seen you around much. Everything working out?"

"Yes, thanks," I assure her, taking the seat she is gesturing to beside her desk. "I just have a question of protocol."

"Shoot."

"My patient had a little problem during PT a while ago."

"May I ask what it was about?"

"I'm not sure yet. I think it's emotional. He's moody. He's in no condition now to go to OT or his afternoon PT. Is there anything I need to do about this, like file a report or speak with the therapists?"

"We make allowances for the patients with depression, illness, and the like, so long as it's a legitimate problem. Let's see. Eric Simon, isn't it?"

"Yes."

She rummages through the charts lining the walls, finds Rick's, and looks through it. "He's been doing well in physical therapy. The notes say that he's fully committed to his goals, which are getting up on his own two feet and getting his bladder and bowel function back. I think he can be excused for the afternoon. Notify the therapists that he has permission to skip and"—she looks up—"do let me know if you find out why he broke down today."

"Thanks, Terry. Rick can be maddeningly difficult to draw out, but I'll do my best."

"In the short time he's been here, he seems to have gained a reputation for being, um, somewhat contrary. Our nurses are very happy to have you here."

"He is a challenge," I agree. "Thanks again."

Back in the room, Rick is as I left him—sleeping, I assume. I sink back into my chair, but feeling restless, I get up again and go to the window. The air-conditioning truck is gone. It's probably been working for a couple of hours, and I never noticed the difference. Before I settle back in the chair, I reach for the phone to call the therapists. Then I open my magazine and prepare myself for three hours of sheer boredom. I don't really mind the boredom though. Frankly I prefer it to dealing with Rick in his current mood.

Redbook's book feature starts out pretty well, and before too long, I am engrossed enough in the story not to fall asleep. Though it's still hot in the room, at least the air-conditioning has taken out some of the humidity, and I'm not sticking to the chair anymore. The next time I check my watch, an hour has gone by, and I realize that, as far as I know, Rick hasn't eaten anything all day. It's three thirty. I'm still concerned about the PT problem, but I let him sleep, and I go back to my story.

"Maggie?" My insides leap at the sound of his voice. It is startling after two hours of cocoonlike silence, and I lay the magazine aside.

"I'm here. Are you all right?"

"How long did I sleep?"

"About four hours."

"I missed afternoon therapy?"

"Uh-huh. Do you remember you had some difficulty in PT this morning?"

"Of course I remember. Why?"

"We need to talk about it." I pull a visitor chair over to the bed.

"What is there to talk about?"

"The floor administrator needs to know what happened to you and why it happened." He doesn't say anything, which is like déjà vu and makes me uneasy. "Don't play games, Rick. The time for that is past."

He takes a deep breath, lets it out slowly. "I don't want to talk about it. Let's just say I had a tantrum."

"That's not an answer."

"Come on, Maggie. It's over. What difference does it make now?"

I'm about out of patience with his "so what" attitude, and I fix my eyes on him in what I hope comes across as a penetrating stare. I'm hoping to make him uncomfortable enough to say something that will explain what caused him to break down this morning. Minutes pass while he sits, face turned away, fingers picking at the threads in his thin woven sheet.

Just as I'm thinking it's a good time for me to duck out for a large cup of strong black coffee, he says softly, "Shit."

Soundless at first, it takes a second for me to register the movements in his chest, his snuffling attempts to breathe back the dripping from his nose. *Dear God, he's crying.*

This is not uncommon among male patients, but it's the last thing I would ever have expected from Rick, and I'm caught totally off guard, unsure whether to comfort him or let him get it all out. I move briskly to the bed, pull his pillow from beneath him, and replace it behind his shoulders. Then I crank up the bed and sit down on it beside him. "It's okay, Rick," I tell him in my best calming nurse voice and brush his hair away from his eyes. "Just let it out."

It takes a while for him to wind down, but finally the tears stop flowing, and the shuddering subsides.

"I can't do this anymore, Maggie," he croaks. "It isn't working." His eyes make me think of shiny panes of dark, wet glass. He wipes them with the palms of his hands, and I grab a couple of tissues from a box on the night table and dab at his red, runny nose.

"What isn't working?"

"Therapy. No matter how hard I try, I don't get any better."

"That's not true, Rick. Didn't I tell you before how well Curt said you're doing? He said you're one of the hardest workers he's ever seen, and that you're making great progress."

He shakes his head. "Great is not good enough."

I take his hand. "Look, you're depressed and frustrated right now, but it'll pass, and then everything will be okay."

"No, it won't. It'll never be okay."

"Why do you say that?"

"Because okay is the way it used to be."

And I thought my mother was obstinate. "Well, it can't be like that anymore," I snap, the little patience I have left deserting me, "and you'd better get used to the reality of it if you want to get better."

I almost never let on when I'm angry, and Rick reacts with a startled expression, followed by a deep blush that spreads over his face, coloring his prison-pale complexion so that it now blends in with his nose. "I haven't cried since I was little."

"It's a natural reaction," I say. "Right now, you're scared, but you'll feel much less helpless after you've adjusted to your situation."

"I have adjusted to it, Maggie," he protests. "That's the trouble. I've done nothing but think about it. I lie awake at night worrying about the future, what's going to happen to everything I've been working toward. There's no way out. Everyone wants me to keep fighting, to bust my back," he snuffles at the irony. "For what? To be a useless cripple for the rest of my life? To have people drag me around, tie my shoelaces, wait on me? I'm twenty-two years old. Drinking a gallon of prune juice before I stick my finger up my ass and push on my stomach twice a day doesn't seem like much to look forward to."

"It's not going to be like that, Rick. You're 'busting your back' so that it won't."

"You even have to wipe my nose for me."

"For heaven's sake, I didn't have to do that, but I'm a nurse. It's a reflex. When I see a nose that needs wiping, I wipe it. It's my job to make sure my patients eat properly and to take care of all the other things they need."

He looks at me for a long time without speaking. With his red nose and bloodshot eyes, his hair hanging down his neck in unattractive coarse, damp clumps, and his three-day growth of beard, he doesn't look much like the magnetic man Kathy introduced me to in my apartment last September. Yet, at this moment, I want him in my life more than I ever have. Not in any romantic or physical sense, but because of what he's given me this past year, the impact he's had on our lives—Jenny's and mine—in the time we've known him. "It isn't what we want that's important, Rick. It's what you want. Everyone working on your case is confident that you can beat this. Would we push you so hard to be something we know you can never be? Believe me, the goal of everyone on the staff is to see their patients leave here on their own two feet."

He sighs heavily. "It might all be part of your job, but there are some things you shouldn't have to put up with."

"I don't mind it," I assure him. "Just keep doing what you're doing and time will take care of the rest . . . Are you okay now? Can I run over to the cafeteria for a cup of coffee?"

"I'm fine. Get me one too, okay?"

By the time I've disposed of the mound of soggy tissues in the bathroom, straightened my uniform, and finger-combed my hair, he has pulled the tray table bearing his books and writing materials into position.

I make sure his glasses are within his reach before I leave the room.

It's Tuesday, and Jennifer and I both had dental appointments this morning, so by the time I get to work, it's a few minutes past eleven. Rick is sitting in his wheelchair, staring out the window.

"Good morning. How was PT today?"

"Back to normal," he replies sullenly without turning around.

"Good. Nice to see you sitting up."

"'Snot like you haven't seen me sitting up before."

I've only been here for two minutes, and I already don't like the direction the day is taking. "I mean in a chair by the window."

"Guess where I was at eight thirty this morning," he says, as if he's about to blame me for wherever it was.

"I don't know, Rick. Where?"

He swivels the chair around, and—*uh-oh*—I imagine I am seeing sparks shooting out of his eyes. "I was in the psychiatrist's office waiting for him to show up for my appointment. Of course, you wouldn't happen to know anything about that, would you?"

"No. Why would I?"

"Because he knew about the episode in PT—"

"From Rob, not from me," I protest mildly.

"Curt didn't know about what happened in here when I got back from the session."

I stand here, at a loss, when suddenly it dawns on me. "Oh! I did mention in my notes for yesterday that you were 'somewhat teary' when you got back from PT."

"You take notes on me?" This discovery apparently takes precedence over the fact that I condemned him to a psychiatric session over the word "teary."

"You know that all attending nurses keep notes on their patients. You've seen me writing in your chart a hundred times."

His shoulders slump, and he looks down at his hands, lying idle in his lap. When he looks up, the sparks are gone. "You're right, Maggie. I'm sorry," he concedes after a moment or two, like a child who's been caught misbehaving. But Rick is not a child. He's a man who has been devastated by catastrophe, has accepted his situation, but has yet to make peace with the changes in his life. How can I be angry or annoyed with him? It isn't fair.

"And what did the psychiatrist say?" I ask briskly, determined not to show any emotion.

He looks up. "That occasional crying jags are normal for men at my stage of recovery, and I shouldn't be embarrassed or worried about them."

"And?"

"He wanted to give me pills for depression, but I refused. I already have enough junk in my body."

"So that's it?"

"Pretty much . . . Oh, yeah, he said he wants me off the bed and in the chair except for sleeping during the night and an occasional nap."

I immediately brighten. "Terrific. That must cheer you up."

"Maggie, I've been in this place for almost two months with my entire existence bounded by this room and the therapy wing. I've done nothing for the past six weeks except read newspapers and make stabs at my dissertation. I'm so anxious to see the outside of a building that I'll go anywhere, do anything just to breathe real air."

Finally! He's found the light, and he's ready to follow it. "I've been waiting for this for weeks, Rick. I was about to give up hope." I point out the window. "See that nice green area to the right? If you want, we can spend some time out there during your afternoon free period. There's also an outdoor café up on the roof. We can take a look at that too. Are you interested?"

"Outta sight!" he exults, then he adds, "for starters."

I'm as elated as he is and encouraged by this sudden turn of events, but I put my excitement aside and go back to the previous conversation. "Rick, did you tell that to the psychiatrist, about how trapped you feel?"

"Not in so many words, but I think he got the idea."

"What did he say?"

"He told me to have my nurse or an orderly take me outdoors and walk me around, so long as we don't go off the grounds."

"We can do that today at three, if you want to."

"It's a date," he declares and lights up my day with a smile that threatens to make me fall in love with him in spite of myself.

During Rick's rest time after lunch, I walk across the building to see if Curt has a minute. He's eating lunch at his desk, but he invites me in and offers me half a sandwich, which I decline with thanks. He's happy with Rick's performance at the morning session and feels sure that he will pick up where he left off without difficulty. He, in fact, gives me a crash course on the ups and downs of spinal cord injury recovery, what to expect, and what not to be worried about. By then his next PT class has begun to arrive, and I return to the room.

In the time before Rick's second PT session of the day, I do a body check on him for bedsores and related problems and give him a short massage. After Tim, the orderly, settles him in his wheelchair, Rick thanks him and informs him that he'll be wheeling himself over to the therapy wing from now on. Tim flashes a 'thumbs up' and says, "Way to go, man!"

I am excited about Rick finally taking some control of his life. Maybe yesterday was the catalyst to get him back on track. This a big step toward independence, and a welcome sign that the tide is turning.

I meet him and Tim in the corridor on the way back from the session. Rick is wrung out, as usual, and I toss him a damp towel. "Clean yourself up. We're going out for a walk."

Tim winks and relinquishes the pushbars without an argument. "This guy give you any trouble, just holler," he says.

To which Rick mutters, "I bet he says that about all the cripples."

For the next half hour, Rick and I stroll the grounds on the landscaped side of the unit. Here there are manicured lawns, flower beds, benches, and smooth white paths. The second the door of the building closed behind us, I felt like I'd been shoved into a steam room, but Rick, who seems to be totally unaware of the intense heat, doesn't say a word. Nor does he speak at all while we're out, just spends the time taking it all in and, every now and then, lifting his face to the heat-hazy sky. When we return to the room, he gives himself a proper sponge bath in the chair, changes his shirt, and without my assistance actually lifts himself up with his arms so I can get him into clean pants. I am stunned by this further progress but don't comment on it. For all I know, he's been able to do this for weeks, but hasn't because of anger, stubbornness, or self-pity. It doesn't make sense to me, but neither does the way some people laugh when informed of the death of a loved one. I've seen that happen more than once.

Rick dozes, but only for a few minutes. He has OT at four. He's tired, but insists on wheeling himself back over. Chances are he's going to sleep well tonight. I leave him a note explaining that I've gone out to pick up dinner, which he'll have at six o'clock. Rick and I haven't had dinner together since the accident, and I want to do something special for him to celebrate what he's accomplished. I've already arranged for Erin to stay with Jennifer until eight.

I have no idea whether Rick and I even have a personal relationship anymore, and I'm more than a little nervous about how this will turn out.

"Is the food all right?" I ask hesitantly. I took a big chance with dinner, but I think I made a good choice. On my way to the deli where I normally get Rick's food, I noticed a small Chinese restaurant. I remembered Jerry mentioning once that to New Yorkers, Chinese food is "comfort food." Jerry always acts as if New York City is the state. It's like saying that Chicago is Illinois, which is ridiculous. We live in Illinois, and to people I know out in Clearyville, comfort food is purely American. I'll bet most of the people out there have never tasted anything more exotic than Italian food. With that, at least we know what we're eating.

Rick was surprised when I opened the bag and took out those little white containers with metal handles, even identified each dish upon sight. "Great choices," he proclaimed, reaching for the chopsticks that were included. "m*oo goo gai pan* and Happy Family." I confessed that I'd asked the owner to recommend a chicken and vegetable dish for myself and that I had picked the other one because I liked the name. After dividing each dish in half, he eats as if he's ravenous. I haven't yet tried his part of the order, but I am enjoying the chicken thing, for which I'm using a good old American fork.

"Have you talked to your mother lately?" I ask. "Usually she calls me once a week, but I haven't heard from her for two, maybe three weeks. Is everything all right at home?"

"Everything's fine," he says around a mouthful of rice. "They're on Cape Cod this week. We have a summer place there."

"Good. I was worried."

He spears what he calls a snow pea with his chopstick. "So how do you like the *moo goo gai pan*?"

"Pretty good. I've never tasted anything like it."

"I'm proud of you, Mary Grace. Want to try the chopsticks?"

"That's okay. Maybe next time."

His big white smile makes my heart skip. If I'm not careful, I'm going to be the teary one tonight.

When we're finished eating, there's still a lot of food left over. I wrap it up for tomorrow, but Rick insists that I take it home and share it with Jennifer. I'm not sure about doing that—not that I don't trust the food, but because it's so different. Rick says it's only meat and vegetables, but still . . ."Then throw it out," he says amiably, but I was raised never to waste food. In the end I agree to take it home after all.

"Thanks for the walk," he says with another smile. "It was the best walk I've ever taken."

By now it's seven thirty, and I promised to be home by eight. "And this was one of the best dates I've ever been on," I reply, squeezing his hand as I stand up, "but I have to—"

He grabs my arm. "Don't go, Maggie. Please." He doesn't sound exactly desperate, but I do detect a hint of urgency.

"I promised I'd be home by eight."

"Call the sitter. Tell her you have to stay a little longer."

"Is anything wrong?"

"Not exactly . . . I just feel a little funny."

I knew I shouldn't have brought that strange food."

Erin says she has nowhere to go, so I can stay as long as I want. They have just watched a program on the TV in Jenny's bedroom, and now Jenny's about to go to sleep.

I thank her and tell her I won't be late. "The social hour isn't over yet," I remind Rick as I hang up. "Don't you want to go over to the lounge?"

"Hell no!"

I don't know what his problem is, but I don't detect anything physical. Fatigue maybe. "Would you rather be in bed? You've been in the chair all day."

"Maybe . . . I am tired and kind of achy. Yeah, that sounds good."

He pushes the orderly button on the wall over the bed, and I set about clearing the little table we used for supper. Then he slowly wheels himself over to the bed, and we wait without speaking. He nods off once or twice, but pulls himself back quickly and shrugs at me. We've overdone it a bit today, but all in all, he's held up well. Tim arrives with his transfer board and, as Kathy says, "does his thing." He's a big man and handles Rick easily. I ask if he thinks I'll be able to manage transfers myself before too long.

"No problem," he says, "once Rick can help you a little more. When you're both ready, I'll bring you your own transfer board."

Rick immediately starts to undress, and Tim closes the door on his way out. I get a basin and a couple of towels from the bathroom and sponge Rick down, do another bedsore search, check his catheter. He still won't let me do the bowel care; that will be taken care of by his night nurse. He pulls on his shirt, and I pull his shorts over his legs. Amazingly he actually lifts his buttocks so I can get them the rest of the way up. Because the occupational therapist dresses him before I get here in the morning and because he's catheterized, I didn't know he could do this. I make a mental note to arrange an appointment to meet with the OT. I don't much like surprises from my patients.

"Do your parents know about all this progress you've made?" I inquire.

"I don't think so. I haven't discussed my potty habits with my mother in twenty years. We have a tacit agreement that those things are private."

It's been so long since Rick has made me really laugh. Thank you, Lord. But the minute the prayer has been formed, I think, "*What's the Lord got to do with this?* then am ashamed of myself for asking, though less ashamed than I know I should be.

I realize that the bed is still cranked down and Rick is lying there, watching me. "You just said a prayer about me, didn't you," he says smugly.

I don't know whether to be surprised or embarrassed. "How on earth do you know that?"

"I can always tell. What did you pray for this time?"

"It wasn't a prayer, it was a thank-you."

"For what?"

"For you making me laugh."

"What exactly did the Lord have to do with that?"

"You know something, Rick? I just asked myself the same thing."

"No shit," he says.

I smile a half smile. "I really should go now."

"Not until we take care of some unfinished business."

As happens so often lately, I don't know what he's talking about. "Can't it wait?" I ask anxiously.

"No. It's too important." He pats the bed next to him.

"Okay, but we'll have to get it over with quickly," I insist and sit down beside him. He immediately hooks his arm around me and pulls me toward him. "Lie next to me, Maggie."

When I accepted this job, was it for the remote possibility of someday ending a shift this way, in bed with my paraplegic patient? I admit that I often daydream about being in bed with Rick, but he's always whole, undamaged. I can't do this. It goes against everything I am as a nurse. I'm grateful that Rick opened my eyes to how life could again be with someone I care about and am physically attracted to, but no, I won't let him manipulate me into compromising my ethics.

"Ten minutes, Rick. I will lie next to you, but I will not take off any of my clothes and I won't let you take them off me either. I want to be with you again so badly, but I cannot compromise my ethics or my career."

"Nobody will know, Maggie. The door is closed. It's against hospital rules for anyone to enter a room without knocking first. Besides, there's no one in the wing. Most of them are at the social hour, so—"

"Okay, but I'm only lying down next to you," I interrupt, "and only because, well . . . I need you to hold me. That's all. You understand?"

"Ten minutes," he says.

My heart starts hammering so hard that my entire body feels like it's inside a drum. As Rick tries to twist his torso sideways, I do my best to maneuver his legs accordingly. It's less of a struggle than it was a week or two ago, when he asked me to turn him from his stomach to his back, and we eventually reach some semblance of the position he wants to achieve. Timidly I lie down facing him, so close that I can feel his accelerated heartbeat and rapid breathing. He locates my left hand and holds the palm against his chest. I am suddenly aware that I haven't heard any sounds in the hall for a while—no squeaky wheels on carts or chairs, no swishing of cleaners' mops, no footsteps. Instead we are surrounded by an eerie stillness. I move my head a fraction and kiss his stubbly cheek. His hand tightens on mine. After a short while, long before I'm ready to let him go, his hand goes slack, and I know he's fallen asleep. I reluctantly extricate myself from his arm, straighten my clothes, and call Erin to let her know I'll be home in twenty minutes. Then I tiptoe back to Rick and lightly graze his lips with a good night kiss.

I apologize to Erin for being so late, and we chat for a while about how she and Jennifer spent the day. She seems to be very good at finding great things to do and exciting places to go for children Jenny's age. In the course of the conversation, I tell her I'm planning to take Jennifer with me to the hospital tomorrow and would she mind picking her up at the rehab unit at 10:00 a.m.? I had no idea I was going to do this; it just came out of the blue. Erin has no objection, so I give her directions.

As soon as she leaves, I check on Jennifer, as I always do, before changing into my nightgown and settling down for the rest of the evening. I turn on the fan in the bedroom, pour myself a glass of iced tea in the kitchen, then return to my room, which already seems a bit cooler. I am immersed in the *Redbook* story I started on Monday, when Kathy calls and invites herself and Todd over tomorrow night around eight thirty.

"Why don't you come up for dinner around six?" I ask, immediately making a mental list of food I have on hand.

"We can't," she says, not sounding the least bit sorry about it. "We already have plans with some friends of ours."

"Oh. Well, eight thirty's fine. See you then." I haven't seen Kathy in more than a week and I wonder, for the first time, if we're growing apart. Not because this is the first time she's ever declined dinner, but that she's been different lately, kind of distant, as if she's at a point where she wants to have a life of her own, apart from family. Maybe it has to do with loyalty to our mother and the feeling that she's caught in the middle of our conflict. In any case, the reason really doesn't matter. I made a commitment to look after my sister when she moved to the city, and I intend to honor it until I'm satisfied she can take care of herself. I've been so taken up with Rick and the new job that I haven't had much time to get to know Todd, who she's been seeing for three months. I don't know if he's on Mother's approved list already, but it's my responsibility to make sure he's a good choice for Kathy before she starts getting seriously involved with him. I'll know better after I've seen them tomorrow evening.

I read for a while longer, then turn off the light and settle in again. I quickly fall into a deep sleep, but wake up with Rick on my mind at five forty-five, an hour before the alarm rings. I linger in bed, trying to conjure up the glorious sense of tenderness and closeness I felt last night, but it's no use without him. When I feel myself beginning to get to a little—what's the word? maudlin?—I decide to to get out of bed and start the day.

Jennifer is already awake, dressed, and reading a book that Lenore brought her last month.

"Guess what, Mommy! Erin's going to take me to the 'quarium today!"

This is news to me. "I didn't know that," I say carefully. "Unfortunately, we've had a small change in plans since you went to sleep last night."

Her face drops. "You mean we can't go?"

"No, you can go, but it will have to be later. Something's come up, and you'll have to come with me this morning. Erin will pick you up around ten, and then you can go to the Aquarium.

"Oh, good," she breathes. "I was afraid we couldn't go at all."

"You will."

"Are you and me going to stay here and wait for Erin?"

"Nope. We're going somewhere too. It's a surprise."

"Where?"

"If I told you, it wouldn't be a surprise, would it?"

"Will I like it?"

"I hope so . . . Do you have everything you need to go to the Aquarium?"

She nods enthusiastically.

I quickly pour out some Cheerios and milk and cut some peach slices into her bowl. "So have your breakfast and we'll be on our way."

We leave the car in the front parking lot and walk toward the building, which from the front looks more like it houses a number of medical offices than it does like a part of the hospital. Jennifer clutches my hand tensely. I lead her into the lobby, waving to the receptionist as we pass. We push through the double doors to the right wing and move down the corridor to Rick's room, once or twice maneuvering around wheelchairs and slow-moving ambulatory patients. Jennifer's eyes dart back and forth, and she looks up at me curiously. She tightens her grip on my hand. When we reach Rick's door, I ask her to stay put for a moment, while I poke my head inside "to see if we're in the right place," in this case actually to make sure he's dressed appropriately for company. He is, and he's in his chair, reading one of his daily newspapers. I rap lightly on the door, Rick looks up, and Jennifer gasps with joy. Before I can say a word, she takes off across the room and jumps up on him, knocking the paper to the floor and more or less knocking the wind out of him. I panic for a moment. "Jenny, wait! . . . Rick, are you all right?"

He looks up, face flushed, eyes shining. "Fine. You should have warned me!"

"I guess I should have warned Jenny too, but I wanted to surprise both of you."

"I'm extra surprised!" Jennifer pipes happily.

"Me too," Rick agrees and starts to wheel toward me with her on his lap. Jennifer tenses at the movement. He presses her closer to him and whispers, "It's okay." He shakes his head. "Let's take a walk. Okay?"

"Where?" Jennifer asks warily.

"Outside in the garden," he answers, adding, "Sometimes they actually let me out of here."

"It will be better for Rick if you walk, Jenny," I cut in quickly.

Rick rolls his eyes and helps her down.

And so we walk and we talk. Rick does a good job of drawing Jennifer out, especially about the new sitter and what they've been doing over the past few weeks. After a while, he decides he would like to see what the roof café is like, so we take the ramp, which stretches across half the side of the building so the incline will not be too steep. Rick has no problem navigating. The building is surrounded by a continuous bed of flowers, dozens of lawn-type chairs, and stone parapets topped by tall clear protective shields around the perimeter of the roof. A sign on the café door says they are open from eight a.m. to five p.m. We move inside to a glassed-in, air-conditioned cafeteria, decorated with plants and paintings. It's quite pleasant up here and I have a feeling that Rick will want to come again.

"Do we have time for a cup of coffee?" he asks.

I look at my watch. "The sitter will be picking Jennifer up at ten, and it's almost a quarter to now."

"Next time then. Jenny can be my date."

"What about Mommy? Can she come too?"

"She'll be our chaperone."

"What's a chaperone?"

"A person who watches to make sure nobody does anything he shouldn't do, like me sneaking you a sip of coffee."

"Ugh! I don't want any coffee anyway," Jenny emphatically informs him.

"Then she'll come as my mommy and your nurse."

"Rick, you mixed that up!" she exclaims. Like me, she has no sense of whimsy.

When we get back to the room, Jennifer starts to explore, looking at the cards on the wall and staring intently at pictures of Rick's family that his mother sent him just after he came out of the coma. I rescued them recently from a drawer they'd been tossed into and taped them to the wall. I doubt he's even noticed them.

Jenny makes her way back to Rick in his chair near the window and asks, "Do you have to sit in that chair all the time?"

"No. I sleep in the bed."

She is still for a moment, then asks desolately, "We can't ever go back to the park, can we?"

Rick ignores her question. "Will you come back to see me again?" She looks in my direction.

"Yes. We'll work it out," I promise.

Jenny knows that school will be starting next week and we may not be able to for a little while, but I think she understands that Rick's time with us is short, and I want to give both of us something to look forward to.

Rick puts his arms out and lifts her onto his lap. He can't feel her weight and looks down at one side and then the other to see where she's sitting.

Jennifer says quietly, "I wish you didn't get in that accident. I say lots of prayers that you'll get better soon."

"I do too, Jen," he confesses with a wistful smile.

"We have to go now, Jenny. Erin might already be outside waiting for us."

She stretches back toward Rick's shoulder and kisses him on the side of his face. He in turn kisses the top of her head. A lump forms in my throat as I watch them together.

Rick, who is due at PT just about now, comes along with us to the reception area. Erin is waiting outside the door. "Have a good session," I say to him. "I'll see you in an hour." He moves off toward the other wing, and I hustle Jennifer out to Erin's car.

When he returns an hour later, he's tired, but in a good mood. I wonder if I'm losing my mind. Less than forty-eight hours ago, he was crying. Yesterday morning, he was furious. If he was a woman, I'd assume he was going through menopause. Never mind, I tell myself. Take him as he comes. I hunker down in front of him. "Rick, last night, those few minutes before I left . . . it was . . . for me . . . the greatest sense of peace I've ever experienced. I just want to . . . I know I'm being awkward about it . . . I just want to thank you . . ."

"For me too," he whispers, looks into my eyes with genuine sincerity, and cups my face in his warm, steady hands the way he used to. I could never say it out loud to anybody, but at this moment, I truly believe I love him, and the thought of it scares me.

"There are many kinds of love, Maggie," he says softly, with his uncanny knack of somehow knowing what is in my mind.

The intensity of last night and the last couple of hours is beginning to overwhelm me, and I'm suddenly close to tears. I stand up abruptly, smooth my uniform, and turn away. "I have some errands to do, Rick. I'll be back in about an hour. Do you need anything before I leave?"

"No. I just want to sit here for a while. I have a lot to think about."

"The cafeteria is still serving lunch. Why don't you go over and get something to eat?"

"I'll think about that too. See you later."

I let Jennifer stay up late because we haven't seen Kathy and Todd in weeks, and also because Jennifer is uncharacteristically overexcited by seeing Rick and going to the Aquarium. As promised, they ring the bell right at eight thirty, which is pretty radical for Kathy, who has always tended to do everything at her own slow pace. Todd must be a good influence on her. She has brought a present for each of us—a Spirograph for Jennifer and a bottle of Jean Naté after bath lotion for me—"for no reason," she says. This is something we never did in our family, so I am astonished. Again, it must be Todd's influence.

To our collective surprise, Jennifer dominates the conversation about her visit with Rick. She is driven to recount every detail. I notice Kathy all but squirming during this recital, so I take the first opportunity to interrupt by opening the Spirograph box for her. I quickly tell her how to use it, since it seems to me that it might be quite a challenge for a seven-year-old, and then ask Kathy to set it up for her on the dining room table. As soon as they're out of the room, I apologize to Todd for not having gotten to know him very well, using my new job as an excuse. He says he understands. I ask him to tell me about himself, and he says there isn't much to tell. He's twenty-six, grew up in Des Plaines, works for the telephone company, and in a few weeks will start night courses toward being an engineer. This is as far as we get before Kathy comes back in and sits down next to him. She puts her hand on his knee, and he smiles at her.

"So what have you two have been up to?"

They look at each other like two cats that have swallowed the cream, then Kathy lifts her other hand and waves it at me. Oh my God! It's sparkling. They're engaged!

"Is that real?" I blurt.

"Yes!" she blurts back. "We've been engaged for"—she glances at Todd's watch—"three hours and forty-seven minutes. Todd proposed in the parking lot of the restaurant, and I said YES! Are you happy for us?"

For a minute all I can do is look at them with a foolish smile on my face. "How could I not be when I see how happy you are with each other?" As if directed to do so, the three of us stand up and come together. "Congratulations. I'm very excited for you." I give Kathy a peck on the cheek and Todd a handshake. "Welcome to the family, Todd." This sounds strange to my ears, since I've pretty much cut myself off from the family I'm welcoming him to. "Have you told Mother and Dad yet?"

"Not yet," Kathy replies, "but I'm not worried about it. She likes Todd."

"Well, good."

I ask about their plans, but they haven't made any yet. I then offer them lemonade or my standard iced tea, but they take a rain check, explaining that they promised to rejoin their dinner friends. We go through another round of hugs and congratulations and they hurry out the door. A sense of foreboding creeps up on me. Am I going to lose Kathy, too?

Lenore Simon calls a while later. "We haven't talked in so long, Maggie. You must think we dropped off the face of the earth."

"Oh no," I protest. "I asked Rick if you were well, and he told me that you were on vacation in Cape Cod."

"If you can call it a vacation," she sniffs. "The house belongs to Richard's family and we usually take turns, but someone messed up the schedule this year and there were so many boisterous kids there, including our youngest three, that it was like a zoo. Even the parents were manic. We ended up sleeping in a little cottage on the grounds and seeing the others only on the beach and for dinner. Even so, noise travels far in the summer, and it sounded like a playground at recess until about eleven every night. We took our kids home after a week and a half. Richie managed to charter a nice yacht with crew, and we went on a quiet seven-day cruise to Bermuda, just the two of us."

I don't know how to respond to all that, since I have no point of reference for what she described. "At least you were out in the fresh air," I bumble. "We've had temperatures and humidity in the nineties for almost a week, and the air-conditioning in our wing broke down for a couple of days. Luckily, they didn't waste any time fixing it."

"I know. Ricky mentioned it to my husband when they talked the other night."

"Oh. I didn't know they talked."

"It was in the evening. You'd probably gone home already. I'm surprised Rick didn't tell you."

"Why? I'm just his nurse."

"No, Maggie, you're much more than that to us. He never tells you that I send my love to you and Jennifer?"

"He's probably forgotten it by morning."

"Well, please don't think I've forgotten about you. As it happens, my blood pressure was beyond acceptable limits by the time I got home from my last visit, and my husband took over the telephoning and made me promise I'd stay away from the situation until my pressure returned to normal. He's been speaking with Ricky once or twice a week and with the hospital administrator once a week." *Didn't someone say that power has its privileges? Apparently it's true.* "But I don't care about that. I want to hear what you have to say. Is he doing all right?"

"He's doing better than all right. After a little breakdown on Monday—"

"Richie told me about it, fortunately after it was over."

"Well, he came through it fine except that he was furious with himself that it happened, and the next day he was feeling so much better that even his attitude was improved. I took him for a walk around the grounds. Lord, it was a steam room out there, but he was so happy just to be outdoors that he didn't seem to notice the heat. I also took Jennifer to see him for the first time, and I think that pepped him up more than anything. He rode her on his lap, and I'm sure that helped to counteract her shock at seeing him like he is now."

After a short silence, Lenore says, "Maggie, thanks for telling me all this. I can't express to you how relieved I am. I'll bet my pressure has gone down ten points during this call."

"I can hear the relief in your voice. But keep in mind that this is only the beginning. There will be more ups and downs, more pain, maybe some more depression, as Rick goes through the process. But he's definitely on his way."

"Due in large part to you."

"But mostly to your son. He's the one doing the hard work. All I do is take care of his medical needs."

"And change his diapers and put up with his tantrums and his rage. That's a lot."

"It's all part of the job and I'm happy to be doing it."

"Well, Maggie, it's almost my bedtime, so I'll let you get back to whatever you were doing. Give my love to Jennifer and send our regards to your sister."

"Thank you, and our regards to your family."

"We'll talk soon."

"Thanks for calling, Lenore. Sleep well."

Except for the heat, everything is looking good for today. After Monday's crisis, Tuesday morning's anger, and yesterday's excitement over Rick's physical progress and dramatic attitude improvement, my nervous system, like Lenore's, can really use some peace and quiet. I don't see anything potentially stressful on today's schedule, so I'm hoping for an uneventful shift. Weather permitting, I want to get Rick outdoors for a while every day. Maybe I can even get him to have lunch on the roof.

His door is open today—a good sign. He's at the table near the window, which appears to be his new headquarters now that he's not spending most of his time in bed. He looks up and smiles when I enter the room, wheels himself toward me.

"Where'd you get the jeans?" I ask, surprised to see him in anything but his sweatpants.

"Joyce stopped by on her way home from work last night." I look more carefully and see that the waist has been pinned smaller with an extra large safety pin and that the bell-bottoms are almost spilling off the edges of his footrest. "She misjudged the size."

"By a mile," I agree.

"Must have confused me with Orson Welles."

He says this so earnestly, so seriously, that I can't help laughing. Besides, the pants do look funny on him. "How much did you weigh before the accident?"

"I don't know. One fifty-five, one sixty maybe?"

"I'll go out during PT and get you some clothes."

His face lights up in total relief. "Thanks, Maggie. Get my credit card from the administrator's office and go to Marshall Field's. One pair of straight leg and one pair of bell-bottoms, but no balloon or elephant . . ." He must have been planning this; he has it all figured out. "Did you bring the doughnuts?"

"I did, but I'm only going to every now and then. Healthy food is more important for your recovery."

"Yeah, yeah," he complains, "but I slept so well last night and I woke up feeling so good, that I can't face another bowl of fruit and yogurt."

"Okay, go back to work. I'll get you a doughnut."

"And coffee, black."

"And then I'll go downtown if you don't need me. I'll be back by eleven."

I'm in the men's department at Marshall Field's. Though I've passed here many times, I've never gone inside; it's a very expensive store. Every year I pop in to Montgomery Ward to get my father a pair of pajamas, a conservative tie, maybe a plaid sport shirt for Christmas. It usually takes me less than a half-hour. But in this store, I am so flustered that it takes me a while just to find the escalator, and now that I've found the right place, I'm really at a loss. I look around me. I just cannot imagine Rick dressed in anything that's on display in the young men's department. Where are the ordinary shirts and pants? I make my way over to the salesman at the counter.

"I'm buying some clothes for a young man, but he's rather conservative. Do you have anything a little less, uh . . ."

"Bizarre?" he supplies.

Thank you, Lord. "I'm sorry if I offended you, but yes."

"You didn't offend me, ma'am. My teenage son, maybe, but definitely not me. Anyway, you're in our disco section. What you want is our regular men's wear, which is right over there," he says, pointing.

I thank him and follow his finger to the area that has the traditional styles. I give the clerk there Rick's height and weight, and he leads me to the right racks. Rick has called in to authorize my use of his American Express card, so there is no problem at the register, and I eventually leave the men's department with one pair each of the jeans he asked for, a long-sleeved blue oxford shirt with a button-down collar, and a short-sleeved cotton with a thin gray-green stripe. Thanks to the Simons, I will be able to clothe Jennifer more expensively, and I am tempted to check out the children's department for a nice first-day-of-school dress for her. But but I'm on business time, so I locate my car in the parking garage and head back to the hospital.

Rick is still in therapy, so I lay the packages on his bedside tray and collect the things I need for his bath and bladder session. Fifteen minutes later, Rick wheels into the room, all sweaty and flushed, and goes directly to the bed.

"You look like you had a hard session," I remark.

"Good one too," he responds and lifts himself from the chair to the bed for the first time.

I look at him in astonishment. "When on earth did this happen?"

"Last night," he replies with a self-satisfied smile. "I worked on it yesterday morning at PT, then at the afternoon session, but I didn't have such good luck either time. So, after you left last night, I took a little nap, then kept trying by myself until I had done it three times back and forth."

My first instinct is to remind him that he should never attempt such feats when he is alone—one wrong move could seriously set him back—but I am so in awe of his will and perseverance that I let it go. "You're amazing, Rick," I tell him and gently push him down on his back so I can begin checking his catheter. Before I finish, the intercom buzzes. It's the front desk, telling me that Rick has company. He can hear both sides of the conversation, and I turn to him. "Are you expecting anybody?"

He shrugs and looks puzzled. "No, but I'll see whoever it is."

I relay his message and ask to have the visitor wait in the lounge down the hall from us until we call. Then I finish what I'm doing and bring Rick the basin, the razor, and the towels so he can bathe himself. "I bought you two pairs of jeans and two shirts. They're on your tray. The credit card is in the bag."

I go out to the kitchen to refill his ever-present water pitcher, and when I return, I notice he's shaved off his beard.

"I'm not the beard type," he explains tersely. He picks the short-sleeved striped shirt and the looser jeans.

I watch him nervously. "I hope these are okay. I didn't think you were the leisure suit type either."

He smiles. "These are fine, Maggie. Polyester makes me itch." He still needs help with his pants. "My next challenge," he informs me with a modest grin.

I help him back into the chair, and he immediately returns to his books and papers. "Might as well tell whoever it is to come down now." He flashes me another quizzical look and shakes his head.

A few moments later, there is a polite knock on the door. Rick calls, "Come in," and the horde descend on us, larger than life and filling the room with noise, excitement, and joy. I've never seen anyone turn as white as Rick is at this moment. Total shock. I know instantly that these kids are his brothers and sister.

"Jesus," he utters. "What are you guys doing here?" He lowers his head to the table and buries his face in his arms.

"Come on in," I say to the three boys and a girl who have already cannonballed into the room and are now surrounding him.

The tallest boy—blond, tanned, good-looking—looks up. "Is he going to be okay? Is he all right?"

"He's fine. Just a bit surprised . . . Are you Andrew?"

"Yes. And you're Mrs. McLean?"

"I'm happy to meet you."

"Mom told us how much you've done for Ricky. I'm pleased to meet you too."

By now Rick has raised his head and merely looks dazed. Andrew holds back as the others crowd in on Rick, hugging him, the boys lightly punching his arm, and all of them studiously avoiding looking at his legs.

"Hold it," Rick says after a minute or two, and the boys disperse to other areas of the room, leaving only the girl with him. "Let's get organized. This lady is Mrs. McLean, my nurse. Maggie, I see you've already met Andy and you know Susan and Jody. This is the rest of us, Matthew over there by the door, Brian, in the chair, and this is Kerry." They each say hi to me in turn. My brain registers them in order as the Mature One, the Quiet One, the Adolescent One, and the Sensitive One.

"What are you guys doing here?" Rick repeats. "Nobody told me you were coming."

"Somebody did," I cut in.

"Who?"

"Remember the postcard you got in the mail? 'Expect delivery by air'? You said it was your father's handwriting."

"Oh, yeah. I forgot. He does nutty things like that sometimes." He looks at the kids. "Did you all know about this?"

They look at each other. "Didn't say anything about it to me," says Andy.

"To me either," Matthew adds.

"He just handed us the airplane tickets last night and said, 'Surprise,'" Kerry says.

"It's just like something he would do though," Brian says, making it sound like a bad thing.

Kerry, standing quietly a few feet from Rick, moves next to the chair, crouches so that she is looking up at him, and asks anxiously, "Ricky, are you really going to be okay?"

"Of course I am. It's just going to take a while." He kisses the top of her head gently, the way he does with Jennifer. He turns to the boys. "You're all probably wondering what's going on here, so if you have any questions, you might as well ask them now and get it over with. If I can't answer it, Maggie can. So shoot!"

I don't think Rick expected the torrent of questions that pour out of the two older boys. While Brian fiddles with some sort of game that fits in his hand, Kerry, now sitting in the upholstered visitor's chair, listens intently to the give-and-take flying back and forth between the others. Andy and Matthew have obviously done their homework on spinal injury and paraplegia. I sense a kind of adrenalin rush between them and Rick. The intensity doesn't waver until they finally run out of questions, at which point Andrew turns to me and asks what my "prognosis" is for Rick. Do I think he will be able to go home soon?

All I can tell him is that nobody can say for sure. "He's progressing fast, but he has to meet certain criteria in order to be discharged, and he's not there yet. Also, complications can arise, even with the best care. Hospital patients, especially ones like your brother, whose spleen has been removed, are susceptible to infection"—Matthew nods knowingly—"but he is doing well, so if it continues to go the way it has been, he might be ready to leave by Thanksgiving."

"No!" Kerry wails. "That's three more months! Ricky, you can get help in New York. There are loads of hospitals on the Island. You don't have to stay in Chicago."

"It's not that easy, Kerry," Rick tells her calmly. "I need to be here now. I came to do something and I can't leave until I get it done. If I'm ready to go home by Thanksgiving, I will, but if I still have a lot of work left to do here, I'll have to come back." Kerry opens her mouth to protest again, but Rick shakes his head and adds firmly, "That's the way it has to be."

She shrinks down into the chair, pouting.

Brian rolls his eyes at the ceiling, then quickly flicks his tongue at her like a snake.

Matthew, expressionless once again, stares at his feet.

Andrew checks his watch and cheerfully announces that it's lunchtime. He looks in my direction. "Is there a restaurant within walking distance?"

Before I can answer, Rick chimes in, "You'll have to go without me. I'm not allowed off the grounds."

I say, "There are two cafeterias downstairs, one in this building and one in the main building. But I think you'll like the one on the roof. It's only four flights up, but there's a good view of the surrounding area. And Rick can go with us, if he feels up to it."

The boys babble among themselves for a minute before deciding on the roof. Rick says he's feeling great and asks Kerry, who is still moping, if she's going with us. She thinks it over for a second, then nods her head.

"Hey, Ricky, why don't you ride the baby on your lap," Brian suggests sarcastically.

"SHUT UP, you creep!" Kerry barks at him. "You're the baby! I'm ten minutes older than you are. Remember?"

"Cool it, Brian," Rick orders in a softly menacing voice I haven't heard him use since he told Kathy off the day she found his shaving kit in my bathroom.

"Excuse my sister, Mrs. McLean," Brian oozes. "It's her hormones."

"Thanks for the analysis," I respond curtly. *I don't know about her hormones, but you're the problem here, you obnoxious little brat.* I glance at Rick to see how he's reacting to this little outburst, but he's watching me and seems to be amused by my reaction.

As we troop out the door, he warns me. "Just a taste of what's to come, Maggie. Teenagers: A Whole Different Animal," he intones dramatically, as if it's the title of his dissertation.

We take the ramp up to the cafeteria. The kids prefer to eat lunch outdoors in spite of the heat, so Rick stays outside, holding a table for six in the corner. He asks Brian to keep him company while the rest of us get the food.

The meal goes by with no further unpleasantness. Brian behaves well, and Kerry says little but seems to be enjoying herself. Afterward Rick leaves us in the lobby and goes for his 2:00 PT. No visitors are allowed there, so I decide to spend the time with the kids in the comfortable air-conditioned lounge. We settle ourselves in a group, and little by little in the course of conversation, I get to know them. Andy, who is going into his second year at the University of Miami in Coral Gables, is the one I like most. He's easygoing, amiable, and passionate about his major, which is oceanography.

I like Kerry too. At fifteen, she's a sweet, gentle girl, vulnerable, and quite different from Susan. She has a passion too. Ballet. It doesn't surprise me. I've already noticed how graceful she is. I sense that, in spite of belonging to a family of self-confident achievers, she doesn't have much confidence in herself. I have a feeling she gets lost in this big outgoing family.

Matthew is even more of a puzzle than Rick. He's friendly, but like Rick, he isn't forthcoming about himself. He tells me he's a high school senior and he's already been accepted to Caltech, where he will study something called biomedicine, but he's hard to draw out about this or anything else.

At this point, all of them except Brian decide to take a walk around the rest of the grounds and then try to intercept Rick on his way back from therapy. I take the opportunity to talk to Brian without them around. I don't know why I need to do this, unless it's that I'm feeling guilty for passing negative judgment on him when all he's done is be a boy teasing his sister. "Brian, would you mind staying a few more minutes? You're the only one I haven't had a chance to get to know."

He looks skeptical for a moment, then says, "Sure. What do you want to know?"

"You're in the tenth grade, right?"

"Yeah. My sister and I are twins."

"I know, though it is a little surprising, since you're not at all alike."

"I don't care about ballet, if that's what you mean." He smiles mischievously.

"What do you like to do?"

He doesn't have to think about it. "Wrestle."

"You mean, in a ring?"

Now he flashes me a look that says, No, lady, in a bathtub. "I'm on the varsity wrestling team in my high school," he answers with exaggerated patience.

"Are you any good?"

"I guess. You usually have to be a junior or senior to be on varsity."

"Your family must be really proud of you."

Hint of a nod. "I guess my parents are."

"Not your brothers and sisters?"

"I doubt it. They just think I'm a dork."

I take this to mean a jerk. "Why do you think that?"

He looks to be sizing me up for a minute, then confides, "Okay. They're always making fun of me because I'm short . . . Sometimes they call me Runt . . . I act like I'm mad, but I'm not . . . It just kind of hurts . . . and, well, sometimes I take it out on Kerry."

"Why Kerry and not your brothers?"

"They'd probably laugh at me even more. Kerry's really sweet. You see how she acts."

"What about your parents? Do they know about this?"

"My mom warns them and tries to make me feel better, but it doesn't help." He lowers his eyes. "I don't get along real good with my dad."

"Why not? I met your dad and he seems like a good man."

"It's my fault. I get kind of mouthy sometimes, you know? Then he gets angry and everything gets kind of out of control." He lifts his eyes and says seriously, "I'm working on it."

It never occurred to me that the Simons' household could be anything but perfect. "Brian, have you given any thought to what you'll do when you get out of high school?"

"No. My grades aren't all that good either, so I might not even go to college. I'll probably just knock around for a couple of years until I decide what to do." He smiles at me again, but this time it's a sad smile, as though he knows the future doesn't hold much for him.

It must be awful not to make the grade in a family like his. I want to hug him, to let him know somebody understands, but I hear young voices talking in the hall. "I hear them coming back," I say. "I think you're wrong about your future, Brian. You're a terrific kid, and I'm glad we had a chance to talk. I know things will begin to look up soon. You'll see."

"Thanks, Mrs. McLean. You're—"

The door opens, and the discussion in the hall spills into the room.

Rick admits to being tired when he returns from PT, and I inform the kids that he has to rest for a while. I suggest that they go down to the lounge or one of the cafeterias for a Coke. Andy says he'd rather go to the Aquarium, and Matthew and Brian want to go downtown, maybe take a bus or boat tour. Kerry wants to stay, but I advise her to go with Andy, who is happy to take her along. Rick encourages them to do whatever they want, so long as they're back by six. They promise they will be.

In a way I'm glad they've gone. I can have some time alone with Rick. Besides, in all the excitement, I missed the 1:00 skin inspection, and I wasn't looking forward to asking the others to leave when it's time for the bladder business. I check his skin, which is clear; he hasn't had a lesion yet, *thank You, Lord.* I arrange his pillows and pull the sheet up over him. He can do these things for himself, but today I'm feeling the time we have together is disappearing fast. Rick is out like a light. I touch the side of his face softly.

I go into the kitchen and get myself a glass of iced tea, then get comfortable and pull my new book from my bag. Rick wakes up in time for OT at four. At five, just as he gets back, Kerry calls to tell him that they stopped at the law office to see the Greens, who invited them to their house for dinner and to stay overnight. The plane back to New York leaves at 10:00 a.m., she says, but they'll be back in time to have breakfast with him. Rick actually seems relieved to hear that they won't be back until tomorrow. He is already working at his little table and barely responds when I say goodbye. Feeling both wound up and fatigued, I leave for the day.

The kids and Joyce Green have just arrived when I get in the next morning. This time they've brought gifts for all of us: for me, a way-too-generous gift certificate for Marshall Field's from the Simon family, stick-on paper dolls and a pretty illustrated book called *A Birthday for the Princess* for Jenny, and for Rick, a brand-new IBM Selectric typewriter so that he doesn't have to handwrite his whole dissertation. The Simons are the most giving people I've ever met. I can't imagine what it would be like if they celebrated Christmas. Mrs. Green tries to get Rick to show her a part of his dissertation, but he replies, "Not until it's typed up."

She winks. "How fast do you type?"

"Not very fast," he responds seriously, "but it doesn't matter. I'll have to find a typist to do the final draft."

"If you can't find anyone, let me know," she says. "I'm sure we can get one of the girls in the office to do it."

"Thanks, Joyce. I'll remember that."

When the time comes for the family to leave for O'Hare, the boys ply Rick with hugs, punches, and horsing around. They're more subdued than they were yesterday, and I'm sure it's hard for them to go home without him. Despite the moods and the squabbles, they are a close family, and their cohesiveness is beautiful to watch. Kerry is last to say good-bye. She kisses Rick's cheek and says tearily, "I wish you were coming with us."

"It won't be long," Rick says reassuringly. "You be good and if anybody tries to mess with you, just ignore him, okay?"

"Okay," she promises dutifully. He plants a kiss on her cheek in return and lets her go.

The visit is over.

I leave the room to get our coffee and Rick's doughnut. By the time I get back, he has taken the typewriter out of its box and made room for it on his table. He's sitting in front of it, staring into space.

"Anything wrong with it?" I ask. Since he's been out of bed, staring into space is not something he does a lot, so what else could be bothering him? He doesn't answer right away. Then his eyes move from the stratosphere and fix on me. "Rick, what's the matter?"

Another minute passes, and he says, "I felt something."

This is important. "Where?"

"In my right foot."

"What?"

"Tingling."

"Are you sure it's not just a phantom pain?"

"Yes. It's like my foot went to sleep."

"How many times have you felt it? Do you feel it now?"

"Three. No."

"Well, let's get Dr. Stern in here and see what he has to say."

"Okay . . . Maggie, do these things tend to be false alarms?"

"Not necessarily, but let's not get uptight until we hear from the doctor."

"Right." He sits and plays with a pencil, staring into space some more while I make the call.

"Stern's nurse said he'll be here tomorrow morning to check you. Darn, tomorrow's Saturday. I'll come in to be with you while he does the examination. I'll be here by eight. Okay?"

"Don't bring Jenny."

"I won't. I'll take her over to Kathy's on my way."

He lapses into silence once more. I feel his fear because it's my fear too. It would be a crushing disappointment if it's just a phantom sensation, and I can't bear the thought of him reverting to his depressive state if it is. *Please don't let him be hurt.*

He has a wooden look on his face, and we hardly talk for the rest of my shift. *He's come so far. Just let him be strong enough to make it the rest of the way, no matter what happens.*

He refuses lunch, and by the end of my shift, he's been sleeping for three hours.

I don't like this.

If I pointed out to Rick that prayers do get answered, he would either be annoyed with me or laugh at how naïve and brainwashed I am. But they do, and God's proven it today. Dr. Stern's tests showed that the feelings in his foot are genuine. There is hope for further recovery, hope we didn't have yesterday. I simply cannot understand why people will not let themselves believe.

By the time I get to Rick's room, Stern has come and gone. Rick, dressed and in a good mood, is punching away on the typewriter with his index fingers. It's not going very fast, and every now and then I hear him growl or sigh in frustration. But his heart is in the right place, even if his fingers aren't. I bring him a sandwich and a cup of coffee and tell him how happy I am for him that everything worked out well.

"Me too," he murmurs absently, scowls, and grumbles disgustedly. "Damn. I can write faster than this." He doesn't look up.

I know he doesn't owe me anything, I think peevishly, *but couldn't he be a little less rude?* Nevertheless, I say, "I can show you a better way if you want. "I got pretty good at it when I worked at the college. Just let me show you before I go."

He makes room for me at the table, pushes the typewriter over in front of me. Our close proximity is slightly distracting, but I manage to show him where to place his fingers on the home keys. He absorbs the information quickly and proceeds to work quietly, except for the curse words he utters at regular intervals. I'm not in any hurry, so I decide to stay a little longer. *Just grin and bear him,* I tell myself. We all have our own ways of dealing with frustration. I tell him he's coming along fine and he shouldn't give up.

He looks up from the typewriter. "Thanks for coming in today, Maggie. I know I haven't said it enough, but I appreciate everything you're doing for me. I'm lucky you're here."

"Oh well," I sputter lamely, instantly feeling foolish about my intolerance toward the cursing and what I perceived as coldness. "I'm happy that I'm able to help you."

An awkward silence fills the space between us, until he says, with a smile that threatens my composure, "So . . . see you Monday morning." The familiar heat rises inside me as if I'm standing too close to a fire. Why, after all this time, all of my resolutions, all of the unpleasant messy chores that come with caring for a patient who can do almost nothing for himself, am I seeing Rick not as the male paraplegic I'm nursing, but as the man I ache to lie beside, the man whose body I have a desperate need to feel pressed against me? All of a sudden I don't want to go home; I want to stay with him. And I want him to want me to stay. Yes, I know that what I want is not important, that I'm lucky to have as much chance to be with him as I have, but that isn't enough.

"Monday," I echo softly, reluctantly forcing my feet to move in the direction of the door.

I'm halfway out when he calls, "Hey, wait! I, uh, just had an idea." Tensing, I turn slowly. *Don't listen, Maggie. Just go.* "Instead of coming in

Monday morning," he suggests, "why don't you work the late shift, like from three or five till whenever you want to leave? It's Labor Day and there probably won't be more than a skeleton staff here. You can teach me typing after supper without interruption, and then we can, I don't know, watch television or whatever you want."

I knew it. He's doing it again, reading my thoughts. And he hasn't lost his knack for sounding like he has nothing on his mind but what he says. No matter how hard I try to resist, my willpower is no match for my need. "I'll see what I can do," I tell him with as much indifference as I can squeeze out.

"Great! See you Monday, he says enthusiastically."

"I hope so," I say, but I don't sound sincere to myself. How can I when I'm praying that by Monday I will have convinced myself that I will not be charmed or coerced into doing something I don't want to do; at least, not like this, when I'm giving in because I don't have the control to say no to him.

September doesn't start off the way I expected it would. Over the weekend, Carol and Larry are out of town for the holiday, Kathy and Todd take Jennifer to Clearyville with them, and I spend a fair amount of time on the sofa looking forward to Monday night.

In addition, Rick wakes up sick on Sunday, but I know nothing about it until I get to his room at two forty-five on Monday.

One of the nurses is coming out of his door as I am about to go in. "Your patient woke up with a stuffed nose, clogged ears, and a fierce headache early yesterday morning," she informs me curtly and hands me Rick's chart. "The doctor on call stopped in to take a look at him. His report is in the folder." She sounds like she's annoyed with me for not being here when "my patient" decided to get sick, which makes no sense, since they all know I don't work on weekends.

It's not unusual for a patient to get sick, especially a patient without a spleen. Since the spleen is the organ that filters out foreign organisms, a person who doesn't have one is more susceptible to infection by contact with anyone—another patient, somebody else's visitor, even a staff member. Most often it doesn't amount to anything. I open the chart and read the doctor's scribbled note: Lungs clear. Negative for pneumonia. Liquids and meds as ordered. Bed rest. Relieved, I step into the room, move toward the bed, and watch Rick breathe for a minute or two, then check him out. His pulse is still normal, his forehead warmer. There is no need to check his heartbeat, but I put my hand under his shirt and lay my palm on his chest for a minute just to feel his heart beating. Whatever he had in mind for us for tonight is obviously out of the question now, and I try to reassure myself that there will be another opportunity before he leaves Chicago. This doesn't give me a whole lot of consolation.

He sleeps for most of the evening, waking only around eight thirty to take half a cup of tea and half a cracker. After this interlude, during which he doesn't utter a word to me, he lies listless and silent, though awake for a while, before he drifts off to sleep again.

I spend most of my time in the chair, reading a lot and knitting a little. Around nine fifteen, I give myself a break and take a short stroll outdoors in the well-lit garden, which, though still too warm and sticky for nighttime, is touched intermittently by a slight breeze. Could this be a sign that our horrendous heat wave might be winding down? I go to the cafeteria to buy a sandwich for supper, then lazily shuffle back to the quiet room. Rick sleeps on.

The only thing I am nursing tonight is a distinctly uncomfortable feeling of emptiness. Since Saturday, I've been alone, looking forward to tonight. I should be glad that we're not able to go through with what I believe Rick really had in mind though; I'd never get over the disgrace if we were found out. Nevertheless, I'm disappointed.

At nine I call Kathy's apartment. She sounds out of breath and explains that they'd just walked in the door. I tell her I'll be over soon to pick up Jennifer and not to wake her if she falls asleep.

"She can stay over, you know," Kathy points out.

"I know, Kath, but tonight, I would just rather bring her home with me."

"Is anything wrong? Is Rick okay?"

"I'm with him now. He has a cold, but he's sleeping it off, and everything else is good. I just feel like having Jenny with me tonight."

"Well, all right," she says in that injured tone she uses when she's feeling rejected.

"But! Are you too tired for me to stay for a few minutes so I can hear about your weekend?"

She brightens. "No, not at all. Suppose I have a cup of tea ready for you too."

"That'll be great. See you in about twenty minutes." I hang up and start packing my tote.

"How's Kathy?" Rick's croaky voice startles me. It's the first sound I've heard in this room in five hours.

"Oh, they're fine. They just got back from Clearyville. I'm getting ready now to go pick Jennifer up on my way home." I cross the room to the bed. "How do you feel?" His color is better than it was a few hours ago, his breathing is easier, and his pulse is normal. I fight the urge to put my hand under his shirt and check his heart rate—for comparison with my earlier check of course.

"I think you should check my heartbeat again," he suggests.

I freeze. "What?"

"I was awake when you did it before. I definitely prefer that method to the stethoscope."

"Dear God, Rick! You scare the stuffing out of me when you do that mind reading thing."

"What do mean mind reading? How could I know what you're thinking? . . . Do you really have to go now?"

Yes, Maggie, you do. "Yes, I do. I need to get Jennifer home and into bed. It's almost nine thirty and besides, you're still sick."

"Yeah, I know, but I don't get it. I'm in a hospital, for Christ's sake." He looks at me apologetically. "Sorry, it just slipped out. How can you get sick in a hospital?"

"Hospital infections are pretty common," I inform him and remind him of the ramifications of living without a spleen. "And now I really have to go, Rick. Do you want me to do your catheter before I leave?"

"No, you go on. The night nurse can do it."

"Thanks. I told Kathy I'd be right over. See you tomorrow morning."

"We'll have a lot to do tomorrow," he says in his froggy voice. Then he adds, as I open the door to leave, "I'm sorry tonight didn't work out. I really wanted it to."

"I did too, but it's not your fault. You just concentrate on getting better."

He smiles and settles back into the pillows, and I go on my way.

September moves on. Rick decides to give up on his typing lessons and asks me to type up everything he's done to date. He continues working in longhand, and the impressive new typewriter, which even has its own correcting tape, is all mine.

Now my days are spent transferring his thoughts onto paper. I think I have a pretty good grasp of grammar and spelling, but my typing itself is a little rusty. It looks like he already has enough here for a book, and he wants to edit it as soon as possible, so I don't really read most of what he's written, just type it mechanically. By Wednesday of the second week of the month, he is feeling better, and my typing is improving dramatically on this incredible machine. My free time no longer passes slowly.

I know from Rick's medical charts that his birthday is on the eighteenth, which is a Tuesday. I would like to have a little party for him, but I don't know if he would enjoy that kind of thing. And who would I invite besides his cousins and my family? He hasn't mentioned knowing any of the other patients in the unit. All he has told me is that he writes in the evenings, so I've been assuming that's all he does. I'd better call Lenore before I plan anything. I haven't spoken with her since before the Simon kids visited.

School started last week. Jennifer is now officially a second grader. I drive her in the morning, and Erin picks her up and stays until I get home, which is usually between five thirty and six. She is always welcome to stay for supper, and occasionally she does. She has also offered to babysit in the evening. For the first time since I took Jennifer back from my parents, I am free to meet Carol or Kathy for dinner, to do a little shopping, or to go to a movie. Not only can I do these things, but I want to do them.

When I look back on the years that I spent my nights on the couch with scrapbooks and old letters, I find it hard to believe that that poor, lonely, hurting woman was me. All those months fretting about my relationship with Rick, the most intelligent, magnetic, and unpredictable person I'll ever know . . . Soon he will be gone, and I'll probably never hear from him again. I can actually think about that now with sadness, but without feeling a pang of anxiety or fear. I doubt I will ever again know a family like his—loving and caring and fun to be with. I bless and thank the Lord every day for bringing the Simons into my life to save Jennifer and me from myself.

Rick

I was born into a privileged family and grew up in a big white house in an exclusive neighborhood on the north shore of Long Island. Thanks to three generations of our family law firm, my siblings and I have had every advantage: good background, best schools, and money to travel anywhere. We've always been able to do anything and have anything we want. The only thing we've never had in our family is the typical rich people's arrogance. We don't throw our weight around or wave big bills in front of people like a lot of the families we grew up with do. Our parents would cut off our trust funds if they ever caught us doing anything like that. I'm no saint, but acting like a big shot is not one of my vices.

I've always been more of a pain-in-the-ass type. For instance, when I was five years old, I thought it was fun to disappear from our oceanfront summer house at night. I really got off on the commotion of all the neighbors searching and calling for me and the police cars charging in with their flashing lights. When I was in high school, I sneaked out of the house late at night two or three times a week. Everyone except my sister thought I was in my room studying or sleeping. She knew I was out getting drunk with my buddies or messing around with girls. It's amazing what you can get away with when you're an A student who can hold your liquor really well at night and still do all the right things during the day. It also helps to have a sister who never tells.

Maybe my behavior had to do with an experience I had that even my parents don't know about, the memory of which I somehow managed to keep from surfacing until after the accident. It happened when I was thirteen and more interested in school than girls, when a woman who was probably older than my mother accosted me in the woods on our property and forced me into, let's say, an early manhood. The only one I told was my sister, who was twelve at the time, and I made her promise she'd never say anything about it to anyone. To my knowledge, she never has. But after it happened, I turned into a moody teenager who knew what "going all the way" felt like and didn't have the control not to go there. I looked eighteen when I was fifteen and took advantage of it.

My sister told me that the girls in school were crazy about me because I was "sweet and vulnerable," which made me want to barf. I was also immature and insensitive, and I ended up hurting many of them without meaning to. Needless to say, when I graduated from high school at sixteen, I was already pretty fucked up, but nobody except Susan seemed to know it. It took giving my college girlfriend an engagement ring one Saturday night, then dumping her two weeks later at our engagement party, for my parents to admit to themselves that I wasn't the golden boy they'd always deluded themselves into thinking I was. Just the horrified look on their faces should have made me see what a bastard I was, but it didn't. I cringe when I think about what I was like back then.

I've lived all my life in New York, except for my undergrad years in Massachusetts, where I earned simultaneous bachelor's degrees in American history and political science. The following year, I returned to the city for my master's in journalism. Last September, I came to Chicago for my postgrad.

I like Chicago, the feel of it. I've never felt like a New York City kind of kid, maybe because I've lived mostly on Long Island or maybe because my father, who is a Californian, is the person I most admire and want to be like. He doesn't have a New York mentality, which is the way I've come to identify a lot of my friends' smug, pushy fathers.

At least when he's at home, my dad is laid-back and easy. Unless we do something that really bugs him or disappoints him, he supports us in every way. One thing is strange though. I've always thought that he knew what I was into in high school, yet he never confronted me about it, which is not like him. I don't know. Maybe he didn't want to upset my mother; it takes a lot less than that for her to freak out.

I'd been petitioning him for a motorcycle ever since I'd gotten my driver's license. When I was accepted to Columbia for my master's, he presented me with a brand-new BMW bike, most likely because I graduated cum laude. I learned later that he and my mother had fought for a year about my having one, because she thought I was not responsible or mature enough to be use it safely. She knew me well.

That summer, I had visions of unlimited freedom once I started at Columbia: living in the city with no restrictions or obligations to anyone except my professors and myself and owning my own wheels to get me wherever I wanted to go. I was almost sorry about having to leave for Europe on a preplanned six-week graduation trip with a couple of friends from Amherst; at that point, Europe seemed irrelevant. At least until we got to Paris and the fun really began. All in all, that summer was about as good as life gets—until August, when my father informed me that I was expected to live at home while I was at Columbia. No arguments; that was how it was going to be. I was still technically a minor and would be until the middle of September. After that, I would be on my own. My parents would pay for tuition, food, books, and commuter fare, but not off-campus living expenses. I believe to this day that it was payback for ruining the engagement party, not to mention Devon's self-esteem, at least for a little while. But she eventually survived me, and I survived Columbia without my own pad. I credit having to live at home for my finishing the program in one year.

While I was at Columbia, I decided to go on for a PhD and chose the University of Chicago, where my grandfather and great-grandfather had gotten their law degrees and had founded their firm. Besides, I'm no stranger to the city, having been here several times with my parents to visit relatives. How do I feel about the year I've spent here? I guess I have mixed feelings. The university's been great. I have enormous respect for my dissertation advisor and the other professors I've met. Somewhere along the line, I've developed a real passion for my topic, which explores how the new media influence the ways people view life on this planet. Of course, I'm equally interested in the way my dissertation will affect my life, and I have worked harder than I've ever worked before. If things had gone differently, I'd have been happy to stay till my work here was done.

There are things I don't think I'll miss, like the sorry news station I picked to get television production experience, or the brutal winters. But there also are things I will miss. The bookstores, the Art Institute, Maggie, and Jenny.

When I first met Maggie, she seemed depressed and repressed. By the end of the evening, I felt sort sorry for her. Yet I kept thinking about her and her little girl. One Saturday, I stopped by her place and asked if I could take her daughter, Jennifer, to the park across the way. Unexpectedly she said yes. I can't explain what happened next. I never wanted a relationship with them, but the more I got to know Maggie, the more I wanted to score with her. She was a challenge.

Sometimes I babysat for her when she was working the late shift, and we would talk a little when she got home. I saw right away that she was obsessed with her MIA husband, who she refused to believe was dead, even after six years. At the same time, I could sense that she was . . . well, attracted to me; and one night, though I knew it was wrong for me to do it, I came on to her pretty strong. Her resistance was formidable, but I wore her down. We had sex in her bed, and I could literally feel her sense of release after six years without it. It was like me after five or six weeks without it.

I didn't love her; I don't think I'm capable of loving anyone outside my immediate family. But I began working at her place in the evenings when she was on day shift, and we kind of drifted gradually into my sleeping at her place every night. Over the months, I discovered that she was—and is—a genuinely gentle and kind person, someone who couldn't be cruel even if she wanted to be. It made me hate myself for taking advantage of her, but when I tried to tell her what kind of person I am, she refused to believe me. It was after she helped me through a bout of pneumonia that I knew I just wanted her in my life for as long as I would be in Chicago. I'm selfish; I know that. I also know now that sometimes I hurt her feelings and sometimes I didn't treat her very well. I never realized it when I did it.

Then I had the accident. During the weeks after I came out of the coma, I did nothing but stare at the ceiling and think about people in my life past and present, and how I've treated some of them, until one day I saw what I was and what I'd done over and over without a second thought since I was a kid. They say that severe trauma changes a person. I don't know about anyone else, but that's how it changed me.

Maggie made me see other things. I was a tough sell, but she didn't give up on me; and finally, just because of who she is, I saw myself for who I am. I owe her more than I can say, much more than she insists she owes me for the changes she thinks I made in her life.

At the least, we can call it a draw.

September 15-18, 1973

I'm excited. After giving a lot of thought to the idea of a party for Rick's birthday on Tuesday, I decide to do it, and it's all Jennifer is able to talk about.

Before I left yesterday, I stopped off at the PT office to ask Curt if Rick was friendly with anyone in his sessions. He said there were two men he liked to hang out with during free time and the after-dinner socials and that he would mention the party to them. He cautioned me, however, that word gets around quickly here, and since each of those guys lives in a four-bed ward, I should be prepared for unexpected guests to drop in.

"Well, I'd be grateful if you could stress that it's a surprise party, so Rick won't find out about it before Tuesday. I'm sure he'll be back in PT on Monday. Oh, and of course you're invited, Curt, if you don't have a session."

"Thanks, Nurse McLean. That's very nice of you. I'll make it a point to drop in if I have a minute. Tuesday at . . . three?"

He isn't psychic. Free time is at three.

"Right."

So today, which is Saturday, Jennifer and I are headed downtown to what Jennifer calls "the big store," to buy a gift and party things. Birthdays in my family were never a big event. One gift and a cupcake was about it. I can only guess that Kathy is responsible for the festive parties my mother gives for Jennifer. Mother agrees to them and supplies the plates and cups, but she never really gets into the parties the way we do.

I know what I would like to get for Rick, but it's a bit odd for a birthday present—or maybe not, given his circumstances. I've never bought one before, and I have a feeling the good ones are expensive, but I've made up my mind that if I see one I really like, I'll buy it, no matter how much it costs. We locate the right department, and Jenny and I look them over and over and over again.

"Mommy, this is a pretty one. The color is pretty and feel it, it's so smooth." She takes it and walks around with it. "But my hand is too small for it!" she complains with a frown.

"Good thing it's Rick's present, not yours. I like it too. We'll take it." Next we need her present. She quickly spots the umbrellas and pulls me over to look at them.

She walks round and round the display case, then chooses one. "I don't think that kind of design is Rick's type," I say, looking at a splashy floral in red, pink, and orange. "How about this one? It's bigger too. More of a man's umbrella."

"It's black! It's ugly," she wails.

"But that's the kind that men like."

She twists her lips into a pout, something she never used to do. "I don't like it."

"Well, we can get something else then."

"Nooo. I have to get Rick an umbrella. What if it's raining when he comes home from the hospital? He'll get all wet and maybe he'll get sick again."

Dear Lord, how am I going to deal with my little girl when her best friend has to go away?

"You're absolutely right, Jenny. It is a very thoughtful present. An umbrella is a perfect choice. If you want Rick to use it, though, you'll have to pick one in a plain, dark color."

She looks around again and finally chooses a very dark green. We take our purchases to the clerk and pay for them.

Next we visit the stationery department and buy plenty of gift wrap and party supplies. She picks out a dozen hats and noisemakers and some confetti. The cleaning people are going to love us. Last of all, we stop at a bakery in our neighborhood, and I let her pick out a large sheet cake. "What do you want the lady to write on it?" I ask her.

"Ummm, I know! 'Dear Rick, I love you with all my heart. From Jenny.'"

Another choke-up moment. "The cake is from all of us, Jen, but you can make Rick a birthday card and write that on it and it will be especially from you." She accepts the compromise—her second in an hour—and I ask the woman to write simply, "Happy 23rd Birthday, Rick, from All of Us," and tell her I'll pick it up on Tuesday morning.

Later, after Jennifer has gone to bed, I call Lenore.

"I'm so glad you called, Maggie," she said cheerfully. "How is everything going?"

"Fine. Rick had a little cold, but he's pretty much over it."

"Yes, we talked for a few minutes last night. He sounded very good, very *up*."

"He's been in excellent spirits and hard at work on his dissertation."

"He said you're being a tremendous help to him."

"I started off teaching him to type, but he was too impatient to put his mind to it, so I'm brushing up on my typing by transcribing the whole thing. Fortunately, his handwriting is easy to read."

"It is. We used to say it was a good thing he chose political science and journalism. He could never have graduated from medical school with his handwriting."

I laughed. Having read thousands of doctors' notes, I could vouch for that. "I called because I'm planning a birthday party for Rick on Tuesday at three and wonder if you and Mr. Simon are planning to be out here that day."

"As a matter of fact, we are. The older kids are all back in school, but we were thinking we would bring Jody with us. We'd come just for the day."

"Great! I've ordered a large sheet cake, but I asked the baker not to make it until I know how many are coming. Do you think Mr. and Mrs. Green would be interested?"

"Definitely, if they're not away. They'll already be downtown too. Do you want to call them or shall I?"

"It would be better if you did."

"I'll do it and let you know if they can make it."

"I'm going to have Erin, our sitter, bring Jennifer up from school. Jenny's very excited about this."

"I am too. It's wonderful of you to do this, Maggie. I won't insult you by offering to pay for the cake, but—"

"Thank you for that, Lenore. It's important for me to be able to do this for Rick."

"I understand."

"I'd like you to meet Erin, by the way, so I'm going to ask her to stay when she brings Jenny. Rick hasn't met her either, but they're both working on their doctorates, so they'll have something in common."

"Wonderful idea. We'd like to meet her. And it will be interesting to see how Jody and Jennifer relate to each other this time."

"I'm looking forward to that too. She's not the same little girl he met in the spring."

"Well, we'll see you on Tuesday then. Would you mind if we brought our housekeeper with us? She's been very anxious to see Ricky."

"The more, the merrier. And we'll supply the snacks, so don't buy any—and don't argue! See you Tuesday."

The high point of Saturday is when I call the bakery with the cake dimensions and ask them to deliver it to the hospital between two forty-five and three. Otherwise the weekend seems to go on forever. Monday is easier because typing keeps me busy during most of the shift. Lenore calls on Monday night to assure me that the Greens will attend and that they will arrive at the rehab between two and two fifteen, while Rick is at PT. Mr. Simon, whom she says is a master at organization, has offered to handle the logistics of the guests, such as how we can hide seven adults and two children in the tiny bathroom and where the gifts will be stowed. I eagerly accept the offer.

At last it's Tuesday, September 18. On the way to work, I stop at the market to pick up some ice cream and then decide that some kind of decoration—a banner or some balloons—might make the room more cheerful. When I get to the rehab parking lot, I dash frantically to the building, willing the ice cream not to melt on the way to the freezer in the nurses' lounge. Rick is at OT, and he usually goes straight to PT, so there is plenty of time before he comes back to the room. Still, I feel skittish as I go about my regular routine. I probably won't be able to calm down until the cake is on the table and ready to be sliced.

I keep myself busy by making up a clean bed for Rick and generally straightening the room by putting the chairs in a conversational arrangement. I've been given orders not to touch the worktable, so I attack the cards on the wall, taking away the old ones and rearranging the newer ones. A few still come in every week. I also run down to PT to ask Curt to detain Rick until I let him know we're ready. When I get finished with this, it's 2:05, and the family will be coming soon. I go down to the lounge to get ice for Rick's water pitcher and breathe a sigh of relief when I find the ice cream in the nurses' freezer, untouched. People have been known to help themselves to other people's items, even when they are marked or bagged.

Five minutes after I get back, I hear a polite knock on the door, and the three Simons and a black-haired woman, whom Lenore introduces as their housekeeper, Carly O'Hara, come into the room. I'd pictured their housekeeper as a kindly older person with gray hair and rimless glasses, but this woman, who is quite nice looking, seems to be closer to my age! Didn't somebody—Lenore or Susan—tell me she'd been with them since Rick was eight or nine years old? She must have been a teenager at the time.

"I'm happy to meet you, Ms. O'Hara, and I'm glad you're all here." I suddenly feel frazzled again. "Um, I don't know what to do first. Should we—"

"Why don't we let Richie take care of everything? He loves challenges," Lenore suggests in a casual voice. "While he's working out where to put everyone, you can tell us what you want us to do."

"Okay," Mr. Simon says enthusiastically, after he looks over the bathroom, "here's how we do it. Three in the shower stall, one on the toilet seat, and three standing up against the door with Jody and Jennifer, so they can easily clap their hands over the kids' mouths when they start to giggle. It might be a bit . . . intimate in there, but it will only be for a couple of minutes." He looks at me for confirmation. "All right?" I nod, wondering why I thought it would be so difficult, working out the logistics. "Great!" he says. "So that's it. Can I go home now?"

Lenore and the housekeeper look at each other and roll their eyes, but I notice again how much what he said sounded like something Rick would say and how alike Rick and his father are in appearance and personality.

Now Mr. and Mrs. Green step through the door, followed by Kathy, Erin, and Jennifer, and the excitement I can already feel in the atmosphere rises a couple of notches. After a flurry of hugs and handshakes, Jennifer and Jody head for the wall with the cards. Lenore brings Ms. O'Hara and Mrs. Green to where I am standing, next to the square old table that I borrowed from the recreation room for the food. Mr. Simon and Mr. Green go over to the window to talk. I explain about the delivery of the cake, then open the bags with the decorations, party hats, and balloons. Mrs. Green, or Joyce, will manage the decorations and commandeers the children to help her blow up the balloons. I always thought the rich look down on people below them on the social scale, but Rick's family insist that everyone be on first-name basis. Lenore has brought snacks, so she will take care of the food. Mr. Green, I mean Greg, and Uncle Richard—I can't bring myself to call him Richie—will hang the banner and take care of the cake when it comes. My job is to put out the tableware. None of these things will take much time, but a glance at my watch tells me it's almost two forty, and I still feel tense, even though I know it's foolish. If we six adults are not capable of setting up a birthday party in a half hour, I don't know who is. Of course, we get done with ten minutes to spare. I direct Greg and Uncle Richard to the lounge for the beverages. We won't bring in the ice cream until we're ready for the cake, so we can relax for a few minutes until they hustle themselves into the bathroom.

The basically drab room is now colorful and festive. I'm delighted when I see a camera in Uncle Richard's hand and watch him take pictures of the scene. At three on the dot, everyone is in the bathroom, and the murmur of quietly excited voices fades out. I call Curt, open the bathroom door a crack, and whisper, "He's on his way," then sit down and wait, breathlessly, aware only of an intermittent "shushing" sound from the bathroom. Four minutes later, there is a bump at the door, and though it isn't necessary, I go to help Rick come in. He is flushed and damp from exertion, and with all the activity, I forgot to have a wet towel ready for him. But no matter. In seconds the bathroom will be empty.

He stops the chair short when he is fully inside. "What the—?"

"Don't say it!" I warn. "Somebody might hear you."

"What's going on here?"

With that, the bathroom door behind him bursts open, and everybody shouts, "SURPRISE!" and stampedes into the room so fast that he doesn't even have a chance to turn the chair around.

As they surround him, he puts his hand over his face and says softly, "Oh, geez."

For the next ten minutes, there is total bedlam, everyone trying to get to him at once. Nobody even notices how disheveled he is. Jennifer runs over and jumps up on him, leaving Jody to hang over one of the chair's arms.

"Jenny, let Jody sit first. He's Rick's brother," I cry out, but no one pays attention. By now Jody is standing on the footrest, and Rick, his face radiant, swings him up easily onto his other knee. A little later, when I am standing apart watching the action, I find him looking at me with an expression that says, "How could you do this to me?" I smile. Shaking his head slowly from side to side, he grins back. I've never seen him so happy, with two young children on his lap, surrounded by people who love him.

Bit by bit, the commotion dies down, and when the cake arrives, I go out to rescue the ice cream from the freezer. The room is filled with the family's laughter, as well as music coming from the small radio on the shelf. I think of Carol and Jerry's barbecue during the summer when their parents were there, and how I envied their easy camaraderie and humor. Here, I don't have to be an observer. The Simons are as warm and friendly to Jenny and me as they are to their each other. I don't think I'll ever understand why they're so good to us; it can only be that they are a gift from God. Carly and Erin light the candles, and we all sing "Happy Birthday" as Rick blows them out. Lenore and I cut the cake, while Kathy dishes up the ice cream.

Around four o'clock, there is another knock on the door, and Curt sticks his head into the room and asks if we have room for a few more. Without waiting for an answer, he opens the door wide and steps in, followed by two wheelchair patients I've never seen before. I stand with him and watch the men wheel over to Rick and instantly get caught in another round of handshaking as they are introduced to the guests. They are made welcome with cake and ice cream and an invitation to help themselves to whatever they want.

A few minutes later, Jennifer and Jody come up to me with ice cream on their faces and cake on their hands. "When are we going to open the presents?"

It's almost four thirty by now, and the party was supposed to end at four. "Oh, I forgot. We'd better do it now. Go get the gifts from the corner over there and put them on the bed. Okay?"

Rick riffles through the pages of the books from the Greens. "These will be helpful." Next he turns to my gift, hefts the cane, and smiles. "Great motivator, Maggie!" When he sees Jody's Magic 8 Ball, he intones theatrically, "Will I ever get out of here?" Then he shakes the ball and reads, "You may rely on it." Hugging Jody, he laughs. "Right on, man." Then he picks up the last gift. It's from Jennifer, who has been squirming in anxious anticipation. Rick unfurls the umbrella and gives Jenny a little kiss on the top of her head. "This is great! It better be raining when I leave here." Smiling shyly, he says, "I don't know what to say. I think I'm kind of . . . overwhelmed. Thanks again, everybody."

At ten past five, I announce that the party is over and everyone will have to clear out quickly. Rick has things that have to be done now. Curt and Rick's two friends leave first, followed by the Greens, then Kathy and Erin with Jennifer and Jody, who persuaded his mother to let him have supper with us. I lead the Simons and Carly to the lounge to wait while Rick goes through his bladder care routine. He also uses the bathroom on his own for washing up. He's getting good at doing these things by himself. When I think he's done, Lenore, Carly, and I go back to his room to clean up. Neither he nor Mr. Simon are there. He's probably taking his father on a tour of the facility.

As soon as everything is back in order, the three of us go out to the garden to look for them. It doesn't take long for us to encounter them, since they're on their way back to the building. The sun is still bright, but clouds are beginning to drift in our direction; and since Rick shows no particular inclination toward going back to the room, the four of us take possession of a bench near one of the flower beds, and he situates himself on the path facing us. Nobody says anything right away. For some reason, this seems like a perfect time to sit quietly and reflect on the loveliness of the garden, the sunshine, and the success of the party. I'm thinking about time and how little of it we have left. I'm thinking about how Rick is Curt's star pupil and progressing faster than anyone could have hoped for. I'm truly happy for him and his family. They'll have him back a lot sooner than they expected. But even though I've accepted the reality of his leaving, I'm sad for Jenny and me.

Rick breaks the silence. "Thank you," he says softly, looking at each of us in turn. When he gets to me at the end of the bench, his eyes fasten on mine and hold me with an intensity I can't break away from. "Thanks for everything," he says again, but this time, in a way that is unmistakably meant for me. If I don't get out of here right now, I'm going to do something embarrassing.

I bite my lip, just to make sure I'm capable of moving, then stand up. "I'm sorry to break the mood, but I really have to get home now," I say feebly. "I want to thank you all too, for making the party a success." They smile broadly. "And I want to tell you, Carly, how much I've enjoyed meeting you and"—I look at Lenore and Mr. Simon—"and seeing both of you again."

Lenore laughs and holds her hand up. "Hey, wait a minute, Maggie. You're not going to say good-bye now, are you? With our little boy at your house? We are going to pick him up, you know."

Dear Lord, where is my head? "Oh yes, of course. I'm a little . . . tired."

She puts her arm on her husband's. "Maybe we should pick Jody up now, Rich. I'm sure Maggie's more worn out than she admits."

"It's almost six. Aren't we supposed to meet Joyce and Greg at seven?"

"Oh yes. I forgot. It's been quite a day for me too," she says. Then she adds, "They're meeting us at the hotel restaurant for dinner. We'll follow you home."

"I'll see you tomorrow, Rick," I say, wishing I could kiss him before I go.

He nods. "Don't forget to bring breakfast," he calls as I walk away.

So ends a joyful, sad, wonderful day.

<u>*October 1973*</u>

"Thanks for everything."

It has such a final sound, like when you've spent a weekend at the home of a friend who obviously went to a lot of trouble to make you feel comfortable, or when someone has volunteered to drive you to the airport. You usually say it just before you say "good-bye," and you can't get much more final than that.

It's Saturday evening. Supper's over, Jenny is in bed, and I'm reading the newspaper in the living room, or to be more accurate, trying to read it. For no reason at all, my brain would rather rerun scenes from Rick's birthday almost three weeks ago, than focus on columns of print. The party must have made even more of an impression on me than I realized at the time. Or is it that I'm so sick of reading about Watergate, my brain is rebelling?

Work is going well. My routine is pretty well established now, and I've been so busy that the days seem to be over almost before they've begun. I still have a ways to go before I finish Rick's notes and bring his drafts up to date, but my typing speed is improving, so I'm confident that I'll soon be able to manage the new corrections and rewrites as they come to me. While Rick is at therapy, I type the part of the dissertation he wrote during his nine months in Chicago before the accident. Now that his energy has returned and he's feeling so well, he's bursting with ideas, so I have to drop whatever I'm doing and take down his thoughts in shorthand, a skill I learned in high school along with typing. Whenever I have a few minutes, I transcribe the notes and file them away until I can get to them. It's slow going, but we're making progress.

Every day, it seems, Rick advances physically. The feeling in his good foot has been steadily increasing, as well as spreading a ways up his leg. He recently felt numbness in his other foot, and that's also been intensifying. His new goal is to be on his feet before he leaves rehab. And yesterday, Dr. Stern, who is much encouraged by the improvement, gave him the go-ahead to start weight-bearing sessions three times a week. He admits he's not sure how much Rick can achieve at his current level of recovery, but Rick's set on giving it a shot. I wonder how long he'll be willing to stay in Chicago to finish his research, but I don't say anything because part of me still thinks it was my pressuring him for information that led to the accident in the first place. I dread the thought of him leaving, but since he never drops a clue to what he's thinking, I'll just have to bide my time until he's ready to say something.

I happened to run into Curt in the hall the other day, and he told me he sees Rick in the recreation room a couple of times a week after dinner. Rick stays for about an hour playing cards or table tennis or just hanging out with other patients, some of whom, Curt stressed, also have advanced college degrees. In fact, Rick told him there is a PhD who is interested in his dissertation. I'm glad to hear he's meeting other people, especially people he can communicate with on his own intellectual level. I've always felt I was never a good companion for him. Too old, too unsophisticated, too uneducated, too boring. I noticed him watching Erin at his party. Even back in August, when I hired her to babysit for us, his ears perked up when I told him she was also working on a PhD, though not at U of C. He could have befriended a doctoral candidate on campus, so why he chose me, I'll never know. The Lord works in mysterious ways, and it's not for me to question.

The telephone rings. I don't feel like talking to anybody, so I waver a bit before I lay the paper on the couch and head for the dining room. "Hello?"

"Hi, it's me. I was about to hang up. Did I wake you?"

Rick? He's never called me at home before. "No. I'm just sitting here and reading the newspaper."

"Woolgathering, my grandmother used to say."

"What's that?"

"You know, daydreaming, fantasizing."

"Rick, you've never called me at home before."

"I know. I just felt like talking to you."

"The truth is, I was kind of woolgathering about you when the phone rang. Is everything okay?"

"Everything's fine. After dinner, I went to the rec room and played chess with this guy who has a doctorate in sociology. We play a couple of games whenever we run into each other. I got back a few minutes ago and thought I'd call to see how your day went."

"Oh, everything's fine here, too," I say. "Jenny and I went to the zoo and then we went to Marshall Field's to find her a winter coat. That's about it."

"That's cool." Slight pause. "Well, I guess I'd better get back to work."

I seem to have exceeded his small-talk limit in one sentence. What do I say now? "I'm glad you called, Rick. You should do it more often."

"You don't see enough of me during the week?"

He must be joking. How can he not know? "It's getting late, Simon. Go on back to work."

"Right on, McLean. See you on Monday and don't forget the bagels."

I'm beginning to wonder if he really does like bagels or if it's just become a habit to say this instead of goodbye.

Kathy and Todd are over for Sunday dinner. It's been six weeks since school started, and time has been going so fast that it's almost been that long since we've seen them. This is the strangest mealtime we've ever had together. Jennifer immediately takes it upon herself to be the chatty hostess, initiating conversations apparently about anything that comes into her mind—school, her new friends, Erin—and then putting her two cents' worth into whatever the grown-ups are discussing. Kathy finally puts down her fork and watches Jenny with a look of perplexed amazement. I know how she feels; I've barely gotten used to my daughter's new personality myself.

Lucky for us, Todd would just as soon watch sports on television as sit with women and chat, so Kathy and I have plenty of time to talk in the kitchen while we're cleaning up. All through the meal, I had the feeling something was on her mind, and we're not alone for two minutes before it gushes out.

"We got our church date! Tomorrow we're going to start looking for an apartment and next weekend we're going to shop for wedding clothes and dishes and silver patterns. It's so exciting, Maggie! I can't believe it's really happening."

Visions of a runaway train fill my head. "Hey, wait, Kath. Slow down. I thought it wasn't going to be until next summer."

"It wasn't, but we changed our mind. Why should we wait? If we get married now, we can be together that much sooner. And I always wanted to go someplace warm—"

"What do you mean by 'now'?" I interrupt. This rushing rashly into something without considering the consequences is exactly the kind of thing I was supposed to protect Kathy from getting involved in.

Her face turns pink. "We know what we're doing, Maggie," she says in a quiet, defensive voice. "We aren't children. Todd is a very sensible person."

I back down. "I know that, Kath. I didn't mean to throw cold water on your plans. What date did you decide on?"

"November 18." I start to remind her that that's only a month away, but she heads me off. "It's going to be a very small wedding. Ceremony at church, reception at home." *Oh Lord!* "We decided we'd rather save the money we'd spend on a fancy wedding and put it toward a house instead. Do you think that's a dumb thing to do?"

"No. I'm just a little surprised. I always thought you'd want a dream wedding like Carolyn Cleary had."

She smiles wistfully. "When I was in high school, we called them 'cheerleader' weddings. You know, like only the prettiest, most popular girls had. Now, a lot of things that used to be important just aren't anymore. The only thing I really want for my wedding is for you to be my matron of honor."

Ceremony at church, reception at home. Can I get through this? "Of course, I will," I promise, hugging her and trying to keep my anxiety from showing. "Who are you having for bridesmaids?"

"No bridesmaids. Just you and Jenny for flower girl, if that's all right with you. Todd's brother Jeff will be best man and his nephew will be the ring bearer. That's all we've worked out so far."

"Are you happy with the plans?"

"Oh yes," she breathes with a grin of such joy that I feel it spill over onto me.

It's really strange when you realize your baby sister is now your peer.

For the past two weeks or so, Rick has been breaking for lunch at eleven forty-five and taking me with him up to the roof café. Already it's become a routine within a routine. I'm especially pleased about it because it means his appetite has definitely improved and he's eating at least one healthy meal a day. I've noticed that the younger girl behind the counter always perks up when we come in the door and maneuvers it so that she can wait on him. She's a cute little thing, around eighteen or nineteen, I'm guessing, and she never fails to flirt with Rick when she waits on us. I'm a little jealous; I admit it. It's been months since Rick and I have so much as brushed fingers; curbing my longing for physical contact with him is an ongoing struggle for me. It's obvious he's gotten past me, while I'm trying hard to deceive myself into believing that I've gotten past him.

We give our orders at the counter and settle down at our usual table by a window.

"She's cute, isn't she?" I ask Rick teasingly.

"Who?" he returns nonchalantly, pouring two cups of coffee from the pot on the table.

"The waitress, the young one with the blonde hair. What's her name?"

"Why would I know her name?"

"Rick, she waits on us every day and she always flirts with you."

He shrugs his shoulders. "If she does, she's wasting her time. I'm not interested." He narrows his eyes and smiles slyly. "Are you thinking of arranging a date for me? With *her*?"

"Of course not."

The smile vanishes. "That's good. I already have one Jewish mother. I don't need another one." He peers over my shoulder toward the counter, then pulls his silverware out of its napkin sheath and arranges it next to his plate. "Food's coming."

"Hi," says the perky waitress and looks at Rick. "How are you today?"

He mumbles something.

"We're fine," I translate. "Thank you."

"Cool," she bubbles, efficiently setting out our orders. "I'll be back with more coffee when you're ready. Anything else you want, just let me know. My name's Cherie."

"Cool," Rick assures her, and she moves on. He says to me, "You reminded me of something I've been meaning to tell you."

My stomach quakes for a change. "What?"

"Nothing big. It's just that I've gotten approval from Stern to go off the grounds for a few hours. You'll have to accompany me, of course. Hospital rules."

"Oh, Rick, that's big!"

"Getting out of here for good is big. This is a baby step."

"Any idea where you want to go?"

"Yes. Your apartment."

Now my stomach does a triple flip. "But you can go anywhere, do anything. Why do you want to do something so boring and familiar?"

"Because it is familiar, Maggie. I just want to be normal again for a few hours. Is there a problem with us going to your—?"

"No, no!" I cry, practically tripping over my tongue to convince him.

"Perfect. I figure we can go out for lunch and then back to your place. What time does Jennifer get home from school?"

"About three thirty."

He smiles broadly. "Good."

"When were you thinking of doing this?"

"I don't know. How about Halloween?"

"Well, Kathy and Todd are coming by around five thirty to take Jenny trick-or-treating. Will that interfere with anything?" I refill my cup from the pot, which is lukewarm now.

He looks disappointed. "Shoot! I was counting on the three of us playing a few high-stakes games of Go Fish." He watches me for my reaction, which is to respond as I usually do when he gets playful. I roll my eyes to let him know that I'm merely tolerating his tomfoolery. To this he puts up his hands as if to ward off danger. "No, Maggie! Don't throw that cup! They have a rule here that anyone who's involved in a food fight in the rooftop café will not be permitted to attend dance classes for three days."

I look around warily, but nobody seems to be noticing his silliness.

"Sometimes you act like you're three years old," I tell him.

"Sometimes you have to act like you're three years old. Try it sometime."

"I don't understand," I say uncertainly.

In an instant, his face goes dark, as if he's been reminded of something unpleasant. "I'm scared, Maggie. I have to go out into the world for the first time in a sitting position. From now on, everything I do or see will be from the vantage point of a six-year-old."

I move my hand toward him on the table, and he clutches it. "That's not true, Rick. You know you're only steps away from walking. You're just having jitters. You'll be fine," I tell him.

He looks into the distance for a few seconds, then lifts the corners of his mouth into a little smile. His fingers tighten. "Still . . ." he says.

One touch and my body is in flames. *Time alone together in my apartment. Can I handle it?* Maybe I ought to consult Rick's Magic 8 Ball when we get back to the room.

In nursing school, I had a teacher who was a dragon when it came to nursing notes. She stressed over and over the importance of our notes being complete, legible, concise, and, above all, 100 percent accurate. Rick would've passed that class with flying colors. I'm acclimated to using the erase key now, so I don't need to concentrate so hard on the typing and can read as I go along. To my surprise, his writing is not way above my head as I'd expected, but in plain language that is easy to understand. And it's interesting. In fact, I've taken to writing down the words that I've never heard of or don't know the meaning of, then looking them up in the evening. Another surprise is that most of the time, they fit what I guessed he was saying. Right now I'm typing the part that deals with political journalism from the late '60s into the1970s, and while I don't claim to know anything about the subject, it occurs to me that in spite of all Rick's painstaking research, he's left out something pretty important. I've been working nonstop to get as much done each day as possible to satisfy this sense of time running out. Rick writes like lightning, and it's a struggle to keep up. Yet I'm too curious to ignore his oversight.

"Rick? How come you haven't written anything about Watergate? Isn't it supposed to be the 'news story of the century'?"

He puts down his pencil, pours himself a glass of water, and takes off his glasses. "Can't yet. Everything has to be researched and documented before I can use it."

"But you read so many newspapers. Don't they tell you what you need to know?"

"This is just a first draft. Before I can write anything for submission, I'll have to read transcripts and everything else that's been written about Watergate so far, and come to my own conclusions. Besides, I'm convinced the public only gets part of the picture from the news, that the government withholds anything they don't want known. We might have to wait years for something like a book or a movie to learn the whole truth—if one ever comes out that tells the truth."

I'm staggered by this. "Our government would do something like that?"

"Always has and always will."

"But our family has always read the *Chicago Tribune* and believed everything it printed. My father swears by it."

Rick shrugs. "It's a good idea to keep an open mind and not believe everything you read, even—no, especially—in the newspaper."

"But then, what should we read? What newspaper does *your* family read?"

"Primarily, the *New York Times*."

"I know you get that one. And you believe what it says?"

"Depends. But maybe I'm not the one you should talk to about this. Political journalism is my field of study. I probably look at news articles with a more critical eye than people who haven't had that educational experience."

Rick is so matter-of-fact about this. To me, however, the idea of distrusting major newspapers and news broadcasts is totally alien and mind-boggling.

He puts his glasses on again and glances at his watch. "It's one. Want to do the skin check and go to lunch?"

I look at him blankly. I'm still fretting over the *Chicago Tribune*. "Uh, yes. Sure. Take off your shirt."

The exam is more habit than protocol at this point, since it's unlikely he'll develop any lesions now. He no longer lies motionless in bed for a long enough time. I give him a quick, cursory inspection, which, of course, is negative. My own reaction is less negative, as a blush of warmth mushrooms inside me. Since Labor Day, Rick has not made a single overture or indicated that he is still interested in me in the physical sense, and I'm too timid or conventional or something to initiate the subject. I sigh audibly without meaning to and hand him his shirt. He takes it from me, places my hand on his body just above the waist of his jeans, and says softly, "I know, Maggie. I think about it all the time. It was good, wasn't it?"

I can hardly breathe.

After a minute, he lets go of me, puts his shirt back on, and we go to lunch. We both act as if that moment in the room never happened, and lunch is as usual. Cherie flirts, Rick ignores her, we make occasional small talk. When we return to the room, we both resume our work, but I can't stop thinking about his response to my sigh.

In the evening, I call Carol. We haven't spoken in weeks, for which I always take responsibility, and as usual, I apologize profusely.

"I didn't call you either," she reminds me, "so we're even." Her way, I'm sure, of saying, "So what?"

We get the trivialities out of the way quickly and make arrangements to meet for a one-hour breakfast on Monday. I don't tell her during the call that Rick is scheduled to come to my house two days later and that I could use some advice on how to handle it. I haven't mentioned Rick's visit to Kathy either. It's so close to the wedding, she's bound to be too immersed in preparations to think about anything else. I do tell Carol about Kathy and Todd, and she utters appropriate expressions of delight. The conversation is short, and we hang up after reconfirming our breakfast plans.

Lenore and I haven't been in contact for two or three weeks either, and I think about calling her now, but I don't do it. Rick talks to one or another of his relatives every few days, so they know he's doing well. I expect she'll call me when she knows when Rick is leaving.

I pick up the book I've been reading for the past week, but my eyes are smarting from typing and poor lighting. I'm not up to reading right now after all. Instead I lie back on the couch and go over in my mind what Rick and I discussed today. I had no idea how much went into a dissertation, and now that I do, I can understand his anxiety and bad temper before he was able to get back to work.

I fall asleep imagining the smooth firmness of him beneath my palm and hearing the echo of his gentle voice: "It was good." *Please let it be good again,* I ask whatever is out there. *Just once more.*

The bus to Jennifer's school stops on our side of the boulevard at the next corner. She has been pestering me to let her wait for it with the four or five kids we pass every day. This morning, Monday, she doesn't pester me, she pleads with me, and I finally compromise and watch her from our front window until she turns the corner. Then I rush outside to play "hide and peek" until she is safely aboard the bus.

Driving over to meet Carol at a small coffee shop near the hospital, I can't help wondering once again how, when I am so cautious with Jenny this year, I could have handed her over to Rick before I even knew him. It was a stupid thing to do, and I consider myself a very lucky woman that nothing horrible happened.

Carol is sitting at a table in the back of the shop, sipping a cup of coffee and reading from a file folder. A waitress appears with filled plates and a pot of tea before I am even seated. "I took the liberty of ordering for both of us," Carol informs me, "since we don't have a lot of time." She quickly stows the file into her briefcase.

"How did you know what—?"

"You order the same thing every time we meet for breakfast, Maggie. Two scrambled eggs and toast with butter. You can change the order if you want to."

"No, this is what I would've said."

"Then let us begin." She folds her hands in front of her and looks at me encouragingly.

"How is—?" I ask.

"Sarah's fine. Enjoying day care and talking up a storm. Jerry is also enjoying his work and talking up a storm . . . So what's happening with you?"

Carol's obviously in no mood to put up with evasions so, for a change, I get right into it. "Okay. Rick's made such excellent progress that he's gotten permission to leave the unit on a kind of field trip"—she says nothing but smiles and nods complacently, as if she knew all along it would work out this way—"and he wants to come to my apartment on Wednesday."

The smile widens a bit, and she nods again. "How do you feel about that?"

I was hoping she wouldn't ask. "Fine."

Her expression doesn't change, but she cocks her head about two degrees to the right. "I mean, of course I'm pleased that he wants to come, but I'm also nervous about it."

"And why is that?"

Another question that makes me feel uncomfortable. I can't even explain why to myself, let alone to a friend who happens to be a therapist. But I plunge ahead. "I think because I don't know where I stand with him. It's different now, the relationship, I mean. He's been pretty much self-sufficient for weeks, and . . ." *I wish she'd stop staring at me. It makes me feel even more uneasy.* I shrug. "I'm not sure how to handle the visit."

"Why not? You see him every day, Maggie. Why is it different at your house than it is in his room?"

"I don't know. That's why I'm here. I don't know what to do with him at my house."

"What do you want to do with him?"

For the second time in two days, I feel an embarrassing rush of heat spread across my face, hotter now than when I was with Rick yesterday. It's like a year ago, when I was unable to control my reactions whenever he came near me. I was sure I'd gotten past that long ago.

"You don't need me to tell you what to do. You know what to do," Carol says.

"What if he doesn't feel the same way?"

"Look. He's been in the hospital for what? Five months? I'm willing to bet he wants it just as much as you do, if not more."

"Why would he, Carol? He can't experience anything. Some feeling has returned, but it's only to his legs. Why would he want to put himself through the disappointment and frustration?"

"He'll let you know if he can't handle it, no pun intended." I look away from her. Carol's the closest thing I have to a best friend, but her crudeness does tend to put me off. "For God's sake, Maggie," she says. "If he doesn't take the lead, then you do it. I bet he'll take you up on it. Human beings are sexual animals. Anyway, if I'm wrong, you'll be no worse off than you were before you asked. Take a risk!"

I don't say yes, and I don't say no. I say, "I'll try."

"Then good, we can put that one to bed. Oops, sorry. Another unintended pun."

Conversation stops until she has finished her food. Then, rubbing her hands together as if she can't wait to hear what it is, she asks, "So what's next on the docket?" The clock over the counter says she has a client in twenty minutes; it's now or never.

"Kathy's getting married in three weeks."

"So soon? I thought they'd decided on summer."

"They changed their minds."

She glances at her watch. "And how is this a problem for you?"

"The wedding is at the church in Clearyville and the reception is at my mother's house."

She wrinkles her nose. "Ouch! How do you feel about those plans?"

"Conflicted. The church wouldn't welcome a sinner like me, and the same people will be at my parents' house, but Kathy still wants me to be her matron of honor, and I don't want to ruin her big day. She'll be hurt if Jenny and I leave immediately after the ceremony."

"I can understand your not wanting to go back to that church, but why are you afraid to face you mother?"

"Afraid to face my mother? I'm not afraid of her." *Am I? I never thought about it that way.* "And I don't mind seeing my father, but frankly, I don't want to be anywhere near my mother ever again. I don't even want Jennifer to have anything to do with her, but she's her grandmother, so of course I have to send her with Kathy when they go."

"How does Jenny feel about her grandma?"

"During the summer, she told me her grandmother was mean."

"Then that problem's solved too."

I start to protest, but she puts her hand up.

"We reap what we sow, Maggie, and your mother has caused you enough harm. You have to make the decision about seeing her and then abide by what you choose to do. And I wouldn't push it if Jenny doesn't want to go. You're in charge of the situation and it's all up to you."

The waitress comes with the check, a fresh pot of coffee, and a carafe of steaming water with a teabag and a slice of lemon on the side. Carol takes the check and waves away the refills. We have about five minutes left. "I'll pay this time," she says.

"No, you won't. I called you. It's on me."

"If you insist," she responds airily. "I never argue about a check. Besides, I have to get going." I take out a few bills, leave a tip, and pick up the check. At the door, Carol says, "You'll let me know how everything goes?"

"I'll call you later in the week."

"Great. Just do what feels right and you'll be fine." She gives me a hug and a peck on the cheek. "Talk to you later. Have a good day," she calls as she hurries down the street to her car.

Well, that was good! We just solved all of my problems in forty-five minutes. If only life was always that easy.

This year, Halloween is the event of paramount importance in Jennifer's life. It's dress-up day in school, and her friends, Lisa and Debby, will be going trick-or-treating with her. After two weeks of secret talks with them, she has narrowed her costume choices to cheerleader, ballet dancer, and Dorothy from *The Wizard of Oz*. Kathy and I were forbidden to observe Halloween when we were children because our church said it was pagan. Instead we had a kind of reverse trick-or-treat, in that every Christmas, the children dressed up as Biblical characters and brought goodies to the less fortunate of our congregation.

Today, I am picking Jenny up at three fifteen to buy her costume. Last year she was Lady "Abbalin," and Kathy and I took her around the block for maybe half an hour before she was ready to go back home. This year she's fizzing with excitement. Talk about change! It's been quite a year for all of us.

"Mom! I know what I'm going to be for Halloween," she announces as she throws her books in the backseat of the car and scrambles up beside me. "Guess!"

"A ballerina," I say, thinking about a pretty paste tiara I saw in an ad for a local costume shop.

"Wrong. Try again."

"Oh, well then, it must be Dorothy. Right?" This is my personal favorite. It won't take much time to stitch together a blue and white gingham apron, and she can carry a stuffed dog in her arms.

"Nope." She smiles smugly.

Just as well. The ruby slippers might have been difficult to find on short notice.

"You get one more guess," she adds, crossing her arms.

"Oh, let me see . . . I don't know . . . Uh . . ."

"Mom, there's only one left. Don't you remember it?"

"Let's go to the costume store. Maybe I'll remember it when I see it."

Miraculously the store still has a small supply of orange and black pom-poms and a miniature megaphone. They don't sell sweaters, and their short skirts have all sold out in Jenny's size. I take a larger one to alter. Jenny spots a little blonde wig she wants to wear, so we take that too. "I'm going to wear lipstick. My mom said I could," she tells the elderly couple who own the store.

"You'll be the most beautiful cheerleader in Chicago," says the wife and gives her a big sparkly barrette to hold her wig in place. "No charge. A little gift for a lovely little girl."

Jenny beams. I want to cry with happiness. Instead I decide to buy a film cartridge for my old Kodak Instamatic. Her excitement has made me realize that memory alone is not always enough.

I work on the costume until 1:00 a.m. Considering that Rick is coming tomorrow, it's just short of amazing that I fall asleep the minute my head hits the pillow, and I don't budge until the alarm clock wakes me at 7:00 a.m.

October 31, 1973

Rick and I make a good pair today. I'm preoccupied, and he's distracted. Neither of us seem to be able to concentrate on our work, and several times

I glance at him and find him staring straight at me dreamily, but without making eye contact. It's as if he's not seeing me at all. I try to concentrate on the words in front of me or think about Jennifer in her classroom, wearing her cheerleader outfit, but I always come back to Rick's visit. We hardly talk either. It's eerie and nerve-wracking.

When he returns from an 11:00 a.m. physical therapy session, he takes a short shower and lies down on the bed in his underwear, with a thin blanket over him. Ever since he started using the writing table, he has taken short bed rests whenever he's needed them. For one thing, sitting up for prolonged periods of time is hard on his back, even in the brace. For another, he refuses to acknowledge pain or spasms unless they're severe. Kathy says he's too "macho" to admit he's hurting. I say he's too stubborn. His only concession to the pain is the twenty or thirty minutes he lies down, and even then, he always reads while he's resting. Except for today. Today he's not reading; he's staring into space.

"Are you up for lunch yet?"

His voice jolts me out of whatever reverie I've been in and, for some strange reason, also reminds me that I have to call Erin about not picking Jennifer up from school anymore. I check my watch: one o'clock. *The adventure is about to begin . . .*

We're riding down the boulevard near my house, looking for a likely place to eat. Rick is kind of appalled that I don't know any restaurants in my own neighborhood. It is sort of funny. I drive down this road every day, but ask me to name a single restaurant in the area, and I can't. Fortunately he can.

"Stop!" he orders. "Make a right at the corner and come back around. We just passed a great Hungarian restaurant I went to a few times. Go slow. I'll look for a parking space."

We find one on the other side of the street about three-quarters of the way up the block. It's been raining on and off all day, and the temperature is in the middle forties. I pray that the wheels on the chair have good traction and that Rick doesn't get a chill in this weather. He "doesn't wear hats," he insisted before we left, and I've been trying to hold an umbrella over him, but it's hard to keep him covered as he weaves around people on the sidewalk. The light is red when we get to the corner, and I take the opportunity to ask him what kind of food Hungarians eat.

"You'll like it," he assures me. "It's food you're used to. Just the seasonings are different."

The manager leads us to a table where Rick, in his chair, will not be in the way, and hands us each a menu that is—*thank you, Lord*—in both Hungarian and English. I leave to call Erin and tell her to take the rest of the afternoon off; I will pick up Jennifer. When I get back to the table, the waiter has just come to take our orders. Rick asks for a stew for me and chicken for himself. We're both hungry, and we tacitly agree to eat without talking for a while.

He's right. The food is very good, so much so that I'm thinking I might buy some paprika the next time I go shopping. The room we're in has a fireplace with a glowing fire in it. Rick says it's a gas fireplace, but still it makes the room cozy and warm enough that I forget the rawness of the weather. We manage to find a lot to talk about, including how easy his dissertation is for me to understand and how interesting I am finding it. I confess, though, that I do have to look up some of the words when I get home from work.

A broad smile lights his face. "You know something, Maggie?" he says with an appraising look. "You're an intelligent woman. You should think about getting a degree."

"Me? What could I ever get a degree in?"

"Anything you want. Your problem is that you weren't brought up in an environment that puts much stress on formal education. But you're smart. You just have to believe it and keep trying to use what you have." I can't quite take in what he's saying to me and assume he's being funny. But he seems truly sincere. "I mean it," he adds suddenly, as if he's once again reading my mind.

"I don't know if I'm really what you say, but thank you, Rick. When you say things like that, I feel as if I'm more than I think I am. If only," I say tentatively, "you could stay in Chicago."

"I can't," he says shortly, "and it's time we went to your house. It's getting late." He signals the waiter, pays the check, and we venture back into the rain. At the car, Rick easily transfers from the chair to the front seat and insists on folding the wheelchair, which is not as heavy as it looks, so I can put it in the backseat. "Lesson 9—Folding," he informs me. "Lesson 10—Stowing, maybe next week."

On the way to the apartment, he turns somber, staring through the windshield like he is riveted to a screen that is showing a movie that really grips him. I try to pull him back to reality. "Did you enjoy the lunch?"

"Sure," he responds after a moment. "It was fun and the food was great. Didn't you like it?"

"Oh yes. I was thinking I might buy a Hungarian cookbook."

"Good idea. Doesn't hurt to introduce Jenny to new foods. Kind of enrich her experiences."

"Before you came, we never went to restaurants. I don't know why exactly, but I never had the urge to."

"So do it from now on. You can never be exposed to too many things."

At this point, we're just about home. I find a space three houses away on our side and get out, open the umbrella, and hurry around to the passenger side. I open the back door and pull out the chair, while Rick opens the front and arranges himself for the transfer. I place the chair where he needs it, and he slides in without difficulty and arranges his legs. Before we start toward the house, he looks up at me with a little grin and says, "I must be the guy that Hertz took *out* of the driver's seat."

I chuckle and squeeze his shoulder, once again keenly aware of the substance of his body beneath my fingers. But touching his shoulder is not enough for me anymore. I want more, and at this moment, I can't imagine a time when I will not want it, not want him.

Fortunately the apartment house has a concrete path leading to the front door and only one shallow step to conquer with the wheelchair. Rick grudgingly concedes that there is no way we can win that battle by ourselves, so I ring the super, Mr. Wagner's, button and tell him I need some help. As he emerges from the building, he pauses for a second, his eyes darting from me to Rick, and a hint of confusion on his face. *We must have managed to keep our secret.* "Mrs. McLean . . . and Mr. Simon!" he crows. "Hey! Me and the wife a-been wonderin' how ya turned out from the accident. Here, lemme help ya with this thing." I hold the door open as he tilts the chair back with no visible effort and pushes it through. "C'mon inna back. I'll open the freight elevator for ya." Rick and I both thank him. Then, as the elevator wends its weary way up to the next floor and we bump down the corridors to my apartment in the front, we repay his kindness by answering a stream of questions about Rick's life in the past four and a half months. "So whut happened? Ya meet in the hospital where Mrs. McLean works and find out you live in the same building?" Rick is patient and polite, and his answers are brief; he knows as well as I do that the information will reach all four corners of the building by tomorrow. Mr. Wagner leaves us as I pick up the paper from my mat and put the key in my door.

And here we are.

Rick situates himself in the center of the living room rug, which makes the room suddenly seem much smaller. He looks around almost solemnly, and I wonder what he's thinking, but I don't ask. I move toward the kitchen. "I'll make coffee."

I don't know much about the psychology of this situation. I suppose everyone reacts differently. With Rick, it's always hard to tell what he's thinking or needing, so I give him time to himself. I lean against the stove, looking at the wall above, struggling with what to do if he disappears into one of his untalkative moods. We see each other every day, and we've already talked at the restaurant. I'm aware that it's ridiculous to go on about this the way I am, but I want today to be a special day for him—and for me. I load up the tray, turn, and gasp. He is sitting in the doorway, looking directly at me with a sweet smile.

"Good Lord, Rick, you startled me! How long have you been there?"

"About five minutes. Sorry I scared you."

"I'm only getting the coffee."

He shrugs his shoulders. "I know, but I wanted to watch you do it . . . It's one of those ordinary, familiar things I was talking about the other day . . . Here, I'll take the tray." He backs into the dining room and holds out his hands for it. We stand here looking at each other for a moment. "Uh," he points out with a quizzical expression, "my hands are full. You'll have to push."

I arrange his chair facing the couch, take the tray, and sit down opposite him. He, in turn, sets up the chair's lap tray, takes the tray back, and peers at me with a trace of a smile. "Let's not play with the tray anymore . . . You're nervous, aren't you?" I nod sheepishly. "Me too," he admits.

"But why, Rick? We spend so much time together. We're working on the same project. We go to lunch together every day. We're never nervous when we do those things—at least, I'm not."

"Neither am I, but—and I can only speak for myself—we have a different relationship there. We're in a hospital. You're my nurse. I'm your patient. The typing? That's business. Here, it's as if we're like our old us . . . Maggie, do you remember what happened the day of the accident?"

"Yes."

"Will you tell me about it?"

I hesitate. He never seemed the least bit curious about it before. Now I just want to forget it and move on. "Does it matter anymore?"

"I'm missing two weeks out of my life. All I'm asking for is one day."

It matters. “Well, it was a Monday and I was on the three-to-eleven shift. I was upset about something. Anyway, I wanted to get home early, but a couple of my patients were having problems, so I wound up staying almost to midnight . . . I always went through the ER to get to the parking lot, and that’s where I was when a nurse I’d worked with before called me back to tell me about someone they’d just brought in from a motorcycle crash. It was so strange, Rick. I knew you were home babysitting Jennifer, but I got the weirdest feeling that it was you. I called my apartment and Kathy was there, said you’d had to go out. So, in a panic, I went back to the ER to find out what was happening, and . . . well, you know the rest. I was there all night . . . didn’t get home till eight or nine in the morning.”

He looks at me curiously. “What were you upset about that night—I mean, that day?”

The days before the accident are still fresh in my mind, painful to think about, hard to talk about. “Oh, I can’t really remember,” I say lightly. “It was probably something that wasn’t important.”

He frowns, shakes his head. “No, you wouldn’t have let something that wasn’t important bother you. Not then. In those days, you were kind of . . . detached, dealing with your grief over Steve. It was almost as if you were on automatic pilot a lot of the time. No, it had to be something big to really upset you, and I think what it was is the thing that’s been nagging me for months, that I can’t remember. I think I’ve even dreamed about it, but I could never seem to get hold of it. Maggie, if you know what it is, please tell me.”

I put my face in my hands to shut out his dark eyes, beseeching me like people in church beseech God for help. “Let me think about it, Rick,” I say tentatively. “A lot has happened since then, but maybe it’ll come back if I concentrate on it.”

He nods, but it’s clear that he’s deflated. We sit in silence for a few minutes, until a sudden, loud clap from his hands smacking the arms of the wheelchair interrupts the lull. “So,” he inquires cheerfully, “do we have any plans for the rest of the day?”

“Whatever you want.”

“I don’t know. What do you want to do? Play Scrabble? Go to a movie? The guys on the unit tell me that basket weaving is a lot of fun.”

I check my watch. “Oh dear. I have to meet Jennifer’s bus in five minutes. I’d better leave now.”

“To go around the corner?”

“It might come early.”

"It's déjà vu all over again," he exclaims. "Only before it was with my mother."

"I guess all mothers are alike when it comes to their kids." Except mine. I grab my jacket from the closet and turn on a lamp against the darkening day. "I'll be back in a few minutes."

"I'll be here."

I toss the newspaper at him, somehow landing it right on his tray. He looks at me like he's both amazed and impressed.

The bus is ten minutes late. I spend the time patrolling the short block between our corner and the bus stop, feeling like I am, as my father used to say, "between a rock and a hard place." What if Rick should need me while I'm out? Will he get worried when we don't come right back? This tiny unexpected glitch in the day has me off balance. *Lord, what is wrong with me?* Did Jennifer remember to put on her rain hat? Suddenly I hear my mother's voice. *Stop it, Mary Grace. Right now. Get hold of yourself.*

Finally here's the bus, lumbering along, stopping for the light on our corner, then lumbering on. I sprint back to our corner and around the turn, then peek out to watch the doors open and the children start to exit, one, two, three, then Jennifer, her books in one arm and her rain hat in her pocket. She ambles along, splashing in puddles. When she is one storefront from our building, I make a beeline for the lobby, hurtle up the steps, and let myself into the apartment. Rick is just coming out of the bathroom.

He laughs when he sees me. "You look like you're training for the Olympics. Where's Jenny?"

"She's on her way. I didn't want her to see me, so just before she got to the corner, I ran like the blazes to get home before she did. Everything all right?"

"With me or the bathroom?"

"Just answer, please."

"We're both fine, thank you."

I sit down on the couch just as Jennifer comes through the door, calling, "Mom, Mom, the bus was—"

She stops short and drops her books on the floor. "Rick's here! Why didn't you tell me he was coming to our house?" She rushes over to him and is promptly swept off her feet and onto his lap, after which a kissing fest ensues, which I have to admit makes me wish I was in her place.

"Jennifer, your raincoat!" I cry. "You're getting Rick all wet!"

"Mom, the rain stopped before I got on the bus," she retorts petulantly.

"Well, then take it off and hang it up. You don't need it in here."

She takes off the coat and goes into her bedroom. I turn to Rick, but before I can say anything, he asks, "Is there something wrong with a little affection between two people who are fond of each other?"

"Fond? She adores you, Rick. You're like her very best friend."

"Oh boy, if that's so, we're both in trouble. But answer the question. Have you developed a dislike for affection?"

"No, of course not, but—"

"Forget it. Just thought I'd ask."

I look at my watch again. The day is going way too fast. "Rick, do you mind if I go help Jennifer get into her costume? Kathy and Todd will be here in a little while to pick her up for trick-or-treating."

"Do what you have to. I'm feeling kind of tired anyway. Would it be okay if I lie down somewhere and rest?"

How stupid of me. He must be exhausted. His first real day out of the hospital and I'm treating him as if he was . . . What kind of nurse am I? "I'm so sorry. I just didn't think. Go into my room, close the door, and lay down on the bed. Sleep as long as you want. I'll keep Jennifer away, and I'll explain to Kathy and Todd. If you feel cold, let me know or just pull the spread over you."

"Thanks, Mags. I'll manage. I'm just going to take a little rest. I'll be up before Jenny leaves."

"I'm going that way, so allow me," I say in my nurse voice. He doesn't argue, and I push him the ten or twelve feet down the hall and into the bedroom, then go next door to Jennifer's room.

"Is Rick going to stay here again?" she asks hopefully.

"He'll be leaving while you're out. He has to be back at the hospital by nine thirty."

Her face clouds in disappointment. "But he's getting better, isn't he?"

"Yes, he is. Maybe the next time he'll be able to stay over. We have to be patient, Jenny. It takes a very long time to recover from the kind of injuries he has." While we've been talking, I've been collecting the various pieces of her costume. "Put on what you can now. I have a little more ironing to do. I'll be back in a few minutes."

"Will Rick be able to see me in my costume?"

"If he's awake. If not, I'll take a few pictures of you for him."

Jennifer is dressed and ready to go by the time Kathy and Todd arrive. I'm glad for the opportunity to use my new camera, a Polaroid that the salesman convinced me I would be very satisfied with, though I'm a bit unsure how it works. Todd is happy to help me with it, and Jennifer is excited about having her picture taken. He takes three and I take one, and we wait anxiously for each to emerge.

"I'm so disappointed that Rick couldn't see Jenny, the cheerleader, in person," Kathy remarks.

"Maybe he wouldn't know it's me. I'm wearing a wig," Jenny says.

"I wouldn't worry about that, pumpkin," Kathy replies. "He'll always know you." She turns to me. "You know something, Maggie? I think Jenny looks a lot older and taller than she did in the pictures Mr. Simon took at Rick's party"—I glance at her doubtfully—"even if it was only six weeks ago."

I draw Kathy aside as they head for the door. "Can you keep her out until about nine?" I whisper. "I'd like a little more time with Rick."

"Sure. She'll be here when you get back from dropping him off." I listen to my little cheerleader talking a mile a minute as they go down the hall, then dash to the window to watch them go off to wherever Todd parked his car.

And now it's just Rick and me, and I'm more nervous than ever.

I wait about a half hour before going to my room. Rick is asleep on top of the bedspread, so I just sit down on the edge of the other side of the bed and watch him the way I did almost a year ago, when he had the bout of pneumonia. His face is different now, older, and of course scarred, though the scars are much less noticeable than they were even two months ago. It's amazing to me that they've healed at all when I think back to how he looked in the days after the accident: his Gemini appearance—one side of his face smashed and the other, except for cuts and bruises, perfectly intact.

I reach over, brushing my fingers lightly down the left side of his face, grazing his eyelid, his lashes, skimming his slightly bristled beard, then sliding gently off his chin. I'm compelled to continue the journey, down his arm, over his hand, onto his hip, down his thigh. I feel so free, unimpeded by my uniform, here on my own bed with this man who has given me back my life. But I know for sure that if I don't stop this now, I'll lose total control of myself—*you just watch yourself, missy*—and, at the very least, wake him up. Resolutely I manage to pull away and pick myself up off the bed.

"Oh no, don't stop now. It feels so good," says his sleepy, quiet voice behind me. I look back at him, but his eyes are still shut, and he hasn't moved so much as a facial muscle. As if drawn by a magnet, I lie back down on the bed and travel the route all over again. This time, when I stretch past the hip to the perfectly intact catheter, then across to the right, the voice says, "A little more to the left and down . . . little more, little more, not there yet, keep going." He feels nothing.

I want to cry because it's so sad, but in another way, it has a funny side to it too, so instead I say softly and truthfully, "I can't, Rick. I've already passed the catheter. I'm at your right hip now."

A moment of complete stillness passes, and then he reaches up and puts his right hand on my head, starts twisting my hair gently around his fingers. "Shit. I miscalculated. I didn't realize you were already in the Graveyard of Good Feelings." He picks up my hand, places it on his chest, and moves it down his body in small circles, the way he did that first night in my apartment when he was whole. Only ten months ago, but it was like another lifetime. I've heard the expression "three's a charm," and I think it must be true, because when my fingertips tiptoe around his midsection this time, his breath catches, and then at the approach to his groin, he gasps out loud. The nurse in me gropes urgently around in my mind for his current injury level stats, but my pleasure-crazed brain refuses to give them up. I move my hand a bit lower, stroking now, and he cries out, "Don't stop. I'm coming!" and begins to shake and move his head frantically as if he's undergoing a seizure. For a moment I am so frightened that my wits desert me, but in a matter of seconds, the tremors calm considerably, and his breathing quiets to panting.

"God, Maggie, hold me," Rick says between gasps. "Just hold me."

Oh Lord, I never prepared for this. I don't even know if the catheter should be removed before sex. What have I done? Witnessed a miracle or caused Rick terrible harm? I keep my arms tight around him until he is no longer trembling and his breathing is almost normal. His face is blotchy, and he's drenched in sweat, which has also dampened my shirt. After a few minutes, he pulls himself up to a sitting position and leans against the headrest. "God, my head is killing me! What happened?"

"I'm not sure, Rick, but I think you had an orgasm," wondering, even as I say it, *How? This wasn't real sex—was it?*

"But I'm not supposed to be able to do that, am I?"

"I'm not sure about that. But we can call Dr. Stern in the morning. Did you feel anything?"

"I felt your hand on my stomach, then nothing. Is the cath still in?"

"I checked it at about the time I moved my hand down from your stomach"—*Lord, this is embarrassing. It's one thing to be doing it but another to have to analyze doing it without the uniform on*—"and it was fine then. Do you want me to check again?"

"Yeah. Please." For the first time in months, without a protective glove I unzip his jeans and carefully pull his shorts down over the cath. Everything looks good. The area hasn't been involved at all.

"Did I have a har—an erection?"

"No, and I don't see any sign of discharge."

Disappointed, he looks at me for a long moment. "Well, at least I didn't mess up the bed." I set his clothes right and feel around under his legs.

"No, perfectly dry."

"Then what was it? I could feel everything I was supposed to, the tension escalating, my heart beating like crazy, and then my head exploded. All I feel now is this awful pain in my head and neck. But if there's nothing there, then . . . nothing could have happened, right?"

"No, it was real. When I got down to your stomach, you started groaning, and when my finger touched you a bit lower, you made that kind of soft hiccup sound like someone threw an ice cube down your pants. I'm not good at describing things, but you know what I mean."

"Dry," he says, as if he hasn't heard me. He shakes his head. "Would you mind moving the chair back over here? I want to call Stern now." He looks at the clock. "It's only around six fifteen." He sits up and maneuvers his legs over his side of the bed.

"You don't need to get up. The phone has a long cord. I'll bring it in."

He reaches the doctor at his office, and they talk for about ten minutes. I'd been planning to broil a steak, but I decide to wait and check it out with Rick first. He might not even be hungry.

Just as I'm pouring myself a cup of tea, he wheels into the kitchen. "He said that what I experienced is not uncommon. He's had other male patients who had the same thing. He told me that, and this is really weird, there was no discharge because nothing happened in my body. It was all in my head."

"You mean you imagined it?"

"Uh-huh. It's unbelievable, isn't it? In a sense, I screwed myself."

"I don't know what to say, Rick. I've never even heard of anything like this before, let alone seen it . . . How do you feel? Do you still have that pain in your neck?"

"It's gone. The doctor said it was from the tension."

"It's so strange," I muse. "I was lying right next to you the whole time. I can't believe that it was just in your head!"

He seems to think about this for a minute. Then he asks, "What's for supper?"

As it turns out, neither of us are hungry, probably because we're both still a little rocky. I make omelets instead and a fresh pot of coffee, and we sit down at the kitchen table. It's the first time just the two of us have ever done this before, and it's as if we're a real couple, companionable, like Steve and I once were. We talk about family news, mostly his family's news, and then he mentions casually, "You haven't said anything about Clearyville in a long time."

"I haven't been back in a long time, but I'll be going for Kathy's wedding in a couple of weeks. Want to come with me?"

He laughs. "I don't think that would be a very good thing to do. From what Kathy's told me, your mother wouldn't exactly welcome me with open arms."

Kathy never told me that she had discussed this with Rick. It must have been at an evening hospital visit. "I've broken off from my family, Rick, and I have no interest in going to Clearyville."

"Why?"

"I love my father, but my mother is . . . someone I just don't want to know anymore." I shrug.

His brow furrows, and he looks into my eyes. "It's because of me, isn't it?"

"Only indirectly. You were basically the . . . accidental catalyst. I was always uncomfortable in my family and in the church, and too stupid to know I was brainwashed into thinking I belonged there. My mother is a nurse and that's what she wanted me to be. She never left me alone about it, so here I am. I didn't want to go into nursing, but I was afraid even to tell Steve that. My mother's the one who wouldn't let me get on with my life after I lost Steve, drummed it into me that I was a widow in the eyes of the church until he returned or was declared dead. Now I'm an adulteress and a sinner, unfit to raise my own daughter. Last summer, she started in on Jennifer about church. I can't let her do to Jenny what she did to me. You've made me see so many things that I never realized before, and you've given me the confidence not to be intimidated by her anymore . . . and . . . well, I think that's all I want to say about that."

He puts his hand over mine on the table. "I'm sorry you're going through this, Maggie. But you have to do what's good for you and Jenny. Your mother's Lord will take care of her."

"And there's something else I want to tell you."

He pushes his plate away and pours another cup of coffee. "Okay. Shoot."

"Before Jennifer got home from school, you asked me if I remembered what I was upset about the day of the accident and I said I needed to think about it. I'll tell you now, if you still want to know."

"Okay." He shifts uncomfortably in his chair. "But first, can I lie down again? My back is beginning to ache."

"The brace is in the bag. I can—"

"No, it's okay. I need to take the leg braces off too."

"All right. Bed or couch?"

"Bed."

And then it dawns on me. He wants to try again.

I look around the kitchen. "I'll do the dishes while you get comfortable."

Rick finishes his bathroom chores, then comes fully dressed, as I am, to bed. It's around seven thirty, a cloudy, dark night. Though he prefers light, he doesn't argue when I turn off the lamp. And now we lie beside each other as we used to. We don't have much time left, so as soon as I sense he's as comfortable as he's going to be, I bring up our last night together. "Do you remember your invitation to California for a seminar?"

"Yes."

"How you needed to register by the fifteenth, and it was the tenth and you still hadn't said whether you were going or not?"

"I remember. I was under a lot of pressure from my advisor, my dean, and my parents. They all wanted me to go. Even you were crowding me about it. But I was worried about my dissertation. I was at a difficult and frustrating point, and I was afraid if I put it down, I'd never pick it up again. And I was beginning to drink again. I was in a bad place."

"You never let on about any of that."

"I know. I've never been a good communicator when it comes to feelings."

"I just needed—"

"I knew you were upset and I knew I was being unfair to you and Jenny, but I couldn't deal with it. I had my own shit and I could barely focus on anything."

"And I was a regimented person. I couldn't cope without everything being in its place and without knowing what was ahead of me. And you wouldn't tell—"

"I didn't know how to tell you without having to face your reaction."

He sounds saying it as he must have felt living it. This is probably not the best time to be discussing this.

"Anyway, I had already made up my mind that Sunday night that I was going to force you into making a decision when you got in. Of course, you got in late, a lot late—"

"Stopped somewhere for a drink—"

"And you just wouldn't—"

"I blew you off."

"I was going to give you an ultimatum. It would be Monday night or never. But, of course, you never came home again—until today." I take a deep breath. "For months I felt guilty, sure I had driven you to have the accident."

"Believe me, Maggie, I don't have any memory of what was in my mind that night, but your doing what you did was just part of the whole thing. If you caused the crash, then everyone else who was on my case caused it, so get that out of your head. Okay?"

I say okay, but even with his permission, I don't know if there will ever be a part of me that truly believes I don't bear some responsibility for what happened to him. And I suspect he knows this, because he follows the order with, "And by the way, that was a good pun when you said you were sure you *drove* me to have the accident." I smile weakly. "So is that it or is there more?"

"Just one thing. Do you remember what you were going to do about going to California?"

"Yeah, I thought about it for a few days and decided I had to go. I could always pick up again on the dissertation, but this was a rare chance to be with all those newspeople together in one place. I would have been crazy to pass it up."

So he knew all the time. I feel a kind of sick feeling in my stomach. "Why couldn't you just have told me, Rick? It was awful not knowing whether you were going to stay in Chicago or just leave us flat."

"As I said, I have never been a good communicator when it comes to feelings, mine or anyone else's."

I lie back, wanting to feel angry with him for putting me through all that misery, but I can't be angry. So, like the wantonly ravenous woman my mother thinks I am, I set about living up to my reputation. If Rick gets back to the hospital late, what are they going to do? As he himself would say, "Sentence me to hard labor?" Praying he hasn't fallen asleep again, I lay my hand on his smooth, hard stomach. He responds immediately by holding it there. "One more time?"

And so in the darkness of my own room on the evening of Halloween 1973, I do things I never imagined even existed, graceless things, things that disgust me until I do them. I realize now how considerate he was of who I was over the six months we were together. All that time he was acting by a rote I had approved. Tonight he is a how-to manual, and this time, I am open to everything.

I wake at eight forty-five, dirty, disheveled, and exhausted. Rick wet the bed a little while ago, as I expected he would when I discovered early on that he wasn't wearing his catheter. I don't care; I wanted him to feel free of apparatus and tubing, free of the hospital just this one night. I quickly shower and change my clothes. Then I wake him from the sleep that literally knocked him out when we were finished. He opens his eyes and makes an unhappy sound.

"Rick, get up. They'll be here in fifteen minutes."

He raises himself up on one arm, shakes his head groggily, then wrinkles his nose. "Something smells," he utters in a hoarse whisper. I die a little for him as I watch the light dawn and his face redden. "Oh shit," he mumbles and covers his face with his other hand.

"Well, not quite that bad, but yes, you wet the bed."

He is mortified. "Jesus! I don't know what to say, Maggie. I'm . . . I'm . . . sorry."

"There's no need to say anything. It was an accident, the first of what will probably be many. When I realized you didn't have the cath in, I knew it would happen. There was nothing you could do."

"But it's your bed. Why didn't you say something?"

"Because I wanted this night to be as normal as possible, with nothing in the way to divert us. And it was, wasn't it?"

"Yes, but your bed! It's ruined."

"No, it isn't. The linens can be washed, the bedspread was on the floor, and the mattress has a covering." Rick looks like he might cry. "Just get up and clean yourself off. Give yourself a sponge bath or take a shower if you want to. But do it now, before they get here. I'll be in once I get the bed stripped." He hustles into his chair and heads toward the bathroom. "There are clean clothes in the bag behind the seat," I call after him.

The sheets are a mess, and I mentally pat myself on the back for using the waterproof mattress cover. I feel achy from the strenuous exercise, but it was worth every moment. I'm sure it wasn't anything like I've heard people call "rough sex," but it was more than enough for me. I laugh to myself. By next week I should be fine.

Kathy calls about nine fifteen to ask if they can bring Jenny back. They arrive at nine thirty. Jenny is sound asleep, and Todd kindly carries her into her room for me. I'm sure he and Kathy know exactly (well, I hope not exactly) how Rick and I spent the evening, but they're good about not letting on. Rick emerges from the bathroom in his fresh clothes about five minutes after they get here. I can hardly face him for fear of blushing in front of Kathy and Todd, but he acts as if we were watching television all evening.

We manage to get back to the hospital by ten and sit in the car for a few minutes, just kind of setting things straight.

"Maggie, what I made you do tonight, please forgive me. I don't know what got into me, but once I started feeling something, or imagining I was feeling, I had to keep it escalating, anyway I could. Can you understand? I treated you like something you're not, never were, and never will be, so please don't hold it against me. I'm ashamed of what I asked of you."

I run my fingers down the side of his face. "Did it make you feel normal?"

"Probably as close to normal as I'll ever feel."

"Then I have no regrets. I'll see you in the morning." He leans over, and we kiss, a sweet gentle kiss, what I will always think of as a Rick kiss.

He starts to wheel himself up the path, then turns back and calls, "Doughnuts."

This morning I wake early with yesterday fresh in my mind and the realization that after having spent hours with Rick outside the rehab building, the time has come for me to face facts. His ability to get around and do just about everything he needs to do for himself almost certainly qualifies him for discharge. This is the way it is, and all I can do now is accept it and go on with my life.

When I get to his room at eight thirty, he is already surrounded by his materials and deep into whatever he's doing. He looks up briefly with an expression that says, "I know you're here, but right now I'm too deep into my own thing to care." *Good morning to you too, Rick.*

I get myself organized and settle down to my own work, but I can't get the uncertainty about his leaving out of my head. In spite of the craziness yesterday, I feel as if we were closer than we've ever been and that we talked more honestly than we ever have. Yet he never said a thing about going back to New York. I can't believe he's repeating the way he handled going to California. Not after all we said about it . . . *Give it up, Maggie. He'll leave when he's ready to leave, and that day will be the first day of your future. The Simons promised you would have another job to go to and you should be thinking about that. Call Lenore. Find out what's happening with that and then use your energy to deal with whatever changes come about. Look ahead, Maggie. Let go and move on.* Rather than sitting down to type, I decide to attend to a few things that I've been neglecting lately—namely, filing and organizing about three weeks worth of mail. It's an easy job. Rick himself is highly organized, and he dates each item and puts it in a separate folder as he goes through his mail. All I have to do is label the folders, magazines, and periodicals and file them alphabetically and chronologically in storage boxes for reference here or for transport when he leaves. The amount of material that has accumulated in the past three months is astonishing, but the system is second nature to me now, and these won't take long to do. Rick is still in his own little world, so before I start, I help myself to his small transistor radio on the table next to the bed, plug in the earphones, and listen to whatever is playing in order to keep troubling thoughts at bay for the moment. I've never cared much about music, but what I'm hearing is very pretty and soothing, and before long, I stop what I'm doing and just sit still and listen. I don't know what it is, and I suspect it's classical music, something I know nothing about.

"Maggie?" Rick's voice brings me out of my reverie.

I look up and find him watching me. "I didn't want to interrupt you, so I borrowed your radio."

He smiles and nods. "I suddenly realized I wasn't hearing the typewriter clacking, and when I looked up, you were a thousand miles away. That was five minutes ago."

"The music on your station is really beautiful. I guess I got a little carried away."

He wheels the short distance to my table. "Listen to it whenever you want . . . You know, you don't have to be working every minute you're in this room. You can take a break whenever you feel like it. As it is, we're just about caught up, so there's no need for you to knock yourself out."

"I know you don't think so, but I do, Rick. Blame it on my work ethic. You don't need a nurse anymore and I'm not being paid to do nothing."

"Right. But you're also not being paid to type yourself into the ground." He looks at me steadily for a moment. "Are you thinking about moving on to something else?"

"No, of course not," I reply, swallowing the urge to ask, *Are you?* "I just want to earn my pay."

He smiles again, but shyly now. "You earn it just by putting up with me. I didn't mean to blow you off when you came in, but I was in the middle of a syntax crisis."

I'm not sure what that means exactly, but as usual, I don't want to sound ignorant, so I don't ask. Instead I venture, "Is everything okay in your family? I haven't heard from your mother in a long time."

"No problem that I know of. Everyone's back in school and doing whatever they do otherwise. She's probably just been busy with her own stuff."

Suddenly I feel peculiar about having mentioned it as if I'm really a person in his mother's life. "I just wondered."

"She cares a lot about you and Jenny. She'll call when she has time."

The sincerity in his voice touches me. He leans forward and kisses my forehead, my cheek, then my mouth, and a rush floods through my body like wildfire. "I want to do another day trip," he whispers. "But not to your place this time."

"Where do you want to go?"

"I was thinking, maybe a nice hotel."

Hotel? That's strange.

"Is that all right with you?"

"I guess. When?"

"One day next week? I'll let you know later."

"Is this a date?" I tease.

"Call it whatever you want, Mags. I just need to get out of this place."

I don't get it. We don't have to go to a hotel to eat lunch, and if he has sex on his mind, I don't want to go with him. I won't get any better at it, and neither will his body. He'll only be disappointed again. "Okay," I agree, but I feel sad for him. He has a few facts to face too.

In the evening, after Jennifer has gone to bed, I try to find the station that was on Rick's radio, but I can't locate it and give up in favor of silence. I pick up my book, but instead of reading, I start thinking about how different life will be without Rick. Where in the hospital will I be working? Will our lives be changed in other ways?

Change. The only change I've seen recently in my day-to-day routine has made no difference for me. Rick's given up afternoon OT to participate in the wheelchair games in the gym, which leaves me with an hour to myself. I can always find some way to fill it, but these days, for some reason, I tend to end up thinking when I am alone. I've done more thinking in the last year than I did in my whole life before Rick came. Thinking about the wedding makes me anxious. What am I supposed to do? Pretend I'm happy to see my parents? I'm not worried about church but the reception at the house—how can I keep myself apart from them without people noticing? I doubt very much that my mother has let on to anyone about the distance between us; that would be like airing our dirty laundry in front of everybody they know, and she would never do that. But after the reception is over . . . ? I refuse to pretend that I feel one way when I really feel another, and that will make her even angrier than she already is. So what should I do? Kathy would be the best person to talk to, but she has enough on her mind without this. I need to work it out myself this time, but how?

I guess I could ask Carol how to handle the situation, but I've asked her for so much so many times already, I really don't want to bother her again. She's supposed to be my friend, not my counselor. On the other hand, she's the one who's always bringing up what's happening in my life so, hoping we can meet next week, I call her after supper. It turns out that she has a patient in crisis, Jerry will be attending a conference, and Sarah has to have tubes inserted in her ears. We will have to put off meeting until after Thanksgiving.

I think again about calling Lenore but let it go. Jennifer and I watch a children's special on television, then we read a book after I tuck her in. For the rest of the evening, I sit on the living room couch and mull over my family situation again, and for the first time, I find myself wondering whether my attitude toward my parents is unreasonable. They are who they are, and I am who I am. After three months without contact, maybe my mother would be willing to bend a bit, and we could find a meeting point. But where would that point be? Am I willing to go back to church? No. Well, not to their church, but maybe to Steve's. Am I willing to let Mother take Jennifer to church with her? Never! Will I consider asking her to sit down and talk it all over? Maybe. If she doesn't start name-calling and being mean, I might give it a try. Would she be willing to discuss our differences? I do know one thing; if she starts putting Rick down or his parents, or his religion, she'll find herself sitting in an empty room. I no longer believe in that kind of bigotry talk.

The next four days pass quietly and routinely except for late Saturday afternoon, when Jennifer and I stopped at the supermarket on our way back from visiting Rick. While we were in the checkout line, I felt a tap on my shoulder. I turned to find a woman, who evidently already knew Jennifer by name. She introduced herself to me as the mother of a child who takes the same school bus as Jenny. She asked if we might set up a time for our kids to get together. We chatted about our Jenny and her son for a moment before she noticed the person ahead of me leaving, and she hurriedly handed me her business card and invited me to give her a call next week. It might sound silly to most people, but I was excited. This was the first time in six years that I actually met someone in the neighborhood. I dropped the card into my handbag without looking at it and made up my mind to call the woman if Jennifer wants to play with her little boy. It didn't take long for me to find out. While we walked home, I asked Jennifer how she knew the lady.

It's Jason-in-my-class's mom," she said.

"Would you want to play with Jason some afternoon? Do you like him?"

"He's my friend, Mom. We read books together in the reading corner. He's really nice."

I will definitely call Jason's mother to set it up.

It's been a while since Rick has called to ask me to come to the rehab on the weekend for one reason or another. I've adjusted to it, and it no longer bothers me. I didn't do anything to make myself feel different about it. It just happened. Sitting here tonight, I feel as if there's no limit to the changes Jenny and I can make in our lives. We just have to be open to them. I almost feel like going to a church on Sunday morning and thanking the Lord for all the good things that have happened to us this year—and asking Him to allow them to continue. Except I'm not really ready to go back to church just now, and I know what Rick would say about it. *You're the one who's making the changes, Maggie. Just pat yourself on the back and keep up the good work.* I have to confess that I'm still a little uncertain about who's responsible for what.

Late Monday afternoon, Rick asks me whether I would prefer to go to an old hotel that has a history or a new, modern one. I don't know, and I really don't know how to answer, so I tell him to decide. He looks at me for a long moment, then shrugs and says, "Maggie, I'm not asking you to *pick* a hotel. I'm just asking what *kind* of hotel you want to go to."

"Don't be so impatient," I chide. "Let me think a minute . . . Would you be disappointed if we went to a very old one, the kind that's elegant on the outside and grand on the inside?"

"Is that what you would like?"

"Yes. But—"

"Do you have a particular place in mind?"

"Oh, I couldn't tell one from another." I laugh.

Actually I do, one that Steve visited on an architectural tour he took after we were married. He'd been interested in all of the historic buildings he saw that day, but this one hotel had made a big impression on him, I recall. I wish I could remember the name of it.

Rick says, "I'll make the reservations. I have to meet with my advisor in his office on Wednesday at ten thirty, so why don't you come in around ten and drive me over to the university. The meeting will probably take an hour and a half to two hours. When we're done, I'll call you at home and you can pick me up and we'll go downtown from there. Okay?"

"So you're ordering me not to come in to work as usual?"

He looks directly into my eyes and says with almost menacing patience, "Mary Grace, listen carefully. I, your boss by proxy, am instructing you not to come in to work tomorrow. What this means is that you may sleep late, have a leisurely breakfast, and do whatever you feel like doing. Can you dig it?"

"If you mean, can I handle that, yes, I can."

He leans over and kisses the tip of my nose. "Good. Now let's finish up here. I have a chess game with the professor after supper."

"Is this the tiebreaker you've been hoping for?" He nods. "Think you'll win?"

"I don't know. We're pretty evenly matched. But winning doesn't matter to me."

"What else is there?"

"Knowing that I played well."

It's when he says things like that that I think I could love Rick Simon . . . if everything else between us was equal, of course.

On my way home from work, I stop off at Kathy's place to pick up a dress of hers that she says will be appropriate for lunch at a fancy hotel. Not that she has any more experience with such a place than I have, but she does know what women are wearing these days. Not counting her wedding, the last time I bought anything remotely dressy was for Jennifer's christening in 1966. I don't trust myself to choose a dress for an occasion like this.

The dress Kathy left for me is made of black wool jersey and has a round neck, flared skirt, and thin black belt. It fits me well. She also set out a pretty scarf with fall flowers on a black background. Thank heaven Kathy and I are the same size.

Tuesday morning. I am still worried that I'm not dressed right. But when I pick Rick up, he is wearing a wool sport jacket over a dress shirt and jeans, so it can't be too fancy.

The dress turns out to be perfect.

I'd never been inside the Palmer House, but this has to be the place Steve was so enthusiastic about. The lobby is magnificent and, while Rick checks in, I stand in the middle of the huge space, eyes fixed on the wondrous ceiling, so rapt that I hardly notice people sidestepping around me. I'm still uneasy, though. All we talked about was having lunch, and I've been praying he isn't planning a repeat of the night at my apartment, but I can't think of any other reason he would get a room. I look over at him in his chair at the desk and suddenly feel an almost overwhelming sadness. My mind's eye conjures up a picture of him as he used to be, standing tall and confident on long straight legs, his jacket hanging on him in a way that makes him look, well, sexy. I haven't thought about him like that in months, and it hurts, so I shake the image away and instead try to imagine how this very room looked half a century ago, when both men and women wore hats and gloves, and nobody would even dream of setting foot in a place like this in jeans, if they wore jeans in those days.

Rick comes toward me, at least sitting tall and wearing a heart-melting smile. "We're all set." He hands me a key with a fifth-floor room number stamped on it. "Are you ready for lunch or do you want to stand here and ogle a little more?"

"Ogle? Am I ogling?"

"You and everyone else who sees it for the first time. Come on. Let's head toward the restaurant."

The restaurant is very busy, but the hostess has reserved a table for us against the wall so the wheelchair isn't in the way. A waiter immediately appears, fills our water glasses, and asks if we would like something from the bar. I ask for ice water. Rick orders a Coke. After a waitress takes our food orders, Rick smiles at me and says, "You look nice. That dress really looks great on you."

"Thank you," I respond, both pleased and embarrassed by the compliment, though I suspect he's just reacting to my not being in uniform for a change. I don't mention that the dress is Kathy's; I don't want anybody at the table but us. After the waitress goes off with our orders, I look around the room, noting the cloth napkins, the flowers, and the sparkling goblets.

Most of the tables are occupied, and the noise level is a lively hum, the lighting is low, and the atmosphere is subdued. No matter how many times this hotel must have been modernized, I can still sense its history all around us. It's exactly the kind of place I was hoping for.

"What made you choose this hotel?" I ask Rick, who is absorbed in the menu.

"It's one of the oldest and best in the city." He looks up. "Is it what you had in mind?" He shifts his upper body in the chair as if he's uncomfortable. I automatically rise to get him the cushion he sometimes sits against, but he motions me not to bother, so I sit back down.

"Exactly. It's beautiful." I take a long drink of water. "Rick, remember when your family took us all out for dinner at that wonderful restaurant, and it turned out to be the place where Steve took me the night he proposed?"

He looks at me, perplexed. "My family? No, I don't remember that. When was it?"

"During the summer. Remember we—?" Then it dawns on me. "Never mind. You weren't with us. You were in the hospital. In fact, it was the day you woke up! That's why we went out, to celebrate you coming out of the coma."

"Ah."

Our waitress suddenly materializes beside me. "For you, ma'am," she says, setting my plate in front of me, "the quiche and the garden salad. And for you, sir, the split pea soup and the turkey club. Is there anything else I can get for you right now?"

Rick and I look at each other in tacit agreement. "Thank you, no," he says.

"The reason," I continue, "that I mentioned that night your family took us out is because the restaurant they took us to happened to be the one where Steve proposed to me—"

"That's cool." Rick glances at me as he brings his soupspoon to his lips.

"—Wait, there's more. One day, not long after we were married, he came home from an architectural tour very excited about a hotel they'd been to downtown. The thing that had left the biggest impression on him was the ceiling in the lobby. I've seen picture postcards of this lobby, but I many other old hotels must also have ornate ceilings. It's funny though. The minute we walked in here today, I just knew this was the hotel Steve had been talking about."

I look at him expectantly for a sign of mutual wonder at this revelation, but all he says, and blandly too, is, "Could have been."

"But don't you think that's a pretty big coincidence?" I press. "That you and your parents just happened to pick two places that were important in my life?"

"It is a coincidence, but what's significant about it? I mean, if you and I had never met and we passed each other in the street twice in two days, what would it be telling us?"

I've never thought about this. "I don't know. That we were meant to pass each other? What do you think it would mean?"

"Probably that we lived in the same neighborhood, but usually took different routes. Most likely, it would mean nothing . . . Anyway, I think you're talking about fate, not coincidence. I don't believe in fate . . . Eat, Maggie. Your quiche is going to get cold."

We both settle down to our meals, eating leisurely and not talking except to remark on our food every now and then. I'd never tasted quiche before, but Kathy said it's popular now, and in fact, the caterers insisted that it was a must for the wedding reception. This gets me on the subject of the reception and the big flap about having it catered. "My mother is furious about having a caterer in the first place. Everyone in our church—their church—does their own cooking. She says Kathy must be trying to fool people into thinking she's marrying a rich man."

With a mischievous smile, Rick says, "Gee, I wonder who she blames for giving Kathy this clever idea to begin with."

"Not me," I contend, a bit defensively.

"At least not directly."

I start to object, but I can't lie. He's right. According to Kathy, Mother blames both of us—Rick for "putting heathen ideas into my head" and me for planting them in Kathy's. Rick shakes his head in amused disgust. I say nothing. That's when I know for sure that I no longer feel any loyalty to my parents, just resignation that they are who they are and relieved acceptance that I'm not like them.

The waitress interrupts to remove our plates and ask if we'd like dessert. Neither of us would, so Rick gives her a credit card, and she goes off with the tray. "Shall we go up to the room?" he suggests after the bill is settled.

I'm not any more comfortable going up to the room than I was before. I feel as if the tiny threads of apprehension I've tried to ignore all through lunch have tangled themselves up into knots in my stomach. I can no longer deny to myself what's coming.

The room is much smaller than I expected. Even though it has a double bed, it's obviously meant for one person. Rick immediately removes his shoes and hauls himself out of the wheelchair and onto the bed—*Lord, please don't let this be more difficult than it has to be.* "I'm having a little trouble with my back today," he admits, sinking into the pillows with a groan.

"Is there anything I can do to help?"

He pats the bed next to him. "You can come over here and sit next to me."

I go.

He takes my hand, raises it to his lips for a moment. "I have so much to say to you, Maggie, but I don't know how to say it . . . I'm not good at getting close to women, except with my body. You probably figured that out early on, so just please bear with me . . . First, I want to thank you for being here for me through this whole stupid accident thing. Which, by the way, I did not cause, either consciously or subconsciously, no matter what my family thinks. I still don't remember anything about it. I just know I'm too selfish to do anything that dangerous. Something I do remember is taking unfair advantage of you too many times to count, and I'm sorry for that . . . and that's another thing I have to thank you for. You've shown me what an insensitive bastard I am . . . I don't know . . . the only defense I can come up with for that is that while my intellectual growth soared, my emotional growth never got beyond early adolescence. I know I'm moody and sarcastic, and I don't have a whole hell of a lot of patience, especially with people who disagree with me . . . but you've put up with all my shit. I think you were nuts to do it, but I'm grateful that you did. I doubt I would have made as good a recovery or come so far so fast without you, not only as a nurse, but as a friend. I really believe that. I owe you so much."

My head is spinning. This isn't what I was expecting, and I'm at a complete loss for words. I just sit here dumbly, holding Rick's hand, my eyes, as if held fast by a magnet, unable to look away from his face. As though he understands that my brain needs a moment or two to start working again, he doesn't say anything more.

How else can I respond? "I only did my job," I say.

"You did much more than that." He gently pulls me down next to him.

I've told myself over and over that this is the last thing I want to do. "Rick, we shouldn't," I protest lamely, but I don't resist.

"This is as far as it's going to go, Maggie. I promise," he says and buries his face in my hair.

We lie like this for a short time before the nuzzling becomes kissing, and soon his arms move around me, and I feel like I'm floating. The ticking of the clock on the bedside table is barely audible, but even its steady sound adds to the sense of peace that I wish could last forever. I don't know how long we remain in what I can only think of as a cocoon. I'm not even sure whether I'm still awake. I move my head to look at Rick. His eyes are closed. I don't want to disturb his sleep, and I settle back in. It could be ten minutes or it could be an hour before I hear, out of the blessed nothingness surrounding us, Rick's smoky voice say, "I'm leaving on Thursday."

I instantly snap back to reality. It comes like a sniper's bullet, this moment I've been dreading for months, the moment I've rehearsed over and over in my head. I've told myself a dozen times that I will react calmly and matter-of-factly when he tells me, but now that it's here, how can I pretend to be calm when he can probably feel my heart pumping like crazy? Why is it nothing goes the way you expected when the thing you've feared most actually happens?

"Maggie, did you hear me?"

I take a deep breath. *Calmly and matter-of-factly.* "You mean next Thursday."

"No, I mean the day after tomorrow." He pulls himself up on his elbow. "My mother will be calling you tonight to discuss your job situation."

Matter-of-factly. "I see." It's not as if I'm not prepared. I know in my loudly beating heart that the sooner he goes, the easier it will be for me, but still . . . so soon. "Will you be able to say good-bye to Jennifer?"

"Sure." He smiles, but I detect a touch of sadness. "I wouldn't just walk out on her. Or you."

"You were going to once before."

"I'm not that person anymore."

That's true. "I'm sorry, Rick. I shouldn't have said that." It's strange, but I do feel calm now—or numb. No, not numb. In control. Just like that. "So what happens between now and Thursday? Do I come in and finish what I can?"

He lets out a long breath. "No. I can finish the rest myself. I think it's best if we just leave it the way it is."

"You don't want me to come back to the rehab at all?"

"I think a clean break is the best way to end it . . . unless you want to bring Jennifer in tomorrow after school to say good-bye. The packers are coming early, and we can meet in the lounge. Or I can take a cab to your place when she gets home from school."

"You don't have to call a taxi. I'll pick you up."

He shakes his head. "No."

Without warning, tears rush to my eyes. *This is real. He is going.* I look away quickly.

He takes me by my shoulders and gently turns my face toward his. "Maggie, you knew this had to end."

"Of course I did. It's just that I thought you would be here for three more weeks. Until Thanksgiving."

"I can't wait any longer," he says, all of his recent frustration suddenly rising to the surface. "I have to get out of here. I can't live in that room anymore. I'm not an invalid. I don't need a lot of help. It's like I have a second chance at life and I have to get on with it. Can you understand that?"

I can and very well. But right now I feel like walls are collapsing around me. I'm sure it's a temporary reaction that I have to ride out until it goes away. "Your family will be happy to have you home for Thanksgiving,"

"Yes, but it's just for a little while. I have an uncle in California. He lives alone in a house, and he asked me to come out and stay with him for a while. I'll probably go out after the first of the year."

I force a smile. *Pull yourself together, Mary Grace.* "So you're going to get to California after all."

"Better late than never."

"How are you getting to the airport on Thursday?" I ask, hating the hopeful note in my voice.

"The cab I take to your house will wait—I'm not going to stay very long—and then he'll take me downtown to the office. I'll stay with Joyce and Greg overnight, and they'll get me to the airport in the morning."

I can't quite get hold of the fact that he won't be here anymore, that he won't be depending on me for what he needs.

"You're not making this trip by yourself."

"Why not? Is there a law against cripples traveling alone?" he counters flippantly.

"No, but what if you run into something you can't handle?"

"Like what? It's not like I'll have to use the bathroom. Besides, I'm sure some stewardess will take it upon herself to look out for me . . . Please stop protecting me, Maggie," he adds irritably. "I don't need a nurse anymore."

Though his short fuse no longer intimidates me, I let a moment pass before I say, "I'm going to miss you, Rick." *So much I can't even imagine tomorrow.*

"I know, but think on the positive side. Soon you'll have a new job to get used to. You won't have time to miss me for very long. Just forget the past and concentrate on the future." He eases himself up to a sitting position. He appears to be energized, as if he's just awakened from hours of restorative sleep.

I get off the bed, straighten my pretty dress, and push the wheelchair over to him. He transfers himself with perfect ease; and within minutes, the room, the hotel, and the fourteen months we had together are pretty much behind us. I feel better as soon as I am outside breathing in the brisk dusk air. This almost surreal episode in my life is over, and though I don't know how it's happened, I'm confident that I'll be fine—eventually.

Wednesday, November 7, 1973

Rick stays for fifteen minutes the next day, just long enough to say good-bye to Jennifer. He brings her a musical dancing clown with flowers in its hand. Jennifer gives him two drawings that she made for him last night, one a self-portrait so he "won't forget what I look like" and the other a picture of both of them in the sandbox in the park. He tells her he'll treasure them forever, and she climbs up on his lap, hugs him tight, gives him a kiss, and promises to write him a letter someday. He gives her a peck on the cheek and sets her back on the floor.

"Will we ever hear from you again, Rick?" I ask him at the door.

"Probably not, but that doesn't mean I'll forget you." He smiles his endearing creases-under-the-eyes smile, but it fades quickly. "I need you to believe something," he says in the shy way he has when the something is not comfortable for him to talk about. "When we first got together, I was a bratty rich kid just playing around, looking for a little-brother substitute and, hopefully, some convenient sex. Not only did I luck out with both of those, but I ended up with a good friend, the kind of fulfilling physical relationship I'd never had before, and the maturity I should have had years ago. You are very special, Mary Grace. Don't ever let anybody, *anybody,* convince you you're not." He reaches up and takes my face in his hands and kisses me, lingering for a moment before he pulls away. "It's time for me to go . . . and it's time for you to let me."

I close the door behind him and join Jennifer at the window. The cabdriver is smoking a cigarette and waiting patiently for Rick to emerge from the house. When he does, I open the window a bit and breathe in the chilly fresh air. As Rick maneuvers out of the chair, Jennifer shouts, "Bye, Rick! I love you." He turns, looks up with a dazzling smile, waves, and lets the driver settle him and the chair into the cab.

As they disappear across the boulevard, Jennifer turns to me with a serious expression on her face. "Mom, I'm locking Rick in my heart, so I can always love him." She hugs the clown to her chest and wanders off to her room.

I stand at the window for a while, thinking about that night more than a year ago, when Kathy brought Rick Simon over for dinner. In my wildest dreams, I could never have imagined the joy, the excitement, and the heartache that first meeting would bring, or the effect it would have on our lives. Rick might have left Jennifer with a big expensive doll, but he left me with the most valuable gift anyone could ever receive. Thanks to him, I know who I am and where I'm going. And I, too, am anxious to get on with it.

Study Questions

1. Maggie doesn't regret Rick's having used her. How has she used him?
2. Why did Rick choose Maggie when he "could have had any girl he wanted?"
3. At book's end, Maggie's relationship with her mother is unresolved for the reader. Do you have any ideas about what the outcome will be and why do you think so?
4. Maggie's story is as much about letting go as it is about losing. Discuss what she has lost versus what and whom she decides to let go.
5. There are several instances in the book where Maggie refers to Rick as a father figure for her daughter, Jennifer. Do you think this is a mature and honest assessment for Maggie to make? If so, why? If not, why not?
6. Do you think Jennifer regards Rick as a father figure, a friend, or a playmate?
7. How do time and setting of the story lend themselves to the development of each character?
8. Maggie tells her story as it unfolds for her, pulling the reader into what could be considered the ordinary. What techniques does the author use to point out the extraordinary?
9. What role does family play in Maggie's concept of herself?
10. What does the future portend for Maggie?
11. As Maggie works through her mixed emotions over her MIA husband, who gives her the most difficult, yet most practical advice?
12. In her desperate need for a compassionate mother figure, why do you suppose Maggie does <u>not</u> turn to Lenore, a person she deeply respects and admires?

Edwards Brothers Malloy
Thorofare, NJ USA
May 7, 2012